BECOMING PART of the CHRISTMAS SCENES

Andy G. Collidge

Published in 2016 by FeedARead.com Publishing

Copyright © The author as named on the book cover.

First Edition

The author has asserted their moral right under the
Copyright, Designs and Patents Act, 1988, to be identified
as the author of this work.

All Rights reserved. No part of this publication may be reproduced, copied, stored in a retrieval system, or transmitted, in any form or by any means, without the prior written consent of the copyright holder, nor be otherwise circulated in any form of binding or cover other than that in which it is published and without a similar condition being imposed on the subsequent purchaser.

A CIP catalogue record for this title is available from the British Library.

CHAPTER ONE

"Look Thomas. Look at all the pretty lights on that snowy little village."

Thomas, a small, four year old boy, who is being held aloft by his mother, is staring, mesmerised, by the Christmas model village display mounted on top of a piano in the bar of The Bell Inn, which is situated in a village called Witherford, in Devon. The exhibit itself is made up of fourteen different pieces, all of which are lit, representing various buildings of an Elizabethan era and covered with snow. Three of the models are longer than the rest, comprising of three to four houses, and or a church, the rest are singular representations, depicting different shops from the same period in time.

Thomas's father joins them, places his beer down on the bar and takes his son from his mother, allowing the boy, with his extra height, to see the display more clearly. Thomas initially tries to reach out to the models, but his father sharply pulls back from the exhibit, warning him not to touch. The landlord had begun to move forward when he thought the lad was about to handle his display, but quickly relaxed as he observed the father to be in control of his child.

"That's really quite magical," comments the boy's mother.

"Thank you," the landlord replies. "I collect a new piece every year. It won't be long before I'll need a considerably larger platform to display them all on."

"It's quite stunning and so life like," she concludes.

The family walk away from the piano and take their seats in the window of the bar. The landlord goes round to give them menus, pointing out the daily specials on the blackboard that is situated directly above the bar.

The landlords name is Alex. He is a tall man with greying brown hair and a long Mexican style moustache. His dress is quite casual, as in jeans, shirt and jumper, but his shoes are immaculate and highly polished. He is a reasonably large framed man who sports the obligatory beer belly, which on many occasion he has stated 'comes with the job'. His demeanour with the customers is always professional, but he is known locally to be extremely strict with regards to his staff. He simply does not tolerate mistakes, slovenliness, laziness or idle chatter, being of the opinion that if you are here to work, then bloody well work. The only chat he ever wants to hear is business, absolutely nothing else.

Alex and his wife Anne had acquired the pub some fifteen years earlier and over the years they had grafted to turn its reputation from an all night drinking joint, into a cosy, inviting pub of quality with a restaurant and a small hotel. To a more or less greater degree they had managed to achieve their goal.

A waitress enters the bar, crosses directly to the seated family and courteously takes their order, displaying complete attentiveness to their every word. Alex smiles to himself as he watches the young girl work, very pleased with her approach and canter.

As she leaves the room he observes Thomas to be staring intently towards the village scene. His father again gets up, gently lifts his son and takes him back once more to see the display. Thomas cranes his head trying to see into the tiny windows of the models, straining to inspect every one, his eyes darting as if following something that is moving inside. This inspection carries on for some minutes, until his father who is now tiring from holding him up, places him gently onto the floor and encourages him to return to the table. Thomas however, is having none of it, and immediately fights against any distance that is being placed between him and the display. His father becoming slightly less tolerant now applies more pressure in his quest to make Thomas return to the table. As the battle of wills over their direction reaches a head, Thomas's father pulls the boy towards him and asks him, "Thomas what are you doing? You've seen the model, now let's sit down and wait for our dinner. It'll be here very soon."

"I don't want food," the lad shouts almost in tears, "I want to see all the small people talking to me in those houses."

"What?" His father replies glancing up at the village scene. "There are no people in those houses Tom, not real ones anyway. It's only a model." He picks Tom up and takes him back to his seat, placing him down and firmly ordering him to sit still.

Shortly the food is served to the family but between mouthfuls Tom's gaze remains firmly fixed on the display, chewing at his food but never blinking, his face full of pending anticipation.

His parents finish their lunch but Tom is not even half way through his sausage, chips and beans. His mother tries to tempt him into a couple of extra spoonfuls, but he is way too preoccupied to eat. Suddenly, he slips from his chair and darts back over to the model village. His father immediately gets up stating, "I've had enough of this."

He follows his son to the display, lifting him from the floor, sternly stating, "Thomas, you do not leave the table until you are excused."

Alex smiles to himself, nodding at the man's sentiment.

Thomas starts struggling, flinging his arms about and kicking his legs out yelling, "Let me go, let me go, they're talking to me."

Tom's father places the lad down, turns to face him and says, "Stop it, there are no people, I will show you."

He picks Tom up again and walks across to the piano, allowing him to see right inside the tiny buildings. As they stare at them, he notices a slight flickering from inside the replica of a toy shop.

"There daddy, see them? There are lots of them."

"I see them son, but they are only lights. They are a reflection of the bulbs which light up the model. That's all, they're not people."

He fondly cuddles his son towards him and takes him back to their table. Placing him down on his mother's lap, he goes to the bar to pay their bill.

"I'm sorry about Tom's little outburst there, he's never done anything like that before."

"No problem," Alex replies. "It's funny really, but he's not the first child who has thought they could see people inside those models. Perhaps that's why so many people come to see them," he muses.

Tom's father smiles and returns to the table. They collect up their belongings to leave and on his way out into the hall Tom turns and waving to the display he says, "Bye bye little people, sorry I couldn't hear you."

CHAPTER TWO

The date was Monday the second of December, and although Alex and Anne had already retrieved the Christmas village scene from the store room and set it up on its usual place on top of the piano in the bar a day earlier, nothing else to do with the Christmas decorations had been done at all. As they slowly make their way down from their second floor flat to begin their days work, Anne stops off on the first floor to collect a couple of boxes of decorations. Alex continues on his way to the kitchen, to make a cup of tea and some hot, buttery toast for them both.

Anne plonks her boxes down in the bar and joins him for breakfast, where as usual they discuss the coming day's events. As they finish, she clears the plates and cups away while he plods back up to the store room, returning with the Christmas tree.

Now, this artificial tree had been purchased some ten years earlier, and at the time had been a very expensive outlay due to its incredibly realistic appearance. According to Alex, the only problem with it was, that it came in sections and therefore it had to be put together every year. This was a process that annually became the overall biggest mission of the entire Christmas period, followed pretty closely by the never working fairy lights. Alex found both of these tasks so emotional that he needed a couple of days to prepare for the utter confusion that they caused to his life. Anne was purely philosophical about the whole issue, and simply ensured that she was out when these operations were due to begin.

Firstly, Alex clears the area of the bar where the tree is to be placed, then he erects the stand and the trunk section of the tree until it is standing proud in its entirety. He then leaves the main stalk and opens up the cases which house the branches. They are all colour coded and had been stored away the previous year in order. The trouble is, every year on, Alex cannot remember what order exactly they were placed in, or what the colour codes stand for, so the cases are emptied and he begins the process of assessing which branches are longer than the others, placing them in piles as he goes along.

Anne disappears into the restaurant and starts adorning this room with the decorations that have been allotted to that area, shutting the door behind her, only too aware that the air is going to be full of colourful metaphors in the not too distant future.

As Alex labours, cussing under his breath every time the branches cause a problem, he hears the front door open and close. He leaves the task in hand to see who has entered the building. On entering the hall he is met by Fleche, who is one of two chefs in their employ.

"Morning, morning sir," Fleche cheerfully greets him with.

"Good morning Fleche," Alex replies grumpily, "you're early, not that I'm complaining as it makes a change."

"It is five to twelve sir, we don't open for five minutes," he continues undeterred.

Alex glances over to the big clock on the wall above the bar entrance and responds with, "Christ I didn't realise that was the time. Give me a hand to get this bar tided up will you, we need to get this place open."

They enter the bar and as quickly as possible, clear away the cases and left over branches, tossing them in the hall under the staircase.

"If it is quiet enough today, I'll continue with this lot after we have the doors open," Alex informs him.

Anne emerges from the restaurant, greets Fleche and beckons to Alex to view the result of her labours. They enter the room and gushingly marvel at the lights, baubles and tinsel that embellish it. The room oozes with Christmas ambience.

"It's beautiful, just stunning." Then Alex pauses, glancing back towards the bar and adds, "You can come and sort out the tree next if you'd like?"

She laughs loudly and replies, "Oh no, no that's your job, besides I couldn't possibly swear as well as you do," she adds with her tongue in her cheek.

Fleche giggles to himself but as his eyes meet Alex's, he curtails the notion and swiftly walks off in the direction of his sanctuary in the kitchen.

Alex strides to the front door, opens it, turns on the exterior lights and returns to the bar to continue with his mission of the tree assembly.

Monday lunchtimes were usually pretty dire and this one was no exception, as between the hours of noon and two thirty in the afternoon, no one at all came in. This didn't particularly bother him as he was completely engrossed in the task of constructing his annual nemesis. By one thirty he was standing back and admiring the tree, blatantly obvious to all that he was chuffed to bits with his endeavours. He then packed up the empty cases and returned them to the store room, collecting the next box needed to adorn the tree. This was a big box, not overly heavy, just large and he carefully manoeuvred it downstairs and into the bar. He placed it on the floor, opened the top and pulled out the Christmas lights, holding the string out in front of him.

"How the hell have they got knotted up?" he seethes quietly under his breath. "I know I packed them away in structured order, so how come they are now in a big, snotty mixed up ball?"

He places the bundle of lights on the floor, gets down onto his knees and starts the process of untangling the unsightly mass. While he is sat on the floor, Fleche walks into the bar and hands him a cup of tea. He gets down on the floor to help Alex with the unravelling process. When they have managed to run the lights all around the bar floor without a knot in sight, they both stagger to their feet with creaking joints and smile at each other with a certain satisfaction evident upon their faces. They go to take a well earned sip of their now lukewarm drinks. Before they have managed to take a step forward they halt, gawping at the far end of the bar closest to the piano and the Christmas scene. There, all sat in a row, were the three pub cats, completely motionless with their ears pricked up, staring across at the snow clad model village.

Alex slowly moves around the room until he manages to reach a position where he can see the cats from the front. Ellie, a long haired tortoise shell and the oldest of the three cats, was perched at the very edge of the bar, whilst Bobs, also a tortoise shell but smooth haired and Charlie, a much larger ginger cat, were sat further back. Ellie was poised for action, looking as though she was about to leap forward at the display at any second, her eyes rapidly shifting left and right but her head never moving, staring at the various buildings.

"What are they doing?" Fleche whispers.

"They seem to be watching the Christmas village," Alex replies with bemusement.

"But why?" he questions, as he moves across to join Alex at the fire place in order to gain a better view of this spectacle.

"I really don't know, but they all appear to be concentrating hard on the same thing."

"Bloody odd don't you think. Have you ever seen them do this before?"

"Nope, well not in here, like this, but their poise compares to when they hunt something of interest, usually a mouse."

Alex moves over to the wall switch that lights up the model village and turns it off. The cats, their trance broken, in turn, all leap from the bar and leave through the lounge area, disappearing in different directions, totally uninterested now and without so much as a backward glance.

Fleche walks up close to the piano and closely examines the display, moving slowly from one model building to the next. Have checked every unit, he then peers over the top of then and checks the back of the display where all the wiring is, gently moving each strand in turn.

"What the hell are you looking for?" Alex asks him.

"I'm not sure, but the cats were staring at this thing for some reason. I wondered whether there was indeed a mouse or something back here."

"Don't be ridiculous man, if the cats had spied a mouse they would have probably demolished the entire display trying to reach it by now. I don't know what their problem was, but it disappeared as soon as I turned the lights off, so no more time wasting on that village. Let's get these lights on that damn tree."

Fleche reluctantly ceases his search and the two men carefully drape the Christmas illuminations around the tree. On completion, Alex plugs them in and switches them on, half expecting some of them not to work, but much to his surprise, the string of bulbs burst forth into action, creating a sparkling cover to the green tree. Next are the baubles of every conceivable shape, which are cautiously and somewhat artistically placed on appropriate branches, finishing off the eye catching centre piece. They both stand back to admire their work.

Anne wanders into the bar, sees the tree and comments on its beauty, congratulating them both on a job well done. Having praised them, she immediately goes across to the tree and starts rearranging odd decorations here and there until they meet her liking. They glance at each other raising their eyebrows, but no protests are spoken, both assuming that it obviously needs the final touches that can only be applied by a female hand?

Two thirty comes and Fleche says his goodbyes, leaving the Bell Inn to return home; he is not due in again until the following evening. They close the pub and Anne goes up to their flat, while Alex continues to hang the remainder of the bar's decorations.

By four o'clock he has finally completed this task, cleared away all the empty boxes and vacuumed the area, making sure all is clean and tidy before he opens again at five o'clock. Having satisfied himself that everything is in order, his gaze falls once more upon the model village. He slowly walks over to it and inspects it from every conceivable angle. Finally he backs away, placing his hands on his hips and slowly shaking his head.

"I really wonder what that was all about?" He questions out loud.

He walks to the kitchen, makes two cups of tea and goes upstairs to join his wife.

At five, Anne is downstairs promptly to open the pub. Within minutes Alex joins her and immediately sets to work lighting the open fire in the bar, to create the welcoming ambience for their patrons to admire then he goes around turning on all the lights, including those on the Christmas tree and the little village. As the electrical devices burst into life he admires the room with uncontained glee. He loves Christmas time even though it is nothing but hard work.

He turns towards the bar as Anne enters the room and he comments, "We need to get that string of lights you got off eBay last year and hang them across the top of the bar."

She nods and says, "I know exactly where they are, I'll get them down later and you can put them up."

Alex then goes into the old skittles alley at the side of the pub, where the cats are now congregating hungrily and he prepares their evening meal. Having put their food into their respective bowls, he places them down and they tuck straight in. He then returns to the bar.

As the cats finish their dinner, they use the cat flap to regain entry into the main building and head straight back towards the bar. One at a time, as they enter the room, they take up their strategic positions, the same places that they take every day in which the weather is cold, damp, wet or snowy. At this moment in time it is simply cold, but the weather forecast has predicted snow over the next few days and apparently quite a lot of it too.

Ellie always climbs up onto the corner of the bar nearest to the piano and curls up on the newspaper, daring anyone to disturb her. She is sixteen years old, known by all the regulars at the pub and very intolerant of anyone upsetting her in any way at all. She will endure the odd bit of attention or the gentle action of being stroked, but no one pushes their luck with this psychotic cat.

Bobs always makes for the table nearest to the fire, selecting the chair that will afford her the most warmth from the fires blaze and settles down there. Charlie however is a little more transient, choosing various venues for his relaxation. He can be found on the main staircase, the back lounge or on the settle in the main bar, reclining with the appearance of the lion king. Charlie is one big ginger cat.

This particular evening, both Ellie and Bobs take up residence in their usual places, but Charlie situates himself on one of the bar stools at the end of the bar, very close to Ellie. The one thing that all three cats appear to have in common on this particular evening is that they are all either sat or curled up facing the Christmas village. Alex observes this straight away.

His attention is drawn away from the cats as John, one of the pubs regular early door customers, enters the bar.

"Evening John," he welcomes, "the usual?"

"Evening Alex, ohhh yes a bottle of the Beast please," he purrs.

Alex lifts a bottle of Beast, a seriously, strong ale that John only drinks over the Christmas period, takes the bottle top off and hands it to him with a glass. John takes them both and pours the liquid, surveying it with definite relish.

Four more people enter; two couples in their forties. Alex welcomes them and offers them a table as they are looking to dine. He hands them menus then pours the drinks they have requested. As these people have decided to eat in the bar he takes their order which he passes out to the kitchen. By now Anne has two staff with her, both waitresses, and as Alex glances at them, they shoot off in different directions, heads down and the kitchen clicks into action. He returns to the bar.

On entering he observes both women admiring the Christmas village, peering at it and commenting on how beautiful it looks. He smiles and glances down at Charlie who is straining his neck in order to see the display around these two people who are now clearly blocking his view. Alex then checks the other two cats. They appear to be doing exactly the same thing.

"Are you seeing this John?" he questions.

"No, what's that?"

"The cats, they can't seem to take their eyes off the Christmas Scene."

John glances at each cat in turn and replies, "It's probably because it's new, besides everyone wants to take a good look at it for exactly that same reason. They'll get used to it."

Alex raises his eye brows and concludes, "Perhaps you're right, but I must admit, I've never seen them maintain such an intense vigil before."

John laughs, "Perhaps there's a mouse living in them."

Alex glances at the two women and then back to John. "Fleche suggested that, so I checked the whole village and there's nothing, besides as I said to him, the cats would have wrecked it by now if there had been anything like that in there. No, I don't know what their problem is, but it's nothing to do with mice."

John downs his beer, places the empty glass on the bar and says, "Well landlord who cares, but I will give it some serious thought while I'm drinking another one of those delightful Beasts," as he raises his eyebrows.

Alex smiles, caps another bottle and places in front of him. "You do that John, I am sure you will come up with a non sensible conclusion for me."

"That I will," he giggles, "that I will."

The waitress, Nancy, enters the bar and lays the cutlery on the tables which the group have chosen to sit at. She carries out this function fully aware that she is under the ever watchful eye of her boss, as he is very strict concerning the way they all act and perform their tasks. He cannot abide sloppiness and is always observing them. Having carried out her duty she smiles at the clients and scuttles away back to the kitchen.

The evening proceeds with more customers arriving as the time moves on. People are eating and drinking, listening to the sixties and seventies music playing in the background with the odd Christmas hit scattered in between, all appear to be generally enjoying themselves. Various customers comment on the Christmas decorations, congratulating Alex and Anne on their efforts, but it is without a doubt the Christmas village which steals the day, as nearly everyone on spotting it, feels compelled to walk over to the display in order to observe it closer. The interesting thing about it all is that having perused the scene, the customers always return to their seats afterwards and proceed with their own private conversations. The three cats on the other hand, never relinquish their vigil of the model.

CHAPTER THREE

A year earlier, almost to the day, a package arrived at the Bell Inn at noon, addressed to Anne. Alex signed for it, took it into the kitchen and handed it to her.

"What have you been buying this time?" He questions with a slight grin.

She takes the parcel and replies chuckling, "It's probably a string of fairy lights. I got them from some witchcraft shop on eBay."

"What?" he stutters, "You bought them from a what?"

She laughs out loud as she begins to unwrap the parcel. "A witchcraft shop, they were shutting down and selling everything off cheap. I saw the lights and knew you wanted something to go around the top of the bar, so I bought them for you. I thought they might be a bit different from all the ones you can buy in the supermarkets."

Alex raises his eyes to the ceiling and leaving the kitchen he adds, "Lights from a witchcraft shop, brilliant, can't wait to see these things work."

Anne smiles as she continues un-wrapping the lights.

Within a couple of minutes she appears in the bar carrying the newly acquired decorations and a set of step ladders. Positioning them at the side of the bar beside the piano she starts to hang them around the canopy above the bar. She slowly moves around securing the illuminations until she has completed the job. Alex watches, hides the excess flex and plugs the apparatus in.

When she's finished she climbs down the steps, stands back and instructs, "Switch them on. Let's see what we've got."

He throws the switch and the little lights burst into life. They are intensely bright, white lights that shortly begin to fluctuate. Initially he concludes them to be defective, but as he watches he becomes very pleased with the way they seem to react. Anne tilts her head a couple of times, obviously not over enamoured with the twinkling spheres and suggests that they are not quite what she expected and perhaps they should be taken down. She receives a sharp, negative response from Alex.

"I like them. You were right, they're different," he exclaims.

"Are you sure Alex, they look as if they're defective to me."

"Why?"

"Because they're not changing their rhythm, they are simply going in and out. There's no control thing making them do that, so they must be broken," she concludes.

"They're not busted, they're fine. I like the way they do that, it's different."

She sighs, "Okay fine, they are over your bar so you can explain them to the customers."

"Explain, explain what? They are obviously doing exactly what they are supposed to be doing. Don't forget that they are witchcraft lights," he chuckles. "Has it not occurred to you that maybe they were designed to be different?"

She raises her eyebrows, "Whatever, as long as you're happy with them."

"I am," he assertively states, "they're just perfect."

She gathers up the ladder and leaves the bar. Alex can't take his eyes off the new lights. He is more than happy with them. As he gazes along the string, suddenly they dim. He walks towards the bar, climbs on to a stool and starts testing the bulbs. Having tried a couple, the penny drops as he realises that LED bulbs mean that a broken bulb would not affect the rest of the string.

His hand brushes over several of the bulbs and he quietly says, "Come on guys, I like you, don't let me down, shine brightly when I need you to."

The lights burst forth so brightly that he falls off the stool and staggers backwards until his progress is halted by one of the tables.

"Hey, that's bright, tone it down a bit!" he shouts.

Immediately they tone themselves down to an acceptable level of illumination.

"Better guys, that's much better," he laughs.

"Who are you talking to?" Anne yells from the kitchen.

"The new witchcraft lights you bought, they're great," he responds.

"I'm glad you like them. I hope you can get them to behave," she chuckles to herself.

He smiles, staring at the lights. "No problem, me and these lights seem to have a great understanding."

"Glad to hear it. Is there any danger you could get a good understanding with the draymen because they are outside waiting to deliver the beer?"

Alex turns to the window and sees the lorry parked outside, throwing the bar into darkness because of its size.

"I'm dealing with them, my sweet little piranha fish," he calls out.

"Get some new lines Alex, Basil Fawlty just isn't cracking it today," she shouts back.

"Running all the way dear," he simply retorts.

He smiles with an enormous cheesy grin and makes his way to the old skittles alley, that in years gone past was where the horses from the coaches were taken through to be stabled. Nowadays it was the route to the rear of the building that housed the entrance to the cellars. Alex opens the big double doors and allows the draymen access. They lug the kegs through and deposit them in the cellar. On completion they leave, the paper work signed and the doors are closed and locked off behind them.

He walks back to the bar. As he enters so the little lights start to sparkle, gently, but sufficiently enough to be evident to him. He gazes at the illuminations, resting back on one of the tables, extremely pleased with their appearance.

"Well guys, I reckon you make this bar. Welcome to The Bell Inn and always be what I need you to be."

The string of tiny bulbs, very slowly decrease their intensity before returning to their previous brightness. Alex cannot contain his pleasure over how they seem to respond to him.

The bar is thoroughly vacuumed, cleaned and all done and dusted by five minutes to twelve. Alex checks the change situation in the till then walks towards the front door to open up for the lunch time trade. He then returns to the kitchen where the ice machine is housed to fill the little metal ice bucket before returning to the bar. Just as he places it down he hears the front door open and close and he heads for the hall to see who has entered. There he sees Duncan, their second chef. He is a man in his forties, tall and lean, with short cropped hair, clean shaven and always immaculately dressed.

"You're late yet again Duncan," he simply states.

Duncan glances down at his watch, then up at Alex and he replies, "Christ boss, a couple of minutes and you feel the need to chew me out for that?"

Alex expression changes, his annoyance becoming very apparent. "Chew you out, how eloquent. No I'm not chewing you out as you put it, not for the couple of minutes that you are late today, but for the fact you've been bloody late for just about every shift that you've had in the last six months!"

Duncan glares at him, places his hands on his hips and sarcastically quips, "Oh so you have been present at the beginning of every one of my shifts since I've been here? Is that correct?"

Alex raises his voice, "Who the hell do you think you're talking to? If I have said one thing here that is incorrect, do feel free to point it out."

Duncan backs down a little, realising that he is heading for a conflict that he won't win. "What I'm saying boss is that I start at twelve......."

"That's right twelve o' clock, not two minutes past," Alex interrupts loudly, "get some decent work ethics. Get in here ten minutes before your shift or find another place that will put up with your lateness and you're attitude problem!"

Duncan turns and walks towards the alley where his locker is situated and Alex strides off towards the bar. Anne remains quietly in the kitchen. Although she is completely in agreement with Alex over this issue, she often feels that he could be a little more subtle with his approach. She knows that if her husband has one major failing, it is with the way in which he is so direct with his thoughts and opinions in not allowing anyone or thing to deter him from what he intends to say.

As Alex approaches the bar from the back, he sees the room aglow with intense light. He walks over to the plug that powers the string of lights to observe that it is switched on. He glances at the bulbs and in his mind he says, "Who turned you on and why are you so bright? You'll burn yourself out at this rate."

The lights begin to fade back to their normal radiance as he watches with a perplexed look across his face. He feels that there is a question that he should ask, but he can't because the concept is too ridiculous. 'Do these lights understand him in some way?'

Still annoyed at Duncan's attitude he decides to give him a verbal warning. He is sick of the apathetic regard this man seems to have to both the work place and his employer. He strides out to the kitchen and bursts into the room. He scans the room but there is only his wife who is busy at the cooker. He makes his way down to the alley to where Duncan's locker is, but the door is still locked shut. He turns and glances behind him, nothing. He slowly returns to the kitchen.

"Anne, where's Duncan, have you seen him?"

She turns round and replies, "No, he hasn't been in here yet."

"That's bloody odd."

He turns and leaves the kitchen striding towards the front door. He pulls it open and glances both left and right. There is no sign of him. Alex leaves the front door ajar as the pub should by now already be open, turns on the sign lights then returns to the hall.

"Duncan where the hell are you, I want a word," he barks out.

There is no reply. Anne is the only one to enter the hall. "What's going on, where is Duncan?"

"I've no idea. He seems to have just vanished."

She looks disgruntled and rather irritated as she asks, "What else did you say to him in the hall? Have you fired him? If you have, the only person that will cause any inconvenience to is me, not you."

Alex's face displays his anger at this implication and he retorts, "You heard all that was said. I haven't been able to find him since then."

"Perhaps he's stormed out."

"No chance, I can see two hundred yards each way up and down the road from the front door. There is no way. Even if he had run, he couldn't have travelled that far in that short time."

"Then you explain it. You were the one that decided it was time to have a go at him with regards to his lateness, not me.

"Great sliding shoulders Anne, fantastic. I suppose you feel that I should let him get away with it again?"

Her lips tighten. "No Alex, I think you were well within your rights to reprimand him, but ploughing in to him like a rampaging train didn't help the discussion, did it?"

He storms off towards the bar aggravated by her innuendo. The new lights begin to increase their brightness once more as he enters the room.

"Cool it you lot, I don't want a fuse blowing," he orders as he walks in. "We've had enough drama for one day and we've only just reached lunch time."

They quickly dim down, beginning to twinkle. Strange as it is, these illuminations seem to calm his mood. He likes their appearance and approves of the way in which they seem to respond to him.

The lunchtime session finishes and there is still no sign of their chef. Anne is completely peeved over his absence and during the lunchtime she rings his house. His wife answers and as the discussion continues it becomes apparent that he has not returned home as yet. When she finishes the call, she goes into the bar and informs Alex of the news. He is totally flabbergasted at his disappearance and comments that when he does emerge, he is fired anyway.

Anne just walks away adding, "Then I suggest you start advertising for a replacement, and soon, as Christmas is less than three weeks away."

Two days go by and Duncan still hasn't been seen by anybody. By now there are plenty of rumours floating around the village with regards to his whereabouts and theories as to why he has gone, but that's all it is, mindless gossip. By the end of the week, Duncan's distressed wife calls the police to list him as a missing person. They come out to see her, logging the details and attempt to put her mind at rest, trying to reassure her that he will turn up soon.

The police call in to the pub to interview the landlord and his wife. They reiterate their story of the last time they saw him and the police leave with their information. Alex and Anne are now becoming quite concerned as to what has happened to him.

Alex posts an advertisement for a new chef, although he feels slightly guilty about doing so under the circumstances, nevertheless, having discussed it with Anne, he has no choice but to keep the kitchens going in the man's absence. Within two days of the advertisement going live he has received several responses and he arranges for interviews to be carried out over the following few days.

Anne undertakes the main part of the interview, as after all it is she who will be working closely alongside them. Alex sits in, but offers very little input. As far as he's concerned, just so long as they have the qualifications and they are presentable, he's happy.

Having interviewed six people, four men and two women, Anne concludes that she has found the person who she would like to try. They discuss the attributes of the man called Fleche, agree that he seems suitable for the post, call him and offer him a three month trial. He is pleased to accept and agrees to start working the following lunchtime.

CHAPTER FOUR

Back to the present.

The following morning Anne arrives downstairs first, but before she has even had a chance to put the kettle on, there sounds a knock on the front door. She quickly fills the kettle, sets it on its mount and goes to see who it is. As she opens the door, stood on the doorstep are a man and a woman.

"Can I help you?" she asks with a welcoming smile.

"Yes Madam, I am Detective Sergeant Marcus and this is Detective Constable Criss. May we come in please?"

She checks the credentials that Marcus is holding out to her and offering for inspection, then she ushers them both inside. You never can be too careful these days. As they enter the pub, Alex appears. Anne introduces their two visitors and they take themselves through into the bar.

"What's this all about?" he questions.

The sergeant answers, "It's quite simple Sir. It's to do with the disappearance of four people from this village and the surrounding area."

Alex and Anne glance at each other then Alex continues.

"Yes of course. We've heard of these disappearances, well of course we have, we live in a village and the rumours are rife, but what's that got to do with us?"

"Please don't become agitated Sir, we are only checking with all those who were acquainted with the missing people."

"Were acquainted?" Anne interrupts, "What's happened to them?"

"Bad choice of words," Marcus concedes. "As far as we are aware, they are simply missing, nothing else. We have been unable to discover anything about them since their disappearance, hence this new line of enquiries. We are now, because they have been missing for over a year, attempting to put a more detailed picture together of the last days in which they were seen."

"Okay," Alex says, "So what you want to know is did we see them the day they vanished?"

"Yes, that's exactly what we would like to know."

Alex sits back in his chair and creases his forehead in concentration. "What date was that exactly, I can't remember? It was late November wasn't it?"

Anne slightly nods her head and then adds, "Or early December. Duncan left here the first week in December because the Christmas decorations were already up."

"That's right they were," he agrees.

"The second of December," Criss interjects and Marcus nods in agreement.

"Well in Duncan's case," Alex explains, "he had come into work late yet again and we had a few words."

"Words sir?" Marcus enquires.

"Yes words, I was annoyed with his continual bad time keeping and attitude, so I pulled him up on it."

"Did you argue?" Criss asks, "Was it heated?"

"They did not argue," Anne interjects. "Alex was quite forthright with him. I heard the conversation but there was no argument, just a very straight reprimand."

"That's right," Alex agrees. "Having said my piece, he walked out to where his locker was and I concluded he was going to get ready for his shift, albeit ten minutes late."

"Then what happened?" Criss asks.

"Well as I told your lot when they came round last year, I walked back into the bar having watched him go towards his locker and I decided I was going to give him an official verbal warning in the hopes that it would jolt him into a better frame of mind, but I couldn't find him."

"Did you search?"

"Yes, yes of course I did. I checked the alley, the kitchen and then the street. I asked Anne if she had seen him but it was as if he had simply run off or something. The other officers checked his locker and all his working clobber and clothes were still in there. It was most bizarre."

"Bizarre indeed Sir," Marcus quietly says.

Alex abruptly asks, "And what the hell is that sarcastic remark meant to imply?"

Marcus straightens up in his chair and defensively answers, "Nothing Sir, nothing at all, it wasn't meant to be sarcastic. I really do believe that the incident you described was quite bizarre."

Anne places her hand on Alex's leg and his mood relaxes a little.

"What can you tell me about Paul and Tara Lucas?" Criss enquires.

"Huh, those two, in my opinion I am glad that they have moved on. I don't think they are missing at all, I reckon they just did a runner."

"Not too keen on them then?" Criss observes.

"They were problematic to say the least," Alex states, "always trouble as soon as they walked through the door."

"In what way?" Criss continues.

"They were alcoholics, the pair of them. If they weren't having a go at each other, they were trying to cause a problem by winding up someone else in the bar. Then there was their cash flow problem."

"Cash flow problem?"

"Yep, cash flow, the fact they were normally broke and trying to sponge of other customers. To be honest, I had banned them both some months earlier but they kept pushing their luck to get back in here. If I had turned them away once, I've turned them away a dozen times. As I say, they were just trouble."

Criss, who has been taking notes the whole time glances up and asks, "So when was the last time you physically saw Lucas then?"

"About two days after Duncan left," Anne answers. "I was just coming out of the kitchen with two plates of food for some customers when they tried to get into the bar via the lounge round the back. It was Alex's night off and Julie Husky was front of house. Alex was upstairs. I stopped them and told them that they had better leave. Yet again, they were drunk and Paul went straight into a loud abusive rant. I told him to calm himself but he carried on shouting and then Tara joined in. Julie came round to see what was going on and then Alex appeared."

All eyes turn towards Alex as he continued the story. "I could hear the ruckus all the way upstairs, so I came straight down. As I entered I saw what was going on. Paul was towering, threateningly over Anne and she was backing away from him. I stepped between them and pushed him away. He wobbled a bit and then began cursing at me. I told him emphatically to get out or the police would be called. He clenched his fists and started to gesture in an aggressive manner. I told him I wanted him out and if he and his wife didn't go, I would throw them out myself."

"Was that advisable?" Criss asks.

Alex tilts his head towards her and replies, "Indeed it was. If the police had been called, they would have taken a good thirty minutes to get here, that's the usual response time out here in the sticks, and by that time this hostelry would have been empty and its reputation wrecked. Besides, licensing law is quite clear, I am allowed to defend myself if I'm attacked."

"Okay, okay," Marcus quickly interrupts. "So they left?"

"Yes," Anne says, "slamming the inner door and cracking the glass in it, yelling and swearing as they went. Alex started to go after them, telling them that they would pay for the damage they had caused, but I stopped him, not that it was difficult, and he returned to the bar to calm down and reassure the customers."

"And that was the last you saw of them?"

"Yes," both Alex and Anne said at more or less the same time. "Never saw then again, as I say, I think they just did a runner," Alex adds

"Regarding Julie Husky, who as you have previously stated worked here. When was the last time you saw her?"

"New Years Eve," Alex replies. "She was due to work right through on that night."

"She was due to work that night? What exactly happened then?"

"She came in ten minutes before her shift, as she always did to find out the state of play before she started work and informed me that she had been invited to a party and needed to leave by ten o'clock. As I'm sure you can appreciate, I wasn't best pleased with this situation, especially as I wasn't being asked, I was being told."

"And that annoyed you?" Marcus questioned.

"Well, yes and no. It initially peeved me, but as the evening progressed it was blatantly obvious that she hadn't got her mind on her work and mistakes started happening all over the place."

"Mistakes?"

"Yes, errors, cock ups, mistakes. For example wrong change was given, glasses were broken, a bottle of wine was dropped and smashed, her manner was extremely curt, bordering on rude with some customers, food orders were taken incorrectly, that kind of stuff. Then there was the continual clock watching, this is when I really started to get annoyed."

Anne takes over. "It was strange really, Julie was good, a really competent bar maid, efficient and honest, possibly one of the best bar staff we have had, but that night, her persona was completely out of character. She even came out into the kitchen with a disconcerted attitude, slamming things down, snapping at the others and the glares she gave me, well, I had always got on well with her. I have no idea what was wrong with her that night. I called Alex to one side and quizzed him about her behaviour. He was as confused as I was. I could see that he wasn't going to put up with it for long. In this case, he was right, something needed to be said."

Both Marcus and Criss turn their attention towards Alex, waiting for the next instalment.

"It was at about nine o'clock when I felt I couldn't tolerate anymore of the fiasco with Julie, so I literally ordered her out from behind the bar. Just past the kitchen, before you reach the alley, I had it out with her. I knew that Anne would be able to hear what was said from the kitchen, which is why I chose this particular place for the pending face down and that is the only way I can describe it as a face down."

When we got there, I stopped her and said, "Right, come on, what's the matter?"

"I told you," she replied aggressively, "I need to be out of here by ten and that's all there is to it, so I'll do my job till then, and then I'm out of here."

I can remember just gazing at her, almost in disbelief. "Julie is there a problem, talk to me."

"Oh yeah, talk to the boss, the one that rules with a rod of iron and perhaps he can help. I don't think so. Ten o'clock and then I'm gone."

I was shocked at her belligerence, but more confused at her unfamiliar manner towards me. "Look if that's the way you feel go now, go and get whatever you have to get sorted out, get it done."

She slumped back onto the wall. "Oh yeah great, kick me out why don't you, bastard."

I raised my voice and said, "That's enough, go now before you say something you'll regret, just go."

"Stuff you," she retorted and she proceeded to enter the bar and collect her belongings. As she came out she said, "I need paying."

Totally shocked, I went across to the till, worked out her hours and took the cash out and handed it to her.

"This is not enough," she yelled, "It's double time on new year's eve."

Now I was angry. "Double time is after midnight as well you know, take your money and get out and don't come back."

She stormed out of the bar and as far as I was concerned she left. I had to work the bar on my own from then on and it was a busy night, as you can imagine.

They both nod, appreciating the gravity of Alex's last statement.

"So that was the last time you saw her, either of you?" Criss quizzes.

"Yes," Alex replies, glancing across to Anne, "I never saw her again."

Anne agrees, "She stormed out of the building and that was that."

Marcus gets up from his seat and walks around the bar. "On that night, or on any of the other instances regarding these missing people, did anything else happen that you can recall, anything that you may consider to be a little odd, different or strange?"

Both Alex and Anne quickly glance at each other and back to the officers. They reply in unison shaking their heads in turn, "Nope," with Alex adding, "Nothing. It's not as if management and staff relations haven't been stretched before and this was no different."

Marcus and Criss thank them both for their time and they leave. Alex saunters back into the bar, grabbing the vacuum cleaner on the way to begin his morning chores of a general clean up. Anne resumes her earlier task of making the morning cup of tea, with many thoughts regarding the last half an hour's meeting dancing about in her mind.

Afterwards Alex proceeds to carry out his routine stock check, followed by the task of bottling up the bar , always a point of contention with him, always feeling his staff should have had this covered before the end of their last shift. In a way, he believes their failure to carry out this function is probably his own fault because he always tends to return behind the bar a good forty minutes before the end of any shift, often letting them go home early. Behind the bar there isn't much room, so if he sits talking to regulars at the far end of it, the staff cannot function properly with him there, so he lets them go. He smiles to himself and gets the job done.

"Howdy doody," Fleche spritely calls out as he enters the building. This is his usual opening exclamation on his arrival at work, unless he is in a poor frame of mind, in which case a grunt with a pained expression will be the order of the day. Again, Alex smiles to himself, at least everyone knows he is in a good mood today anyway. Fleche pokes his head into the bar as Alex acknowledges his presence. He then takes himself off to his locker in order to don the appropriate attire for his chef's duties. Having changed, he makes his way to the kitchen, where he and Anne discuss the day's events along with any necessary prep that needs to be carried out.

Alex, having seen him come in, knows it must be mid day; he always cuts his starting time fine. He switches on the main ceiling and bar lights and makes his way to the front door to open up. He returns to the bar via the main entrance and heads for the power point to illuminate the Christmas tree. As he bends down to turn the switch on, he notices that the lights adorning the canopy of the bar are already glistening. His head lurches up, but on closer inspection, he sees that they are not actually turned on. He shakes his head and crouches back down again to carry on with what he was doing, but keeps glancing up, as if trying to catch the lights out.

"What are you doing?" Alex mutters to himself under his breath. "There are no super powers here. They are just a set of lights." He pauses for a second as he stares at them again, "Albeit the greatest set of lights I've ever seen."

He turns to the tree, which now is shimmering beautifully, then heads behind the bar to illuminate his favourite twinkles. He disappears back through the main entrance, down the hall, into the back and enters behind it. He walks to the switch and flicks it on. "Come to life my beauties," he coaxes them.

As these loving words leave his lips, two couples in their fifties stroll into the bar. Alex greets them, enquiring as to what they would like to drink. They occupy a corner table and having taken menus along with them, they sit and peruse what is on offer, glancing from time to time at the specials board written on the canopy above the bar, now enhanced by the fabulous new Christmas lights. Alex leaves them to contemplate their choices for fifteen minutes or so and then takes his pen and pad to wait on their table.

He strides off towards the kitchen to present their order to the chefs. On his way, he sees six or so more people entering the premises. He acknowledges them on his way through, stating that he'll be with them shortly.

He enters the kitchen, hands the order to Fleche and enquires, "Where's Jack, I thought he was working this lunchtime?"

"He is," Anne replies, not turning from what she is doing. "I guess he is running late. He did say he had to go into town early this morning. Perhaps the bus was late returning."

"Jesus," Alex grumbles, "welcome to The Bell Inn, work when you like, finish when you like, do what you like. Why can't we find some staff that actually work when they are supposed to and have some kind of ethic about them?"

Fleche begins to titter quietly and Anne warns, "Let us not judge until we find out the facts Alex."

He leaves the kitchen muttering under his breath, but on appearing behind the bar, his professionalism once more kicks in and with a broad smile he says, "Afternoon folks, how can I be of help?"

Drinks are ordered and like the other four, they too are on the hunt for food. Alex explains the menus to them and invites them to choose their table. This they do, just as John walks through the door beaming, "The Beast, feed me the Beast."

Alex smiles and reaches down below the counter, emerging with the said Beast. He caps the bottle top and hands it with a glass to the now seated John. "There you go, one pint of the wee beastie."

A huge smile spreads its way across John's face as he gently picks up his dense black liquid, which he then slowly sips.

Just then, the front door opens and closes and the patter of feet scampering up the hall can be heard. Initially Alex thinks it is probably someone shooting in with some urgency looking for the toilet, but when he doesn't hear the loo door go, he deducts that Jack has probably arrived. Then he hears the steps disappear along the hallway towards the alley. Yes, he now knows it is Jack.

Alex moves from behind the bar to attend to the six who are seated, gazing at the menus to ask if they are ready to order. When they all nod their readiness, he proceeds and relays their order out to the kitchen. There he sees Jack, who is rapidly explaining his lateness on shift.

"Then to cap it all, the bus pulled out early," Jack complains, "driving away from the bus stop while I'm chasing after it. It didn't stop though, I know the driver saw me, but the git just kept going."

"Probably thought you were going to mug him," Alex quips.

Anne glares at Alex, replying to Jack, "Oh well, you're here now, safe and well, so let's get our heads down and get to work."

Alex smiles at her even tempered nature, winking at her. Jack glances at the food order and begins to collate all the necessary bits and bobs, cutlery, condiments and napkins required to set the customers places.

Alex returns to the bar only to be confronted by Ellie the cat, sat on the bar, poised on its extreme edge as if about to leap into the air at any second. He follows her line of sight until he ascertains that she is looking intently, yet again, at the Christmas scene. Slightly agitated, and using the palm of his hand, he shoos the animal off the bar and onto the floor, where she shoots off. She bounds out of the main entrance, up the hall and reappears once more behind the bar, leaping onto the low shelf of the glass washer, then onto the back bar until she is firmly back in exactly the same position where she was previously unceremoniously removed from. Alex just stands looking at her in total amazement.

"Did you see that John?"

"Indeed I did, that cat knows where she wants to be I reckon and nothing you are about to do, is going to change that," he erupts into laughter.

A couple of the customers have also watched the spectacle, one of whom, a woman in her thirties, gets up and walks over to the cat. She slowly extends her hand towards Ellie to stroke her head, when the cat, just as the woman's hand is about to make contact, lashes out at the incoming limb, all claws out, just missing the hand. The woman withdraws her hand with masterful speed and agility, letting out a very nervous giggle.

"Oooo, she's fast."

"You okay?" Alex enquires.

"Yes, yes, she never caught me."

"I'm so sorry. I have never seen her do anything like that before," he continues apologetically.

"No problem, it was my fault. I disturbed her concentration of the flashing lights up there," she replies gesturing over at the Christmas scene.

Ellie, who remains staring at the scene, seemingly oblivious to anything apart from what she is watching so intently. The woman turns and takes a step towards the display, moving along it, examining every model in turn. As she moves, obscuring Ellie's view, so the cat cranes her neck to maintain a constant vigil of the display.

Finally when the woman has finished her examination, she smiles at Alex saying, "That is quite beautiful, a fantastic display." She then returns to her seat.

Alex smiles, thanks her and Ellie resettles herself, once more able to watch the display without hindrance. John bursts into laughter yet again, saying, "I told you, that cat knows where she wants to be and low and behold anyone who might try to change that." Again he follows this statement with more rapturous laughter.

Jack enters the bar, laboriously laying up tables and chatting with the customers, taking time to be polite and attentive. As quick as he appeared, he is gone, returning within minutes with the plates of food, which he serves professionally, again taking his time to appease the customers.

Alex smiles to himself, knowing full well that this young man is very good at his job, even if he is a little slack with his time keeping. However, he feels that one thing outweighs the other and to replace Jack would prove difficult.

The lunchtime period, not overly busy, finishes and both Jack and Fleche leave fairly promptly, knowing that they only have a two and a half hour break before they are back in for the night shift.

As they leave, Alex calls out, "See you later lads, do try and get in on time this evening. It would be novel if you could just try it."

They both reply with, "See you later", with Jack cheekily adding, "At five....ish!"

CHAPTER FIVE

Anne places a cup of tea on the bar as Alex is completing his final clear up, before she takes herself upstairs to their private domain. He is vacuuming around the tables, muttering under his breath and complaining as to the fact that 'customers seem to keep missing their mouths and letting the food drop to the floor'. He moves a table to see not only peas, crumbs and chips squashed into the carpet, but serviettes screwed up, littering the floor underneath the settles. He sighs and moves the chairs away, then lugs at the big heavy wooden table which stands in front of the settle, trying to gain access to the paper napkins strewn around. Bit by bit, he budges the table away, cursing under his breath as he labours. Suddenly, from behind him, the bar brightens, with light emitting all around him. He immediately stops what he's doing, turning to see where the illumination is coming from. He can't pinpoint the origin of the light as he is temporarily blinded by the intense brightness.

He straightens up, hesitantly enquiring, "Is that you guys? Calm it down or you'll blow a fuse."

Instantly the glare subsides and the individual lights above the bar once more become evident. Slowly, they return to a low glimmer. Alex watches them, with yet again, that feeling of pleasure and power concerning the fact that they seem to react to his voice. He walks straight over to them, placing his finger on various bulbs, checking their heat and closely inspecting the cable.

"Bloody hell guys, what woke you lot up? Glowing that intensely could cause you a problem, be careful," he chides.

The lights start to sparkle, changing colour as they do, but this time with a more gentle, peaceful radiance.

Alex surprised, steps back saying, "I didn't know you could do that, I thought you were just white lights."

The illuminations speed up, dancing and showing off as they go through their routine.

He turns around and returns to his task of cleaning the area in front of the settle. Having moved the table far enough away to allow him to squeeze behind it, he crouches down to crawl underneath. Having manoeuvred his way to where the napkins originally where, to his total amazement he finds that he cannot see them anymore. He looks left and right, but there are no serviettes, they have simply disappeared.

He clambers out, places his hands on his hips and stares at where he had previously seen the screwed up items to be saying, "I must be losing it."

He pushes the table back, vacuums around the area and then replaces the chairs. Finally happy that the bar is ready for action for the night time session, he unplugs the cleaner, winds up the lead and puts it away. Returning to the bar, he turns out all the lights, leaving the top ones until last, stating, "Have a rest guys, I'll be back in a couple of hours."

At ten to five, he appears downstairs, routinely going to the kitchen, turning on all the cooking appliances and lastly turning the kettle on. He places two mugs next to it, then heads for the hall, turning all the lights on there, then the restaurant, the outside pub lights, the sign lights and then finally, into the bar. Here, the order of illumination is very precise, firstly the wall lights then the ceiling lights, followed immediately by the lights behind the bar. He then switches on the Christmas tree, bringing it to life, smiling to his self as he throws the switch. As he turns his attention to the lights across the top of the bar, he takes a second look as they already appear to be turned on, dancing and flickering with real vigour. He glances at the electric point where they are plugged in, walking over and examining it.

Shaking his head and under his breath he says, "How the hell did that happen, I know I didn't turn you lot on?"

The tiny bulbs increase their brightness, filling the bar with such intense radiance that once more he becomes concerned that they will blow themselves up with their power. He snatches at the power point, snapping the switch off. For a moment, nothing happens, but then the lights extinguish within the blink of an eye.

Suddenly, Anne appears behind the bar, asking, "Is everything ok Alex, I could see a very bright light in here, what the hell was going on?"

"I'm really not too sure," he concludes, "the voodoo lights seemed to switch themselves on, and then they got so bright, that I felt sure they were going to blow a fuse or worse, so I killed their power."

She smiles, sliding past him and checking the electrical point, placing her hand gently on it. "There doesn't seem to be any problems here as the point is not even warm, in point of fact, it's bordering on cold."

"I know that," he grumps, "I've already checked it."

Anne raises her eyebrows, squeezes past him and as she leaves she adds, "Well I did say that they might be defective and they are a year older now. Maybe we ought to throw them away and replace them?"

"There's nothing wrong with the lights, probably a power surge or something," he retorts slightly aggravated.

He throws their power switch again and the lights burst back into life, this time sedately, slightly shimmering, but reacting quite normally. Alex smiles, quietly he says, "Be good you lot, no more stupid antics."

The evening gets under way with various locals calling in, some eating but most just in for a drink and a chat. John as usual, situates himself in his standard seating position in a corner of the bar, supping his Beast. Ian, a local artist, is sitting mid room in front of the fire, enjoying a bowl of soup and as always two rolls, as one is never sufficient for him. This is accompanied by a cup of coffee, then a second one before he will partake in an alcoholic beverage. Marvin and Ella, a couple from London, are seated at the opposite end of the bar from John, next to the piano and the Christmas scene and as usual they are joined by Trev and Rowena. Trev is a bloke from the South East and Rowena is a local lass. In the far corner of the bar are Steve, Maddie and their daughter Charlie, who are dining. They often come in and being good friends with Alex they frequently have a good old banter together. There are others as well, some local but not frequent visitors and a few who are completely unfamiliar to both Alex and Anne.

This is mid week, so Anne and one waiter, in this case Jack are staffing the kitchen and Alex is front of house, running the bar and watching over the ambience. By ten in the evening, the parties who were eating have all paid their bills and left, with most of them casting the Christmas village scene a pretty thorough examination and all of them without exception, commenting on how beautiful it is.

At ten fifteen, almost to the minute, Rob and Michael walk in. They are real night owls who always like to push the last orders of licensing to the limit. They are good friends with Alex and Anne, having all moved to the village within a few months of each other. Michael has been in a couple of times a week on his own recently while Rob has been in America on a tour. The latter is a man in his late fifties, fair haired, clean shaven, over weight and is a major participator in the world of psychics, having written books and given numerous lectures on this subject matter. Even now he jets off all around the world, to see, speak or participate in various aspects of his work. Michael is older, in his seventies, a retired barrister and an extremely intelligent man. He is over six feet, slim, with a full head of white hair and an abrasive manner that he somehow manages to get away with, although at times, both Alex and Anne cringe at his witless retorts.

By now, the three cats have taken up their positions in the bar, occupying vacant seats that will afford them the best view possible of the model village, while all the remaining people in the room have now taken stools around the bar. Jack has finished his evenings work and gone home. Anne has entered the bar and poured herself a large red wine. She is now sat with the late door patrons, all chatting amiably.

Alex and Rob greet each other with Alex enquiring as to how his latest trip had gone, when Rob suddenly catches sight of Bobs the cat. Her stature attracts his attention, the way she has craned her neck to look at something which appears to be obscured from her view. He attempts to trace her viewing line, but can't quite make out where it finishes. He then catches sight of Charlie and Ellie, who are staring at exactly the same point.

"What are they looking at?" he questions.

"Oh, they're looking at the Christmas scene," Alex replies sighing.

Rob glances over at the village scene, then back towards the cats, scrutinising each one of them in turn. "Well, that's bloody odd, what do you think they can see in it?"

"Dunno," John slightly slurs from the other end of the bar, "but they keep doing it. I reckon there's a wee beastie in there, talking of which landlord, any chance of another bottle?"

Alex smiles, reaching down behind the counter to get a fresh bottle and a general titter can be heard from everyone present at John's wit.

"There's no wee beasties in the scene Rob, both Fleche and I have checked it thoroughly, there's nothing there."

"Well, they think there is. Cats don't take on the behaviour of these three without them believing they are waiting for something to appear. If it's not the village scene, then it's something else in this corner by the piano."

In unison, everyone turns and surveys the piano and its surrounding area.

Alex watches this action, placing his hand on his chin, seeing the spectacle as amusing. "When all you Sherlock Holmes have finished analysing the supplied data from Rob, is there any danger you could all drink up and piss off home so I can go to bed."

This statement causes a chorus of groans as Anne gets to her feet, collects up the cats, placing them on the stairs that lead to their flat, bids everyone a goodnight, gives Alex a peck on the cheek and takes herself upstairs to bed.

Rob, almost oblivious to everything that has just taken place, is still looking puzzled, inspecting the scene, the piano, the shelf above it and any nooks and crannies that he can observe.

"Give it up Rob," Marvin jokes, "those cats need to see a shrink."

Alex notices that although everyone in the bar is giggling, Rob's face remains serious. He allows the situation to calm itself down, cracking a few jokes that on completion, sparks off others to join in on the act, especially Marvin, who loves a joke night. After a few more minutes of searching and watching the cats, Rob returns to his stool, his eyes still studying them, his demeanour remaining attentive.

By midnight, Rob and Michael are the only ones left in the bar, all the others have wound their weary and alcohol induced way home.

"Should we have one more?" Rob asks.

This is a phrase that annoys Alex, feeling it to be so American. "I don't know mate, should we?"

Rob's head leans to the right, "Can we?" he asks again.

"Don't be so obtuse," Michael grunts, now three sheets to the wind.

"Do you do that on your own Michael," Alex sarcastically questions, "or are you plugged into the mains again?"

Rob giggles, Michael glares.

Alex grabs the bottle of wine and pours them both a drink. He then tops up his own glass.

"Rob," Alex says, "what do you think the cats are looking at?"

Immediately Rob glances at the village scene. "I really don't know, but their reaction to this model is strange. Bobs was ready to pounce and Ellie and Charlie's pose was very similar, but they were more inquisitive than she was, watching to see whatever it was that they could see."

"Which is what? I've checked, you've checked, there's nothing there."

"Nothing we can see, but that doesn't mean there's nothing there."

Suddenly, the canopy lights begin to dim. It's Michael who initially observes this saying, "Your sparkly little lights are on the blink Alex."

From where Alex is standing he can't see the lights but he replies, "Naw, they're fine. They just perform some peculiar illumination things at times. That's all."

"Nope, they're fucked," Michael quips simply.

Rob takes a fleeting look at the display and states, "They really don't look quite right. Is this the same lot that you had up there last year?"

"Yes, they're the same ones and they're fine. They are just doing their own thing. It's late, so they're allowed to," Alex chuckles.

Both men look directly at him. "They're allowed to do their own thing? What the hell is that supposed to mean?" Michael stabs.

"Exactly what I said," Alex replies, raising his voice, alcohol enhancing his agitated mood. "They react to me and that's fine, if they want to climb down from the canopy and have a frigging drink with me, then that's fine too ok?"

"He's a lunatic, a complete nutcase," Michael retorts.

Rob begins to laugh, trying to make light of the contention, but Alex's eyes narrow as he states, "Don't upset me Michael. Go home."

Michael easies himself down from his stool glaring at Alex, dons his coat and leaves the bar grumbling under his breath. Rob grabs his glass, smiles at Alex and just as he about to speak the canopy lights blast with a blinding radiance.

"Jesus!" Rob exclaims. "What the hell are they doing now, turn them off!"

Alex reaches for the switch, just as both men hear the front door of the pub slam shut. The lights are extinguished and the room falls once more into a calm light.

"Sorry Rob," Alex concedes, apologising for his behaviour. "Sometimes when he's had a few, he annoys the hell out of me."

Rob laughs, "No shit, it didn't show. Besides when he wakes up tomorrow, the likely hood of him remembering the last hour here is extremely doubtful."

"Yeah, I know, but I still feel bad when I argue with that old fart."

Again, Rob laughs. He picks up his beer, drains it and says, "Is there any, remote as it maybe, chance that I could indulge in a final, no, ultimate glass of wine?"

Alex pauses for a second, places his hand on the bottle, but then stops before asking, "What about Michael, will he be okay getting home?"

"Of course, he will take three steps forward, two back, one to the side and then three more forward. The whole exercise will eventually get him home. Besides, he is such a stubborn old bastard, that after having had words with you, his whole mission will be to get home and devise ways to get back at you, which by morning, he will have forgotten, scratching his head as to what happened the night before."

Alex shakes his head, "That's harsh Rob, very harsh."

"Maybe, but it's the truth. You must understand, Michael thinks the world of you. He regards you as a close friend. That's the problem, a friend to Michael is a person he can ridicule, but there is no real malice in his actions."

Alex gazes at him, his eyes wide open, "Very deep, no, I mean it, that was very deep. Shall we just finish our drinks then I can hit the sack, trying very hard to blot out what occurred tonight with Michael."

Again, the canopy lights enhance, but this time changing their colours as they flicker.

"I thought you turned those things off?" Rob remarks.

"So did I?" Alex replies, reaching down to the switch.

When his finger reaches the power point, the display shuts down, going completely blank. Alex's finger twitches the on, off lever, but the small lever is definitely in the off position. He glances up to Rob, who is just draining the last dregs of his glass, saying, "Okay, now they're off."

"Good," Rob jokes, "I was beginning to believe they had a life of their own."

Alex chuckles a false chuckle, "Naw, just hadn't hit the switch right."

Rob, rises from his stool, smiles at Alex with slight disbelief and quips, "Well, just as long as you're in control of them and they are not in control of themselves, eh?"

Alex gives Rob a sideways glance, "They are lights Rob, not a flipping living thing."

Rob carefully puts his coat on, his eyes never meeting Alex's. Once attired, he smiles and says, "Goodnight my friend, watch your cats very closely, they see something I cannot pick up on. Watch them."

These words uttered, Rob makes his way to the front door and leaves. Alex returns to the bar, having seen him out, he locks up and shuts down the bar. Having systematically turned off all the electrical appliances he stands in the middle of the room. The only light afforded him is that from the fire place, as the last of the logs burn slowly down. He stares at the lights adorning the canopy over the bar, slowly allowing his eyes to settle on the dead and unlit bulbs along the expanse.

"You guys are doing some really weird stuff. Do me a favour and be something different when I need you to be."

Abruptly the lights spring back into action. Their light not content to illuminate just the bar, but their radiance spills out over the curtains that shroud the window and into the street. Alex stumbles backwards with the force, glancing across at their power point, fully aware that he has already turned it off, before steadying himself by clasping onto one of the table edges. The lights begin to change colour, oozing a glow that seems to leave the bulb and partially enter the room. For a second he senses fear well up inside him, but as the bulbs begin to soften their appearance once again, his empathy towards them returns.

"Sleep you lot and that's an order," he sensitively commands.

In an instant, they go out and darkness, apart from the fire, again fills the room. Although the fire as always has the ability to cast out its eerie shadows around the room, this time he is aware that even though the lights above the bar are out, there remains a distant and vague flicker, deep down inside the bulbs. He places the guard in front of the fire, checks the main bar door is locked and takes himself off to bed, his mind constantly pondering the hold which these set of Christmas lights seem to have over him.

As he climbs into bed, he hears the phone ring. He glances at the clock to see that it is past two in the morning. He slumps his head down onto the pillow, feeling the worse for his late night drinking, thinking to himself, 'I don't give a toss whoever that is, the answer machine can get it'. He hears the answer machine click in, turns over to snuggle up to his wife who is sound asleep, totally oblivious to his current dilemma, and finally he too drifts off into a deep slumber.

CHAPTER SIX

"They must have gone to bed," Julie Husky states, trying to see out of the small, frosty window.

"You mean that it's gone dark. That's brilliant, I think we've all gathered that," Paul Lucas grumps.

"Calm down Paul," Duncan soothes, as he sits huddled up against an unlit fire place, "we're all in the same boat here."

"Where exactly is here?"

All three crane their heads to see who has uttered these words, as none of them recognise the voice.

While Duncan is slowly getting to his feet staring at the silhouette in the doorway, Paul replies, "In the Christmas scene and who are you?"

Michael slowly and apprehensively shuffles into the room, the effects of the wine he was drinking earlier still evident. The only light apparent to him is emitting from outside the window, an orange glow. "My name is Michael and what do you mean exactly, 'in the Christmas scene?'

"Precisely that dopey," Paul retorts, "in the bloody Christmas scene. Have I got a speech impediment or something?"

Duncan intervenes for a second time saying, "For Christ sake Paul, he is obviously new here and hasn't a clue about anything, so why don't you stop being part of the problem and concentrate on helping to be part of the solution for a change."

Paul glares at him and walks towards one of the other doors, leaving the room, grumbling under his breath.

"Well Michael," Duncan states, "welcome to hell. To put this in a nutshell, we are in the Christmas village scene that stands on top of the piano in the bar of the Bell Inn, which if anything like us, you were just leaving, when you found yourself here. Am I correct in my assumption?"

Michael shakes his head in disbelief, blinking his eyes, vowing never to drink again and replies, "What, how, make sense man, I do not understand your gibberish explanation."

Julie, who is still trying to see through the window, bursts forth into rapturous laughter, "Like the man said, welcome to hell."

Michael supports his frame against one of the walls, surveying the room which he finds himself in. It is a small area with no furniture, with the exception of an uncomfortable looking settee that appears to be constructed out of plastic, even down to plastic cushions. There are two Georgian type windows on one wall, but the glass is frosted heavily and again, their construction appears suspect, almost artificial. When he glances up, he observes there to be no ceiling as he can see where the pitch of the roof begins. While examining the building, he notices that at some time in the past, it appears as though there would had been another room above, as the windows remain around the lofty expanse, but again, very little light is coming from them, just that same flickering orange glow.

"So," Michael enquires, "I will refine my question, what is this place?"

Duncan walks over to the settee and takes a seat on the hard surface. "As I have already told you, this is a model village, the one in the pub which you were leaving, when you suddenly found yourself here. As to how you got here, how any of us got here, we don't know the answer to that question. We arrived in a similar manner to you, the only difference being that we came here last year."

Michael stands up straight and with a certain degree of urgency in his voice he asks, "Are you trying to tell me that you three have been here for a year and know nothing about the way in which you arrived?"

"That's correct Einstein," Tara Lucas states, entering the room with Paul. "We know very little more than we did when we arrived, but now that you're here with your obvious, superior intellect, we should be free fairly soon," she smugly states.

Michael now recognises the Lucas's and recalls how problematic they used to be. He simply replies, "Well, yes my dear, you are undoubtedly correct, I will apply myself to the task first thing in the morning."

The light in the room decreases until finally the five of them are plummeted into total darkness.

Morning arrives way too soon for Alex, as his eyes flicker open to see the daylight flooding through the bedroom window. Anne has already risen, washed, dressed and left to tend her pony, which she has stabled a few miles away.

Alex's feet touch the carpet and he flexes his toes in its deep pile. He leaves the bedroom, going to the bathroom to wash and wake himself up. The air is cold and as he passes a window, he sees a layer of snow covering the landscape. It looks beautiful, causing him excitement just to see it. He rushes to get dressed and downstairs, knowing there will be work to be done clearing a path to the pubs door. He heads off downstairs to the kitchen to make a cup of tea. While he waits for the kettle to boil, he walks through to the front door, opens it and takes a look at the state of play of the snow clad ground. He raises his eyebrows when he sees that although the fall of snow is wispy, there must have been a fairly strong wind in the night as the snow has drifted, leaving two feet dumped against the front of the building.

"Morning Alex," Chris one of the local doctors calls out as he meticulously drives along the snow covered road towards the far end of the village.

Alex raises his arm to acknowledge the greeting and turns, shuts the door and heads for the kitchen; tea is paramount on his mind. On finishing his first cup, he sets the cup up for a second then heads off to find a stiff bristled broom. Having tracked one down in the garden shed, he passes through the kitchen and back out to the front of the pub to start sweeping the snow aside, carving a defined, non-slippery pathway to the front door.

"Alex!" he hears someone shouting. "Have you seen Michael?"

He turns to see Rob precariously making his way up the snow ridden path and replies, "No mate, not since last night when you saw him. Why, where's the old reprobate got to now?"

"That's my whole point, I don't know."

Alex can see the concern etched on his face and he stops what he is doing, waiting for Rob to reach him.

"Slow down Rob, when was the last time you saw him?"

"Probably the same time as you did and I haven't seen him since. When I got home last night, he wasn't there. I searched the house, even came back here in case he had fallen and I'd missed him going home. I even rang you, but got the damn answering machine."

"Ok, ok," Alex interrupts, "let's think about this logically."

He leans his broom up against the wall and they both enter the building whereupon Alex makes two fresh cups of tea.

Alex begins. "So the last time either of us saw Michael was when he left this bar, correct?"

"Yes that's correct."

"And as far as you are aware, he had no early morning appointments or anything?"

"No, there was nothing like that, he would have told me, besides I searched the house after I got home last night, he wasn't there."

"Hmm, then I don't know, where the hell can the old fart be?"

Rob looks pensive then says, "Shit I'm worried, where in the hell could he have gone to?"

Alex gets up from his seat, peers out of the window and replies, "I don't know, but I think we ought to rummage around the locals in the village, see if anyone has seen him today."

"It's daylight," Julie announces, running to the window that she still cannot see out of. "Michael, wake up!" she orders.

He stirs, as do the others, rubbing their eyes and slowly rising to their feet.

"Another day in hell," Duncan morosely announces.

Michael pushes back his hair, straightens his attire and walks to the window where Julie is stood. "First things first," he states, "get this window, either open or removed. We need to see what's out there."

"Tried that one," Paul claims, "but the bloody thing won't budge."

"Then try harder," Michael stabs, "we need to be able to establish our bearings and if this window won't open, then find one that will."

Duncan stares at Michael and says, "Do you not think that after a year of being in this place, we haven't tried every bloody window there is, tried to open it or smash it. Hell, we've even tried to bore a tiny hole so that we can look through it?"

For a minute Michael looks thoughtful then he enquires, "How many windows are there in this place?"

"Which building are you referring to?" Julie questions.

"Obviously I asked the wrong question. How many buildings are there?"

""Fifteen plus a couple of additions, structures that seem to be randomly placed," Paul informs him in a matter of fact manner.

"Interesting," Michael declares. "Then would it be possible for you to provide me with a guided tour of our, my, new surroundings."

Julie jumps down from the window ledge which she has been perched on, grabs his arm and excitedly says, "It would be a pleasure, come with me."

"Wait," Duncan orders, "we stay together, always together, that way nothing can happen without all of us being there."

Michael stops, turning his attention towards Duncan, his head slightly tilted to one side, he says, "Duncan isn't it? Well young man, if nothing has changed in one year then the chances are that nothing is going to change. Whatever managed to place us here is insular with its planning to believe that we, the five of us, are secure, as far as this presence is concerned. Working as a group is good, but a recognisance of our immediate surroundings, especially with a fresh pair of eyes, is essential and I do not require either your support or an audience."

"But what if you find something we haven't already found, something dangerous?" Tara interjects.

"Oh please, then I will eloquently request that it comes to meet you, so you may interrogate it. Oh and by the way, while I am gone, could you rustle up some breakfast, as I am beginning to feel a little peckish?"

Tugging at his arm Julie informs him, "Oh yeah, that will pass. We haven't eaten for a year. There is no food here and somehow we don't seem to need it either."

Michael sympathetically glances down at her before he replies, "Ok if you insist. Come on young lady, shall we let the tour begin."

Having already called into the local stores / post office with nobody there having seen or had anything reported to do with Michael, Rob walks across the square to the paper shop, to see if better luck can be had there. Alex, who has informed his wife as to what is going on, walks through the village taking his time to question anyone he sees as to whether they have seen Michael or not. Receiving a negative response from everyone he speaks to, he slowly makes his way back to the pub with his fingers firmly crossed, to hopefully find Rob and check on his progress.

As the pub comes into view, he sees both Anne and Rob sitting at one of the external round tables talking. He strides out expectantly to reach them for an update.

"Anything?" he questions urgently as he approaches them both.

"Nope," Rob replies, his concern evident on his face.

"You?" Anne hopefully asks, but already knowing the answer.

"No, no one seems to have seen him since yesterday or even the day before."

Rob pulls himself to his feet and says, "I'm going back home. I'll leave things as they are until this afternoon and then I'm going to report him missing to the police."

"I suggest that you spend the meantime ringing the hospital and anywhere else that you and he usually frequent," Alex suggests.

Rob nods as he dejectedly walks away towards his house. Alex and Anne enter the pub to continue with their daily routines of preparing for opening time. They discuss the mystery of Michael's disappearance on and off throughout the day, but try as they may, they can't seem to make anything remotely resembling a satisfactory conclusion as to his abrupt departure, especially as one minute he was at the pub and twenty minutes later he had apparently simply vanished.

The lunchtime period comes and goes, not a busy one, but then again the lead up to Christmas is always a funny time of year with people either Christmas shopping or saving their pennies for the holiday. The pub closes at the usual time and the instant the door is closed, Anne jogs across to Robs place to see if there is any further news. Alex takes himself upstairs as he has a quiz to put together for Thursday. This is a task that takes him a good couple of hours every week. She returns an hour later, joining him with the updated news.

"Rob has called the police to report Michael missing," she simply informs him.

He stops what he is doing to asks, "So I assume that Robs searches hasn't produced anything more?"

She shakes her head. "He rang all the local hospitals and spoke to the doctors, then various places in town where Michael frequents, but nothing. He even rang the bus company to see if anyone had reported seeing him, on the off chance that maybe he had lost his memory, fallen ill or something, but again nothing."

"This is bloody odd," Alex concludes. "Michael is no fool, in point of fact he is one of the most intelligent men I know, so where ever he is, he was either forced to go there or he fell sick and someone has taken him somewhere safe."

She stares at him and quietly says, "I am inclined to agree, but where?"

Julie leads Michael through a couple of rooms which closely resemble the one in which their search began, before finally they arrive at a hole in the floor, which she hesitantly peers down into.

"Down here," she beckons him.

"Why down there?" he says standing with his hands clasped behind his back.

"Because it's the only way out," she replies glancing back at him.

Looking perplexed he says, "What do you mean, it's the only way out, don't the doors work?"

She sighs. "The doors are like the windows, they are simply a moulded look alike, they don't actually open. To leave this model we need to go down here, past the wiring looms and transformer, across to the next model."

She disappears down into the hatch. Michael walks across to it and peers down watching her as she reaches the bottom. "You do understand that I am a man who is in his seventies and mountaineering is a thing of the past for me."

She takes a momentary look up at him and replies, "Seventies? You're still just a kid then. Come on, get down here," she chuckles.

He sniggers to himself and slowly he makes his way to the orifice, negotiating the steps down. These are not purpose built treads, but protrusions of unfinished plastic which due to the fact that they are encased inside the model, have never been smoothed off properly. Gradually he manages to make his way down to where she is.

"I do hope there are not too many of those to undertake."

She smiles as she continues to lead him forward. They pass all the wiring with Michael stopping from time to time in order to examine his surroundings and finally they reach a petite crack in the models casing, just wide enough from them to squeeze through. Michael crouches down and looks through, evaluating the lay out ahead.

"It appears that there is a way to leave the models just here, where there is a gap between them."

She laughs, "You'll see when you get out there."

He turns his attention back towards her, now staring straight at her he requests, "Please clarify your last statement young lady."

She crouches down beside him looking out of the fracture and pointing ahead. "Do you see the other building over there? Yes? Well, as we squeeze through this hole, we will not actually be out in the open but somehow we will simply find ourselves inside the next building."

He frowns, beginning to make his way slowly through the crack. He moves with deliberation, inching his way forward, awaiting the unexpected. As he eventually manoeuvres his entire frame from inside the first building, he does indeed find himself within another building. He looks back at her, still crouched down and watching him.

"Come over," he directs her.

Within an instant she is climbing through the crack and just as quickly, she is stood beside him.

"I told you," she quips.

"You did indeed," he says smiling. "This is a strange phenomenon, but it is exactly as you described it to me." He then turns and surveys his new surroundings, striding to the middle of the room and looking up into the ceiling, which climbs steeply upwards before it tapers away into a point.

"This is a church Julie, look at the structure."

She joins him, staring up in to the buildings lofty heights. "It might be. I can't remember what it looks like from the outside."

He gives this statement a few seconds thought before he replies, "Those are interesting words young lady. What exactly can you remember of this display as it appears from inside the bar?"

She ponders for a moment before she replies, "It's laid out on two levels with three longer collections of buildings at the back. You know like a couple of houses and a church in each one."

"Very good my dear, now can you recall the ones at the front?"

"Sort of," she replies, "the trouble is that there are at least seven of them and I can't remember the order which they are arranged in."

"I understand, so take your time and try to envisage the scene. Present me with the best layout you can perceive from your memory."

She seats herself on the floor just inside the room, using the wall as her back rest and ponders. "Working from right to left as you look at them from the side of the bar, right?" Michael nods his understanding. "Ok the first one is the model of a pub, The Mitre Inn. It is a two storey building with a room in the roof and a small single storey annex type thing adjoining it to the left. Next to that, there is the tea room and then comes a church."

"Do you think that the building we were in is that church?" he interrupts.

"No," she emphatically replies, "the one we are in is part of a model which consists of several buildings, the one on the bottom shelf is just a single church and it's much smaller."

Again he acknowledges this information with a nod.

"Now," she continues, "it's what comes after that I can't remember clearly. I know there's a house scene with a merry go round, a sweet shop and three others, one of which is a single house with trees around it and it has fibre optic lights all over it."

"Ok young lady, that was very informative and I thank you. If you do fathom out the exact order please let me know."

She beams with satisfaction and slides her body up the wall, getting to her feet. "You're welcome, so what now, do you wish to continue with the tour?"

"Indeed I do, please lead on."

Once more the pub opens its doors for the evening session and the early period produces a dozen or so of the locals who maintain this ritual a couple of times a week. In turn, they all buy a square or couple of squares on the Christmas draw. The prizes for this are on display for all to see at the end of the bar. Alex had spent part of his afternoon putting this all together, three draw sheets, each one containing one hundred and ten squares. If he managed to sell all three sheets, he will have raised three hundred and thirty pounds for charity. He was always proud of the monies he had raised for various causes over the years and worked hard at promoting them.

Early evening moves on to mid evening and now the pub is fairly full with people dining. Fleche is duty chef with Nancy and Jo waiting on tables. Alex is fronting the bar while his wife has the evening off from the kitchen, but she is upstairs in their private quarters working away on the annual accounts of the business that the accountant will be demanding in the New Year.

As usual all three cats are positioned strategically around the area in the bar, their eyes peeled, watching the Christmas village scene with immense interest. Alex cannot help but notice that various customers are also intrigued by the way in which the cats continue to stare, eventually bringing them to ask the inevitable question, 'exactly what are they staring at?'

The Christmas scene itself is visited and gazed at by nearly everyone present in the pub at one time or another as they examine the models with great gusto. As the newfound interest of the cats over the models escalates, a few people venture up to undertake a more thorough inspection of the plastic lit display, some joking that they can even see movement inside.

"Don't be ridiculous," Alex grumps, "how the hell would anything get in there?"

There are various theories offered, but he merely 'poo poo's' them all saying, "I think I had better shut the bar, as it appears that you lot have had quite enough to drink already."

This statement cause a ruckus of laughter with a variety of humorous jibes and the evening continues, joviality rife, speculation regarding the Christmas scene growing, with several groups of people discussing the display.

By eleven, only ten people remain in the bar, two of whom are Anne and Alex. Rob is there, still deeply concerned as to Michaels whereabouts. He has now been visited by the local police, who have taken all the particulars with regard to the missing man and the time leading up to his disappearance. Rob informs them both of their imminent visit from them too, in the not too distant future.

"Oh bleeding brilliant, that lot are becoming more regular visitors here than my locals."

"Well, think about it Alex," Chris the local doctor interjects, "Michael, and the other four who are missing from this village, were actually all lastly seen here."

For a few seconds total silence reigns, the only audible sound being the CD player, randomly selecting the music it chooses to play.

"He's got a point," John adds with a lopsided frown.

"We don't know that for sure," Rob states, "Michael definitely. The other four were here too, but we don't know whether anyone else saw them afterwards as we are not privy to all the facts relating to their disappearance."

Alex's face turns as each person airs their thoughts on the matter, his manner becoming slightly agitated as he finds his thoughts becoming defensive.

"Well we are all aware that even if they didn't disappear from here, they were definitely all here on the day preceding their evaporation into thin air," AP concludes.

AP is the nickname of a man in his late thirties, real name Andy Peter Elmsford. He is a tall, lean man, dark haired, sharp features, sporting glasses. He lives in the village with his wife and daughter, but travels all over the country as an inspector with plant machinery, always in great demand by his many customers for his expertise in the field.

"True enough," Chris concurs, raising his eyebrows in agreement.

Alex gets up from his stool, placing his beer down on the bar. "Think about it. All five of these people were either leaving here, or had recently left. If there is any connection between this pub and their disappearances, then it is tentative to say the least as they were all known to have left the building."

Slurring a little due to the amount he has consumed throughout the evening, John laughs out, "In which case, there must be a gang of kidnappers watching the pub around Christmas time, zapping various people for no apparent reason at all."

"And that's another thing," AP interrupts, "they have all vanished coming up to Christmas, all within the month of December?"

Again, silence fills the room, everyone present pondering the words which have just been spoken.

"Perhaps Santa has run out of elves and is trying to get some more help by stealing people from outside the pub," John breaks the silence with.

Alex glares at him, replying, "Perhaps it is time you went home."

The others smile and titter, but Alex is beginning to tire of all this speculation.

"Right that's it people, time to go home, me and the missus need to hit the sack, so grab your glasses and drink it or lose it."

There is a substantial amount of moaning from those gathered around the bar, but without exception, they all begin to sink their drinks and empty their glasses, fully aware that when Alex says 'that's it' he means it and if challenged, the culprit will never be invited to stay late again.

Shortly the room empties, leaving Anne and Alex alone in the bar. Alex follows Chris to the door as he is the last to leave, then locks everything up, securing the building for the night. When he returns to the bar, the canopy lights are glowing with a hazy radiance, slowly brightening their lights before dimming them once more. He walks behind the bar and turns them off for the night. He can hear Anne in the kitchen making their night time drink and goes out to join her, picks up his cup and returns to the bar. He sits, contemplating what has been said throughout the evening and staring into space without really seeing anything at all. Anne breaks his concentration when she enters the bar, kisses him on the cheek and bids him goodnight.

As he hears the door to the stairs behind him close and she goes up to their home, he gulps down some of his drink preparing to follow her upstairs, when his attention is caught by something in the Christmas village. He leaps to his feet to take a closer look at the scene. Slowly and methodically he inspects each model, picking them up one at a time to turn them over and look underneath each item. Nothing, he cannot see anything wrong.

"Bloody hell, now I'm seeing things," he says out loud to nobody but himself.

He returns to his drink, downs the cup and returns it to the kitchen, placing it in the sink and then retires himself. Shutting and locking the door to the stairs behind him, he climbs the first flight. As he turns the corner, he is struck by an intense splurge of light shining through the glass doorway from behind the bar. The shock causes him to stumble on the next stair, his mind frantically searching but fully aware that he has turned everything electrical off. He attempts to turn around to see what has caused the blinding flash. When he manages to regain his composure and footing, all he can see is darkness. He stands watching for a few moments, shakes his head when nothing unusual happens, thinking he's finally gone mad, he continues his weary way up to bed.

CHAPTER SEVEN

The morning breaks and snow is falling, settling as it goes. The sky as a whole is a soft yellow and pinkish grey, with no sign of a break in the weather for the foreseeable future.

Across the road from The Bell Inn are several detached houses, all old, listed and a little down at heel. The one immediately opposite the pub and the most run down of them all, is occupied by a widow called Gladys Stanford, a strange woman with five cats that she completely worships. She is not very tall, white haired with a reddish complexion, beady eyes and a broad Devonian accent. She dresses extremely matronly and is always to be found watching by her front window, anything and everything that is going on outside. This particular morning she is gazing at the pub, at the bar window to be precise, observing the light display taking place there. The dawn is just breaking so its visibility is obvious to her and she finds it quite intriguing.

While she watches two of her cats join her on the window sill, purring and nudging her, wanting to be fed. When the third one arrives she bows to their demands, leaves her observation point, heading for the kitchen to feed them. On her return, she immediately checks the window once more but to her dismay the glowing opposite has ceased and the room seems now to be enveloped in darkness. She leaves the window, walks to the hall, pulls a coat around her and leaves the house, leaving the door wide open and cautiously shuffles over the road to the pub window. Using her hands to form a tunnel, she places her head on them and peers as best she can in order to see inside the room. Narrowing her eyes she can make out the layout of the bar, but there is no illumination visible. Suddenly, the canopy lights burst into life, shaping the shadows into a vision which Gladys perceives to be a human shape running towards the window and directly in her path. She stumbles back from this sight, slips on the path and tumbles off the curb, falling into the road.

"You ok Mrs Stanford?" Cyril an early bird villager calls out, having just left home to collect his morning paper.

For a moment she doesn't move a muscle, assessing the situation to see if she is hurt anywhere before she slowly heaves herself into a sitting position and curtly replies, "I think so, come and help me up."

Cyril raises his eyes at the order snapped out by Gladys and shuffles through the snow to where she is sitting. He stands behind her, crouches down and puts his arms under her arm pits, clasps his hands and hauls her to her feet. Having a struggle to lift her, as he is in his sixties, he huffs and puffs and after a couple of attempts he manages to haul her on to her feet.

"Have you finished groping me now?" she sarcastically says once upright, brushing herself off.

"If groping was to be my intention my dear, I would have chosen a much younger model of woman than you. I can assure you of that. I was purely trying to aid your assistance," he barks back at his in defence.

She scowls at him and begins to shuffle through the snow back towards her home muttering, "Ghost light, slippery surfaces and old perverts, it's not a great start to the day."

Shaking his head, he turns away from her and proceeds with his journey down the street to the newsagents. He enters the shop to see Edna, a lady in her seventies, smiling at him.

"I can imagine how nicely you were complimented for your gracious efforts by her," she says.

"Accused of groping, that was my thanks," he huffs.

She bursts into laughter saying, "Wishful thinking on her behalf I would say."

Cyril raises his eyebrows, takes his paper, pays his money and leaves the shop saying, "The next time I see that old cow on her arse, I'm just going to walk the other way."

Early morning moves on to mid morning and Alex and Anne are in the pub cleaning and preparing for opening time. Alex is cleaning out the big, old open fireplace and laying the kindling ready to light it up again at noon. He places a firelighter underneath, leaving just enough poking out in order to light it, then he grabs the coal scuttle, shaking it a couple of times and ascertaining that as usual it needs filling. He lets out a deep sigh as he feels that he always seems to be the one with the job of refilling the scuttle and makes his way out to where the bags of coal are stacked. He places the receptacle on the floor by the coal bags, grabs a sack and empties the contents into it. He then takes the top handle, lifting it carefully as it is now very heavy, and makes his way back to the bar. As he turns the corner the handle shears away from the carrier and both the receptacle and its contents fall to the floor, but not until they have grazed his shin and landed on his foot. He lets out a shrill cry as the pain of the accident registers with his brain. Glaring down at the broken scuttle, his anger rapidly begins to swell inside. The bar canopy lights glare into action, filling the room with an intense red light. Initially this startles him and his concentration is momentarily removed from his stinging wound, to the display that has now illuminated the entire area. He stumbles backwards, falling over a chair and landing on the carpet, staring up at the canopy in disbelief and cursing under his breath. Hearing the commotion Anne runs into the bar. Instantly the lights shut down, plunging the room back into the normal light afforded from the solitary window, which is quite dim in comparison to the canopy display. She trips over the coals now strewn around the floor and ends up sitting on the floor right next to Alex who is now pulling up his trouser leg to inspect the damage caused to his leg and foot.

"What the hell is going on?" she grumbles.

"The bloody handle sheared off the scuttle, scraped my leg and landed on my frigging foot!" he loudly explains.

She scrambles to her feet saying, "Why and how did you manage to turn the lights out when I came in?"

"I didn't, the bleeding things just came on and then went off. I didn't touch them!"

She glances around the floor then moves around behind the bar. She turns on the main lights. Surveying the area she glances across at Alex then she continues with her inspection of the room.

"Where's the scuttle?"

"Here somewhere, stupid bloody thing," he complains.

"Where?" she presses, "I can't see it."

Alex, now on his feet, but still disturbed by the graze down his shin and the bruise on his foot shouts, "Here, here, it can't be far! The bloody thing is metal and heavy and it fell on my foot, how far could it go?"

She moves slowly around the room, crouching to look underneath the tables, collecting up odd pieces of coal strewn around the floor. Having searched the entire area, she turns again to him saying, "Well, I can't find the big, black heavy scuttle that could not have possibly gone far. Did you throw it by any chance?"

Alex, who is now rolling his trouser leg down, slowly raises his gaze to meet her eyes and slightly agitatedly, he retaliates with, "No, I did not throw the scuttle, as I originally stated, I dropped the bleeding thing down my shin and onto my foot."

She raises her eyebrows and with a smile says, "Then it should be here, shouldn't it? I cannot see it, so I will leave you to search for it. I am going to get on with what I was doing if you are ok now?"

He grits his teeth and nods but doesn't look up or cease with his perplexed and methodical search.

"I can hear voices out there," Duncan states moving towards one of the heavily frosted windows.

"I heard a crash as well," Julie adds, following him to the aspect.

Tara giggles her small, nervous laugh that causes everyone in the room to glance at her.

"You okay love?" Paul asks.

She drops her head into her hands and says, "What do you think, are we ever going to be allowed to leave here? Will we eventually just die in this place?"

Silence hits the room before Michael calmly answers her question. "No my dear but I really do not think that we are simply going to be released. Whatever mystical power put us in here in the first place quite obviously had its reasons for doing so, reasons that are not apparent to me at present, however, the answer to our liberation will be within our incarceration, I am sure of that, and we all need to start searching for whatever that is."

Duncan turns his attention away from attempting to see out of the window and questions him, "Look Mike..."

"It is Michael," Michael aggressively interrupts, "not Mike, Mickey, Mick or any other abbreviation of the name, please be clear on this point."

Duncan, obviously taken aback by this statement, clears his throat, and then continues with his question. "Michael, have you any idea what we are supposed to be looking for, any inkling of where the key may lie?"

Michael begins slowly pacing and thoughtfully answers, "I must admit, the answer to your enquiry is no, nevertheless, having given a great deal of thought to our predicament it has become obvious to me, that the prison which we find ourselves in, is designed to limit our contact with anything or anyone outside of its boundaries. When Julie and I took our little stroll around, we were always forced, no that's the wrong word, directed in a certain path, making it appear to us as though that were the only way through. Personally, I do not believe this to be the case. We simply need to test our boundaries. Eventually we will find a weakness."

A hush falls across the room.

"Ok," Duncan breaks the silence with, "what exactly have you got in mind?"

Suddenly a crashing sound echoes from the next building. They glance around at each other as Julie runs towards the doorway, closely followed by Duncan. Tara doesn't move, but Michael and Paul, their curiosity aroused, follow them in.

As Julie enters the room, quickly scanning the whole area, she cannot see anything different. Then Duncan enters, walks past her and positions himself centrally in the expanse. He crouches down and methodically completes a three hundred and sixty degree search of the room. Seemingly not seeing anything strikingly untoward, his gaze settles on something in the far corner. He immediately gets to his feet and walks across, with the others close on his heels.

"What is that?" Duncan asks.

Paul leans down and picks up the object, inspecting it further. "It's a coal hod."

"That is a coal scuttle," Michael elaborates. "A hod is what builders use to transport bricks and furthermore if I am not mistaken, that is the same scuttle which resides in the bar of the Bell Inn."

"How do you know that for sure?" Julie asks.

"Because," he continues, "the top handle is missing. It had been loose for quite some time as I remember. Those marks around the very bottom edge, I have noticed them many times before and lastly, because we all went missing from the Bell Inn, so it would follow that this item must also have come from there in order to be transported here."

"Wow," Julies says in wide eyed amazement, "what are you, some kind of detective?"

"No my dear, I am merely a retired lawyer and used to looking through the unnecessary wrappings."

After a few seconds of silence, Tara who has remained in the other room but has been listening to everything calls out, "But why, why has that been sent here?"

"Now that," Michael emphatically states, "is a good question, extremely well put and deserves an answer, but at present I have no real idea. However, it has confirmed one thing and that is as I had already suspected, the Bell Inn is the platform which is used to send us, in point of fact to send anything here."

"Can you get the door?" Alex yells out to Anne, "I'm still trying to get this coal cleaned up, it's gone everywhere."

Hearing his plea she puts down the pastry she is kneading, washes the flour from her hands and heads for the front door. Again the door bell chimes just as she reaches it.

"Christ," she mutters under her breath, "patience is a virtue. You should try it now and again."

The front door is exceptionally large and heavy so she has to pull it with some effort. There on the step, looking a little sheepish at their welcome, are the two police officers from before, Criss and Marcus.

"Sorry to disturb you ma'am, but as you are probably aware by now we have had another disappearance."

"Yes of course we know," she impatiently replies, "I should think the whole village knows by now."

"May we come in?" Criss requests.

She beckons them in, showing them into the bar where Alex is now on all fours underneath the corner table, collecting odd bits of coal which he is muttering, "have managed to hide themselves under there."

"Good morning sir," Marcus greets.

Alex lurches up to see who it is, smacking his head underneath the table in the process, turning it over with the force.

"Bloody hell," he screeches in pain, "what now?"

Anne quietly chuckles to herself and Marcus enquires, "What are you doing sir?"

"Riding a bicycle, what the hell do you think I'm doing? I'm picking up coal, well until you came bursting in I was, then I decided I would break up the bar using my head just to impress you."

Anne creases with laughter, Criss smiles but Marcus remains straight faced, not sure how to react.

"So you are here to interrogate us yet again, on the missing person problem of this village."

Marcus, taken aback by his aggression, replies, "Not at all sir, we are here trying to ascertain what happened on the night of Michael Nisty's disappearance."

Both Alex and Anne take their seats and begin to relate the happenings of the evening in question, describing the facts as vividly and accurately as they can remember. Criss and Marcus listen attentively, scribbling down notes in their pads, never interrupting. On completion, both officers stand, thanking them both for their time and co-operation and Anne sees them off the premises. Alex remains seated, seemingly perturbed.

"What's up?" she asks him on her return.

"Something isn't right here. Those two listened, said nothing and left way too soon, as though they have already made a conclusion and just needed some gaps filling in."

"Oh come on, aren't you taking this too far? The word paranoia springs to mind."

His head springs up, glaring at his wife. "Paranoia is an uninformed frame of a confused mind, what I am feeling is that outside people are collating a bunch of theories and coming up with an answer to a problem that is far from solvable at this moment in time."

Fully aware that her husband's background was in the Criminal Investigation Department of the police force she nods, saying, "In which case darling, you of all people should know very well that they are far from the mark."

He affords her a grin and dejectedly retorts, "Assumptions are like arseholes dear, everyone has one. Clint Eastwood said that and how true it is. These police and other people in this place, capable of an opinion, have already made one and I feel that the finger is pointing this way. "

She walks across to him, kneels at his feet and hugs him, "Alex we cannot afford to be so judgemental and opinionated in a small village. Please do not upset the apple cart over stupid accusations."

He smiles to himself and whispers in her ear, "At least one of us is a diplomat, personally I would just like to meet some of these gossiping idiots."

"I know," she says, rising to her feet, "but I also know that you will look after business before you deal with a stupid set of circumstances, which after all have no real bearing on our lives."

Slowly he nods, reiterating, "Ok, although I have got to say that the authorities and some of the people in this village are firmly pointing their crippled fingers at this pub, I will for the moment, keep playing the impartial landlord of the Bell Inn."

Snow begins to fall by lunchtime, settling on top of the load which had established itself earlier. The temperature is a couple of degrees above zero with very little wind, so the flakes flutter down vertically with no interference to their descent. Initially they are small, almost whimsical, but within the hour their size increases as the load becomes heavier, making it difficult to see across the street.

John gazes out of his window, watching it for a few minutes and then quite excitedly says to his wife, "I'm off for a pint at The Bell, won't be long."

"In all that snow, are you off your rocker?" Carol, his wife calls back, as she hears the front door shut behind him.

He does up his jacket as he begins his way to the pub, carefully placing his feet as he treads, the snow already a couple of inches deep. As he walks into the village square he can see The Bell, both its sign and Christmas lights managing to guide him through the blizzard he is fighting against. Halfway across the square he literally bumps into

Rob, who is on precisely the same mission. As they collide, both men grab hold of each other, creating a slippery ice skating dance, while both men attempt to remain upright on their feet. During their balancing act they erupt into laughter, which doesn't help their efforts to stay aloft in the least. The dance ends with them both falling over, landing firmly on their ample bottoms. Still giggling, John is the first to clamber to his feet before he aids Rob up as well.

"Well, that went well didn't it?" Rob jests.

"We must have looked ridiculous," John replies, "are you ok?"

"Only my pride is hurt, I just hope no one witnessed that fiasco."

"Are you two ok?" A voice from behind John calls out.

Rob raises his eyebrows in answer to his statement and stares into the falling snow, peering to see who asked the question. John has already recognised the voice.

"We're fine Steve," he yells back, "haven't had a drink yet and still can't stand up for long."

Steve, a man who originated from the north of the country, is in his early fifties, short dark hair, bearded with a stocky build, comes into plain view and says, "Nothing new for you two then. Where you off to?"

"The pub of course, well I am anyway," John replies.

"Me too," Rob adds.

"Then let's all go together. I was supposed to drive to Nottingham today, but the snow has brought that plan to a grinding halt, so the pub appears to be a much more civilised option," Steve states.

All three continue to plod their way through the snow, making their short trip to The Bell Inn.

Once there, all three in turn bash their feet against the stone wall outside the main entrance, ensuring that all the snow and slush is off their shoes. They all know their landlords thoughts on ignorant people who walk mud and rubbish into his premises. They enter the building, heading straight for the bar.

"Afternoon lads, what can I get for you on this cold and wintery day," Alex greets them with.

"Have you seen the weather out there," Steve questions, "its bloody arctic conditions."

"Nope, I tend not to gaze out of the window while I'm working, besides it's been lovely in here all morning," he jokes back to them.

Giggles can be heard from around the bar. Hand shaking takes place, a tradition that Alex has encouraged, saying 'friends should always greet each other as friends'. The locals appear to approve of this custom too.

Drinks poured, the three men take their respective stools at the bar. Around the room a couple of families are already eating, with the only other customer being Andy, who is sat at one end of the bar. Alex relays to them the morning's events with the police and all four listen attentively. The cats as usual, have taken up their places, all watching the Christmas Village Scene.

When Alex finishes his story, Rob surmises, "They seemed to leave a little abruptly, don't you think?"

"Yeah, we did."

As if..." Andy starts, but then stops.

"As if what Andy?" Steve asks.

"Well, as if they'd already made up their minds about the disappearances."

Alex glances across at him and after a couple of seconds of thought he asks with some agitation, "What is that supposed to mean, what on earth are you trying to tell us?"

Andy looks a little uneasy at both the man's tone and his question. He reshuffles his position on his chair and then replies, "The way you put it to us Alex, it simply sounded as though they were just going through the motions, not really interested in discovering anything more," he attempts to backtrack.

Silence fills the surrounding area, only the voices of those not privy to this conversation can be heard in the background.

"To some extent I am inclined to agree," Alex states, "but if they have, they are certainly not casting any inclination as to their conclusion."

"Typical of our local law," Steve concludes. "They strut about as if they are in complete control of everything but they bump into things that are staring them straight in the face, not realising the importance of the collision."

"Wow, that was deep," John quips.

Rob hands his empty glass across the bar and Alex refills it. While the drink is pouring he says, "If the police do have any idea where Michael and the others have gone I would be very surprised, because evidence wise, there isn't any. Any theories they might have are exactly that, a guess."

Everyone gathered around the bar and part of this discussion, nod, concurring with his sentiment. Suddenly there is a huge crash. All eyes turn in the direction of the disturbance, only to see Bobs the cat sliding across the front of the piano, taking one of the models partially with her. She slips off the piano, releasing the wire that was tangled in her claws and hits the floor, freeing the model she had dragged behind her. To everyone's astonishment it flips back upwards into exactly the same position as before. She flees from the room, cornering with the skill and dexterity that only a cat can manage.

Alex stares at the model, moving slowly from behind the bar towards the piano, he leans over the previously dislodged model, inspecting it closely.

"Did you see that?" he stutters.

There is a resounding 'yes' from everyone behind him, with Rob suspiciously adding, "I have never seen anything like that before. It was almost completely off the top of the piano and then, as if by magic, it took itself back to its original position."

John glances over at the other two cats which throughout the ruckus haven't moved a muscle. Their eyes, like black holes, continue to stare at the village. "Like magic," he mutters under his breath. He downs his drink, bids everyone goodbye and leaves with a frown firmly fixed on his face.

CHAPTER EIGHT

"What the hell's going on?" Duncan yells out as the room which they are in starts to violently shudder.

Tara and Paul are holding each other tightly, having crouched on the ground with the misconceived idea that this would afford them some kind of safety. Immediately Julie wobbles across to the window, hoping to see what is causing the earthquake while Michael has shakily made it to one of the corners of the room, placing his hands either side of the angled walls to gain some stability. Duncan stands in the centre of the room, arms held out on either side, attempting to maintain his balance.

Suddenly the entire room starts tilting forwards. Michael stumbles before falling, groaning in pain as he lands and begins to slide towards Julie. Duncan is thrown off his feet and only stops rolling when he hits the outer wall. Tara and Paul are forced to a sitting position before sliding down the room. The only person who is not caused too much of a problem is Julie, who on seeing Michael fall, immediately jumps to his assistance, slowing his momentum across the room, allowing him to gently reach a halt by the window where she had previously stood.

The initial tilt rapidly turns into a violent lurch forward as the occupants scream, their bodies pushed hard against the cold wall which they find themselves firmly pinned against. Then within an instant, the brutality of the gravitational energy which is holding them in place is abruptly reversed, sending them all sprawling in the opposite direction. Duncan hits the central structure and is knocked unconscious, while the others hurtle towards the void, not stopping until they meet the other side.

Within seconds, the movement has ceased as quickly as it began. Everyone remains perfectly still as the realisation dawns on them that their limited world has settled again. Julie is the first to move, slowly staggering to her feet, negotiating her way to the nearest corner of the room, then keeping her back to this upright she traverses its expanse until she reaches the far side. Here, she presses her head against the window. Everyone apart from Duncan, who remains unconscious, watches her with anticipation.

"I don't think we have moved at all, although I can't really see out of this window very well. I have become accustomed to the way the light issues from outside and looking at it now it seems the same as it was before."

Shakily Michael gets to his feet. He limps across the room to where Julie is standing, asking, "Are you sure my dear, I mean are you absolutely positive?"

Momentarily she remains silent, still gazing out of the mottled glass, then nodding her head she replies, "I'm as sure as I can be."

"Well that's good enough for me," he says. He turns and walks over to where Duncan is sprawled out on the floor. Having checked his pulse and gently moved various limbs, watching for a reaction he states, "I think he's ok."

"Was that an earthquake?" Paul questions.

"Don't be ridiculous man," Michael protests, "we are inside a model on a shelf. Simple reasoning would conclude that due to the fact Devon hasn't had an earthquake of any consequence, that I am aware of anyway, I can only assume that we were knocked off our perch by someone, or something."

"Ok, Mr Know it all," Tara retaliates, "if you know so much, why don't you get us out of here?"

Michael raises his eyes to the heavens and gently, but sarcastically replies, "I, my dear woman, am working on that exact thing. What are you doing, apart from complaining at every possible opportunity?"

Her eyes glaze, her annoyance evident, but before she can retort, Duncan who is rubbing his head and pulling himself up into a sitting position says, "Come on people, getting annoyed with each other is really not going to help."

Julie immediately goes to him and crouches by his side. "Are you ok?"

A smile flickers across his face and he replies, "I reckon so, it's just my head that is thumping."

He is helped to his feet, where upon he walks, although a little shakily, straight to Michael and says, "Look mate as you seem to be the only one here who has any real idea of what's going on, I think you're hatching a plan to get us out. Am I right?"

Michael turns away, walking towards the next room quietly saying, "The answer to our escape is to identify what exactly sent us here. I use the word 'sent' purely because if indeed we are in the Christmas village, inside The Bell Inn, we are minute, we have been shrunk."

Immediately these words leave his mouth, both Tara and Paul having overheard the conversation, instigate a manual inspection of their selves. Julie smiles at this spectacle.

"That would suggest," he continues, "that we are dealing with something such as the occult."

"The occult!" Duncan spits out.

"Yes as in witchcraft and the like. As far as I am aware, and believe me I am very well read, no one has ever had the ability to shrink people, not in reality and while they remain alive anyway."

Now Tara looks terrified and stutters out, "You mean...."

"No my dear woman," Michael interrupts, anticipating her question, "You are not dead, none of us are, we are plain and simply caught up in some kind of black magic. At least, that's my theory so far."

The others digest this statement for a couple of seconds before Duncan enquires, "If that really is the case, how do we deal with that kind of thing?"

"A very good question, extremely well put and deserves an answer, but at this present moment, I do not have one. We need to carry out further investigation into our habitat in order to discover these answers."

"Then what are we waiting for? I for one don't want to spend another year in this dump. Where do you want to start?" Julie says.

A blue backed file is slung onto the desk and Inspector Henderson, hands clasped on the file, lifts his eyes to gaze upon Criss and Marcus.

"Five people missing, some for over a year and all you can conclude is that it has something to do with the local pub. That's brilliant!"

"But sir," Criss defends, "based on ...."

"Based on what? Just because the last time they were seen was at the said pub. What are we doing now, assuming guilt by association? Bloody hell you two, take this file back and do some real detective work and bring me some sound answers."

Criss and Marcus leave the Inspectors office like two scolded children, not uttering a single word until they are well away from the vicinity.

"That went well," Marcus jokes.

Criss affords a giggle, adding, "If there is any other way we can cock up today, just let me know won't you?"

Marcus suddenly stops in the middle of the corridor. "Are we missing something here?" he asks.

"Definitely," Criss replies, "didn't you hear the governor just kick our arses out his office?"

"No," he continues, "we went in there with the aim of persuading him to allow us a search warrant because we were convinced that the pub would give us the answer to this riddle."

"I still do believe that."

"Think about it Criss. Everyone who had seen the people who'd disappeared, they all said the same thing."

"I know, but I still think the answer lies in that pub."

"It does, you're right, but it doesn't lie in turning the place over."

Criss slumps back onto the wall sighing, "Oh do enlighten me, please."

Marcus casts a sideways glance before continuing, "They all said quote, 'They were leaving the pub'."

Criss's face creases, deeply in thought, she questions, "I'm really not following you here?

"They, the missing people, were all leaving. That is the one consistent fact. If they were all leaving and that means they all must have been in the hall in order to leave the said premises, then we just need to take a really good look around that hall."

"And how are we going to do that, pop in to The Bell for a drink and then loiter around in the hall? Don't you think the landlord might find that just a little suspicious?"

Marcus looks slightly perplexed before adding, "No not really, I thought I might drive out to Witherford, go to the pub and just ask if he minds if we have a look around. Personally, I feel that is a far better approach than your cloak and dagger stuff."

Criss raises her eyebrows and replies, "Ok let's do that, straight after lunch because I'm starving."

Both officers set off again with new direction and a definite spring in their pace, towards the canteen.

Graham and Mandy emerge from the fields having walked their two dogs in the deepening snow. They leave the track on to the road and walk a few yards before entering the grounds of the parish hall. There they meet George and Eileen with their dog Moneypenny, a small mongrel with a big attitude, not nasty but full of life and energy. The dogs are familiar with each other and immediately erupt into a chase, frantically circling the grounds, rolling each other over and over in the fresh snow, all three dogs relishing the soft, white novelty. The couples chat for a while before deciding to go for a coffee at the pub. Checking the time on the church clock they note that The Bell Inn's opening time is in fifteen minutes, so they decide to linger for a short while longer, letting the dogs run and play before they make their short journey to the local watering hole.

When they enter the pub they are confronted by a full house, the bar is steaming.

"Looks like the snow brought everyone out," George grumps, as he begins to fight his way to the bar.

Graham smiles, following him on his quest. The girls glance around, looking for somewhere to sit with three snowy dogs. Mandy spots a couple sitting at a corner table who are only occupying a couple of seats. She makes her way to the table and talks with its occupants. In seconds she and Eileen have taken their seats, the dogs with them, Mandy catching Grahams eye, gesturing for them to join them with the drinks.

Suddenly, one of the dogs begins to growl, a low deep droning snarl that immediately catches Eileen's attention. She follows the dogs stare, attempting to ascertain what it is grumbling about but when her search fails to enlighten her, she reprimands the dog saying, "Shush cut that out."

The dog briefly glances at his owner before returning his stare towards the Christmas village scene, his growl becoming deeper and louder. One of Mandy's dogs joins in on the act, which in turn alerts the other one to the issue. As the volume of their vocal disapproval increases, other people in the bar turn to see what the problem is.

Having fought their way to the bar and ordered their drinks, Graham and George become aware of the ruckus occurring in the far corner. Before they pick up the coffees placed in front of them, they turn to see what's happening. Graham's expression changes from one of interested disquiet, to concerned alarm. He witnesses all three dogs tugging at their leads, trying to cross the room to reach something, which as yet is unidentified. Eileen and Mandy are struggling to hold the dogs back with one of the other people at their table assisting them in their efforts to control them. He quickly moves across the room to help. As he reaches the animals, they wrench their necks to see past him. He quickly glances over his shoulder and then back to the dogs. Various people on tables close to them have by now vacated their seats, moving to a safer distance, watching the animals with a sense of foreboding in their eyes.

Graham and George grab the leads of the dogs from the women and immediately try dragging them towards the exit. By now the dogs have reached fever point, their mouths frothing and teeth bared, lurching and pulling violently in the direction of the model village. They eventually manage to drag the dogs out of the pub and into the street. As they walk the animals away, so they start to calm down and within a minute or two, they are back to their usual relaxed, playful selves. Shortly they are joined by the girls, who are totally perplexed over the dog's bizarre behaviour. They decide to take them home.

Graham and Mandy, who only live a hundred yards from the pub, are home quickly. They take their dogs indoors and settle them into their baskets. Shortly Graham informs his wife of his intention to pop back to the pub to apologise to Alex. He dons his coat once more and makes his way back to The Bell Inn. As he enters he can hear that people are still talking about the incident regarding the dogs. He spots Alex serving at the far end of the bar and when he reaches it, he catches his eye and beckons for him to come over.

"Alright Gray?" Alex greets him.

"Yes fine," Graham replies, "I just wanted to apologise for the dog's behaviour earlier."

Alex laughs out loud, "No problem mate. It livened up a few of the punters."

Graham joins in with his laughter and adds, "Well, while I'm here, I'll have a beer, it would be rude not to."

Alex smiles and grabs Graham's personal glass, a jug which hangs from a hook inside the canopy, where all the other personalised glasses hang. He pours the beer and places it in front of him. Graham begins to search his pockets for his money, when Alex says, "On me mate, you never actually got your coffee earlier and you'd already paid for that."

Graham smiles, Alex is always fair, not a soul on the planet could say otherwise, fair and honest. "Thanks. By the way, did you see what spooked the dogs?"

Alex creases his face, implying 'not really' and he says, "Something over this side of the bar I think, well at least that's the way they were looking."

"The piano, they were growling at the old Joanna," Vic, an old Devonian of large build in is his late fifties informs.

"True enough," Judith, Vic's partner substantiates, "they were definitely pissed off with something to do with that piano."

Graham turns to inspect the item, his gaze instantly falling on the Christmas scene. He takes a pace towards it, scrutinising each model in turn, taking his time, looking in, over and behind every single piece. Having satisfied himself that all as it should be, he then examines the furniture which the models are stood upon.

"It's a piano boy," a local farmer called Julian Canning calls out from the far side of the bar, having watched Grahams investigations.

Graham, who is now crouched, slowly rises, turns back to the bar, ignoring the quip and takes a sip of his pint.

"Even we old Devonians know what that is. You should have asked one of the local, the real locals, if you weren't sure," Canning pursues.

Alex glances across at him. He immediately reacts to the glare. "Oh, is our esteemed landlord going to defend the uneducated outsider?"

A hush fills the room, akin to a Mexican 'stand off' with its imminent gunfight.

Alex inclines his head at Canning's innuendo, the intensity of his stare increasing. "Mr Canning, a local farmer you might be, a pillar of our community you are definitely not. As for a diplomat to the cause of those people who move here or merely visit this village, well? You are a rude, egocentric and arrogant man and in this case you are inebriated as well. You may finish your drink and leave, but please do not linger in doing so."

Throughout this verbal onslaught from Alex, the entire room has fallen silent; a pin could be heard to drop. Anne has lowered her head, knowing that her husband's tolerance with this man has reached the point of almost nonexistence since he started his regime of dumping the waste products from his farm animals on his peripheral fields closest to the village, where the prevailing winds carry their odious aroma, permeating the dwellings that stand throughout. Various committees, including the Parish Council, have tried to rectify this situation, but the man has stood firm, saying 'he can deposit his waste anywhere he likes as long as it is in accordance with the Environmental Health Department'. Fully aware that the act itself has enraged the village, he seems intent on provoking them further by ignoring their complaints. Alex has been looking for an excuse to ban him from the premises, especially as some locals have stopped using the pub because of his periodic presence there.

Canning shifts uncomfortably in his seat, glancing around the room, observing that all eyes are now upon him. As he takes a deep breath to deliver his reply, the canopy lights begin to flicker, not in unison, but randomly, increasing in volume, second by second. Immediately the patron's attention is drawn to the illuminations and Graham stands back from the bar to gain a better view of the display.

"I have, in the whole of my life, never been so insulted with such claptrap. You landlord, are a disgrace to your profession," Canning rants.

"I doubt that," Alex replies, "from what I hear, most people around this part of the world share my opinion. As for my profession, licensing law has made it clear that I am not to serve anybody whom I believe is intoxicated or a problem, and you are both. Now get out of here before I remove you."

Canning leaps to his feet with his two accomplices, slams his beer mug down on the table, the handle of which shears straight off, causing the receptacle to hit the table, roll across it and crash to the floor.

"You can stuff your pub, what you forget is that I have choices!" he bellows.

Alex's eyes widen as Anne gently places her hand on his arm, hoping to temper his mood slightly, but deep inside knowing that nothing at this point is going to achieve that.

"Well you have managed to limit your choices sunshine, you are barred, now piss off and do not soil these premises every again, not even with your pathetic little distorted shadow."

Suddenly the room erupts into light, the canopy Christmas lights intense with their brightness. People turn away, shielding their eyes from the blistering luminosity.

"Calm yourselves," Alex hisses at the lights under his breath and instantly the bulbs return to their usual state of illumination. Anne who hears these quietly spoken words of his, is astounded at the way the lights seem to obey his wishes.

Canning storms from the room, followed by the other two. One of them suddenly stops, lingering at the bar door for a moment before turning around to say quite loudly," You are out of order Alex, well out of order."

Alex smiles and replies gently, but assertively, "Of course I am lad. He didn't get his way because I put a stop to him. Of course you think I am out of order, but if you just take the time to look at what happened here, you will see I am far from out of order. Now go and join your boss without uttering another word, thus far you are not banned from these premises. It's only what you say next that will determine that."

The lad turns and leaves without saying another word. Half the people in the bar begin to applaud, then as the volume increases so the others join in. Phrases like 'nice one Alex' and 'about time you got rid of that bad apple', are heard from certain local parties, while the visitors in the bar merely seem to want to join in with everyone else's appreciation of what had just occurred.

"Are you happy now?" Anne quizzes him.

He casts a sideways glance and replies, "It's been coming for quite a while, you know it has and now it's done. Besides I am not going to be questioned in my bar by anyone, let alone by someone like him."

"Well, I should think you have made that point extremely clear now," she states before leaving the bar area.

The lunch time period finishes slightly later than normal, due to the fact that no one seems in any hurry to go home. No sooner has Alex shut the door and headed for the stairs and his well earned rest, when a heavy knock lands upon it. He lurches to a halt, stooping his head and exhaling with a frustrated sigh, he wanders back to the front door just as a second barrage of knocking occurs. He unlocks the door and opens it wide. To his amazement, the two lads who were with Canning are stood on the doorstep. Initially, he surmises that there is going to be trouble and braces himself for this eventuality, his eyes narrowing, his fists clenching and his stance balanced.

"What's your problem lads?" he enquires aggressively.

The lad closest to the door takes a defensive step backwards. His name is Alex G, an exceptionally tall, lithe lad in his late twenties. He has short fair hair, quite sharp features and was known to be pretty wild in his earlier years. The other young man is known as Sid, an abbreviation for Simon. No one seems quite sure how this nickname came into being, but all the locals call him Sid. He is slightly stockier than Alex, not as tall, dark haired with a bad set of teeth. Both lads are Devonian.

"We be looking for Mr Canning, we can't find him," Sid simply states.

Alex looks a little perplexed, taken aback by the question and then says, "What do you mean where is Canning? I'm not his keeper and besides, I threw him out, he's banned. How should I know or care where the hell he is."

"We know that," Alex enforces, "we were there when it happened, but since then neither of us has seen him or been able to find him anywhere."

Sid, standing slightly behind his mate, nods his agreement to this statement.

Alex, who still cannot understand why they are there, says, "Well, he left Sid, both of you went with him. Alex you said your piece before you finally went, but I don't understand how you managed to lose him when you left within seconds of each other."

"That'd be the whole point," Sid says, "Mr Canning got up and walked out the door from the bar and I followed. I even thought I heard him go out the front door, well at least I heard it click shut and I assumed it was after he had gone out, but when I got outside, not five seconds behind him, there was no sign of him."

"Even his old truck is still exactly where he parked it," Alex G adds.

Alex shakes his head and then says, "Come in lads, just come in, there must be a reasonable explanation as to his whereabouts."

Both lads and Alex enter the bar where they all take a seat at a table. As Alex is about to utter his first words, there follows another thunder from the big old knocker on the front door.

After another deep sigh he once more rises to his feet and says, "Bloody hell, why the hell did I bother closing?"

He goes into the hall again and drags the big old wooden access wide open. For a second time, he is surprised to see his latest visitors.

"Christ, you two are on the ball. He hasn't been missing for more than a couple of hours."

"Who hasn't?" Criss immediately asks.

"Canning, I've got two of his work lads here who are trying to find him at this very moment."

"We are not here about Canning, whoever he may be," Marcus states.

Alex raises his eyes to the heavens and quickly backtracking he replies, "I know. I was just messing with you. So why are you here?"

"Who is Canning?" Criss pursues not allowing this latest snippet of information to drop.

Marcus slowly turns to his colleague and says, "At this moment in time, as far as I am aware, we do not need to know who this Canning person is, or do we?"

Criss glances at Marcus and reluctantly says, "Of course, you're right, for the moment anyway."

"No sir," Marcus continues his attention back to Alex. "We were wondering if you would have any objection to the two of us taking a look around in your hall?"

"What?" Alex exclaims.

"Your hall sir, may we inspect it?"

"Why on earth would you want to do that?"

"It's purely routine sir but from all the statements we have read, it seems that the common denominator of all the missing people is that they were last seen in that vicinity, so on the off chance, we would like to give it the once over."

"Are you serious?" Alex asks.

"Very serious," Criss informs him.

Alex drags the door wide open and beckons them in sarcastically saying, "Why the hell not. Come in, I'm expecting the Vienna ladies choir at any minute, just to top the building up to capacity before it even reaches opening time."

All three of them step into the hall and Alex shuts the front door firmly behind them. The officers immediately begin their inspection of the area, while Alex lingers for a minute watching their efforts, shaking his head in disbelief. Finally, having seen enough, he returns to the bar and retakes his seat with the two lads.

"Now, where were we, ah yes, Canning leaving the building and then disappearing from the face of the earth."

"That's how it seems," Alex G agrees.

Sid leans on the table and explains, "We left here and he was gone. Obviously, we both went to the truck and we waited for at least ten minutes and then, when he didn't join us, we thought perhaps he'd returned here. You've got to follow our thinking here Alex, he was pissed off and a bit worse for wear and after what happened between you and him, well, he be a proud man and all."

"He's a sad old would be tyrant, that's what he is, however I am following what you're saying."

"So we returned to the pub to quickly check around. I even looked in the loo."

"Nothing right," Alex tiredly states, "that spineless old git hasn't got the guts to confront anyone without others behind him, let alone me."

Both lads lower their heads, knowing that what has just been said is about right. Then Alex G says, "The thing is, we walked down to his farm and his Mrs said she hadn't seen hide 'nor hair of him. From there, we walked all the way back up here and as it's so cold out, we checked any places we thought he might have decided to stop and have a kip in like the church, church rooms, the parish hall or the rest awhile over there; but nothing. So me and Sid had a chat and worked out perhaps he was still here."

Alex listens with interest, concluding, "Well lads, you were wrong, he's not here. I know that for sure, because before I shut these premises up I always check the whole area in case anyone is still in here."

"In case of what?" Sid asks with sincere earnest.

Alex's face is a picture of disbelief and he sarcastically replies, "In case pirates are hiding in the cellar and toilets waiting for me to leave so they can get pissed and have a party. Why the hell do you think lad?"

He shakes his head, gets to his feet and strolls out to the hall to see how the police investigation is progressing. Poking his head around the corner of the door, he sees Criss on all fours peering under the big pine dresser which is situated under a huge wall mounted mirror. Marcus is attempting to see behind the mirror, his head pressed hard up against the wall. Alex blinks a couple of times at the absurdity of it all and returns to the bar.

"Right lads, now as you are sure that your boss isn't here, it's time to go."

They get to their feet and follow him to the front door. Alex G glances at the two officers, who are now delving under the stairs, then turns to Alex, begins to open his mouth to speak but Alex beats him to it by saying, "Don't ask, please just do not ask, because I really haven't got a clue what they're up to."

When the door is shut behind them, Alex returns to the hall, striding through it asking, "Coffee you two, if you have time of course?"

A muffled, "That would be lovely," comes from under the stairs, where only two pairs of legs and their feet can clearly be seen.

CHAPTER NINE

Cyril negotiates the corner entering the approach to the square with great trepidation, hoping that Mrs Stanford will not be out of her abode. He skids on the corner in his eagerness to peer around the junction, steadying himself on the building he is now holding on to. On seeing the coast is clear, he cautiously shuffles through the snow, keeping close to the uprights of the houses next to the pavement, he makes his way towards the paper shop. As he draws level with The Bell Inn, Stanford's door springs open, her eyes glued to him as she comes out.

"Cyril, look through the pubs window, see if the lights are on, it's important, do it!" she insists.

He abruptly stops and almost at the window he takes two paces forward, uses his gloved hands to cut out any outside glare as he gazes in through the glass. Still looking in, he calls out, "It's all dark in there Mrs Stanford. There's no light whatsoever."

When he turns to face her, he sees she is stood in her doorway sporting a big smile, wearing a long, woollen dressing gown. "Can I tempt you in to a nice cup of tea and warm crumpets?"

Cyril, who is completely horrified at this prospect quickly replies, "Er no, no thank you Mrs Stanford, I'm late to get my paper, it will miss me."

He quickly turns away and scurries off towards the paper shop, throwing caution to the wind with regards to the snow, slipping and sliding all over the place in his eagerness to get away. Having managed to make it to his destination without falling head over heels, he negotiates the front door with amazing accuracy, almost tripping over the doormat and coming to a halt at the main counter using his outstretched hand and arms to cease his forward momentum.

"Morning Cyril," Edna the shop owner politely greets, "I think that is the fastest I have ever seen you move."

"Quite possibly Edna, when you get propositioned like I just did, you head for cover at the best possible speed."

She erupts into laughter as she hands him his daily paper.

Anne is the first one down on this particular morning, making straight for the kitchen to put the kettle on for their first cup of the day. She puts two cups on the work surface next to the teapot and when the water boils, pours it over the tea leaves. Even in this modern day and age, she prefers to brew a pot of tea the old fashioned way, waiting for the leaves to infuse with the water. To occupy her time while she is waiting for this process to take place, she crosses to one of the cupboards and takes out three bowls. These receptacles are the cats feeding dishes which she places down before leaving the kitchen to obtain a tin of cat food. As she returns she catches sight of a glow emanating from the bar area. At first, her thoughts are that Alex must have left a light on the night before, but then when it suddenly goes off, her suspicions are aroused. She walks past the kitchen and heads directly for the bar. Cautiously she peers in through the door, glancing left and right, trying to ascertain where the light had come from.

"What's up?" Alex greets her with, as he appears at the bottom of the stairs, immediately opposite the door where she is standing.

Anne nearly leaps out of her skin. She spins on her heels shouting, "You stupid sod, you scared me half to death!"

Sleepily, he is taken aback by his wives attack saying, "Whoa, I didn't mean to make you jump, I was just wondering what you were up to."

Taking a second to compose herself, she inhales a deep breath and then replies, "Sorry but you really did make me jump. To answer your question, the lights were on in here but when I came to look, they were turned off."

Looking perplexed, he steps down the last stair making his way around to the front of the bar. He strides in with a serious look on his face, surveys the room, searching every corner, nook and cranny. Having satisfied himself that there is no one there, he walks across to the only window in the room and checks it. He finds that it is locked shut and that there is no damage to it. He turns and paces to the area behind the bar and examines the window there as well. Exactly the same thing as before, all is secure. By this time, Anne has checked the doors, only to find that all is fine, all locked and secure as it should be. She unlocks everything and goes to the front door. Here Alex joins her and they both open the door and step outside, pushing the drifted snow away with their feet.

Immediately Alex spots the foot prints in the snow leading up to the front window. He points this out to his wife, who is staring across the road at Mrs Stanford, who is twitching her curtains as she tries to conceal her vigil on the pub.

"Look at this," he says, "someone has shown real interest in the window just here."

"It shouldn't be difficult to find out who it was with that nosey cow over the road watching the place all day long."

He glances across and frantically starts waving, calling out, "Yoho, morning Mrs Stanford."

Anne begins to giggle and playfully pushes him saying, "Stop it you idiot, she will only become abusive again."

"I don't care, stroppy cow ought to try and get a life."

"Stop it will you please. She's just a harmless old lady, with way too much time on her hands, that's all."

They return inside, closing the front door behind them. Anne proceeds straight to the kitchen, to complete her original task of making the morning tea. The pot is stewed now and as she cannot abide stewed tea or Alex cold tea, she has to repeat the whole thing again.

Alex goes directly into the bar, stands in the middle of the room staring at the lights adorning the canopy and asks, "Are you playing tricks again?" He then tilts his head and under his breath he whispers, "Do not get me into trouble you lot. When I turn you off, stay off, until I turn you back on again." As he begins to walk away, he stops, tilts his head and then adds, "Besides, you wouldn't like to actually enlighten me as to how the hell you manage to turn yourselves on when you are not even plugged in?" The illuminations gently glisten then dimly they dance on and off, repetitively along the entire length of their cable. "Behave," he quietly snaps, "and how the hell you do that, beats me." He shakes his head and walks off to the kitchen to get his morning cuppa.

"What about going up?" Michael questions the others.

They all immediately gaze upwards, with Duncan answering, "As you can see, there are no proper floors in any of the buildings that we have found so far, but no one has attempted to scale the walls to see if there is a way out from the top."

Everyone in the room, without exception, turns and stares at the room adjoining theirs as they hear, "Jesus Christ, where am I now?"

Julie immediately makes her way towards the sound, while Tara says, "Oops, looks like we have a new member to join our escape committee."

Paul smiles and follows Julie on her quest to greet their new arrival. On their return they introduce Mr Canning to the others, not that anyone in the room didn't either know him, or know of him.

"Ah, Canning, so what brings you to our miniature world?" Michael immediately asks.

Canning stares at him for a few seconds, then retorts, "You are one of those they live in the Shilling House, aren't you?"

"Indeed I am, how astute of you to have observed such a fact, but my question still stands. Could you possibly manage to enlighten us as to how you arrived here?"

He surveys the room and its occupants, recognising each person in turn but making no effort to acknowledge them. His gaze returns to Michael.

"Well, it's all a bit fuzzy really. I was in The Bell Inn and arguing with that idiot of a landlord. I went to leave and suddenly I was here."

Michael slightly tilts his head, his expression actually saying it all. "Would you like to try again sir, as I can only conclude that was your abbreviated version, which more than likely, left out a substantial amount of any relevant information. So, as I am trying to ascertain why you are here, could you please in your own time, please tell us exactly what happened leading up to your arrival here?"

Canning, now looking and feeling a trifle uneasy, aware that all eyes are upon him, slides down the wall he is leaning upon and squatting down he relates the full story, from the moment he entered the pub, to the moment he arrived in his current location. All ears are pricked, no one interrupts his oration, they simply listen and contemplate the facts they are hearing.

On his completion, he raises his arms and says, "And that's it, can't see how it's going to help, but that's what happened."

All eyes turn to Michael, who at this point is gently massaging his chin. A few seconds pass by before he utters, "It is very interesting to note that we were all sent here, and I use the word sent very carefully, on leaving the Bell Inn. This would imply that the source of the power applied to the subject is emitted from within the pub itself. Having discussed at length with all of you the time leading up to our individual abduction, it has become very apparent, that we all argued, no wrong word, all aggravated the landlord."

An eerie silence fills the room, until it is broken by Canning. "I knew that bastard was evil and no good."

"Well, he certainly picked on us," Tara states

"That he did," Paul adds, "and what the hell have we ever done wrong?"

Duncan raises his eyebrows and notices Julie smiling as well.

"All very well and likely," Michael diplomatically says, "but the fact still remains that my analogy may well still be correct, giving us at least the answer as to who sent us here."

"But why?" Duncan interrupts, "Why would he do such a thing? None of us were beyond his control. Let's be honest, Alex is no fool and quite forthright, if he bans someone, then they are gone, never to be served in his pub again, but in my case, I reckon I was on the verge of being fired anyway, so why send me here? I would have left and that would have been that."

Most people in the room nod their agreement, all waiting to see how Michael will react to this conjecture.

"If indeed, he knows he is doing it," he peruses. "As far as I am aware, and please feel free to correct me if I am wrong here, Alex has not got the power to shrink people and send them to wherever he wishes," Michael simply states.

Again, a hush then Julie adds, "Then how or what is doing it? As far as I am aware, shrinking people is not a commonplace occurrence in our neighbourhood."

Paul bursts into laughter, "What are we talking about here, magic, voodoo or the like? That's all crap and you know it."

"Who knows it?" Julie is quick to snap back at him, "I've read a fair amount on the subject and I reckon there is such a thing."

"Me too," Tara adds as Paul's head swings around to glare at her.

"You can't read, so I doubt you've been looking it up," he scathingly replies.

"I watched those programs on the tele mostly when I had peace and quiet away from you."

"Enough!" Michael yells, "That's enough of this useless, pointless banter. We need theories that turn to facts, not arguments and squabbling like a load of children, until we have found a way out of here."

Canning nods in agreement before he says, "Well, what we need to do is organise ourselves."

"Oh be quite you idiot," Tara decisively declares, "we have already done that. Michael is our leader, talk to him."

These words cause Michael to puff his chest and proudly stand upright with a huge beaming smile across his face. Julie walks across to him and rubs his arm in an affectionate way, showing that her trust lies firmly with him.

"Ok, I wasn't trying to upset the apple cart here you know, no need to be rude," he defensively replies.

"That'll be the day," Duncan attacks, "We all know how you operate and we don't trust you for one minute."

The lunchtime session is quiet, not too many people venturing out into the cold. Now the wind has got up, whistling around all the old structures of the village, menacingly challenging anyone to leave home and feel its sharp and bitter bite. Although it has stopped snowing, the power of the blustery weather is skimming loose snow from the roofs of the houses, turning them into spinning eddies and sending them in wave after wave down the streets, buffering everything in their paths.

The Bell closes promptly at three o'clock, with Anne and Alex retreating upstairs within minutes of shutting the doors in order to rest their weary legs for a couple of hours. Having just settled themselves in front of the fire and taken to their allotted comfortable chairs, in the distance they can vaguely hear a rap on the front door. They look at each other both hoping that the other will say, 'I'll go', but the silence of the moment says it all. Finally Alex breaks, saying, "It can't be that important, if it's a delivery, they can leave it on the step. We'll get it at opening time."

Anne nods in agreement and sips on her tea. Then the phone rings and both of them turn their heads, staring at the device. After four rings, he begins to lean forward in frustration saying, "This best be important."

"Leave it," she instructs, "let it ring, just sit back and ignore it. In point of fact, for the next two hours let's ignore everything that we don't wish to do and simply relax."

He smiles, liking this idea very much and leans over to her, planting a gentle kiss on her cheek before settling back down into his armchair.

Finally the phone stops and then within a minute, it starts again. Anne slowly gets out of her seat and unplugs it saying, "Now you're done, be quiet," as she firmly nestles back into her seat.

Clive, a van driver for a parcel delivery firm, is at the front door. He prides himself on his hundred percent success rate at delivering his parcels, never returning to his depot with anything remaining. He is a northern man of medium height, stocky build, short dark hair, glasses and immaculately dressed in his late fifties. At this moment in time, he is becoming increasingly frustrated because he cannot get anyone to answer the door at the Bell Inn. Having knocked hard several times and tried phoning three times, he begins to look either side of the pub for somewhere to leave his package. Firstly he strides to the left, disappearing into the car park and calling on two houses on the far side of the expanse. Having found no one in, he walks back out of the parking area and heads to the right of the pub, trying three houses in a row, without any success. He sighs, a very audible sound, before he plods back to the front door of the pub. Here yet again, he thunders on the door, the whole structure slightly shaking with the intensity of his labours. He places his ear to the door and carefully listens, hoping to hear some reaction to his efforts. Nothing at all comes back to him. With this negative result, he feels anger swell inside him and he kicks out at the door, denting the wood and chipping the paintwork.

Suddenly his attention is caught by the bright light which has just appeared in the window to his left. He immediately rushes over, cupping his hands and peering through them. 'Finally' he thinks to himself, someone is at home and he will be able to deliver the troublesome package.

Alex and Anne both emerge downstairs ten minutes before the doors are due to open. She makes straight for the kettle. A cup of tea might help them both to wake up after their afternoon snooze. Alex as usual goes into the dark bar to begin systematically turn on all the lighting. He stands back and admires the illuminations before he strolls to the bar door and opens it once more. From here, he moves to the hall and opens the main front door after turning on the sign lights. He stands in the doorway, glancing up and down the street lit road when he spots a package covered with a film of snow, standing on one of the outside tables in front of the building. He picks up the parcel, checks the address and finding that it is his, takes it back inside, walking into the kitchen and placing it on one of the work surfaces.

"Well, we now know who was banging at the door," he states.

She smiles and adds, "And it would probably explain the constant ringing of the phone too."

"Strange though," he says, "I found it on one of the outside tables. You would have thought they would have left it on the doorstep, closer to the door. Now it's soggy and covered in snow. Oh, by the way, it's for you."

She glances across at the parcel as Alex leaves the kitchen, heading on his way back down the hall to the front door again. Once there, he steps out into the snow and searches the other tables, just in case something else has been left and is now covered in snow. Having completed his rummaging, he notices a white van that is parked a little way down the road with both its rear doors and the driver's door still open. For some reason he stands there staring at the vehicle for a few moments before shuffling through the snow towards it. Having reached the van, he looks in to the cab which is now speckled with snow and notices that the keys are still in the ignition, then he shuts the door. Walking around the van towards the back he glances down at the snow around the vehicle, observing that it is untouched, no footprints are evident. Having reached the open doors at the back, he looks down the other side of the van. Again the snow is pure and unsoiled by any tracks. He gazes into the back of the long wheel based vehicle and apart from some flat packed boxes and various lengths of bindings, it is empty. Alex, now quite confused, shuts the doors, locking the handles in place before checking they are secure. He invades the virgin snow, pacing his way back to the driver's door, pulling it open and climbing into the cab. He picks up a clipboard which is placed on the passenger seat and he starts to scan its contents. Having almost reached the bottom of the page, he sees that The Bell Inn is there on his schedule and that he had placed the time of his arrival in the appropriate box. That was a good two and a half hours ago, so where the hell was he?

He leaves the van, taking the ignition keys with him and goes back into the pub. He finds a note pad and writes a note saying that the keys are with him in the Bell, then goes back to the van and places the note under the windscreen wiper where it will be visible for when the driver should he eventually turn back up. Having satisfied himself that the vehicle is secure, he re-enters the pub, following John into the bar, who is there as always for his early doors tipple.

"Evening landlord," John jovially says, taking his usual seat at the corner of the bar.

"Evening John, a bottle of the wee beastie is it?"

"What a splendid idea Alex, I am more than ready for it."

Alex pours his beer and notices John staring intently across the room in the direction of the Christmas scene. He too glances over, making sure his assumption is verified and then asks him, "What's up mate, did you see something over there?"

John sniggers and replies, "Believe it or not, I could have sworn I saw shadows moving from within the building next to that church."

Alex stares hard at the model, eventually moving himself from behind the bar in order to obtain a better view. The model mentioned by John is on the top row of the village scene and Alex peers right in to the windows of the building. While he is scrutinising the model, he tells John about the van outside.

"I saw him knocking," John states, "I saw him disappear into the car park as well. I suppose the bloke was looking for somewhere to leave the parcel when you didn't answer."

"Well that may well be so, but that was at least two and a half hours ago and why would he leave his van completely open. I have this horrible gut feeling that something isn't right here."

John chuckles, "Come on Alex, what can happen to anyone in Witherford. We're in the middle of nowhere, nothing ever happens out here." There follows a moments silence while both men's eyes meet and they look at each other, and then John quietly adds under his breath and with raised eyebrows, "Well, apart from various people going missing that is."

"Oops, there you go, but nothing happens in Witherford does it?" Alex concludes.

"There!" John yells out, startling Alex, "something definitely moved in that model then!"

Alex spins around on his heels, glaring at the model, moving up and down the row of small houses searching for whatever it was that John said he had seen.

"Have you got a bulb out Alex?" Andy asks as he strides into the bar.

Alex doesn't waver from his investigation, only ordering, "John, go behind the bar and pour him a beer."

"Right," John quips, jumping down from his stool before disappearing out into the hall and re-appearing behind the bar, "And what can I get for you young man?"

"A lager and a cigar please," Andy replies, slowly edging his way to where Alex is, trying to ascertain exactly what he is doing.

John pours the beer, takes a cigar from the tin and places them down where Andy has now settled himself. He tells him the cost which Andy obediently pays, placing the funds in the till, before returning to his seat on the other side of the bar.

"What are you up to Alex?" Andy timidly asks, not wanting to break his concentration.

Before he can answer, Richard who is nicknamed Tricky for some obscure reason that no one seems to know the origins of, bounds into the bar looking around him and saying, "Evening people, everyone ok today?" Then he spots Alex and jokes, "Hi Alex, lost a cat up there have you?"

Alex freezes with his investigation, his head slowly turning to face Tricky, his body almost motionless. "Is that supposed to be an attempt at humour, because if so, I must have lost mine somewhere?"

Tricky places both hands on his hips and replies, "Alex me old mate, you run probably the best pub for a hundred miles around here, but when it comes to humour, I've got to say, as unpleasant at it is probably going to be for me, you have to have had a sense of humour in the first place, to have been able to lose it."

John in mid gulp chokes on his beer, spitting it on to the bar in front of him. Andy is trying to bite his tongue to stop himself from laughing, but Alex has frozen. This time though, he stands up, turning his whole body to face Tricky with an all too familiar frown upon his face. Before he has a chance to speak the canopy lights begin pulsating faster, attracting the attention of everyone in the room, aware that they have changed their intensity.

Alex smiles, laughing as he whispers under his breath, "Behave you lot." He heads back behind the bar and once there he looks across to Tricky and says, "Pint of ale, you sarcastic little toe rag?"

Tricky smiles, "Please sir, if I'm still allowed?"

"I'll let you know when you're not," he says smiling as he pours the pint of beer.

He turns to John, "There are two things my friend; number one, can you get the phone number of the delivery service which owns that van and secondly, there is nothing odd about the damn model village, ok?"

John pulls his phone from his pocket to access the internet. He walks to the window in order to see the van, noting the name of the company to make his search. He returns to his seat, places the phone in front of Alex and says, "There's the number you want and as for the Christmas scene, I did see something," he adds but this time with a serious look upon his face.

CHAPTER TEN

"Hello," an enquiring voice with a northern accent can be heard, "anyone here?"

Julie turns, looking in the direction of the voice. "Looks like yet another person has come to join us."

"They seem to be arriving thick and fast just recently," Duncan quips.

Michael smiles at the flippant attitude of his enforced companions before calling out to the newcomer, "Follow my voice, you are not far away from the rest of us."

A couple of minutes later Clive enters the room. He studies the people there, Michael, Julie and Duncan. The remainder of the group, Tara, Paul and Canning, are presently on a roof studying mission of some of the adjoining buildings.

"I am pretty sure that I don't know any of you," Clive states.

"That may be the case sir," Michael says, "however, I have seen you before. You are a delivery man, aren't you?"

He nods in confusion, saying, "Yes I am, and that was exactly what I was doing before I came here. By the way, where is here?"

Duncan walks over to him, places his hand gently on his shoulder and enlightens him of his current whereabouts. "Believe it or not, you are in a Christmas village display, that sits on top of a piano in The Bell Inn in Witherford, and the fact that you are here, means that you were in that pub."

He firmly shakes his head. "No, I wasn't in the pub. I was outside the front door with a parcel trying to get someone to answer the door."

Michael listens carefully to this explanation, his eyes light up and he excitedly asks, "So you were outside the pub, can you remember what you were doing just before you arrived here?"

Clive tightens his lips and his head drops. Julie and Duncan can see he is reluctant to answer this question, so she jokes, "Come on Clive, it's important and believe me, when you hear what we were doing just before we arrived here, I will guarantee that you will laugh your socks off."

A grin flickers across his face as he quietly says, "I'm not very proud of what I was doing. I lost my temper a bit."

No one utters a word, all faces watch him struggle with his conscience before he finally adds, "I was kicking at the front door."

"What, what did you say?" Julie enquires.

Clive turns to face her and repeats, "I was kicking the front door. I couldn't get anyone to answer and I lost my rag. I always deliver everything before the end of the day and it looked like this was going to be the first time I would fail in eleven years."

Duncan roars with laughter and Julie joins him. Michael affords a grin saying, "Very professional, I'm sure."

Clive tightens his lips again and grunts, "I told you I wasn't proud of it. By the way, that isn't the last thing I can remember."

He has now regained the attention of everyone in the room.

"After I kicked the door, I saw a bright light from the bar window. As soon as I saw it, I thought great, I had finally got someone's attention, so I went across to look in."

"And what did you see?" Julie asks.

Clive's forehead creases as he thinks and then he replies, "Just a huge bright light from the back of the room, fleetingly and then I was here."

Having rung the delivery company, Alex is surprised over their lack of concern and he returns to the bar to tell John. More customers enter with that air of excitement caused because the snow is falling yet again, this time quite heavily.

As the evening progresses, Alex moves all three cats from the bar, placing them on the back stairway, so as to avoid another attack on the Christmas scene in front of the customers. As he collects them all together, there are various jibes and jokes from those who had witnessed the earlier incident with them. Alex merely laughs them off, as he moves throughout the room.

By nine thirty in the evening, several locals have moved outside the front of the building, engaged in a free for all snowball fight, with the snow still falling thick and fast. The joviality of the games is temporarily interrupted by the local police car driving through the village at a snail's pace. The fight stops as it approaches, with all players seeking refuge on the pavements on either side of the road. At this point with the weather, it is difficult to tell where the verges are supposed to be. As the car draws level with the pub, one of the younger lads launches his snowball towards it, connecting firmly with the windscreen. The vehicle stops abruptly. Everyone in the night, snow clad road remains perfectly still with their mouths open silently in trepidation. Suddenly, both front doors of the police car open in unison and two officers partially get out of the car, one of them with a radio in his hand. Everyone present hears him say, "Control, this is Bravo 34, assistance required by any other unit available in the Witherford area." There follows a short silence, until the officer finishes his request with, "Snow ball fight with hostiles outside The Bell Inn and we are taking fire." Immediately both officers grab the snow closest to them and start throwing snowballs at anyone close enough to hit. The tension erupts into raucous laughter and the fight continues, with the majority of the snowy projectiles pelting the police car while others are flung randomly at anyone else in the vicinity.

Thirty minutes later the players are exhausted, flaked out on the sides of the road, sitting or laying in the snow, some returning into the pub in an attempt to thaw out their frozen hands and fingers. Alex invites the policemen inside to warm themselves. They gratefully accept his offer and Anne quickly rustles up coffee and sandwiches, thanking them for their joviality.

By half past ten the pub is packed with tired and happy customers, the officers have left, grateful for their evening's entertainment and to Anne for the welcome refreshments. The main topic of conversation is over the snow, the amount that appears to be falling and to the way the police joined in the fun.

As Alex points out with substantial agreement, "Old fashioned policing, it's bloody marvellous to see."

The others are introduced to Clive on their return, before discussing the findings of their search. It quickly becomes apparent that although the three of them had only managed to cover a third of the buildings, they still hadn't managed to discover a way out. Undeterred, they state that after a short rest, they will continue to search the remaining buildings. After all, they only need to find a crack large enough for them to squeeze through?

Julie, Duncan and Michael decide to show Clive just what he has been thrown into, with Michael eagerly wanting to study the way in which the models are connected to each other again. He has an instinct that if there is a crack in this armour, then it is most likely to be at one of these points of weakness.

After the others have rested, the two groups move off in their different directions, both on their relevant fact finding missions, both with an eager intent to find their answer so they may exit from this god forsaken place.

The pub slowly empties at the approach of closing time and only 'the usual suspects' as Alex calls them linger at the bar, in a hope that they will get that last after hours drink. Being a village pub, the police turn a blind eye to this custom, just as long as it is kept quiet and no trouble emerges from the practice. It is very much up to the landlord to decide who is allowed to stay on and to maintain 'a no noise' policy. He is very strict about having a late night. If he decides he is going to have one, then he will make sure anybody he doesn't want on the premises has left. It is not a regular occurrence, only once a week and the day he chooses will change at his will.

This particular night, due to the great fun and good humour of the earlier evening, he decides that a late drink is a must, besides that, he's in the mood for a couple of beers. He studies the bar and noting that some twenty or so people still remain, he picks up a pile of beer mats and ventures forth.

Now everybody knows how Alex's rules work regarding 'after hours'. If he picks up your glass and places a beer mat underneath it, then you are invited to stay. If he doesn't, then you are to drink up, say your goodbyes with a smile and leave quietly. If you are not invited to stay, it doesn't matter how much you would have liked to, one never questions the fact that a beer mat hasn't been supplied, as that would result in never ever being asked again. Alex hates beer mats, describing them as 'nasty tacky pieces of cardboard', therefore there are no spare mats on any of the tables to fool him into thinking he's given you one by mistake.

This particular night he chooses ten friends who he wishes to join his elite club for the duration. He circles the bar and places his beer mats under the chosen ones glasses. Completing his selection, he heads back to his sanctuary behind the bar. All the time he had been watched carefully by the few who had not been nominated. Most simply drank up and began to leave, with one exception.

Cameron, a twenty four year old farmer's son had in the past been invited to stay. This had inevitably finished with him having just that one too many to drinks and resulted in Alex having to tell him to go home. The last time he was permitted a late night drink was at least six months ago, and to a degree Cameron knew why. This particular evening, he was already at 'the one too many point', even though earlier Alex had refused to serve him anymore and had told him the reason why. However, Cameron had managed to persuade someone else to buy him another pint, which although Alex had witnessed he wasn't over perturbed with, thinking he would just drink it up and be on his way. After all, none of the youngsters wanted to get themselves barred; you see the nearest pub after this one was four miles away, which meant driving. What Alex didn't see however, was that Cameron had a half bottle of whiskey in his inside jacket pocket, which he had been lacing his own drinks with for most of the evening.

"That is time at the bar," he calls out, surveying those still remaining. He spots Cameron sitting with another lad and passes him by to see who else needs to leave. A minute or two later, everyone has gone except for Cameron and his mate, plus the ones previously invited to stay. The lad with Cameron, Stuart a strong, burly lad, gulps downs the remainder of his pint, gets up from where he is sitting, sets the empty glass down on the bar and says goodnight to everyone, raising his eyebrows at Alex in Cameron's direction. Alex smiles and takes the time to shake Stuart's hand before he leaves, then his focused gaze falls upon Cameron.

"Let's have your glass lad, it's time for you to wind your weary way home," he delivers.

Anne walks across to Cameron smiling and coaxing in her friendly manner, "Come on lad it's time to get some shut eye." She places her hand on the young man's shoulder, which he immediately shrugs off. She backs away from him quickly having spotted the aggression in his eyes.

Andy is off his stool ready to jump to her defence, but Alex raises his hand to halt any action that he doesn't deem necessary.

"Cameron you will leave, one way or the other, you make the choice and let me know. In your present state, and you did not get there by drinking what you have had here, you are becoming a problem."

"I ain't going nowhere," he slurs, "I don't see why they can stay and I can't, I'm just as entitled as them."

The canopy lights begin to flutter. No one in the room notices, as all their eyes are firmly fixed on the inebriated youngster.

"Come on Cam," Rob says, "why are you doing this? You're only going to get yourself into trouble."

"Fuck off fatso," he retorts, "I don't need any advice from you."

Rob, taken aback by this attack, turns towards the bar, hoping to make this particular problem disappear.

"Alex," Andy says, "alright with you if I help this little idiot off the premises?"

Alex with a stern look on his face shakes his head, gesturing him to sit back down. He moves out from behind the bar and heads straight to the table where Cameron is sitting.

"On your feet boy," he says quietly but firmly.

Cameron drops his head, but offers no retort or movement.

"I said on your feet," he repeats louder but this time with definite menace in his voice.

"Piss off," comes back the sullen reply.

Everyone present is now aware of the canopies illuminations, as they have burst forth into their frenzied display. Alex can feel the anger welling up inside himself, his fists clenched, staring unblinkingly at the lad.

"Jesus," Graham says, shielding his face from the light, "what the hell is wrong with those things?"

Anne immediately looks at Alex. Deep down inside she is acutely aware that he is the cause of the lights reaction. She also now believes that he too is aware of this. At this moment in time, his attention is completely focused on Cameron and it seems to her that so are the lights. "Alex, control those lights," she calls to him.

There is a delay in his response as his rage is centred entirely on Cameron, but as the penny drops and he realises that she has spoken to him, he spins around and yells out, "Cease!"

The lights fail to respond to his command for a couple of seconds, but then they drop to a glimmer, shimmering with short bursts of lower luminosity. Instantly he turns around, towering over Cameron who remains sat, slumped forward drunkenly on to the table.

"You will get out now, you will present yourself to me tomorrow and in that time I will decide whether I am going to ban you from here or not. Now get out of here!" he orders.

Cameron springs to his feet, shoving his chair backwards. It topples over, crashing to the ground as he strides towards the door, yelling behind him, "Fuck you lot, ban me, huh I ain't going to come back here anyway. Poke your pub!" He staggers out of the front door, continuing his ranting, the last sentence being, "After hours drinking, not when I let the law know what you're doing you bastards!"

"Little shit," he growls, following him out.

Anne steps in his way saying, "Not you, I'll make sure he's gone. With the mood you're in, you're likely to hit him if he gives you any more lip."

The canopy lights once more intensify, sparkling in total disorder.

Alex knows she is right. He turns to Graham grunting, "Follow her and watch over her." A couple of the others also follow her out. Ten minutes later they return.

"I take it he's finally gone home?" Alex growls.

"When we got outside there was no sign of him, that's why we've been so long, checking that the little worm wasn't hiding somewhere, waiting to cause a new problem," Graham informs him.

Alex glances across to his wife while he's pouring a beer and she says, "Where ever he went, as drunk as he seemed, he managed to get away from here very quickly and it's too dark out there to see any footprints."

"The lights have taken him," John interjects, "it's the lights, those dreaded lights," he chuckles.

As the laughter echoes around the bar, Alex goes out to lock the front door. Before doing so he steps out into the night and on to the snow clad ground, initially watching the calming effect of the snowflakes falling gently to the ground, illuminated only by the solitary street light further down the road. He glances up and down peering through the darkness for any sign of the lad, until his gaze comes to rest on the white van which is still parked a little way down the road.

"Is everything ok mate?" Andy gently asks him from inside.

Alex nods, "I think so, but I've got to say, there's some really weird stuff going on in and around this village and now it's beginning to concern me."

They both return to the bar after ensuring that the door is firmly secured behind them.

Michael, who is now feeling quite exhausted, having trudged around most of the accessible buildings, decides to take a much needed rest in the model of the tea rooms. The front window of this building is fairly large. As he sits, legs stretched out, studying it, he suddenly spots a tiny pin prick of light coming into the room through its corner.

"Can you see that my dear?"

"See what?" Julie replies.

"That minute ray of light, just there in the corner of that window."

Julie, Duncan and Clive stare at this new discovery until suddenly Duncan says, "Yes, I can see it, but what of it?"

Michael sighs before adding, "It is a ray of light entering into this room, which would imply that it can also be used to look out from."

Julie and Duncan glance at each other then they madly scramble towards the tiny hole.

"I wish I had thought of that," Clive states dejectedly, slumping down beside Michael.

"Well you probably hadn't noticed it until I mentioned it, my dear boy."

"Brilliant," Clive states enthusiastically, "I'm going with that story. Thank you."

Julie is the first to reach the window. She tries placing her eye as close as possible to the gap, in the hope of finally seeing something that might make sense in the outside world. When she realises that it is way too small for this she begins frantically scratching at it in an attempt to make it bigger. Duncan seizes the opportunity to join in. There toils are brought to an abrupt halt, when as they have witnessed before, the world outside theirs, bursts in to a blinding glare. They rush to shield their eyes from the intense light, with the exception of Michael, who as much as it hurts, watches the tiny pin prick hole begin to fill itself in and close over. The whole incident takes no more than a minute and when the lights go out again, the minute hole is gone.

Julie and Duncan crawl dejectedly back to where they had been working, scraping and thumping the area in question.

Michael begins to giggle, which causes all of them to stare at him.

"What's so damn funny?" Duncan snarls.

"Oh my dear boy, do you not see, we have gleaned yet another tiny fact from this situation."

"And what might that be?" Clive asks.

"Simply that we are not only imprisoned, we are also being watched."

The room falls into a dark silence.

Anne and Alex, both a little the worse for wear after their previous late night session, have spent the morning undertaking their various chores. Anne has been preparing food for lunch, while Alex has been cleaning the beer lines. As soon as he arose that morning, he had immediately come downstairs and checked outside to see if the van remained. It was exactly where it had been left the night before. The snow had stop falling, but it was obvious to him by its depth, that Witherford would be cut off by now, besides there wasn't a tyre track to be seen, just the odd footprint here and there.

He rings the courier company again to tell them the van is still exactly where it was the day before and that he is now very worried for the safety of the driver, especially due to the current weather conditions. He also informs them that he is going to ring the police. The courier company thank him for his concern, but say they will inform the police themselves to advise them of the situation. As he hangs up from the call he gives the situation a few minutes thought before deciding that he will call the police himself anyway. He enters the bar and after searching for a few minutes he uncovers the calling card left by Criss and Marcus.

When he finally gets through, having been passed from pillar to post as usual, he speaks to Criss as Marcus is apparently snowed in at home and unable to get in to work. He tells her what the problem is and of his concerns for the drivers safety. She thanks him for the call stating that 'She will log it and take the appropriate actions'.

Shortly before midday, Fleche comes bouncing into the building, "Good morning, good morning, good morning," he calls out jovially.

"Afternoon Fleche," Alex replies, just as the church bells begin to chime the hour.

Fleche tilts his head to one side, using his hand to bend his ear towards the ceiling and with some joviality he says, "Harken, the bells are chiming midday, the hour that I start work."

"Then how come you are still standing in the bloody hallway and not suitably dressed for work or, am I supposed to pay for the time it takes you to don your work clothes too?"

Anne, hearing the conversation in the hall, laughs to herself, which Fleche can hear as he walks past the kitchen towards his locker. "Morning ma'am," he calls out.

"Good morning Fleche, late again I see," she says chuckling.

"Yes ma'am, sorry ma'am, it will never happen again ma'am," he replies with his usual humour.

Alex walks across to the front door and opens the premises muttering, "Bloody idiot, I don't know why I put up with him, bloody soft touch that's what I am."

As he pulls the heavy, old front door open, to his complete surprise, Cameron is stood on the doorstep.

"I'm here as you told me to be."

"Then you'd best step inside lad, it's freezing out here. How did you get here?"

"I walked. Stuart rang me this morning and told me what an idiot I'd been. I don't recall all of it, but the bits I do, well I guess that he's probably right."

"Oh, he's right alright. The word idiot doesn't really describe it, but then again, at least you were man enough to face me today. Come in."

After turning on the outside lights, he enters the bar to turn the other lights on as well. The canopy lights spring into action, one at a time resembling a line of dominoes falling over in sequence.

"Well Cameron, what should I do with you, you really do not seem to learn, do you?"

Anne walks through the bar and before he can reply she says, "There's no damage done young man, but I would choose my answer carefully," she smiles at him and leaves.

With his lips tightly pressed together and his head hanging down he says, "I've been thinking about that all the way up here. I even left twice, but I knew I had to come back, I knew I had to face you. As for what my punishment should be, to be completely honest, if I was you, I'd ban me."

"My thoughts exactly," Alex smugly states, "excellent idea, get rid of the problem once and for all."

Cameron slumps into one of the chairs, lowering his head into his hands and bending forward to his knees.

Alex sips on a coffee that Anne has just placed on the bar for him and then says, "Listen to me young man and listen well. In my opinion, not all problems are solvable by throwing them out. In your case and I maybe wrong, but you'd better hope I'm not, I'm not going to ban you, but I will place a four pint limit on your drinking for a while. If I catch you conning someone else into upping that allowance, you're done, if you bring any spirits into my pub and drink them on top, you're done and if you ever, dare argue or question my authority in this pub again, I shall take you out to the woods and leave you for dead. Are we clear?" Alex smiles as these words leave his lips.

Cameron lifts his head, his expression one of disbelief and relief, it was now obvious to Alex that the lad had never dreamed the final outcome would be this one.

"I don't want to see you again till the weekend Cameron and tell your friend Stuart from me, that he has a pint in the wood. He's a good lad and you're lucky to have such a friend."

Cameron nods eagerly, gets to his feet and heads for the door. He stops and turns, nods again, the words in his head, but feeling a little too emotional to say them out loud. He leaves the building.

Alex smiles, feeling quite smug with himself over the way he'd handled the situation.

CHAPTER ELEVEN

It is now nine days to Christmas Day and Alex and Anne are woken, whilst attempting a lie in, firstly by hammering on the front door and closely followed by the phone ringing at minute intervals.

He rolls over and glances at the alarm clock, half expecting it to tell him it's ten in the morning or something. Finally focusing on the clock, he sees that the time is a quarter to eight in the morning.

"For Christ sake, can't we ever get any peace in this place, who in hell is banging on the door at this time of the morning?"

Half asleep, Anne replies, "There's only way to find out and I guess it's either you or I that have to go downstairs to see." She quickly turns over, snuggles herself up as if to go back to sleep.

"Great," he says clambering out of bed, "and I can only assume that due to the chain of command, that someone is me."

She giggles as he dresses and leaves the bedroom. On his journey downstairs he can hear the banging on the door and before he manages to reach it, the phone goes off again.

As he begins to unlock the main door, he calls out, "Alright, alright for Christ sake is your arse on fire?"

He flings open the door and to his surprise, Marcus and Criss are stood there.

"Sorry to disturb you sir," Criss states, "but I feel that we need to talk."

"Do you by God, with your approach to raising my attention, I'm just glad I got down here before you brought a swat team in and smashed the whole place up."

Criss backs off slightly under his onslaught and replies, "We just felt it would be better if we had a chance to talk before you got busy and also before anyone else was around."

Alex backs away from the door and turns to the hall, heading for the kitchen, a cup of tea being the only thing on his mind at that specific moment. "Come in, shut the door and wait there," he orders them.

Having completed the circuit from the hall to the bar, he opens the inner door allowing the two officers to enter the premises and gestures to them to sit before he proceeds to the kitchen to make the pot of tea. A few minutes later he arrives back with the steaming pot, a jug of milk, bowl of sugar and three mugs, placing them down on the table in front of them.

Pouring one for himself he places a cup in front of each of them saying, "Please help yourselves, a good old cup of 'rosy lea' will soon warm you up."

Criss immediately takes the teapot and pours one for each of them.

"Ok," Alex states somewhat calmer and reclining in his chair, "what's so important that you two feel the need to take me from my nice warm slumber?"

Marcus, having taken a couple of sips of his brew, cradles the mug and replies, "More missing people I'm afraid, all last seen at, or very close to this pub."

"Ah yes, the van driver and Canning I suppose. would they be the latest?"

Criss sits forward, a serious expression upon her face, "You seem a little flippant regarding this situation, which worries me somewhat."

"Then worry away young lady," he quickly retorts. "I have the feeling that you two have already decided that I, or possibly Anne, perhaps even both of us, have something to do with these disappearance."

Marcus is quick to intervene, "That is not the case at all. We, as in Criss and I, are duty bound to follow up any leads, and in this case, you yourself called in to tell us that Mr. Dobbins was missing."

"Dobbin's being the van driver I presume, and I did not report him missing, I aired my concerns regarding the fact that he had left his vehicle unlocked, wide open to be precise and also that I had been unable to locate his whereabouts."

"Indeed," Marcus sighs, "a poor use of words on my behalf."

"Nevertheless," Criss pursues, "he hasn't been seen since and neither has Mr. Canning, and what's more, is that both men were last seen at this address."

"Look, when Canning left this pub, it was due to the fact that I'd banned him. There were more than enough people in this room who witnessed the entire episode and saw him leave with his two drinking buddies. Canning was drunk and argumentative, to say nothing of rude and arrogant, but when he left these premises, both Anne and I were in this room and I can prove that."

"And Mr Dobbin, where were you when he disappeared?" Criss questions him.

"How the hell should my whereabouts be of concern? From what I've been told, he was outside these closed up premises, he never entered the building, so how would I know what had happened to him. I don't think I've ever even seen the man., but just for the record, I was upstairs asleep."

Criss and Marcus glance at each other and then Marcus says, "We are going to have the van removed as soon as the weather allows, and forensics' will give it the once over. Did you touch the vehicle in question sir?"

He thinks for a moment and then states, "Yes I did. I touched the driver's door, inside the cab and the back doors. In point of fact, as I told you, I have the keys to it. I took them out of the ignition and locked it up. My prints will be in various places."

"We will need those keys sir," Criss requests.

Alex gets up, disappears for a few moments before returning with the keys, which he casually tosses onto the table. "Is there anything else I can do for you because my faith in the police force as of today is dwindling rapidly?"

"Not at the moment thank you," Criss emphatically states, "but if we do think of anything else, we know where to find you."

The two officers get to their feet and are shown out of the building. Having shut the door behind them, Alex locks it and then decides there's no point in returning to bed, so he grabs the dogs lead and takes her out for a walk, feeling that he needs time to think. Things are getting complicated and none of it is his doing, but he needs to get to the bottom of it.

Now, the search for another little opening to the outside world is really underway. Michael and his team, having relayed their findings to the others, are fired up with enthusiasm. Having discussed their options at great length, they have decided to split into three teams, one of three and two, two man teams who are now scouring the buildings. It had been previously agreed that none of them would return to the church, until they had thoroughly completed their designated part of the exploration. Also, it had been previously decided, that if another hole should be found, it was not to be touched, its whereabouts were to be logged but no outside interference was to take place, the others to be alerted.

The lunchtime trade is slack, the snow and ice making people reluctant to venture outside.

At four fifteen Anne is downstairs, checking in some guests who are staying for the night. Two rooms are booked out, to two couples from the southeast. She wasn't sure they would arrive because of the weather, but there they were, knocking at the front door. She sees them in and shows them upstairs to their respective rooms, explaining as always that they can come and go as they please, but the bar and restaurant will not open again until five o'clock. They are more than happy with this, stating that, 'A nice shower and a rest would be just what we need after the arduous ten hour journey we've had getting here.'

She returns upstairs, where Alex is sat at his computer. He is playing a multiplayer shooting game, which he tells everyone is 'doing the business accounts'. He loves it, but his wife regards it as a waste of time which could be much better spent doing something constructive. She informs him that their guests have arrived but receives only a grunt in response, as he is completely engrossed in his game.

Isme and Judith Crackoth and Dan and Jill Peterson are their latest guests. They were travelling to a convention in Cornwall and had decided to take a break in their journey, rather than undertake the long trip in one stint. As it happens, with the adverse weather conditions, it was a plan that was heaven sent.

Having both showered, Isme stretches out on the bed while Judith takes the leather backed arm chair and they both drift off into an exhausted sleep. Dan and Jill do the same thing, except they both flake out on the bed with the television droning in the background.

Abruptly, Isme opens his eyes, staring at the ceiling without moving. "Can you hear that?"

Judith stirs and sleepily she asks, "Hear what?"

Isme, concentrating hard on the sound replies, "A faint screeching noise, like voices which have been fast forwarded."

She opens her eyes and leans slightly forward. She, like Isme, listens intently and then replies, "I can now. Yes I can hear something odd. What is it?"

"I'm not sure, as I said it sounds like distant voices, but due to the speed of the noise I cannot decipher any particular words."

"Where do you think it's coming from? I'm sure it's not on the other side."

"No, it's definitely not," Isme emphatically replies. "These voices are part of this world, but they're not normal, not like ours."

Their attention to the sounds is broken by a knock on their door.

Isme climbs off the bed and opens the door to see Dan standing there. "Come in my friend," he beckons.

"No that's ok. I just wanted you to know that we're going down to the bar as it should be open by now."

"Ah ok, we'll join you shortly."

Alex has already opened up and John, Graham and Mandy are having an early doors drink. When Dan and Jill enter the bar, Alex is chatting to the others in the corner but aware as always, he spots them as they enter and greets them with, "Hi folks, is your room okay?"

They both acknowledge his greeting, replying that 'all is wonderful thank you,' and order a couple of gin and tonics. Ten minutes later, Isme and Judith join them. All four of them remain sitting at the bar and before long, they're chatting freely with the others. It transpires that the conference they are attending in Cornwall is a psychic convention, where some of the world's top specialists within that field will be in attendance.

Mandy seems very interested in the discussion and is quick to ask questions and pose the argument as to the validity of the belief. Isme seems amused by the reaction of the others, especially Alex, who comments in his usual diplomatic way, "What a load of old bollocks. When you're brown bread, you're dead."

As the evening moves on, so the early door's customers leave, to be replaced by those who are dining for the evening. During this time not many locals use the pub. They tend to visit later, maybe nine o'clock or further on.

The guests move away from the bar, entering the restaurant for their evening meal. Fleche is duty chef with Jo as waitresses and Nancy in the kitchen. Alex, much to his disgust, has the bar for the evening. Anne, who has the evening off, arrives downstairs earlier than usual to a caustic comment from her husband asking, "To what do we owe this pleasure? You don't normally emerge until closing time." She merely answers with a glare and heads off towards the kitchen.

"God, you like living dangerously Alex," old George states.

"You know me George, call it as it is and then wait for the explosion."

This causes a general titter from those people close enough to hear.

The evening progresses and the diners begin to leave as the locals start to arrive. The guests have now finished dining and returned to the bar, taking some seats in the far corner of the room. Before long Anne enters, introduces herself and gets involved in their conversation. She has always had a deep curiosity with regards to the physic goings on, so here lays a prime chance for her to feed her interests.

Within a short period of time, the discussion at the corner table has managed to spill out into the room, initially to a couple of people who are close by, standing by the fireplace enjoying its heat, who invite themselves into the debate, then it cascades out to the other tables and finally back to those seated at the bar. Isme and his friends are particularly courteous and attentive people, always answering the questions that come their way to the best of their ability, and fast and furious they come tonight, people all attempting to satisfy their own curiosity.

By ten o'clock the bar is heaving. Isme and his group have moved back to the bar, positioning themselves at the far corner, constantly bombarded by yet more questions. Suddenly Dan's head swings to the left, his whole being staring at the piano. Alex seeing this action becomes aware that Isme is doing the same thing. Both men's demeanour seems to have changed; their facial expressions have become more serious and intense.

"Are you getting that as well Isme?" Dan enquires.

"Most definitely, it's those voices again."

"Voices, yes that's what it is, but you said again, have you heard them before?"

"Yes I did this afternoon, upstairs in my room, just before you knocked on the door."

Alex, at the other end of the bar, can see that they are deep in discussion but is unable to hear what is being said, so he slowly begins to inch his way towards them.

"You ok gents?" he enquires.

Isme instantly removes his gaze from the piano, nudging Dan to do the same. "Yes of course, we were just admiring that lovely old piano."

"Definitely," Dan adds.

Alex looks slightly annoyed by their answer, but goes along with the facade which he believes they are playing, by answering, "Oh yes, she's a beauty, built in nineteen eleven, but she became part of The Bell Inn only eight years ago."

Alex observes Dan speaking softly to his wife, who in turn whispers to Judith, where upon both women say their goodnights and leave, climbing the stairs to their rooms. Isme and Dan remain, again relaxing with the locals, but

Alex remains ever observant as both men never remove their focus from the piano.

Closing time comes around and Alex yells 'last orders' and then ten minutes later, 'that's time', signifying to all that no more drinks will be poured tonight. At this time of the evening, all that's left in the bar are 'the usual suspects' plus their guests, Dan and Isme. Alex is keen to get cleared away, making sure all his locals are aware of this and showing the right respect, they finish their drinks, say their farewells and leave. Isme and Dan do the same. Alex had planned to have them stay for one more drink, due to his desire to talk to them, but as they leave, he says nothing. The bar empties and the building is locked down and finally it's just the two of them alone once more, with Anne sipping at her wine and Alex partaking in a cider.

"What lovely people they are and so interesting," Anne gushes.

"Hmm, quite so," he grunts his reply.

She gazes across at him, studying his face then she asks, "What's the matter Alex?"

He puts his cider down and walks from behind the bar towards the piano, intently studying the Christmas village. "They lied to me and I cannot understand why."

"What, when, how?"

"Both men were staring hard in this direction but when I asked if everything was ok, they replied 'yes' before proceeding to tell me how beautiful the piano was."

"So," she questions, a little mystified, "what's wrong with that?"

He turns to look straight at her, "I am astounded that they even noticed there was a piano over here, they were concentrating so hard on this village and from the moment they spotted it, they never stopped watching it all night long."

"Can you still hear them?" Isme asks both Judith and Jill.

Both women, with their eyes tightly closed, are sitting cross legged on the bedroom floor. Jill nods, "Just about."

"There are at least four different voices, possibly more," Judith informs him.

"They are coming from that display on top of the piano," Dan states.

"I thought the same thing," Isme confirms.

"But these voices are people," Jill says, "and I'm absolutely certain that they're not dead."

"I have the same feeling, but that is why it doesn't make any sense," Isme states. "People on the other side have various ways of contacting the living, normally through people like us. These voices, if they are indeed alive, are inside a model or at least somewhere very close to it."

"Is that not the whole point?" Judith interrupts.

The others look at her as she continues, her eyes still closed tightly shut. "They are not trying to contact us. They are not from the other side and they have no idea what we do. For some reason, possibly because we have the ability to tune in to a different level of sound from most others, we are able to hear them."

Isme slowly nods, "I think you've hit the nail on the head. In which case there is no point in trying to contact them."

"I've been trying to do exactly that," Jill states, "but I can't seem to get through."

"The chances are that we wouldn't be able to anyway as they are still living. So rather than trying to use our psychic powers, perhaps walking up to the model and just talking to it might work. After all, we should be able to hear any reply that's forthcoming," Dan says.

Jill's eyes flicker open and she smiles at him, saying "That's my Dan, pure logic."

They giggle and Judith adds, "How are we going to achieve the plan? The bar is shut now and I somehow do not believe that this landlord is going to like being woken up with our story."

"What about him?" Isme says. "Do you think he has any idea that there's something strange about that model?"

"Hard to say," Dan concludes with a smile, "but I had the distinct feeling earlier that he didn't believe us when we said we were in love with his piano."

Alex picks up each model in turn, shakes it, checks underneath and behind it, before placing it back down again. Anne watches him enquiring, "What on earth are you doing?"

Somewhat agitated he replies, "Think about it Anne, we've got cats that are fixated with this bloody thing, dogs that attack it and now guests who are glued to it and psychic guests at that. There has to be something going on up here."

Hearing his explanation she concludes that he has indeed got a point and gets up to join him with his examination.

The canopy lights gently twinkle, all except one which is situated at the far end of the bar partially covered by some holly. This one is as bright as bright can be, fluctuating with every word that is spoken.

"Jesus Christ," Canning yells out, as the building that he, Tara and Paul are in starts violently moving. They are thrown from left to right, careering from one side of the room to the other, colliding with each other as they find themselves with no control over their movements or direction whatsoever. The commotion lasts only briefly, but for the occupants it feels like an eternity.

After the worst of the uproar, there follow a few more erratic movements, where all three of them quickly anchor themselves to anything they happen to have to hand. Even when all further upheaval seems to have ended, they remain still, apprehensive to move in case it all kicks off again.

"Hope the others are ok," Paul calls across to the other two.

"We'll find out soon enough, but for now," Canning observes, "we were told to finish our sweep of these damn buildings and that is what we are going to do."

"Very caring Canning, your concern makes my eyes fill up," Paul quips.

Tara grins as Canning glares across the room at him, "Come on, let's get this thing done," she says.

They tentatively rise to their feet and then cautiously make their way across to the next building.

Meanwhile on the far side of the display, Michael, Julie, Clive and Duncan have experienced a similar earthquake. Michael is tossed violently across the void, collides with the opposite wall and is knocked unconscious upon impact. His limp body is flung to and fro like a rag doll until the limited world which they live in, finally comes to rest. Like the other party, the others all try to anchor themselves to whatever they can, remaining motionless for a short while even after the unrest has stopped. Julie is the first to move, dashing across to where Michael is laying, straightening him out, allowing him to rest evenly, she places a rolled up jacket caringly under his head.

"Is he breathing?" Duncan calls across.

She nods, "Yes, I think he's just knocked out, at least I hope that's all."

Clive joins her, checking for a pulse, then glancing at his watch. "His hearts ok, ticking strong and regular. All we can do is to wait with him until he comes around."

Duncan nods with understanding. "In which case, two of us need to carry on with the search and the other needs to remain here with him."

"I'll stay," Julie volunteers, "You two carry on. When you get to the end of this run of buildings, come back this way. If he comes round, we'll try to catch you up."

The two men get to their feet and leave the room.

Morning dawns and Anne is up first, down to the kitchens by eight thirty, opening the restaurant for their guests to breakfast. They arise half an hour later and take their seats at the table which she has laid up for them. Taking their order, she returns to the kitchen to prepare their food.

Dan, sipping his coffee, glances over to Isme who suddenly nods. Dan immediately gets to his feet and heads for the bar by way of the back hallway, in the opposite direction to the kitchen. He manages to reach the Christmas village unseen and places his hands on top of two of the models, concentrating hard. Out of the blue the canopy lights burst into action, spilling forth blinding white light into the room. Startled he turns to see what is causing this display just as he finds himself standing inside a darkened room with light glaring through its frosted window. Within seconds the illumination has stopped and he is left alone in a dimly lit void.

"He's taking too long," Jill states.

Isme's lips tighten as he pushes back his chair, standing up with the sole intent of finding his friend. His progress is halted as Anne enters the room, carrying in the cooked breakfasts. He is left with no choice but to retake his seat. She places the plates of food in front of each appropriate guest, enquiring as to Dan's whereabouts."

"He's just popped up to his room, he won't be long," Jill answers quickly.

Anne smiles, leaving the restaurant she returns to the kitchen. Immediately Isme heads for the bar in search of him. He walks into the bar and glances around the room. Not seeing his friend, he turns on his heels and heads directly upstairs to check if indeed he has actually returned to his room. Not finding him there either, he returns to the restaurant.

The two women look hopefully at him as he enters but he simply shakes his head and says, "I've no idea where he's gone. He's not in the bar or up in the rooms, so I'm at a loss as to where he's disappeared to."

Jill, at first appears a little perplexed, but quickly this turns to concern as she says, "This is a small pub with a bed and breakfast, how far can he be?"

Isme takes his seat and begins slowly to eat his lukewarm breakfast. Judith consoles her by saying, "He can't have gone far you'll see. He'll be back in a few minutes."

She closes her eyes for a few seconds and suddenly she blurts out, "No, he's not here anymore, well he is, but he isn't!"

Hearing Jill shout, Anne swiftly comes back into the restaurant, "What's the matter?" she asks.

They reiterate the story to her. She decides there is some urgency attached to their story and uses the intercom to call her husband down from upstairs, believing that he really should be here to hear this. He arrives almost immediately and moves the entire party into the bar where he sits them down and asks them to relate their tale one more time. By now Jill is in tears, with both Judith and Anne attempting to console her.

Alex listens to their account and although slightly annoyed that his guests have seemed to adopt their own hidden agendas, he stays calm and attentive, finally saying, "I've got to say, this is well beyond me. We will search this building and if we don't find him here, then we will scour the village. If we still find nothing, then we will call the police."

He glances at Isme judging his reaction, but only to see him staring at the Village scene. "Isme are you with me on this because I am feeling a little upset over the fact that you people seem to think you can wander all over my business and my home, lose one of your party and then look to blame anyone but yourselves because your friend has disappeared."

Isme slowly turns to face him and quite calmly he announces, "There is something very dangerous and macabre in this place and I personally would like to be out of here at the soonest possible opportunity."

Anne hears this and gets to her feet, staring hard at him and scathingly she says, "We've made you people welcome here, you ought to remember that. We have shown you great respect, a lot more than you have shown us."

Alex makes a couple of phone calls asking some friends of his to help in the search for their missing guest. They arrive within half an hour and the hunt begins for the absent man. Firstly they scour the Bell like a fine tooth comb but find nothing. Then they begin their search of the village, checking the paper shop and the stores even the little electrical shop on the edge of the village but no one has seen anything of him.

CHAPTER TWELVE

The police arrive by midday with Isme and his party still at the pub. Although, as explained to them by the officers in attendance, a missing person is not classed as missing in such a short period of time, but they will never the less still take the relevant particulars and have a good look around. Even Alex doesn't feel overly inspired with their attitudes saying, "Bloody hell, various people go missing, the police start to point fingers but when I call them in, they're not missing until they say they are. Well that's outstanding logic."

One of the uniformed officers over hears his dialogue and slightly agitated by the remark he says, "With all due respect sir, there is a procedure to follow and I will follow it regardless of your unfamiliar knowledge of how we work."

Alex's eyes begin to glaze over and before Anne has time to try to calm him down, he lets rip. "Listen to me you sanctimonious little idiot. The man we are trying to find came here to stay as a paying guest, on an interim stop before travelling on to Cornwall. He knows absolutely nobody here, due to the fact that he has never been here before. This morning he had no reason to leave these premises, especially right in the middle of his breakfast and I don't think for one minute that he would have gone anywhere willingly, without informing his wife and his friends at some bloody point, do you? You add all these facts together and you have a very weird picture or are you, so blinded by procedure, that you are missing that small point?"

An uneasy silence fills the room, until finally the officer calmly states, "I understand exactly what you have said to me, and no I am not blinded by procedure, however as you must appreciate, I still have guidelines to adhere to. I am taking this seriously. I can assure you of that sir."

Alex nods his understanding and thanks Graham, Andy and Steve who all turned out at short notice to help with the search. He grabs the dog's lead, calls her and without uttering another word, he takes her out in the deep snow for a long walk. She loves romping around in the snow and he desperately needs to clear his head and his thoughts.

He has only been gone for ten minutes when Criss and Marcus turn up, precariously driving down the road though the snow and ice, on the one way track, right in the centre of the carriageway which had been ploughed clear by a local farmer on his tractor. The farmers keep the centre of the village clear themselves as the highways department never seem to reach the outlying villages, only concentrating on the major roads, leaving the rest to their own devices. Alex always quips, 'It's funny how we all have to pay the same amount of rates for a completely fourth class service, if any at all'. Scathing some might say, harsh but nevertheless, absolutely correct.

It would be incorrect to say that Criss, who is driving, had parked the car; a more accurate description would be that she had simply abandoned it as close to the pub as she could. They both get out of the car. Criss while attempting to close the door slips over falling heavily on her rear end.

"She'll be fine," one of the uniformed officers states on seeing her, "all that padding on her backside has to be useful for something."

The other officer smiles but carefully shuffles through the snow towards her to see if he can be of any assistance. By the time he reaches her, Marcus has already managed to help her up and the two of them are heading off towards the pub.

Anne spots them coming and glances the other way up the road, in the direction that Alex went, trying to see if he was still in view, but he's gone, by now he'd probably already be at the parish hall grounds. She welcomes everybody in, gets them all settled and makes the necessary introductions, then heads for the kitchen to make them some hot refreshments.

Criss and Marcus question the group, listening to their story, rarely interrupting their dialogue and taking notes the entire time. After a short while, having heard everything, they take themselves off into the more comfortable area of the lounge bar with the two uniformed officers to discuss their viewpoint on all that has happened.

"Well, it's pretty clear on this occasion, that the landlord was nowhere around when this man disappeared," Marcus states.

"True," Criss replies, "and this time, the last known whereabouts of the victim was in the bar, not in the hall or outside."

"Which means?" Marcus begins to say.

"That we now have three different locations in which these people seem to have vanished from, but they are still all in or immediately around the same building."

"Which implies what?" one of the uniformed officers enquires.

Criss glances over to Marcus and replies, "It's got to have something to do with this building. Even those guests said they could hear voices."

"They did. Voices they believed to be coming from that model village over there," Marcus adds.

"Oh bloody hell," the other uniformed officer declares, "we're all stuck in the twilight zone."

The others glare at him, Marcus snapping, "Do try and keep up, this is serious stuff here."

"Yes sir, sorry sir," he replies.

"So, our next course of action..." Marcus begins once more.

"Is to take that village scene to bits and examine it completely ourselves," Criss finishes with.

All four rise to their feet and return to the bar, positioning themselves in front of the Christmas scene, staring at it, with the exception of the disbelieving officer who now has his ear pinned to one of the pieces. "Can't hear anything, I don't think anyone's home in this one. Shall I test the others?" he smiles.

"Please don't," Criss says grinding her teeth, "just find the damn socket which they are attached to and unplug it please."

Both officers begin to follow the mains cable from the model, eventually locating the plug behind the bar.

"You need to cut it out Brian. You're going to get us both a bollocking if you keep it up," the first officer whispers.

"Come on Phil are they really serious, because if they are why don't we just call in all the vertically challenged police officers in this force, provide them with riot gear and send them in to the buildings to do a search."

Phil starts to giggle but reaches out and switches the socket off before calling out, "It's dead, your good to go!"

Brian bursts into laughter, loud enough for everyone present to hear. Criss and Marcus just look at each other in total disbelief.

"Leave it alone," Alex sharply orders on entering the room. All eyes turn to him while they watch him release his dog from her lead and remove his coat and wellington boots.

"I took it apart and looked at every piece of that model myself last night, I even shook them up, there's absolutely nothing up there. They're just models, there's nothing sinister in them."

Criss places her hands on her hips and aggressively replies, "That was then and this is now, so I would like to inspect them myself if I may?"

Alex, much to the surprise of his present audience, merely smiles, "Well, why the hell not, let's be honest, you two seem to be experts in thoroughly searching the strangest places. The halls had a good going over, so now it's the Christmas village. When you've finished, the key to the piano is hanging up behind the bar, you may need a pickaxe to get into the stone wall behind it though."

He then turns to the two officers who are behind the bar and assertively says, "And you two can get out from behind my bar before I become unreasonable. You have no warrant, so move."

His attention then returns to Criss and he adds, "Help yourselves, but they are expensive pieces. Please be very careful with them."

She nods as she begins dismantling.

Michael comes to, gently rubbing the side of his head, "How long have I been out?"

"Not long," Julie informs him, "five minutes or so. Anything else hurt on you?"

He is helped to his feet, whereupon he performs various stretches, testing his joints and limbs. "Everything seems to be working, cannot see that anything has broken off me, so all is hunky dory, shall we go?"

She smiles, "Yeah let's do that, I'll lead the way and we'll take it steady."

"As you command fair maiden, as you command."

They set off following the direction in which Duncan and Clive had left earlier.

Within the hour, not only had they caught up with the other two, but they had completed their part of the search, joining up with the other party. They all sit around discussing their respective findings. It soon becomes apparent that no more than six points of weakness have been identified, three by each team. Also both sides have made a basic plan of where they've been, making it easier for others to commute through this maze of buildings. They decide to rest before preparing to set off again, this time in opposite directions, to verify the findings of the others.

Isme and Judith reluctantly leave the pub to continue on with their journey to the convention in Cornwall. Jill books in to stay for a further two nights, not willing to leave until she has found her husband.

The four officers dismantle and then reassemble the Christmas village scene, thoroughly examining every single piece, and finally having to concede that they cannot see anything amiss with it at all. Having placed it back on top of the piano under Alex's watchful eye, verifying that everything is in its rightful place, Brian with the landlord's permission enters the bar to turn it back on.

Alex goes to the front door, opening it up for the lunchtime period. Fleche enters as he opens the door, the church bell just finishing its twelfth chime. He sidles past Alex who exhales an audibly exaggerated sigh displaying his contempt, which is added to that of the morning's activities.

Almost immediately a family of six come plodding through the snow and enter the hall, removing their wet footwear they enter the bar making straight for the blazing open fire to warm themselves. The family consists of two adults and four children who range from the youngest, a two year old to the oldest at eight.

Alex proceeds to his bar, greeting the customers and signalling to Jo, the day's duty waitress to take menus to them. Smiling, she directs them to a table which is closest to the bar, before handing around the menus. Alex pours them the drinks they have requested, personally delivering them to their table.

Criss and Marcus are sat in the corner writing up the events thus far. The other two officers have left.

The family soon order, two main meals for themselves and three children's meals which they plan to share between the four little ones. Then dad spots the Christmas scene, pointing it out to his family. In the blink of an eye, the oldest child, Prim is out of her seat and at the foot of the piano, gazing up at the twinkling display. Her father immediately follows, picking her up and holding her close so that she can see the models properly, the delight in her face is evident as she looks from one end of the display to the other and from the upper level to the lower one. Suddenly she seems mesmerised by just the one model, this being the 'tea rooms', which she strains to get closer to. Her father allows her to reach a certain distance before pulling her away gently requesting, "Don't touch it please sweetheart."

She bursts into laughter, giggling away, all the time pointing at the model. Her happiness is so infectious that everyone's attention is magnetically drawn to her, with smiles displayed by all, except for Criss who is showing a curious expression across her face.

"They're funny aren't they daddy, can you hear them?"

The man glances at the model and replies, "Really funny darling, now come on, let's sit down, our lunch will be here very shortly."

Prim waves at the models as she is carried back to her seat, a picture that once again brings smiles to the faces of all those watching. Criss observes the whole incident and when the child is seated back at the table, her gaze immediately returns to the Christmas scene.

"What is it?" Marcus asks.

"Did you see that little girl?"

"Yes, everyone was watching her, quite charming really."

"Forget that side of it, she said that she could hear something in that display."

Marcus slams his pen down firmly, startling Criss. "For pities sake, what is the matter with you? We've had the frigging thing in pieces and found nothing untoward but you now want to base our professional enquiry on the fact that a small child giggles at a bloody model. Personally, I feel we've made a big enough joke out of our investigations thus far and would simply like to get out of here for now."

Criss lowers her head and quietly replies, "Okay, let's go, but I'm telling you, there is something wrong with that display."

"Whatever," Marcus dejectedly answers as he rises. He glances across to Alex and thanks him for his time before he heads for the door. Criss follows having nodded to Alex, but she utters no words.

As they leave so more people enter, the bar is filling up fast. Within ten minutes Anne is on the phone calling in reinforcements for the kitchens to help with the increased workload.

By closing time they're both exhausted. They'd been so busy that the take had rivalled that of a Saturday night. Having closed the door, Alex sets about cleaning the tables and vacuuming the bar of all the surplus food scattered around the place, just as Fleche paces towards the door about to leave.

"Where are you off to?" Alex casually asks.

"Home sir, my shift finishes at three o'clock."

Immediately Alex heads for the kitchen only to see his wife, the two girls plus Ryan the young lad washing up, completely buried in a huge pile of pots, pans and crockery.

"FLECHE!" he yells.

"Just leave it Alex, we'll get it done," Anne tiredly says.

"Fleche get your sad arse back in here this minute!" he continues to shout.

He hears the door slam shut and feels the anger inside him. "Lazy bastard!" he hisses under his breath. Striding towards the front door, he stops suddenly as he draws level with the bar, observing the canopy lights brightly fluctuating. "Pack that in, I've got enough problems without you lot blowing a fuse too!"

For a second nothing happens, the lights stay the same. He pauses glaring at the display, then they dim and return back to normal. He proceeds to the front door in pursuit of the departing chef. Having wrenched the door open in anger, he glances left the way that Fleche would normally go home but there is no sign of him.

"Says it all," Alex grunts, "you can bleeding move when you want to even with all this snow, lazy bastard."

He goes back in to continue with the chores that are still in front of him.

Fleche returns home but when he staggers through his front door, Jade, his wife is concerned over his appearance. "What's wrong," she asks him, "come here and sit down for a minute."

He slumps into a chair, cradling his head in his hands. He tries to speak but finds that he can't, his whole body is trembling.

"Jesus," she exclaims in fear, "I'm ringing for an ambulance."

He raises an arm, gesturing her not to, waving his arm frantically at her. He manages to stammer, "No, no don't, I'll be ok in a minute."

She makes sure that he is comfortable before going to prepare him a warm, sweet drink. His young children are both looking scared at his appearance. He manages a smile in an effort to console their fears.

After twenty minutes or so, he begins to rally around, colour returning to his face, he is now able to talk properly. Jade relentlessly questions him to explaining exactly what had happened.

"It started as I left work. I'd just stepped out of the door into the snow and this strange feeling came over me."

"What feeling?" she interrupts.

"Will you let me finish woman, for Christ sake, I'm trying to tell you."

She nods her head and bites her tongue, holding back further questions.

"I heard Alex call out to me but I wasn't going back. It had been a murderous lunchtime; we did over sixty covers and had to call in extra staff. Anyway, I heard him call out but by then I'd decided to leg it. I'd finished my hours and I had no intention of staying on to clear up as well. I'm a chef, not a damn lackey."

Jade thumps her fists on her knees in frustration and says, "Fleche, will you just tell me what happened?"

"I had only taken one pace when I felt it. The only way I can describe it is like a tug, something pulling me backwards, stopping me from moving forward. At first I thought Alex was behind me, dragging me back to the kitchen but as I glanced behind me, there was nothing there. I tried to move forward, away, anywhere but the sensation increased, tearing at me. I felt my chest tighten, but I seemed to be able to breathe ok, then I looked down at my hands. I could feel I was trembling, shaking uncontrollably but what I saw, well what I think I saw was really weird."

"What?"

He looks straight into his wife's eyes and says, "I hope you can believe this because this is what I saw."

"What?" she says again, her eyes now wide in anticipation.

"It was like there was another me, another identical person, and my skin was peeling away from my hands, forming an apparition behind me."

Jade looks horrified but doesn't utter a word.

"It was an outline that bits of me seemed to be filling in. As the seconds passed, I felt weaker and weaker, as if I was ready to pass out and the thing behind me was taking shape, the shape was becoming me, and in its turn, it was moving towards the pub."

A deathly silence filled the room, until Jade broke it by saying firmly, "Kids go to your rooms. I want to speak to your daddy alone."

When they've left the room, she gently asked, "What happened then?"

"That's the odd bit. All of a sudden the sensation stopped, the outline started to fade and everything that it had taken away came cascading back to me. It felt like I was being hit by a train, it hurt like hell, but in seconds I was able to move unhindered. I literally fled. I knew I had to get as far away as I could. Now I'm here, safe and sound I hope?"

"Drink your tea. I'm going down to that pub to find out what's going on in there."

He sat bolt upright in his chair, the urgency in his face paramount. "Please don't. Stay away from that place for now. We'll go together later, when I'm due to go back on duty."

She stops, considers what her husband has said and agrees to his wishes. She sits down beside him, takes his hand and stares deep into his eyes with her thoughts of, 'what the hell really happened?'

"Hello, hello?"

Duncan spins around on his heels, gazing at one of the exit points in the room in which they are all congregated.

"Another one, bloody hell at this rate we'll be over populated soon."

"Hello I know that you people are here."

"Hmm we have another one, but this one is already aware of our presence," Michael observes thoughtfully, "now that is unusual."

"In here," Julie calls out.

Dan enters the room aware of the seven sets of eyes all staring in his direction. He smiles and calmly says, "Well hello, my name is Dan and it's a pleasure to find you all at last."

"Have you been searching long?" Paul asks in a mocking manner.

He smiles and replies, "Not too long. I have only been aware that you were in here for a short time. It was just a matter of locating you."

Michael takes a pace towards him and asks, "So are we to assume you came in here voluntarily to find us?"

Dan sniffs and replies, "Not exactly."

"Then," Michael assertively states, "Tell us how you got here, why you think you knew we were in here, and most of all, why you seem so undisturbed by finding yourself here."

Dan quickly scans the room, noting that all eyes are firmly fixed on him. He quickly ascertains that the man who has just spoken, seems to be the leader and that the others appear relatively happy to follow him.

"Ok," Dan starts, "from the beginning. I am or was staying at The Bell Inn, with my wife and another couple of friends. We are all physics."

"A damn physic!" Clive blurts out, "just what we don't need. Why can't an explosive expert get dropped off in here instead?"

Michael's displeasure at this outburst is evident and silence reigns once more. He gestures to Dan to continue with his oration.

"Anyway, we could hear you. At first it was a high pitched garble that we tuned in on but as we entered the bar, we were able to identify voices and ascertained that it was coming from the Christmas models on the piano. We didn't want to appear nosey, so we decided not to go poking around, especially as the bar was pretty full of customers, so we left it and went to bed that night, deciding to take a look, if possible, in the morning."

"Ok," Michael says, "so the morning came, then what happened?"

"Simply during breakfast, when the landlady was preparing our food, I slipped into the bar to take a closer look at the models. I had just started to apply my concentration on the display when everything behind and around me became enveloped in an extremely bright light, so intense that I couldn't see anything."

"And the next thing you knew was you were in here," Michael finishes for him.

"That's correct, but the strange thing is that I knew exactly where I was, there was absolutely no doubt in my mind. The obvious thing for me to do, was to find you all."

All eyes now fix on Michael, who they can see is deep in thought.

"Clive you saw bright lights, didn't you?" Julie questions.

He nods, still observing Michael.

"Anyone else remember lights of any kind?" she labours.

The room is filled with murmurs but the overall answer is no.

"Not that we saw," Michael interrupts, "Not that we were aware of, but that doesn't mean they were not present at our abductions."

"How do you mean?" Duncan asks.

"Canning and you had both left the pub, as had I. Julie was heading for her locker and Tara and Paul were at the front door. We were all very close to the bar when the dastardly deed was done and now we are being informed of these lights. The only lights that I can think of that could possibly be part of this scenario are the ones that adorn the canopy of the bar."

"I vaguely remember them being up, but can't recall them doing anything strange," Julie informs.

"Don't reckon I even remember them at all," Paul adds looking at Tara who is also shaking her head.

"There is one more thing," Dan adds, regaining their attention once more. "Just before the lights came on, I felt an extremely powerful presence, as if something was actually touching me, a presence that certainly didn't feel as though it was physically from our world. Its aura felt menacing and dangerous. When the lights came on, it felt as though I was being torn from my body by something really powerful. I could see myself, still standing over the model. It was quite frightening."

"We've all experienced that feeling," Canning consoles, "and as you say, it was bloody scary."

"So Dan, having found us and as you said, that was your original quest, how do you intend to proceed? Have you gathered any thoughts together on our method of escape?" Michael doubtfully quizzes him.

He smiles, "It's not what we do next that will make too much difference. Whatever it was that put us here is bound to be ensuring that we don't leave. However, when the time is right, my friends will contact me. It is then, that whatever is holding us here will come to light and manifest its self, as it will have little choice but to fight against their combined powers."

Michael nods, "Interesting theory, but I'm sure you won't mind if we, the non psychic people present, carry on with our meagre endeavours to free ourselves in the meantime."

Dan laughs, "Not at all and furthermore, if I can be of any assistance, don't hesitate to ask."

CHAPTER THIRTEEN

"The carol singers are in tonight," Fleche calls out from the kitchen, whilst perusing the diary.

"What time?" Anne calls back.

"Nine o'clock it says here, but you know that lot. They could arrive thirty minutes either way."

"Free mince pies and glasses of sherry again, that's why they're never on time. It just depends how many they've had at their previous venues," Alex cuttingly adds.

Anne glares at him, "It is, as you well know, a community thing. Besides, they come in here and add a Christmas spirit by singing for us."

"Is that what you call it," he grunts.

A giggle can be heard from Fleche in the kitchen and Anne retorts, "If you can sing better, then why don't you join them."

"Bloody hell," he concludes, "that would definitely bring the building down."

She smiles and this time Fleche calls out loud enough for Alex to hear. "I would pay real money to stop him attempting to sing."

Alex and Anne continue with their morning's chores, while Fleche is cleaning the chip fryers, a weekly task that he abides due to the muck and grease and inevitable collection of incinerated chips that collect at the bottom of them.

By midday, the doors are open and Alex stands on the doorstep watching the snow still slowly fall from the skies. The track in the middle of the road remains to some lesser degree, although it is now fairly well covered with the latest fall from the heavens, but everywhere else, the snow is a couple of feet in depth with the drifts piled substantially higher. He gazes up into the sky, able to see that as far as the horizon, the cloud cover is complete, the whole of its being shimmering with a pinkish blue tinge, informing him that there is to be no let up in these weather conditions for the foreseeable future.

He turns and strides back into the building calling out, "If this snow keeps up, I'll be surprised if we see anyone at all today, let alone the carol singers."

He strolls behind the bar and begins to make a list of the bottles he needs to bring up from the cellar to replace those sold the previous evening. As he labours away, Jill comes down from her room upstairs and enters the bar, taking a stool at the end. From here she orders a coffee and sits staring at the Christmas scene. She closes her eyes, concentrating on the model buildings. Alex takes himself off to the kitchen to place the coffee order and returns to the bar.

"Tired?" he asks her.

"No, not at all," she replies, "I'm just trying to make contact with Dan telepathically. Sometimes we can contact each other using this method."

"Really," he exclaims raising his eyebrows, "you can do that?"

She chuckles, "Sometimes yes, especially if either of us are in any trouble."

"How did you discover that you had the ability to do this?" he questions her.

She sighs from having to break her concentration, but replies graciously none the less. "Both Dan and I are a twin. He had an identical brother and I also have a brother. Obviously we are not identical. Throughout our lives we have been able to contact our siblings using this method. It's pretty common place amongst twins to some degree. Believe it not, I sort of knew of Dan even before I'd met him and the same applied to him with me."

"How did you both meet?"

"In a pub, I was with Isme and Judith, but I knew he was there. Suddenly I saw this man slowly moving through the long bar, staring at various people and inspecting the occupants of every table that he passed. As he approached, I knew he was the one I had been sensing for some time, and then he stopped right in the middle of the room and looked over at me. A huge grin filled his face from ear to ear and he came straight across the room to our table saying, 'I didn't believe that I would ever find you', and that was that."

"Wow," Alex exclaims with a nonchalant toss of his head, "that would make a great chick flick, especially with the 'twilight zone' thing thrown in."

She smiles, "I must admit, being in love before you have actually met the person in the flesh is unusual, but once we were together, well until now it has been pretty much perfect." She hangs her head, "He's not dead. He's here somewhere. I can sense him, just as I could all those years ago."

Alex looks a little perplexed and gently asks, "But where exactly is he? We've searched this whole place twice over, where could he possibly hide?"

Her eyes light up. "It's not where he's hiding but it's where he's being hidden. He is on a different level to us right now."

"Whoa, now it's all getting a bit deep for me, but if there is anything you think I can do to help, just ask," he says backing away slightly.

Jill thanks him before returning her attention to the Christmas scene.

Alex leaves her to it and walks out into the kitchen to get her coffee which has probably gone cold by now. As he picks up the tray, he glances across to Fleche and asks him, "Do you understand this 'plane' thing?"

Fleche looks back with a blank look on his face having not been privy to the conversation and says, "What, the winged type or the wasteland type?"

"What?" Alex pauses, raising his eyes to the heavens, then adds, "Neither idiot, the 'astral type'."

Fleche puts his hands on his hips and sarcastically replies, "Oh that type, well as you didn't enlighten me as to how it was spelt, did you?"

"Brilliant!" Alex snaps, "You're a real help. I now know why we have these little talks, they are so fulfilling." He turns on his heel with the tray to deliver Jill her coffee.

The occupants of the Christmas village scene make their way in unison to the closest point where light can enter the buildings. Having reached their destination, they stand in the centre staring at the tiny pin prick, which permits a single thin strand of brilliance into the room from the middle of an outside wall.

"Well, what's the plan?" Canning asks.

"In its simplest form, if we all attack the hole together, we can tear it open quicker if we all work in unison, then we can possibly making it large enough, quickly enough, so that one of us can get outside before we are intercepted," Duncan explains.

Michael smiles in agreement adding, "That is it in a nutshell. However, we must be quicker than light speed, otherwise our invisible jailer will intervene. What I suggest, and this is where we differ, is that no more than three people take a turn at any one time. If for any reason, any one of the three tires or hurts themselves, then they are to withdraw immediately, allowing the next person straight in to carry on. Speed is of the absolute essence here."

Everyone looks around at each other. The silence is broken by Clive, "Right, I'll be on the first shift, who would like to join me?"

Immediately Duncan comes forward, quickly followed by Julie. Tara, Paul and Canning fall in behind them. Dan watches the operation from the side, not offering any physical help as such. Michael glances across to him and he smiles saying, "I'll keep watch."

"Are we ready people?" Clive assertively asks.

Nodding, they drop down onto all fours with both men using their belt buckles as tools, while the only weapon Julie had to hand was a metal nail file. They gouge away at the holes location, bits of debris flying in all directions.

Michael observes with great interest, looking up and around him every few seconds to make sure everything remains ok. On one of these occasions his eyes lock with those of Dan, who displays an expression of pure horror on his face.

"What is it?" Michael urgently asks him. "Dan, speak to me, what is it?"

Dan slowly turns his head to face him, his eyeballs slipping back into the sockets of his head so that only the whites are showing as he replies, "It's coming."

"What's coming, tell me, what the hell is coming?"

Abruptly, his eyes return to their normal position, his pupils zooming in and out rapidly. His gaze finally focuses on Michael and he stammers, "I don't know but it's awesome, powerful, frightening and vicious and with singular purpose it is heading straight for us."

"Stop what you are doing now!" Michael yells, "Everyone out of this room and make it quick."

After a moment's hesitation, everyone leaves the room, everyone except Dan.

The last one to clear the room is Michael and as he glances back, he sees Dan standing there. "Come on, let's go," he insists.

"I can't, I need to see what we are dealing with."

Michael grabs Duncan and quietly says to him, "Get in there and drag him out, I don't care how but just get him out of there."

Duncan slips past Michael and into the room, making a bee line for Dan, but before he is able to reach him, he is thrown backwards, landing at Michael's feet. Physically, he is lifted off the ground and an eerie outline of a large, shaggy being can be seen holding him by one of its huge limbs. They both stare deeply into each other's eyes, the spectre's pupils glowing with a sickly green intensity. It then turns its attention towards Dan who is tossed like a discarded rag doll across the room, falling motionless on the furthest side away from the others. Duncan staggers to his feet, shaken but eager to reach Dan. Michael holds him back, gesturing that it would be far more beneficial for him to stay still while the being remained in their presence.

The eerie figure turns its attention towards Duncan and Michael, who both immediately flee the room. It then turns towards the spot where the light is entering the room and within seconds, a liquid plastic type substance cascades down the wall, quickly sealing the hole again. As fast as it arrived, it was gone, leaving only an odious smell in the room.

Duncan cautiously peers into the room before being pushed forward as Canning shoves his way past him, curiosity getting the better of him. Duncan looks back saying, "So much for caution. Next time I think we should just send you in Canning then if something is amiss, it will be you who receives the consequences."

Canning glares at him as he strides past, heading straight for where the opening had previously been, inspecting the entire area in case he'd misplaced it. "That thing has filled it in, the bastard."

On entering the room, Julie sprints across to Dan. Duncan glances across then looks back to Canning saying, "Boy you're a real piece of work."

"What?" Canning exclaims, "What's your problem now?"

"He should be our first concern here, not the damn hole."

Canning quickly turns to where Dan and Julie are squatting then he glares back at Duncan saying, "He's got help, he doesn't need me."

With everyone finally back in the room checking that Dan is alright with nothing broken, they survey the scene and muse as to how the hole had simply disappeared. Michael quietly listens as they discuss their latest visitor, the spectre. Speculation was rampant.

Dan is slowly but surely, lifted to his feet and although physically he appears sound, for some reason he is unable to speak. As he regains his wits he becomes extremely agitated over his loss of speech. He clutches Michael by the shoulders, staring hard into his face as if trying to communicate with him by some other method, but Michael can't hear him.

The lunchtime session is finished and the pub is locked up. Alex decides to take the dog for a walk. As he is ready to leave, Anne emerges kitted out for the Arctic Circle announcing that she will join them. They lead up the dog and set off, tramping through the deep snow is hard work but within half an hour they reach the fields behind the village. They stop, gazing about them at the virgin white expanse. Previous walker's footprints would rapidly have disappeared with the volumes of fresh snow that kept falling; the unruffled facade remained untainted.

From where they were, they could see the back of The Bell Inn quite clearly, a three storey, early eighteenth century building, made of local stone with a slate roof. Alex can see the smoke billowing from one of the four chimney stacks and immediately he turns to Anne.

Reading his facial expression she says, "Yes the fire guard is in its position in front of the fire."

He lets out a low huff of relief, "You know me too well."

She takes his arm as they set off around the field. Their dog Twiglet, is a black and tan, medium sized mongrel which has to leap in order to make any headway through the depth of the snow. He disappears completely for some seconds before bursting out of a drift, as if tunnelling his way through.

Suddenly Alex stops abruptly, pulling Anne backwards. His gaze is once more fixed firmly on the pub in the distance.

"What's up?" she asks.

At first he doesn't answer, but when he does, it is quietly under his breath. "How the hell can they be on?"

She turns her attention to follow his line of sight, to see both the back lounge and the kitchen windows full of blazing light, perfectly visible even at their distance. "I know they were all off before we left."

"I know they were too, as I turned everything off myself." Alex confirms.

They turn around to retrace their steps, this time with a certain amount of urgency and as much speed as the terrain will allow them.

Isme and Judith having finished their seminar for that day are sat in the hotel bar where their conference was held. They are in the company of another man who in their circles is known as a 'power house'. His name is Tristan Grantree. He is a big man, six feet four in height, broad, with jet black long straight hair. He is clean shaven and originates from Haiti. They sit together, leaning forward, their heads almost touching. Judith is relating the story of Dan's disappearance. Grantree listens attentively, never interrupting. When Judith is finished, Isme adds his thoughts and anymore facts that he regards as relevant. When the conversation is finished, they sit back in their seats, a pensive silences reigning while Grantree ponders everything that he has heard.

Suddenly he leaps to his feet saying, "I need to think further on this matter. It is obvious to me that if you two couldn't contact him, that there are other, not so evident variables within this equation."

He leaves the bar without another word and Isme and Judith are left looking at each other in awe.

Quickly unlocking the front door, Alex throws it open and strides through the building towards the bar. Anne closes it behind her and follows him in. The room is no longer illuminated, in point of fact, with the winter light fading the room is actually quite dark. He goes behind the bar to turn on the main ceiling lights.

"They're not on now," Anne observes.

He looks around the room, his watchful eyes only halting when they reach the canopy lights. "Think about it, no lights were on when we walked in and I'm bloody certain there were none on when we left this building with the dog, but we both saw how much light was oozing out of this building when we were stood in that field."

Anne nods, "That's all true, so explain it then, because I'm buggered if I can." She turns, undoing her coat and removing the rest of her arctic clobber she disappears upstairs.

Alex slumps down in one of the armchairs next to the fire and gazes at the canopy. "It was you lot, wasn't it?"

The lights blip, as if only a tiny electrical current had been allowed to pass along the circuit.

"But how and why and what the bloody hell are you trying to prove? At this rate you are going to muster so much interest that you will find yourselves replaced."

The display instantly bursts into life, a solid white light, so concentrated and intense that Alex has to shield his face. He can literally feel the heat they are emitting.

"For Christ sake, calm it down!" he says raising his voice.

The lights go out, not a glimmer, only total stillness.

"Light!" he commands.

A slight twinkle passes through the string, each bulb in its turn, dancing.

He giggles, "You lot are bizarre, but sometimes you're out of order too. Listen to me. Here I am talking to a set of Christmas lights as if they understand me." He pauses for a moment then studies them hard adding, "But you do, don't you, somehow you do?"

The lights softly go crazy, displaying an exhibition so colourful and exotic that he simply sits back in his chair and watches their performance, loving every second of what he is witnessing. Suddenly, they go out as the door from the stairs is opened. Alex jumps at the sound, so completely engrossed in the lights that Anne's entrance had startled him.

"What are you doing?" she asks strolling into the room.

Stuttering for a second he replies, "Nothing, I was just sitting here trying to work out how the lights turned on earlier."

"Maybe they didn't, maybe we were seeing a reflection of the evening light or something?"

He tips his head, raising his eyebrows and with a giggle replies, "More like the 'or something' I reckon."

Having returned to their room, Isme and Judith speak with Jill, take a short nap, shower and dress for the evening. On their arrival the hotel bar is busy with a buzz of voices and topical conversation everywhere. They make their way over to the bar, greeting various people who they've met on different occasions. Isme orders their drinks and looks around him for a vacant table.

Suddenly together they hear quite clearly in their heads, "Come to the outer lounge area, I'm waiting for you."

They follow their instructions and as they enter the wide open expanse filled with luxurious high backed chairs and leather sofas, they spot Grantree sitting alone, peering at them over the rim of a coffee cup.

"Good evening Tristan," Isme greets, "that was a novel way of gaining our attention."

He stands and shaking their hands, he replies, "Not at all, it's an ability I mastered some years ago and one that enables me to sit comfortably, instead of fighting my way through the crowds, but still acquiring my desired objective."

They smile as they take their seats. Grantree inhales deeply before he begins."I have given this problem of yours a substantial amount of thought and I have even tried to contact Dan myself through my mind. This should have succeeded, as I know the man and am able to visualise him. However, I could not make any contact, but what I did receive back was a terrifying image. As I was attempting to locate him this image placed itself within my mind and then it began travelling towards me. I broke the link of course. Whatever it was, it was extremely powerful and dangerous."

"What of Dan?" Judith enquires.

"That is probably the only bit of good news. Whatever that image was, I am sure it entered my link because it was guarding and blocking anyone from contacting him."

"And you feel that is a good thing?" Isme questions him, quite surprised.

"Of course it is because it means that he is being held captive and he is not dead. On what level or plane, I cannot speculate at this present time. We need to go to this pub so that I can experience for myself what is there."

"What, now?" Isme asks.

"Indeed now, there's no time like the present. Besides, Dan is obviously in danger."

They sit for a short while and finish their drinks while organising their trip, before they leave the lounge, going straight to their rooms to pack. Within fifteen minutes, they are in reception, checking out.

As the pub opens at five o'clock prompt, there are hungry people already waiting on the doorstep, hoping to be fed. They are invited in, furnished with menus and informed that the kitchen will open in half an hour. Drinks are purchased and they sit admiring the open fire, the interesting decor and of course, the model village.

Anne arrives ten minutes later and sets about feeding the animals before washing up the few dishes that remain from earlier, preparing for the evening ahead. Fleche is already in the kitchen, with Jack the duty waiter.

"What's that funny noise?" Tara questions.

The entire room listens for a second then Clive says, "I can't hear anything."

"Nor can I," Michael adds.

"Bloody hell," Canning interrupts, "at your age, you wouldn't hear an elephant charging through a cut glass display cabinet."

"Shut up you lot and listen," Duncan orders, "Tara's right, I can hear something as well."

He gets to his feet and crosses quietly towards the opening on the far side of the room. As he is about to enter the adjoining room, he jumps backwards and in his haste he crashes in to the wall, as if startled by something approaching him. Everyone else in the room jumps straight up, preparing for whatever is approaching, all eyes straining towards the opening. Briefly you could hear a pin drop, perspiration showing on their foreheads, when finally a cat pokes his head around the corner. It ambles nonchalantly into the room closely followed by two more.

Michael walks forward, staring at them and announces, "These are the pub cats. I recognise them, yes it's definitely them."

"You're right," Duncan confirms, "but how the hell did they get in here."

Julie giggles and they all look towards her. She says, "Well, I'm obviously not Einstein but seeing as how they are perfectly in proportion to us, I assume they were transported here by the same thing that sent us here."

Michael bursts into laughter, followed by the rest of them. Paul slides down the wall holding his stomach, relief evident on everyone's faces.

As they calm down Paul picks up one of the cats, stroking it he asks, still giggling, "But why have they been sent here?"

Michael attempts to answer him, "Why have any of us been sent here? If we knew that, we would be a lot closer to solving this whole problem."

"I can hear them coming," John states at the end of the bar.

"Hear who?" Graham enquires.

"The village choir of course, they who have been around the village serenading the occupants with Christmas carols and annoying the hell out of everybody."

Alex glares across to him saying, "Can it John, I'm not keen either but as Anne pointed out, at least they're trying."

"Yep, they're trying alright," he retorts.

A few muffled, sniggers can be heard from around the bar.

Ten minutes later, the kitchen staff have prepared the warm, mince pies and glasses of sherry and delivered them out to the bar and placed them on a corner table awaiting the singers. Shortly they enter.

"Merry Christmas everyone," Val the choir leader calls out.

In unison, the whole bar in harmony, chant back, "Merry Christmas!"

The carollers bunch together in the window area and burst forth into song. Looking around at the occupants, Alex observes that there is a difference of opinion with regards to the rendition which they are hearing. Some people have big smiles across their faces, happily taking part in the Christmas spirit while others are grimacing as odd notes are sung off key. Alex shakes his head and continues serving drinks. Everyone stops their chores to watch the spectacle. As they finish their rendition there follows a rousing round of applause and cheers, with the choir theatrically taking their bows. When the acclaim quells, the singers, having spotted the pies and sherry on offer, dive straight into the refreshments. Alex notes that he arranged for twenty pies and glasses of sherry to be put out, but that there are only twelve singers present. Nevertheless, everything on the table is consumed. He decides that if the choir are on site, he might as well utilise them.

"Come on you lot, Christmas is a coming, let's sing."

Val bursts straight into song again. In no time at all, everyone without exception is singing at the top of their voices, tunes that can be heard halfway around the village.

Alex observes the canopy lights to be pulsating to the rhythm. No one else seems to notice, but he has to smile at their joviality.

CHAPTER FOURTEEN

Through the dark of the night, a Range Rover containing Isme, Grantree and Judith, slowly negotiates the snow laden roads on its way from Cornwall to Devon.

"I'll ring Jill to let her know we're on our way," Judith says.

"Please do not do that," Grantree jumps straight in saying. "Jill is too close to Dan and will have tried to contact him already."

"Your point Tristan?" Isme asks.

"Quite simply, that whatever knew that I was attempting to contact Dan, will know that Jill has tried as well. This apparition will be in tune with her, even if it has not as yet manifested itself to her. It will be watching."

"I see, but we still need to find out if there's room at the Inn," Judith states.

"Then ring the pub direct please," he insists.

Judith does as she's instructed. When she gets through its Anne who takes the call and as rooms are available, she books them in without any further questions.

"Last orders!" Alex yells out over the music and noise in the bar.

There is an immediate glance at glasses by over half the room, all estimating whether they need a final drink or not before they rush to the bar. By now, Anne used to this late night onslaught when the bar is packed, moves behind the bar to help Alex serve them as quickly as possible.

Fleche has already gone home, insisting that he leaves the building with someone else in case the gremlins come to take him. Since his 'experience', this ritual has been carried out after every shift. He is accompanied by a 'body guard' until he is well clear of the pub. Alex finds the whole thing amusing but seeing the fear in the other man's face, he goes along with this daily fiasco.

Jack finished his shift earlier, but elected to stay on and partake in a seasonal drink. At this moment in time, he has placed his beer down in a safe place and is racing around the bar collecting empty glasses.

When the 'last order' rush is over, Anne pours herself a large glass of red wine, while Alex pours both him and Jack a pint of lager to thank him for his off duty help. The lights at the back of the bar are turned off and Alex calls out, "That's time ladies and gentlemen, that's time!" as he does every night of the week.

Of course, there is always the odd one who attempts to down his beer in the last seconds and then try to get his glass refilled as the bar shuts. This, as most locals know, is a point of contention with Alex and when he's called time, that is it, unless he decides he is going to have a 'lock in'.

Terry, a big man in his forties and an old Devonian with his own fence erection business, drains his glass and heads straight for the bar. Anne is out front socialising with some of the locals. Alex has passed Jack his pint and grabbed his own, about to join his wife.

"Here," Terry calls out bashing his glass down on the bar, "chuck another one in there before you go."

Alex's eyes narrow and ignoring the order he leaves the bar, joining Anne. Terry watches as he emerges into the main room and then grabs his glass and begins to make his way across to him.

When he reaches the corner of the bar, Alex has his back towards him chatting to his mate Steve. Terry slams the glass down next to him and very loudly says, "Are you going to fill this or not?"

All eyes fall on Alex. He slowly turns around, picks up the glass and places it behind the bar next to the glass washer. "Does that answer your question?"

The lights on the canopy begin to flicker in a disorderly manner, but not bright enough for anyone to take any notice.

"What is it with you," Terry seethes, "why can't I get another drink?"

Alex, now on his feet replies, "Because we are shut. When I call time the bar is shut and you know it."

"You could see me waiting......."

Before he can finish his sentence, Alex interrupts him, "Waiting, you were not waiting. You were, as normal, pushing your luck. Well sunshine, in this case you are definitely shit out of luck. Now if I was you and if you have the basic intelligence to understand, I would go, before you completely queer your pitch. I do hope I have made myself clear."

The room falls silent, except for the Christmas tunes playing in the background. Terry looks really angry and Alex studies his eyes to ascertain if he is about to make any rash movements.

"I'm going to find me a decent pub, with a decent landlord," he blurts out, storming out of the building.

"You do that," Alex calls after him. He nods to Andy, who immediately gets up and goes to the front door to close it.

Anne, looking at Alex, signals to him to leave it there and not to pursue. He smiles, turns back to Steve and carries on with his conversation.

The canopy lights calm once more until they are merely glowing.

Isme draws up outside the pub at midnight. Alex is awaiting their arrival, sitting by the fire with the lights out, except for the ones above the canopy. There is a knock on the door and the lights instantly burst into action, not overly bright but with a strong enough glow to illuminate the room. Alex smiles to himself, thanking the display for alerting him to the newcomers. He rises from his chair and makes his way to the front door. On reaching it, he hears, then sees Jill coming down the stairs from her room. He smiles at her before unlocking the big old door and pulls it open.

"Welcome back," Alex greets their visitors with.

Handshakes follow, plus an introduction to their new guest, with Jill hugging Judith and Isme but bowing low to Grantree. Alex shows them up to their rooms, noticing that Grantree keeps his gaze fixed on the bar door as he ascends the stairs. Once he has shown them to their respective rooms, he returns to the bar and turns off the canopy lights. He throws the switch, but they linger on for a few seconds, pulsating, before they finally extinguish themselves.

He leaves the bar, goes upstairs and climbs into bed. After having consumed three or four beers, he falls straight into a deep slumber.

Grantree, having unpacked, showered and prepared himself for bed, sits up, legs under the covers, closes his eyes and slips away into a trance. Within seconds his spirit emerges at the top of a long, winding tunnel. He cannot see the far end but the walls pulsate, guiding him along, inviting him to start his journey. He peers forward, trying to concentrate on Dan but seems unable to identify him, as many other spirits appear to blur the clarity of his aura. He decides to discontinue for now, sensing that this might not be the best time for what he had planned to do.

The entire group, including cats, set off to the church. All gathered in the tall room, they gaze upwards, gauging the distance to the apex of the roof.

"Just there, nearly at the top," Duncan says pointing up.

"Hmm, how the hell are we supposed to reach it?" Canning questions him, observing the ray of light which is shining through the largest hole that they have so far discovered.

"Well, I'm not about to clamber all the way up there," Tara adamantly informs.

Duncan glances over to her and replies, "No one is asking you to do it."

Julie and Dan walk around the room, fleetingly looking at everything, assessing the options open to them. Michael is much more methodical, concentrating intently on one area at a time.

"What we need is more light," Paul offers to the group.

Immediately Dan produces a small key ring torch from his pocket. He grunts and holds it up.

Paul walks over to him, takes the device and smiling he says, "It isn't exactly what I had in mind mate, but it's better than nothing at all."

"We also need something to climb on," Clive adds with raised eyebrows.

"Where do you propose we find that?" Michael asks, sighing deeply, still examining the walls of the church.

"There are all kinds of stuff in some of these buildings, like those battery holders, they would do." Julie informs.

"Then may I suggest, that before we attempt to make any advances to reach that hole up there, we should assemble the items that we require," Michael simply commands.

"Clive, Dan, Paul, you all come with me. Let's get the things we need," Duncan says eagerly.

They leave the church and head off to locate the necessary equipment. Michael and the others remain to continue with their study of the problem in hand.

"We need to get someone to stay at the pub for a few days," Criss states.

"What book in you mean, as in undercover?" replies Marcus.

"Yes why not, it has to be by far the best way to find out exactly what's going on in that place."

"Why don't we just ask the landlord if we can stay for a couple of days and watch over it for him?"

"Basically because he might be in on whatever is going on there."

"Jesus Criss, you seem to really have it in for that bloke."

"He's got a really bad attitude," Criss snaps back.

"Oh that's great police work. He's guilty because you have a problem with his attitude."

Criss glares at him then concludes, "Well he could be, we have so little to go on but the one common denominator so far, other than the location, is that he is probably always the last person to talk to them."

"I'm inclined to agree, with the exception of Dan. So how do you explain that one?"

She frowns, "I can't, but couldn't it just be an exception?"

"It could be but we need facts and an exception to any rule shows that the facts are shaky and in this case, very shaky."

Criss gets up and pours herself another coffee, checking as to whether Marcus would like a refill. "I still think we need to get someone in there."

"Ok, to a degree I follow your thinking on this, but we would have to get the idea past the governor first. Also, bear in mind that the first four disappeared a year ago. With the best will in the world, he is not going to allow us to eyeball that place for very long."

"True," Criss dejectedly replies, "But then again, it seems to be a seasonal thing. Each year, these people go missing in the four weeks leading up to Christmas. We really don't want to wait for next year's body count do we?"

Marcus raises his eyebrows, "Ok, let's run it by him but don't hold your breath."

It's breakfast time and both Anne and Alex are down this morning to cater for their guests, who are seated in the restaurant eagerly awaiting nourishment, with Grantree who is standing at the window staring out.

Alex enters the room carrying two plates of English breakfast, which he places in front of the men. He then advises Grantree that his meal is ready and leaves for the kitchen to return with the ladies breakfasts, scrambled eggs on toast. The guests dig into their food with great relish. Anne is an excellent chef and her breakfasts are renowned.

On completion of their meal, both Grantree and Isme walk through to the bar, where they find Alex vacuuming.

"Sorry gents," Alex says when he sees them, "but the bar's not open until midday."

"We just wanted to take a quick look sir," Grantree explains, "if that is ok?"

"Please gentlemen, a little later if you will. I can't have you in here while I'm cleaning, so if you can give me half an hour or so, I'll be done, then you can come and take a look around."

Grantree smiles, nodding and as he turns he catches his first glimpse of the Christmas village scene, his watchful eye lingering on the display for a few brief seconds. When they have left the bar, Alex continues with his daily chores.

"Why so covert Criss?" Inspector Henderson asks.

A little uneasy in her chair, she replies, "Not covert as such sir, more an unobtrusive, subtle approach."

Henderson lifts his eyes staring straight into hers. "I don't really care how you wish to flower up the phrase, the only way to describe the action you are suggesting, is bloody covert."

"Yes sir."

"And you Marcus, you're in here with Criss, so you must believe this is the way forward too?"

"To be honest sir, I'm beginning to think this is the only option left open to us, either that or to place the building under twenty four hour surveillance."

Henderson slowly rises to his feet, places a folder back on the bookshelf before returning to his seat. "I believe that both options seem a little drastic, however, I will sign off a two night stay there. Who do you propose to send in?"

"I thought Gary Martin would be a good choice," Marcus suggests.

"Does he know about this mission of yours?"

"Not as yet sir," Criss replies.

"Yes he's a good man and he doesn't suffer much crap either. Ok I will pull him away from whatever he is currently up to and briefly assign him over to you."

They both turn to leave the office, when Henderson adds, "And make sure, no one apart from us four knows what is about to be done, understand?"

Together they reply, "Sir," closing the door behind them.

They walk in silence along the corridor with a bounce in their step, until they reach their own office. As they enter, Gary Martin is sitting at one of the desks smiling.

"Hi team, what the hell have you two roped me into this time?"

They return his smile, taking seats themselves as Criss begins to brief him. This process takes a good forty five minutes and apart from the odd question to clarify the scenario, Gary listens attentively.

As Criss finishes he asks, "So let me get this clear, you want me to book in to The Bell Inn and then, basically, to snoop around as much as I can?"

"In a nut shell yes," Marcus replies.

"Ok then, you had best get me booked in at this Bell Inn asap."

Criss immediately picks up the phone and dials the number of the inn. Five minutes later she hangs up the phone saying, "You can arrive as from midday today. You are booked in there for two nights."

"Right," Gary emphatically says, "I'd best go get some equipment and an overnight bag. I'll be back in a couple of hours," he says jumping to his feet and leaving.

"Well, so far so good," Criss muses.

"I've got to say," Marcus informs him, "I didn't think the old man would actually go for it, but here we are, in full flow."

"That's absolutely the maximum amount of stuff that we can drag into here. Some of it we've had to leave behind because we couldn't get it through the doorways," Duncan states.

Michael surveys the rather large and out of proportion, plastic battery holders and replies, "In which case, these are the tools which we will have to work with." He paces over to one of the walls and continues, "Having given the problem a substantial amount of thought, I believe this to be the point where we should begin our construction. When we have reached that rim up there," he says pointing, "we will need to undertake a new assessment from that position. Hopefully it will furnish us with the way forward."

"Right," Duncan says, "let's get some of this stuff stacked up over there."

"Why, just because he says so, does that mean its right?" Canning jibes, leaning against the wall.

Slowly Duncan turns to face him. "Canning if that was only a wild guess by Michael, I would go along with it. In my opinion, his best guess will well surpass an informed effort from you. He has been here gauging this problem while we have been gathering stuff to get this job underway and I would imagine that any input on your behalf has been nonexistent. Now shut up and help, because your attitude is beginning to annoy me and believe me, you really wouldn't want to see me annoyed now, would you?"

Dan, still unable to talk, cannot help but chuckle. He walks across to the battery holders and starts to drag one over to its designated place. Within seconds, Julie and Clive join him.

"Good evening sir," Alex says immediately any stranger walks into his bar.

At the same time Anne enters asking, "Alex, have you seen the cats? They haven't eaten their dinner from last night. Did you feed them earlier? When I think about it, I haven't seen them all day, have you?"

Alex briefly digests this barrage of questions before replying, "Come to think of it, no I haven't seen them today. Well they can't be far, can they? I'll look for them in a bit." He then returns his attention to the stranger who has just entered the bar, "Can I help you sir?"

"I hope so," he replies, "As I'm booked in to stay here for the next two nights. The name is Martin, Gary Martin."

Anne looks up saying, "Ah yes, Mr Martin, you are in room three. If you would like to meet me in the hallway, I will show you up to your room." She disappears from behind the bar and after a brief conversation she takes him to his allocated room.

As soon as the door closes behind Anne, Gary opens his case and removes a mobile phone. He presses a preset number on the keypad and says, "Ok I'm in."

His one word reply is, "Roger."

He hangs up, placing the phone on the bedside cabinet. He then unpacks the rest of his clothes, hanging or placing them in the wardrobe and drawers of the bedroom. He opens his holdall, removing various small, electronic devices before opening a small case, from which he removes a tiny microphone which he places under his wrist watch. He takes a quick wash and goes down to the bar.

"Good evening sir," Alex greets as Gary casually walks in. There are three other locals already sat around the bar, who all turn and greet him with 'Hi'. Surveying the beers on offer, he requests a pint of Exmoor Wildcat, a local ale brewed in Somerset. The pint is poured and handed to him. He takes a sip and smiles saying, "Ooh, now that is good, full marks to you on your beer."

"Thank you sir," Alex replies, feeling a satisfaction which he has felt a thousand times before as these words have been uttered. He prides himself on the fact that his beer is always superb.

Gary takes his pint and walks across to the other end of the bar, closest to the Christmas scene, placing the microphone underneath the bar in the right hand corner. Then having covered his actions by appearing to study the model village, he takes his beer and settles himself in the far corner of the bar, placing another microphone underneath the table, as close to the middle as possible without looking conspicuous.

As the evening wears on he remains in this corner, watching and listening to everything there is to observe. He eats a sumptuous plate of deliciously cooked steak and chips, impressed with the quality of the cuisine, commenting on this to the waitress. Another pint later and the time is now eight o'clock. He goes to the bar to check that everything to date has been placed on a tab for his room. He informs Alex that he is going to his room for a while, but that he will return later.

Once in his room, he removes a laptop from his case, connects it to the internet to check that his 'bugs', as he calls them, are operational. Having satisfied himself that they are sound, he sets up a dual recording program enabling each of the bugs to receive their separate dialogue.

He picks up his phone, again presses the preset number on the appliance stating, "The bugs are up and running, have you obtained a fix on them yet?"

"Roger, monitoring them as we speak," comes back the reply.

"Good, I'll place two more before the evening is done, keep monitoring."

"Roger and understood."

He relaxes back on the bed, turns the TV on and unwinds for a while.

"Well, what do you think?" Duncan asks.

"Looks a bit precarious if you ask me," Clive comments.

They're all staring up at the structure which is constructed of all and anything they could find and drag into the room, winding its way up towards the roof of the nave. Then slowly but surely, every set of eyes turn towards Julie.

When she suddenly notices that she is being looked at by everyone, she asks them all, "What?"

"A good question young lady," Michael says, "but if you think about it, you are without exception the lightest and most agile person here."

Slowly, she moves her attention to the stack of bits and bobs that constitute a platform type structure, reaching up into the lofty heights of the church and says with a resigned sigh, "Ok let's get this done."

Michael takes her to one side to instruct her. "Work little by little, with a short break between each attack at that hole but be very aware that if that ghoul should turn up, we will be hard pushed to assist you in anyway, so on your way up there, look around you for quick escape routes."

She nervously nods her understanding and begins to approach the construction, when Michael adds, "I have calculated that the thing will only be alerted if you continuously work on the hole, so remember, bit by bit." She nods again, smiles at him then begins to scamper up the higgledy, piggledy creation.

Silently everyone watches her, some in awe, as she fearlessly negotiates every level, only glancing down when she finally achieves her goal of reaching the top. There is a big cheer from below and she waves, shouting down, "Here we go then."

Michael immediately walks over to Clive, Duncan and Paul saying, "Right people, you take the next three rooms that way. If it starts coming anywhere near, yell as loudly as you can, immediately you see it."

Then he goes across to Tara and Canning. "We will take the three rooms in this direction with me occupying the furthest one, so keep your eyes and ears open."

Dan is stood at the base of the structure looking at Michael, awaiting his orders.

"You young man, will stay here. Without your voice you are not an option, however you can hear. If you hear us yelling, assist her as much as you can."

He nods his understanding, positioning himself away from the base of the construction to see her clearly. Both teams leave the room to take up their sentry posts.

A high pitched bleeping sound can be heard as Gary reaches for his watch to turn the alarm off. He rolls off the bed, enters the bathroom and splashes his face with cold water to freshen himself up. He returns to the bed, picks up the phone, presses a button and asks, "Anything?"

"Nothing so far just a load of chit chat," comes back the answer.

"Ok well I'm off back down to the bar to plant another couple of bugs in the hallway."

"Roger."

Gary grabs his jacket, leaves his room and heads on down to the bar. As he walks in, Alex immediately spots him, takes a beer mug and points at the pump which Gary was drinking from earlier. He nods and proceeds to fight his way to the bar which is heaving with standing room only. He grabs his beer from a smiling Alex, who calls across to him, "Give it forty minutes or so and it will calm down."

Gary shouts back, "Don't knock it mate, it's lovely to see a busy bar."

He smiles and nods, then carries on serving. Coming up to closing time, there is the usual surge at the bar and Anne jumps into the fray, pouring drinks and generally helping out.

This is Gary's chance. He places his beer down at the corner of the bar and moves out to the hall. Taking a quick look around, he places a bug under the edge of one of the stair risers and another one on the side of the dresser which is located midway along the hall with a large mirror over the top of it. Just as he puts the bug into place, Graham appears from the bar.

"You alright mate, you lost?"

Gary, who is used to thinking quickly on his feet replies, "I'm not lost, just trying to find the toilets."

Graham laughs, "Follow me my friend, I'm heading that way myself."

"Last orders!" Alex bellows out over the noise in the room then yet another rush results at the bar, with just about everyone trying to get that last drink.

At this point, Alex stands back from the pumps and turns off the music. The room falls to a hush.

"Right," he calls out, producing a large cardboard sheet which is divided into one hundred and ten numbered squares. "If you look at the end of the bar you will see a chocolate Christmas cake on offer in this raffle for a local charity. Unless, at least two pounds a head goes on this fantastic opportunity to secure the said cake, you lot are not getting any more beer. Understand?"

A loud groan envelopes the room, followed by raucous laughter. They all know they are going to part with the two pounds and in essence they don't mind as it all goes to a good cause.

CHAPTER FIFTEEN

Julie labours for over an hour, without interruption. Every little bit of plastic she digs out and forces away, she tosses off the platform before she stops and rests for five minutes or so. She begins thinking to herself, 'It looks as though Michael was right, so far so good', and the hole is slowly widening all the while.

Dan watches her labours, frustrated at his inability to shout up and check on her, but his vigil remains firm. The others all remain at their stations, not one of them faltering in their concentration, aware that if the spirit should arrive they would all be in great danger.

After a further hour, Julie is noticeably tiring. She carefully climbs down the structure, aided in her final stretch by Dan. She takes herself off to a corner of the room, crouches down and dozes. Dan disappears from the room to find Michael, informing him of the recent state of play with regards to the hole. In turn, Michael calls everybody back to the church to witness her progress. Finally assembled, they all gaze aloft to see that the pin prick of light has now become a golf ball sized opening.

"Well done young lady," Michael congratulates turning to her.

She sleepily smiles, but doesn't move, quite obviously exhausted with her toils.

"At this rate it's going to take forever," Canning condemns.

"Jesus," Duncan says scathingly, "you really are a bad piece of work."

"What, what's that supposed to mean?" he defends.

"I don't see you up there working. In point of fact, I had to almost wake you up to tell you to get back here," Tara sneers at him.

He merely shrugs his shoulders and takes himself off to the opposite corner to where Julie is slumped.

Duncan walks over to Julie, crouches down he takes her hand and sincerely asks, "Are you ok?"

She smiles, showing him the state of her bruised fingers and broken nails. Both hands are bleeding where she has continuously scratched at the plastic surface. "I'm not sure how much more I can do," she sadly announces not wanting to let the team down.

Michael observes her showing Duncan her hands and joins her. He examines her hands himself, stands up and says, "Right, it is obvious to me that we are all going to have to take turns in this endeavour." Then glancing over to Canning he adds, "And that means you too."

"I'll never get up there and besides as I said, this is going to take forever."

"Then that is precisely how long it will take," Michael snaps back at him. "If you hadn't already noticed, if we don't do anything, then there is a distinct possibly that we will be here forever."

"At least the monster hasn't reappeared," Tara says, "Looks like you were right about that."

Michael relaxes and smiles, his agitation with Canning now beginning to quell. "Yes my dear, but my initial concern remains that as the orifice develops, the greater the chance that our grisly friend's attention will be drawn to its existence."

Clive paces over to the structure and staring up at it, he begins to climb. Various pieces of the debris shudder as his weight is brought to bear upon them, but after each movement he remains still for a split second before continuing upward on his mission. After a few minutes, he has reached the spot where Julie was working and he continues where she left off.

Duncan watches him the whole way, then as he notes concern in Michael's facial expression that they are all stood around watching him, he says, "Ok people, let's get back to our sentry duties. Julie, you replace Clive on his team."

Within seconds the room clears, leaving only Dan who is staring up at Clive working away at the top.

The bar begins to empty, leaving just a few of 'the usual suspects' as Alex calls them who linger at the bar, with the exception of Gary who has now taken up residence in the 'grumpy corner' as the locals call it, a captains stool that is positioned in the corner of the bar, nearest to the piano. He swills down the last dregs of his beer and places the glass gently down onto the bar.

Alex, observant as ever, sees the glass emptied and strolls across to him, asking, "Would you like another?"

He hesitates for a second and then replies, "If I can, but I thought you had closed the bar?"

Alex smiles, "Out here in the sticks there is a difference from being shut and being closed."

"Is there by God," he replies, "and how does licensing view that?"

"Oh they know, of course they know, but they tend to turn a blind eye to it, as long as nothing untoward happens."

"Doesn't make it right though," Gary states, "but if I can get that extra pint, I'm all for it."

Alex giggles, "It seems to have that effect on more or less everyone. It's funny how a simple, clandestine late night drink is so attractive."

He goes to the ale pump and pours the pint. Placing it front of Gary, he immediately notices that Rob and Steve both have empty glasses in front of them too and are looking sheepishly at Alex. He immediately picks up there glasses to refill them. Placing them down in front of their respective seats, he contemplates Gary's previous words, 'it doesn't make it right' and says, looking directly at him, "There's no charge here gentlemen, let's keep this legal, these are on me."

Settling himself on his stool behind the bar, Alex pours himself a cider before engaging himself in the conversations around the bar. Anne leaves to close the front door and turn off the exterior lights. When she returns, it is with some hot chocolate, announcing that she is off to bed. She bids everyone goodnight and then turns to Alex saying, "I'll do the breakfast tomorrow. By the way, have you seen any of our guests tonight?"

He thinks for a moment, glancing over at the key rack and then replies, "No not a glimpse since just after breakfast. I assume they are in though, their keys are missing."

She shrugs her shoulders and takes herself off to bed. Her parting words are, "Make sure they're in before you lock up."

Grantree's room is spacious with a three piece suite, coffee table and a television. He is sitting with Jill, Judith and Isme. They are waiting for the pub to fall completely silent, to enable them as a team in their attempt to contact Dan. They sit, chatting but listening all the while.

As the local church bells eventually chime a quarter to one in the morning, Grantree states, "I reckon they have finally all gone to bed. Now is the time."

Isme and Grantree are both seated in the armchairs, while the two ladies recline on the settee. Simultaneously, they all sit back, resting their heads on the furniture as they close their eyes.

Suddenly Grantree shudders. The others don't appear to notice, deep in their own concentration, attempting to enter their individual trances. He is already in, back to where he was the previous night. He turns slowly towards the angled tunnel, which this time is still and peaceful. The sides as before are pulsating, but the clutter of all other life force is not evident this time. Within seconds, Judith is beside him, her abilities far superior to the others. She observes her surroundings and then, like Grantree, she peers along the tunnel. As she begins to take a pace forward, he stops her, saying, "Wait for the others, whatever is ahead, it is not only Dan, but something which might require our combined minds to overpower it."

She nods her understanding as Isme appears, closely followed by Jill. All assembled, Grantree leads them off along the tunnel.

Back in his room, Gary has turned out the lights, with the exception of a solitary bedside lamp. He is lying stretched out on the bed with a headset on and his mobile phone clasped in his left hand. The headset is plugged into his laptop, which is linked to the recording devices which he placed earlier. He has every intention of falling asleep listening to them. His reasoning is simple, if anything moves around in the bar, or in the main hallway, he will hear it, even if he is asleep, which is going to be pretty likely with the five beers he has consumed throughout the evening. Although he hadn't intended to drink so much, it had provided an ideal opportunity to study exactly how the bar behaved and the locals in it. He places his hands behind his head to make himself comfortable, aware that this night could be a long one.

As the four of them move forwards along the tunnel, the going is slow due Grantree's caution. He seems highly concerned about what he might encounter. The further they proceed, the more they can sense Dan. The tunnel begins to widen. Having travelled along in single file they are now able to journey in twos, not that this makes any difference to the conversational dialogue as they all remain completely silent and attentive.

After what seems an age, but in point of fact is probably only minutes, the passageway begins to disappear, leaving them standing in the open without any cover at all to their side or above. Breaking away from this cover, they glance back to find that the tunnel is no longer there, it has completely vanished, replaced by a huge barrier, that ripples and fluctuates in a myriad of different colours, with faces attempting to emerge from behind it, only to be dragged back as soon as they become visible.

Jill ventures towards it, but is pulled sharply back by Isme. "We are not here for those souls. Remember that we are here for Dan."

In front of them now is a white plateau, stretching as far as the eye can see. The sky, if that's what it is, now has a bluish pink tinge to it, reminiscent of snow. Judith crouches down to touch the surface they are about to walk on. Initially it feels like snow, cold and wet, but within seconds of her taking a handful, the substance turns bright orange, with steam rising from it. Startled she lets it drop and instantly it returns to its original state.

"What do you think it is?" she questions.

"The blood of a million souls I should think, they being the lucky ones," Grantree states.

"Lucky ones?" she enquires, a little apprehensively.

"Yes," he replies, "the ones who have gone. Their miserable existence in here finished."

"I have to say that the feel good factor you are trying to emit isn't working Justin. Shall we just press on and find Dan?" Isme says with a sarcastic smile on his face.

Grantree glances over to him, his glazed eyes returning to normal, "Yes, quite so, we must continue."

One at a time, they step out onto the whiteness, with every step they take, so a small but distinct groan can be heard.

Gary's eyes flicker open like a robots, his whole body instantly tensing. He can hear a faint, but definite hissing sound through his headset. He slowly sits himself up, swinging his legs over the side of the bed and he places his hands over both ear pieces. Again, the hissing becomes apparent, this time he can hear a clicking sound as well. He pins his ears back for a brief while longer, then removes the headset and heads for the door. Once out into the corridor, he creeps along until he reaches the door that will lead him down to the grand old staircase. Once at the top of the stairs, he crouches down. The light here is poor with only small night lights giving out any illumination. He surveys the area below him the best he can and concluding that no one is there, he makes his way down the stairs very cautiously.

In the hall he tries the handle of the door to the bar, but it is locked securely. He then crosses to the doorway into the corridor only to find that locked too. Knowing that there is no way to gain entry to either without waking the entire household, he decides to venture outside to see if he can see anything through the window.

Unlocking the big front door, he tugs it open. It creaks and groans on its hinges. He glances back over his shoulder the whole time. Prising it open far enough to enable him to squeeze out, he leaves it there not wishing to make any more noise than he already has.

Once outside, he realises that he hadn't stopped to put his shoes on, as the snow penetrates his socks, soaking his feet and quickly numbing them. He glances down, shaking his head at his own stupidity, wondering what on earth possessed him to come down like this, he paces out into the snow, along the front of the building to the bar window.

Trying to peer inside, he attempts to climb onto the window sill to see above the cafe curtain which is pulled across the lower section of the window. Having wiped the snow away, he finds it is too slippery to get any sort of grip. He glances to his left and spots one of the bench seats against the wall a little further down. He walks over to it, his feet now beginning to throb with the cold, and he drags it until it is directly under the window. This time he is able to climb up onto it and see into the top half of the window.

He stares inside. Initially, all he is able to see are the dying embers of the fire casting out an orange blush and the beer pump lights, emitting their glow around the room. As his eyes adjust to the gloom he is able to make out the side of the bar and the table where he placed the bugs earlier but he cannot see anything moving, or ascertain what could have possibly caused the hissing sound which he had previously heard.

Peering inside, the glass, either on his side or inside, appears to be misting up. He pulls his cuff over his hand and starts to scrub at the window. In order to do this, he has to lean back a little and it is then that he realises to his horror, he has been trying to look through a face on the other side of the glass which is glaring back at him. It has no form as such, just features, piercing eyes, a sunken nose and a frothing mouth, but there is no outline to the head.

He stumbles back, falling off the bench and landing on his back in the snow. The area of the window abruptly bursts into light, so bright that he has to turn his face away while still fighting to see if the apparitions features remain. Abruptly he becomes only too aware that he is in trouble, not only is the vision still present, but the whole casement of the window is bulging outward as the face appears to be fighting its way out to him.

He feels a sudden tug in his guts, followed by sharp pains in his chest and finds himself struggling to breathe. The face grins and an arm reaches out to him.

Through the pain he tries to move away from the spectre, pushing himself backwards but his feet just skid on the snow and ice. Then to his horror, as he begins to make slight headway with his retreat, he observes a replica of himself sitting motionless, with the hand of the spectre buried deeply into his chest. The duplicates head slowly turns one hundred and eighty degrees to face him, a horrific sight, its eyes bulging, nose splayed, teeth gritted and instantly he passes out.

Grantree and his companions finally reach a misty wall. His head tilts to one side as he surveys this new obstacle. The ladies stand still, while Isme walks close, gently placing his open palm against it.

"I thought it would be cold," he states

"Why?" Grantree asks, "because of the way it looks and how you perceive it to be?"

"I suppose so," he agrees.

Grantree smiles at him. "This plane is not one that has expanded from our minds. It should be, because we instigated the trance but when we tuned into Dan, this became the platform where he is currently situated and we have simply followed it. I personally believe that nothing here will be what it seems. Whoever prompted this astral world is not of our world, of that you can be sure."

Judith marches forward and strides away into the mist, disappearing into it within seconds.

The two lads look at each other as Isme says, "Well ok that's what's called throwing caution to the wind."

"Are you lot coming, time is a wasting you know?" A voice from the haze calls back to them.

Jill chuckles as they all follow Judith into the mist.

The mist rapidly disperses and the four of them find themselves gazing down onto a series of dolls house sized rooms with miniature people moving around inside them.

Grantree recognises that they no longer seem to have any physical form, they are seeing but it is only inside their heads. As he tries to turn away from the scene below, he finds that he can't. It appears that the view they are watching is the only picture that they are going to be allowed to see.

"Can you hear me?" he asks.

The other three acknowledge him in turn.

"I can't seem to move," Jill says, quite alarmed by this fact.

"None of us can," he replies. "I have a strong feeling that we are being shown this scenario, which can only mean that we were expected."

Suddenly from between the rooms which they are floating above, an image starts to manifest before them. Their immediate reaction is to draw away from this materialization, but all too soon they realise that this scenario is being completely orchestrated by something else.

"I can see Dan!" Jill yells out.

For a second, four sets of eyes stare down at the rooms below and there they see one small figure waving his arms about, looking as though he is calling out, but no sound can be heard.

Jill concentrates hard with her mind. 'Dan we can see you, use your mind my love, use your mind' she urges him.

Suddenly they hear at great volume, 'Get out, get away as quickly as you can. It's coming, go now!'

Immediately Grantree tries to break his trance, but the ghost, a writhing mass of faces, bodies and limbs, with a face similar to a Grammatostomias flagellibarba, a fish more commonly known as the Dragon Fish which is found in very deep waters, is almost upon him.

Judith of a similar mind to Grantree has already broken her journey and is back in the room, eyes open, her attention instantly falling on the other three. She grabs hold of Jill by the shoulder and pulls her off the settee, allowing her to fall to the floor. Immediately Judith flies out of her seat and over to Grantree, who she forcefully slaps twice around the face. As he mummers, she crosses to Isme, repeating this process on him. As Grantree opens his eyes, he clasps his chest, falling to his knees and gasping for breath. She cradles his head saying, "It's ok we're back."

"Jesus Christ, what was that thing?" he stammers.

"That," Isme states, now standing bolt upright, "was a spirit from the abyss."

Jill coughs and splutters a couple of times then she sits herself back onto the sofa. Distraught, she says, "It was Dan and we left him there."

Grantree pulls himself together, replying, "Left him there, no we didn't. We were lucky to get out of there with our souls, whatever that thing was, we were in its world and it was controlling everything. Next time we meet that will not be the order of things."

"Next time," Isme splutters, "what do you mean next time? That thing is something else, something I have never, ever encountered before and really don't feel inclined to meet again."

"Don't be naive man. It has seen you for what you are now. Do you really expect that it's going to turn a blind eye to you? The next time which I am talking about, is when it comes to the real world to find us and I don't think that will be very far away."

"Justin's right," Judith states. "What we've just encountered has the ability to move between astral flight and reality. It will come for us."

"Then we need to get away from here," Jill states. "We can't help Dan if we end up in the same place as him."

Grantree takes a seat saying, "Now that is an interesting statement Jill. We all saw a physical presence that was Dan."

"What is your point?" Isme asks.

"He was free to move and to warn us but only with his mind. I think he is incarcerated, to what end I do not know, but he is not in any immediate danger."

"Again, what is your point?" Isme questions him.

"That place where Dan is being held is a prison, a place that this entity has evolved somehow inside this small village."

"How do you know this?" Jill asks.

"He isn't the only person who has disappeared. You saw the others in those rooms and those rooms, as tiny as they are, are the village Christmas scene on the piano in the bar."

"That being the case," Jill surmises, "why don't we just grab it and take it somewhere safe?"

Grantree rubs his chin. "Basically because the village scene cannot be the issue, it is simply the prison."

Isme's eyes narrow, "So what do you think is the issue?"

Grantree starts nodding, "That is a very good question and I do not know the answer............ yet, but I will."

CHAPTER SIXTEEN

Very cautiously Clive descends the rickety tower to the floor, assisted the last few feet by Dan. With red raw hands, he slumps down into a corner of the room to examine his injured digits. Immediately Dan leaves to alert the others that work has temporarily ceased.

Once again they all gather in the church with everyone staring up at the hole which is now clearly visible and resembles the size of a tennis ball. Tara checks Clive's wounds. Dan attempts, using a form of sign language akin to a game of charades, to enlighten Michael as to his earlier experience with the ghoul. Initially, the conversation is hard going with a room full of puzzled looks but Julie, who seems to grasp the ability to understand his attempts, soon takes up the role of interpreter. As Dan finishes his story, he stops gesturing, slowly turning around to stare at the far entrance into the church.

"What is it?" Michael asks him.

Dan turns his attention back to Julie and anxiously gestures to her with further hand signals. She nervously says, "I think he's trying to tell me that we have company on the way."

"Everyone spread out and get ready to move," Duncan orders.

Dan turns to look at him, rapidly shaking his head.

Michael tilts his head, smiling. "I do not believe the company we are expecting is going to be problematic."

Dan nods, smiling, happy to be understood.

With all eyes on the entrance, they wait for only a short while before Gary warily walks into the room.

"I take it that you have just upset someone in the pub?" Canning simply states.

Gary looks him up and down, before assessing the remaining occupants of the room and answering, "By the look of things, I've found all the missing people of Witherford in one go."

"Not exactly," Paul jokes, "to be precise, you have joined all the missing people of Witherford."

Michael walks directly up to him and introduces himself by shaking his hand then in turn he introduces their latest guest to the others. Gary is of course familiar with them all, having studied their profiles before he was assigned to the case.

Alex is the first one down in the morning, slightly bleary eyed from the night before, but working on auto pilot he gets everything ready for his guest's breakfast in the dining room. Not long after, Anne emerges heading straight for the kitchen, to begin preparing their food.

Having placed the orange juice and fresh milk on the tables, he leaves the restaurant and returns to the hall. He stops dead in his tracks, slowly turning his head towards the front door which is lying half open, allowing the snow to blow into the lobby and pile itself up into small drifts. Under his breath he says, "What the bloody hell is going on?"

He walks across to the lobby wrenching the door wide open, which requires a fair amount of effort due to the snow, and he looks out in both directions. Immediately he notices that one of the outside benches has been pulled across underneath the window of the bar. The snowfall of the night has hidden any evidence of footprints, so apart from the furniture removal he is unable to see anything else obviously amiss.

As he gazes across the road he spots a twitching curtain. He beckons to Mrs Stanford to come to her door, but she simply disappears deeper inside her abode. He waits but when nothing happens, he returns inside to the warmth of the pub, muttering under his breath as to, "Where is the nosey woman when you want her."

He strides to the kitchen, picks up a broom and tells Anne what has happened, before returning to the lobby to clear the snow away and shut the front door.

She follows him out to see what's going on. "All I can assume is that one of our guests must have come down and gone out really early."

"Bloody early I would say, with all the snow that's in here. I'd say at least two or three hours ago. Besides, who the hell goes out in this weather and at that time in the morning?"

She places her hands on her hips and with a deep sigh she says, "Alex give over will you. What if one of our guests had an emergency and had to leave unexpectedly, they wouldn't have woken us to tell us, would they?"

He stops his sweeping for a moment, resting on his broom and he retorts, "If that was the case, I'm glad they didn't wake me up but I wish they could've shut the frigging front door behind them."

Just then, the door on the top landing opens and Grantree and his friends begin their descent of the staircase.

"Well, if one or more have left during the night, we will be finding out who it was fairly soon," he quietly whispers to his wife.

Good mornings are exchanged and Anne shows the guests to the dining room, before returning to the kitchen to fulfil their orders for tea and coffee. Alex continues with his task of clearing the snow out of the lobby.

By nine o'clock, Alex who has not seen Gary emerge, makes his way up to his room and firmly knocks on the door. When there is no reply, he uses his pass key to enter the room, observing that the bed has been used and that his toiletries and clothes are still in the room with a small suitcase lying open on the floor. It is then that Alex spies the laptop laying on the bed which is still turned on but has entered into sleep mode. He moves across to the bed and presses the enter key. The machine slowly springs back into life, with the first message up on the screen stating, 'battery low'. He closes this screen. Hearing voices that he recognises coming from the laptop, he picks up the machine and quickly heads downstairs.

As he passes the dining room, he glances in to see the guests sat around their table chatting. Aware of the buzz of conversation coming from the machine, he hurries to the kitchen and places it firmly down on a work surface.

"What do you make of this?" he says with annoyance.

Anne glances around to see what he's found to annoy him this time and replies, "It's a laptop, whose is it and what's it doing in my kitchen?"

He sighs deeply and says, "It's listening to our guests in the dining room."

The lights in the bar suddenly burst forth, pulsating as Alex's mood changes and his irritation increases.

Anne moves across to study the machine. Listening to the voices she asks, "How is that happening?"

"A wild shot in the dark would be that Gary, the guy who was staying last night, but who now is nowhere to be seen, has planted bugs in the building for some agenda known only to his self."

"Bugs!" Anne exclaims in disbelief, "what you mean listening devices?"

Alex raises his hands to the heavens, his mood now becoming quite agitated. "Yes bugs damn it, listening devices, hidden, covert, electrical ears designed to hear and spy on us all. What did you think I meant creepy, crawly things!?"

The canopy lights increase their volume by the second. The laptop shuts itself down, its battery power now totally depleted. The screen goes blank and its mechanism grinds abruptly to a halt.

"Bloody thing, I'll be right back," he grumbles.

"Where are you going?" she asks, totally dumbfounded as to the mornings events to date.

"To get the power cable, we need to see what else has been going on and that thing may tell us."

He bounds up the stairs towards Gary's room. Anne briefly glances at the machine, shaking her head in desperation before going to check on their guests.

From the building next to the church, there can be heard a loud, crashing noise. Duncan, who was about to scale the tower to continue with Clive's work of earlier says, "What now? I'll go, you lot stay here."

"We go in twos," Michael snaps at him. "We all agreed, we go everywhere in twos."

"I'm with him then," Julie says getting to her feet.

They leave the church and are gone only briefly before Duncan returns chuckling and carrying a load of broken pieces. He walks across to the gathered crowd, placing the debris on the floor in front of them and saying, "This must be a new visitor. It's a bit smashed up but I know it wasn't there a couple of hours ago."

Gary crouches down to examine the smashed pieces and firmly states, "I know exactly what that is and where it came from."

"I can see what it was, but do feel free to enlighten me as to where it came from," Michael says raising his eyebrows.

Gary looks up at him, stating, "It is, well it was, my laptop and the last time I saw it was in my room at the pub."

Alex flies back into the kitchen carrying the mains cable to charge the laptop. He paces right up to the worktop where he left the machine, shakes his head and starts to search the kitchen attempting to ascertain where it's gone.

Anne enters the room, almost right behind him asking, "How long will it take to charge? I'm curious to know what's going on here. Also, where is this Gary, have you seen him yet this morning?"

Again, Alex lets out a deep sigh. "No dear, I haven't seen Gary and it will not take long to charge up. As soon as it's plugged in we should be able to turn it on, that is if I knew where the bloody thing had gone to."

She stops in mid pace, walking up beside her husband, staring down at the empty piece of worktop where it had been. "Where's it gone?" she asks.

Alex walks to the end of the work unit, slumping himself down onto a stool. "I don't know. All I know is that things are getting stranger by the second around here."

"We need to find Gary. He'll be able to explain everything to us," Anne simply concludes.

"You're right of course," Alex replies, "but that is bound to be the next mystery, finding Gary."

"Christ Alex, will you start searching for him now? I'll go and ask the others if they've seen him this morning."

By lunchtime, Marcus and Criss have arrived at The Bell Inn. They've listened to Alex's story and now find themselves in the extremely awkward position of either telling all, or keeping Gary's identity secret for the moment. The two officers take themselves off into the lounge to discuss their options.

"If we admit to him that we were spying on this place, he's going to hit the roof," Criss states.

"Of course he is, but I think he already has a pretty good idea anyway. He's not stupid you know," replies Marcus.

Criss glares at him. "Nevertheless, keeping him in the dark for now, even with his theories and suspicions as to what's going on, he should be more inclined to help us and not quite so much on the defensive."

Marcus ponders this for a moment then replies, "Ok we will, for the minute anyway we'll play it that way. Gary is now just another missing person from Witherford."

Duncan has reached the top of the tower and is busy beavering away at the hole. The others, with the exception of Gary and Dan, remain on sentry duty.

Gary, tiring with watching Duncan toil and Dan maintain his vigil over him, decides to take a look around. Having digested the information which the group have provided him with as to his whereabouts, he is finding it somewhat hard to take in.

As he begins to leave, Dan looks at him and nods in understanding even though he is aware that they agreed to travel in pairs. Gary smiles and leaves the church. Wandering aimlessly around he passes the various sentries and continues on his way through the assortment of buildings, testing every window in an effort to find one which he can see out of. Finally, frustrated by any further lack of information as to his location, the thought suddenly occurs to him that he might just have the article to secure their release, or at least to alert someone as to where they are. He immediately begins to retrace his steps back to the church.

Here he gathers together the broken pieces of the laptop before heading off to the room where it arrived to see if any bits had been overlooked. Gathering up a few more pieces, he returns to the church, squats down on the floor and with his knowledge of machinery and computers he begins the arduous task of trying to reassemble it into a working machine.

By the time the pub opens for the evening, Gary has been officially logged as a missing person. Many residents from the village have been out in the bitter weather searching for him, checking any disused farm buildings and the surrounding fields.

The snow is falling again, not quite so heavy now, but still a constant sprinkling, topping up the already well established covering.

Grantree, Isme, Judith and Jill are sat in the bar with Grantree concentrating intently on the Christmas scene. Alex watches the five of them, fully aware of their joint belief that something is amiss with the model, but also that they remain thoroughly perplexed at what exactly it is. He doesn't feel inclined to ask them, he finds all that 'out of body' stuff a little weird and disconcerting.

His thoughts are suddenly interrupted as Rob walks into the bar. "There's another one gone missing I here?"

"Where have you been all day? That gossip is old hat."

"Me?" Rob says with a certain amount of glee. "I have been on Skype, talking to some friends of mine in America."

"What all day?"

"More or less yes, the atmospherics have been playing havoc with the internet. Anyway, they are sending a man over to help us look for Michael and the others."

Alex casts him a sideways glance and sarcastically asks, "What kind of man?"

"He is an expert at finding people or things for that matter. His name is York Dawson and his side kick is called Tom Davies, Druid, Damson or something like that."

Grantree's ears immediately perk up. His attention is drawn to the conversation on hearing the name York Dawson. He tentatively enquires, "Is he coming here?"

Rob turns to him and replies, "Yes, why, do you know him?"

"No, not personally, but I know of his reputation."

"My friends," Rob continues, "say he is one of the best at this sort of thing."

Grantree nods in agreement. "Indeed, I would say he is the very best, but he's also pretty expensive."

Alex pours a large glass of merlot for Rob and asks him, "So when is he going to get here, if indeed he can get here with all this snow?"

"My connections said he was already in England, so he could potentially be here at anytime really, tomorrow, the next day, soon."

"Well if he solves this one, he'll be famous in Witherford as well, not that that counts for much. Personally, I've never heard of the bloke."

Just then a bunch of children, between the ages of twelve and fourteen, burst into song outside the front door. Two of them are playing guitars, but they are hitting chords which are a long way off from the melody of the Christmas carol that they are attempting to sing.

Alex's face cringes. "This must be a new version or something, I've never heard this tune murdered so badly before."

Titters and sniggers can be heard from around the bar, as Alex digs into his pocket to find some change to give to the kids. He leaves the bar as the motley choir enter now reciting, 'We wish you a merry Christmas', at great volume and just as out of tune as the last song.

"Ok that's enough," he yells out, "here's some money, now please go and terrorise someone else. Bloody hell with that racket you're all making, you should make a fortune with people paying just to get you gone."

One of the boys steps forward smiling, he takes the money saying, "Thanks Alex, the guitars make a difference, don't they?"

"Yes, that's it, they make a difference, not the words I would have personally chosen but that is definitely one way of describing it."

Everyone in the bar joins in laughing, most of them handing a few bob to the enthusiastic youngsters as they leave.

Returning behind the bar, Alex says, "I swear those little tykes are nothing more than a Christmas extortion racket. I wouldn't mind, but they are the only carol singers who actually get worse every year."

Criss and Marcus pull their blankets tightly up to their chins inside their unmarked police car which is parked in the square, affording them an excellent view of the front of the pub. They dare not start the engine to keep warm for fear that they will be spotted and their surveillance discovered.

"Bloody hell it's cold. I'm beginning to think this is a crap idea," Marcus moans.

Her teeth chattering, Criss seriously replies, "We've now lost one of our own so we really need to do this."

"If we've got to stay here, let's have some coffee. That might help to warm us up," Marcus says.

"If we keep drinking it now, there'll be none left and then in the early hours, we will freeze our nuts off."

Marcus looks puzzled, "You haven't got any have you?"

"Haven't got any what?"

"Nuts."

Criss sighs, "Idiot, it's just a turn of phrase to describe the situation we will find ourselves in if we drink all the coffee now," she recites without humour.

"Ok point taken," Marcus concludes.

They sit, mist visible with every breath they take, as the temperature of the air inside the car slowly heads down towards freezing point.

As the evening progresses, the pub fills up with locals, with tonight, the main topics of conversation being the latest disappearance and the juvenile choir that is terrorising the whole village, demanding monies for a complete row in the name of 'Christmas carols.'

Half an hour before closing time John walks in, calling out, as he fights his way towards the bar, "A pint of the wee beastie please landlord."

Alex hears the request and instantly reaches for a bottle of 'The Beast'. He pours the strong black liquid into a glass and passes it across to him.

Casting a glare at the person who is sitting in his 'usual seat', he manages to intimidate the occupant enough into vacating it and takes his place with a satisfied look upon his face. He sips at his brew. Alex shakes his head as he has always made it perfectly clear that seating is not a particular person's right. It is always first come, first served, but John with his idiosyncrasies, chooses to ignore this fact.

As the bar empties a little, Alex notices that John and Rob, who by now is beginning to slur his words, are deeply engaged in conversation. He positions himself at their end of the bar to join in.

"What do you think Alex?" John asks.

"What do I think about what mate?"

"The two people huddled up in their car in the square. Surely they can't be that hard up that they can't afford to get a room here for the night."

"Who are they anyway?" Rob questions.

"Don't know," John replies, "but they've been out there since it got dark."

Alex glancing across at the window observes that the snow has started to fall heavily again. He leaves the bar and positions himself slightly outside the front door. Looking down the street he can see the car that John is talking about. He returns inside, taking up his usual position behind the bar.

He walks over to where Anne is sitting with her glass of wine and quietly whispers in her ear, "I think we have company."

"How do you mean?" she questions.

"John says there are two people in a car over in the square, looking as though they are set to spend the night there."

She looks a little mystified. "So what's that got to do with us?"

"Well," he surmises, "I don't know for sure because I can't see who's in the car and I don't recognise the vehicle, but my gut tells me that it's Criss and Marcus, those two coppers."

"You mean, you think they're watching this place?"

"That's exactly what I think."

Anne digests what Alex has just said for a few moments before she concludes, "Well that's up to them, but it's going to get bloody cold out there tonight."

"That's my point," he replies, "they are going to freeze out there and furthermore, I have no idea what they believe they are going to achieve by staking out the pub from the outside."

Then he smiles, beginning to slowly nod his head, "Of course!" he jubilantly says.

"What?" Anne asks, surprised by his exclamation.

"How blind and stupid am I?"

"What, what have you realised?"

He lowers his head, shaking it this time. "That bloke Gary, he must be a copper. They've now lost one of their own, so they've stepped up their surveillance. I told them earlier that the outside table had definitely been moved, so they must be assuming that the abductions are happening outside."

"Well that follows," she replies.

"Not all of them have disappeared from outside, think about it, some have but some haven't."

She nods. "So what are you, if anything, going to do about it?"

For a moment he appears thoughtful then he leaves the bar saying, "If they think something's going on in here, then in here they should be. At least that way they can keep an eye on everything."

He strides out of the front door, along with a couple of the locals who have overheard their conversation, who follow him as far as the door. He purposefully plods through the deep snow towards the parked vehicle. As he approaches, Criss and Marcus spot him and attempt to shrink down in their seats, in the hope that he won't see them in there.

When the realisation dawns on them that he is heading straight for them, they glance across at each other, Criss closing her eyes, gritting her teeth and saying, "Now this is going to be embarrassing."

As Alex reaches the vehicle he hammers on the roof. There is a momentary pause before Marcus lets the window down.

"Good evening officers," he greets them.

"Good evening sir," Marcus responds.

"My guess, and I do not believe I would be far from the mark, is that you two are staking out the pub right now because you've lost one of your own men, who incidentally, you installed in that same building, to watch me. Am I correct in my assumption?"

Marcus and Criss glance at each other with raised eyebrows, then Marcus replies, "Not exactly sir......."

"And please can you stop calling me sir, my name is Alex, could you try using that instead," he snaps.

"Yes sir, Alex. Yes, you are right about why we are here and you are also correct as to the identity of Gary, but he wasn't there to watch you, he was there in an attempt to find out exactly what is going on here."

Alex inhales deeply before he says, "In which case, why didn't you just come to me earlier and inform me of your intentions? It would have been a lot easier, to say nothing of cheaper."

Marcus's head drops in resignation and Criss remains silent.

"Start your car up and drive across to the pub," Alex insists. "If you want to watch my place and check things out, then come and do it, but I warn you, I don't want any more covert stuff. Like you, I would also like to know what's going on."

He promptly turns and plods back through the snow towards the pub. The locals, who had both been keeping an eye on their landlord and also watching the goings on out of interest at the same time, scuttle back inside as they see him begin to return. Marcus starts the car, gives it a couple of minutes to warm up and then moves and parks it directly outside The Bell Inn.

Alex, by this time, is back inside the building seeking warmth. He walks over to Anne and says, "Right we have two more guests, what room shall I put them in?" then he pauses for a moment, adding more to himself than to her, "and a double room is out of the question."

She smiles, saying, "Once a copper, always a copper you old softy. I'll go and get the keys to the twin room then, shall I?"

When Marcus and Criss walk in, the locals cheer. Marcus rises to the occasion by bowing gracefully several times while Criss displays total embarrassment.

Anne returns with the keys and smiling at them both she says, "Chin up officers, come with me and I'll show you where you can run your operations from." Again, there is laughter and sniggers from around the bar as she shows them to their room.

On her return to the bar, she takes her seat and sips on her wine glancing at the clock to note that the time has passed closing time. She looks at Alex and gestures this to him by pointing at the clock.

He glances across and calls out to all those present, "If our two 'Sherlock Holmes' wish to solve this mystery, then we need to carry on as we would, so just be your normal selves," he says as Criss and Marcus enter the bar.

"Drink?" Alex calls out to them.

Marcus nods and replies, "If we may, that would be most welcome, a pint of ale for me and a gin and tonic for my partner please."

She nudges him, still looking self conscious she remind him, "We are supposed to be working?"

"And so we are," he replies, "that doesn't mean we can't take any refreshment, besides it means the coffee will last longer."

She chuckles at this statement and they move into the bar, taking their stools, collecting their drinks and paying their dues before starting a conversation with the others who are sat around the bar.

CHAPTER SEVENTEEN

During the night, both Criss and Marcus patrol the premises from time to time, constantly trying to locate and remember where all the creaky floorboards are. Alex has given them a set of keys to the main rooms so they can move freely around the place.

Alex and Anne don't sleep well at all. They can hear them moving about below them all night. By seven o'clock in the morning they are both up, having given up on any further attempt to sleep. Anne ventures downstairs first, with Alex not too far behind her. They open up the internal doors, then the restaurant, the kitchen and finally the bar. It is there, much to Alex's surprise that he finds Criss and Marcus sitting in the window seat.

"Morning," he greets them with.

"Good morning," Marcus replies. "Did you sleep well?"

Alex lets out a small grunt, followed by, "Not really, not with you two prowling around, trying to imitate a herd of bulls wandering all over the place."

Both officers chuckle, with Criss apologising, "Sorry about that but we did try to creep around. The problem is that the floorboards squeak, the doors creak and not being too familiar with the layout of the building. Well we did our best to be quiet, albeit not very successfully."

"That's the beauty of this building, during the daylight hours, no one notices all the little noises that this place makes, but at night, they are better than a burglar alarm to me," Alex pauses for a second before he asks. "Anyway, how did it go last night, anything to report?"

"Nope absolutely nothing, apart from us creeping about in the dark, there was nothing untoward," Marcus informs him.

"Well, chins up, if something is amiss in this place, I'm sure that one of us is going to notice it."

Criss gets to her feet when she sees Anne entering the room carrying two hot cups of tea. Taking hers, she thanks Anne and then says, "At nine o'clock we will be relieved by two other officers. We won't return until six tonight."

"That's no problem, when you come back on duty later, come straight in. If you want to, you can keep your room keys and use them as you please. As for the two who are taking over from you, please let them know that they can also come in at any time they want."

They thank Alex and Anne for their hospitality and sit back down, sipping at their tea as their hosts return to their current task of preparing breakfast for their other guests.

Having done the best he can to repair the computer, Gary realises that the battery is dead. Work has once more ceased on expanding the hole in the heights of the church, so everyone is there closely watching his activities while taking a rest. Gary, cautiously, presses the start button and watches as the machine attempts to limp itself into action. The screen is cracked but a display appears and he can see that the machine is trying to boot itself up.

"Do you think it's going to work?" Paul asks.

"Only time will tell. My biggest concern is the battery. We need to charge it. At the moment, I reckon we will be lucky if it even sustains the machine for a minute or so."

Paul turns away from Gary and calls across to Duncan asking, "Weren't you a spark once Duncan?"

"I did my training but I never pursued it for a living. Why?"

"Got any ideas on how to recharge the battery on this laptop?"

Duncan, who is sitting with Julie and Michael, pulls himself to his feet and walks over to them. "Well, in theory, yes. This place, when it lights up, is running on a twelve volt system, so it would simply be a matter of tapping into it."

"How do we do that?" Gary asks with interest.

Duncan shrugs, "We find one of the bulbs, remove it and then run wires from the live and the negative and attach it to the battery. That is simplifying it a bit but as I said, in theory it should work."

"Can you arrange to set it up Duncan?" Michael politely asks.

"I'll get right on it boss. Can I take Julie to help me scavenge the bits and bobs I need?"

"That should be no problem," he answers before looking around the room, trying to decide who the next person should be to continue with the excavation of the hole.

Before he is able to make his choice, Gary gets to his feet and says, "I'll go up there and take my turn, there's nothing else I can do down here right now."

Michael nods, smiling and then proceeds to brief him on the way in which the work must be carried out and the reasons why, emphasising that it needs to be only small amounts removed at any one time with lengthy gaps in between.

Complete with his orders, Gary sets off to climb the mountain of debris. Duncan and Julie have already left to locate what they need and all the rest, return once more to their allotted sentry points. Dan takes up his position where he can watch Gary working and maintain lookout but every now and again, staring upward into space, constantly fretting that his wife and the others will attempt to join him here.

The lunchtime opening period produces very little custom. Christmas Day falls on a Monday, so most people are still at work on this Friday before the holiday. Fleche is in the kitchen and Anne is at the stables with her horse, supplying the necessary hay as the grass is firmly buried beneath a blanket of snow.

Alex is sat behind the bar bored as there is little to do, so he decides to do some cleaning. Firstly, he clears all the beer trays and runners, giving the bar surface a good scrubbing. Then he polishes the bar and replaces the trays and runners with clean ones, leaving the others stacked up in the kitchen for cleaning. Happy with his efforts he stands back to admire his work. His line of sight rises and he surveys the canopy. He walks forward, right up close to the bar and runs his finger gently around the lights. In turn, they dim and brighten again as he moves away. This causes him to smile with satisfaction.

"You like that, do you?"

He disappears out into the cleaning cupboard and returns with a duster.

"You guys are getting grubby and we can't have that now, can we?"

The lights burst forth into life, the twinkling starting at one end of the string and cascading to the other, forming an impressive display. Alex carries in a set of steps which he places next to the bar, climbs up and begins to clean both the canopy and the lights. Slowly, he moves along the bar, thoroughly freshening up the display, gently brushing over the small lights to dislodge any dust. Finally, after turning the corner of the bar, with his back to the piano, he reaches the end of the length of lights. Following the flex down the side of the bar he notices that the wire has come loose. He gives it a slight tug and with ease it comes away from behind the bar, the plug which is supposed to be located within the main socket, now swings freely.

"Bollocks," he cusses under his breath, believing that he has just pulled the wire out of the plug.

Just then Fleche appears carrying a cup of tea. "I have your refreshment here sir."

"Ah Fleche, can you, if I poke this cable back through, attach it to the plug where it is meant to be?"

"I should think so sir," he replies, crouching down in the corner.

Alex, painstakingly threads the cable in through the hole towards Fleche, who grabs hold of it, gently pulling sufficient cable through in order to reach the socket. Alex believing him to be reconnecting the lights walks around to the middle of the room to see if they have come back on.

"Brilliant job Fleche, they're all fired up and working again," he says excitedly.

"What?" Fleche retorts and begins to stand up, bashing his head on the underneath of the shelf, "Ouch shit that hurt!" he exclaims in pain.

Alex stares at the bar, waiting for him to emerge. When he does, he says, "What I meant to say is, that really hurt."

"I'd never have guessed," Alex replies laughing. Then he notices that Fleche is still clutching the detached cable. His eyes immediately rise to where the lights are merrily flickering away. His line of sight drops to where Fleche is standing and he slowly asks, "Please do not tell me that the cable you are still holding is the one that powers those canopy lights?"

"Well ok then, the cable I am holding doesn't power the canopy lights."

Alex's head tilts, his eyes narrow. Fleche now appears slightly uncomfortable at his boss's demeanour and he quickly adds, "This was the cable you pushed through the hole to me?"

"Then how," Alex says loudly, "can they still be bleeding working?"

Fleche drops the flex and hurriedly joins him in the main room but by the time he arrives, the canopy lights have gone out.

"Oh, that was a good one and I fell for it," he quips sarcastically.

Alex, now flabbergasted at this vision retorts shaking his head, "No this was real, they were on, they were working, they were bouncing around full of life."

Fleche places his hands on his hips and says, "Yes sir, of course they were. I am now going back to my kitchen, where there isn't anyone to make me look like an idiot."

With a huff he marches out of the bar, leaving Alex still staring at the lights. "Well, are you going to turn yourself on, come on, do it again, I want to see," he orders them.

"It's not going to work boss, I'm not coming in there again to see a bunch of dead, light bulbs, you've done that one already," can be heard from the kitchen.

Alex has to smile at this, but inside he just feels confusion over the behaviour of the lights. He leans across the bar, fumbles around and finally puts the plug back in. Instantly, they burst forth into life. He stumbles backwards, never removing his eyes from the display, until he reaches the window, the furthest point from the bar. He bumps into a chair and without looking down he picks it up and sits down.

His stare is only relinquished when Kev, a local man, bursts into the bar shouting, "Hi Alex, have you seen the weather warning?"

Alex blinks a couple of times, attempting to kick his brain back into gear as he replies, "Weather warning, no, I haven't heard anything today so far."

"They reckon that by tonight we're in for a blizzard with about nine inches of snow, so batten down the hatches."

"Right!" Alex exclaims getting to his feet, "batten down the hatches it is then."

He makes his way back to his usual spot behind the bar and says, "Right young Kevin, what can I do for you today?"

Kev glances along the bar and replies, "Well I wasn't going to have a drink, I just told Rose that I was going to let people know about the alert, but it would be rude not to especially on a day like today."

Alex smiles as he pours him a beer. "You're a real hero putting the residents of the village first, being the one to circulate the warning. How many people have you alerted?"

Taking a huge gulp, he replies with raised eyebrows, "Just you so far."

Underneath the wine rack at the far end of the bar, a laptop is situated. Alex turns it on and begins to surf the internet for a local weather station. Having found one, he searches for the next twenty four hour weather forecast. He raises his eyebrows as he confirms Kev's information, a storm is brewing and it has already hit the northwest of England and Wales and is heading south towards Devon for around midnight.

As he looks away, Kev places his empty glass down on the bar and says, "Cor now that was outstanding. I'd best have another one."

Alex takes the glass and begins to refill it saying, "What happened to alerting the masses then?"

He laughs, "Bloody hell Alex, I'm in the hub of the village. As they come in, I'll tell them."

Alex places the glass down, shaking his head and chuckling at the man's logic.

Duncan and Julie, having traipsed throughout the entire village scene, return to the church clutching and dragging various pieces of wire, which because of their reduced size, now appear more like ships cables in comparison. They deposit them into one of the corners, slumping down beside the pile, exhausted from their efforts.

Dan strolls across and crouching down beside them he writes a question in the dust, 'Anymore to get?'

Julie nods and replies, "We've left a couple of piles back that way, you can't miss them."

"Take someone with you Dan, it's too much for you to manage on your own," Duncan adds.

Dan nods his understanding and makes his way out of the church heading in the direction that Julie had pointed to. He was confident that he would bump into some of the others on his way and recruit their help. He hadn't gone far when he met Paul. Once more he signals his request in the dust, explaining what he's doing and what he wants. Paul smiles, directing him to stay put. He runs further on into the village to find Michael excited with the latest bit of information. Michael in turn tells Paul to carry on and to take Clive with them, while he returns to the church to cease the work on the hole for the meantime as the lookouts have all abandoned their posts. Within a few minutes, both Dan and Clive join Paul and they head off towards the stash that Duncan and Julie have piled up waiting for them.

By two thirty in the afternoon the bar is pretty full, with the main topic of discussion being the pending storm. Both the radio and the television are exaggerating the weather conditions as per normal calling it 'The Great British blizzard snow storm of the century'.

The sky outside appears angry, dark grey with hints of blue shimmering through. The temperature has dropped to zero, in theory it's too cold to snow, but everybody is shaking their heads saying the skies look laden with the stuff.

Rob, looking the worse for wear after the night before, has carried on where he left off. Alex is always amazed at the man's capacity to take in and retain so much alcohol. He is sat at the far end of the bar by the piano and the Christmas village, chatting with Andy and John, who are happily laughing away at something. Kev, who is now on his fifth pint, having not informed anyone of the weather conditions as per his original intention, seemed to be simply enjoying the beer.

Suddenly an enormous clap of thunder erupts, seeming to shake the entire building upon its foundations. The power cuts out, the music stops and silence fills the room. Everyone in the bar applauds, displaying their defiance to the weather; a common occurrence when any climatic conditions threaten the village.

Alex laughs loudly, saying at the top of his voice, "If that's the state of play then the pub will remain open the whole time you lot grumble."

This is met with yet more applause, the locals ecstatic that they don't have to return home just yet. Their enthusiasm is infectious and even Anne is smiling at their boisterous reaction.

Meanwhile Graham, who is sat with friends in the far corner of the bar, calls across to anyone within ear shot, "Look at that over there on the canopy. The power is off but one little bulb is still managing to work."

All eyes turn to see what he is talking about, just in time to see the single bulb, slowly dim and finally extinguish.

"A bit of static there Alex, that's all," Fleche yells out, followed by, "I'll be back tonight, if I can get in?"

"You'll need a better reason than the weather sunshine," Alex calls back, "and don't be late."

"Yes sir," comes back the reply, as he leaves via the front door.

There is a definite air of excitement. It is an idiosyncrasy of the village, being snowed in, power cuts, floods or some other tempest and everyone pulls together. A feeling of comradeship always emerges. A couple of customers ask Alex if they can use the pubs landline to call home as their mobiles never seem to pick up a signal inside the building. Several of the wives join their husbands and the kitchen kicks back into action with late lunches being ordered all around. By the time the staff return for the evening shift there is a back log of orders to be dealt with, even though Anne has been working flat out the entire afternoon.

The job of unravelling the cables is a long and arduous one, attempting to split open the plastic covering and part the strands. They have no proper tools, only two penknives.

The work on the hole has been temporarily suspended due to the lack of sentries on duty. Michael has decided that the business of trying to provide the laptop with a power supply is equally as important as the job of making an escape hole, stating, "It's far preferable to have other options to fall back on."

After some time, Duncan stands up holding a rolled up cable at least twenty feet long.

Michael smiles at him. "So now what is the next step?"

Duncan frowns, "To make two more of these, the same length."

"Oh," he says with surprise," I thought we were good to proceed."

"Not yet boss," Clive joins in the conversation, "but I promise you we'll be dancing about when we've finally cracked this stage."

Sniggers can be heard from around the room, all except for Canning who remarks grumpily, "It's just another waste of time."

Gary looks over at him, his eyes narrow. "Do you know, I haven't been here long, but it's obvious to me that everything is a waste of time to you, but the one thing that you seem to be missing is that we don't care what you think and we are going to try anyway." Silence follows his outburst as he concludes, "The only waste of time I have noticed here, seems to be you. If you are not part of the solution, then you must be part of the problem. Either help or get lost, personally I don't give a damn which."

Michael walks forward in an attempt to calm Gary, placing his hand on his shoulder and saying, "You are quite right my boy, but I would prefer it if we all remained together. We are in this together so let's hope we all leave together."

Gary breathes deeply, nodding but turns to Canning with a glare, "You might just have something to offer if you could keep your gob shut."

"Typical copper," Canning retorts sneering, "big when everyone's on his side."

Gary turns away from him saying quietly under his breath, "I'm not typical because if there were no witnesses here, I think I would introduce you to some police brutality."

Tara giggles nervously and Dan turns away, his eyes watering with the silent laughter he is containing inside.

"Ok," Michael calls out, "We need to proceed with our mission. Duncan, please continue with your efforts, while we attempt to source another hole, preferably a much lower one this time. We might as well have a third iron in the fire. Mr Canning, I believe you have found one such hole, would you mind leading us to it?"

Canning turns, grunting, "It's this way, follow me."

Smiling Michael says to Gary, "Would you mind awfully, staying and helping out here, I would hate for Mr Canning to meet with, how can I put this, ah yes, you're more basic side."

"He's an idiot," Gary states through clenched teeth.

"Indeed he is but he is also in the same dilemma as the rest of us. It is my intention that when we finally manage to escape from here, it will be as one unit."

"You've got it boss I'm at your command."

Michael displays a huge grin. "Gary, I am not the boss, however when a group of people find themselves in a bad situation, there is a need for leadership. I do not relish the post which I have adopted, but I will nevertheless carry it through, even temperedly, until the conclusion of this little adventure."

Gary shakes his head saying, "Naw, I think you're the boss."

It is hard to hear the Christmas songs above the buzz of chatter in the bar. The power has once more been restored. Alex increases the volume, taking the microphone and urging the customers along with, "Come on you lot, sing along to Slade!" The bar erupts into a chorus of, 'So here it is merry Christmas, everybody's having fun, look to the future it's only just begun'.

Another clap of thunder resounds as the lights falter, go out, come back on and finally, darkness. The emergency fire lights click in, casting out their green tinged illumination, but not providing sufficient light to be able to see much. Alex yells out, "Everyone stay still, we'll get some candles lit!"

Jack and Nancy enter the bar carrying huge church candles. They proceed to light the wicks and place them on the tables. The light's not great, but it's quite romantic, with everyone commenting on the cosy ambiance.

It is ten in the evening as Marcus and Criss enter the bar. The locals applaud, and this time Criss joins in with the bowing. Alex smiles to himself pouring a gin and tonic and a beer, and placing them down on the bar in front of them. As Marcus reaches into his pocket for some change, Alex shakes his head saying, "They're on me mate. You two are becoming quite the celebrities around here."

"It's beginning to snow," Andy calls out.

Some of those present excitedly vacate the bar to go outside or rush across to the window, to see the flakes of snow falling. Anne clasps her husband's hand, smiling she says, "Christmas is not two days away, but I have a feeling that it started just a few minutes ago."

He smiles, "You're a real romantic and that's why I love you, but in this case you're absolutely right." He pauses, surveying all those in the bar. "The trouble is though, I have this gut feeling, trepidation that something is going to explode here in this pub, in this room, and I'm dreading it."

Anne looks into his eyes. "Christmas is Christmas and nothing can spoil the feeling of goodwill. Look at these people, they are happy and excited, fully grown adults, but they are full of Christmas joy and a lot of that is produced here."

He looks around and is able to see that what she is saying is right, but deep inside he has a dread, one that he tries to deny. He can sense that the whole thing is about to reach a head. Nevertheless he manages to say with a smile, "You're right, this bar has initiated a great feeling."

She can read his apprehension, but feels inclined not to pursue it. "I'm off to bed, don't let it run on to late, you need your sleep as well."

He turns and tenderly says, "I heard those words, I'll kick them out sooner than later."

CHAPTER EIGHTEEN

Eventually, after a couple of hours, the single strands of wire have been striped and are ready to go. Duncan, Clive, Gary and Julie stand back to admire their efforts.

"Right," Duncan says, "Now we need to source a power supply which we can tap in to and adapt, in order to recharge the battery."

"I'll go and enlighten the others of our progress so far," Julie happily announces.

"There's no point," Gary jumps in, "We might as well get all the ground work done without an audience. Besides, as I recall they should be grafting away on another job?"

Julie smiles nodding and glances over to Duncan, to see if he is also in agreement. He nods too.

"What we are looking for is one of the smaller bulbs; one of those LED types with at least two wires to it. Has anyone seen anything like that?" Duncan asks.

"Can't say that I've ever really looked," Clive answers.

"Likewise," Gary concurs.

Julie is stood shaking her head too.

Duncan adds, "In which case, let's go and see if we can find one. Split up into groups of two and if one team bumps into Michael and company, advise him as to the state of play."

Gary and Clive set off in one direction, while Julie and Duncan go in the other.

As of the previous night, Marcus and Criss patrol the premises but this time, slightly quieter, having now mapped out where the creaky floorboards lay.

Alex and Anne sleep like tops, both extremely tired, not just with their busy day but also due to their lack of sleep from the night before.

Isme and Judith, fast asleep, drift in and out of dreams, but these are not restful dreams, they are laced with menacing visions which remain partially hidden.

Jill is experiencing the same dreams, while Grantree, in his room, is wide awake, sensing the uneasy sleep of his friends. He is aware of who is lurking deeply within the shadows of their dreams, knowing that should he fall asleep, that he too would find the same troublesome slumber.

Outside, the wind is howling, the snow driven sideways across the countryside. As the storm rages, Alex is woken by the wind and the flakes forced at their bedroom window. He carefully climbs out of bed, trying not to disturb his wife and he leaves the room, creeping along to his office. He crosses to the window without turning on the light, hoping to see the extent of this snowstorm. Until his eyes readjust and focus into the blackness of the night, he cannot see anything. Staring at the light in the car park, the sensors having been activated by the size of the snowflakes, he sees the white eddies, climbing and falling, dancing their waltz before finally coming to rest in drifts around any suitable structure to build against. At that moment he senses the wonder, believing that he has never witnessed anything quite so beautiful.

About to turn and leave the room he feels something touch him gently on the shoulder. He nearly jumps out of his skin and with both fists firmly clenched he turns to see what is behind him. There is only Anne looking startled to say the very least.

"Jesus Alex, why are you so jumpy?"

When he sees her, he exhales deeply and replies, "Sorry sweetheart but you made me jump."

"I saw that," she says, raising her eyebrows and looking at his fists. Staring out of the window she quietly says, "My, oh my, that is one hell of a snowstorm."

"Yeah, I know, it's beautiful isn't it. I'm going downstairs to check that everything is ok down there."

"Why? Didn't you do that before you came up? Besides, we have two police officers wandering around, what could possibly be wrong down there?"

Alex hangs his head, "Do you know babe, I don't know, but what I do know is, or should I say I feel, is that I need to go downstairs and have a look around."

She smiles and hugs him. "I know, I can see it in your face, give me a couple of minutes and we'll go together."

They return to the bedroom and don some suitable attire with which to go downstairs. Once dressed, they proceed to the landing door and down the two flights of stairs to the ground floor. Alex slowly pushes the door open at the bottom and steps out into the corridor.

Before Anne has time to follow him out, he is grabbed by the shoulder. Immediately he snatches at the hand, turning the fingers up and backwards. Retaining his grasp he spins around to identify his attacker. Unaccustomed to the gloom, he is initially unable to see who it is, but as Anne moves in behind him and turns the lights on, he sees Criss with a pained expression on her face.

Releasing his hold as Marcus enters the hall, he says, "Sorry about that, but I didn't expect to get attacked by the police, by a burglar possibly, but not by the law."

"What's up?" Marcus says with a certain amount of urgency. "Why are you up and about at this god forsaken hour?"

"That's a good question and I've already asked him that one," Anne replies.

"Ok, I woke because of the storm and decided I was going to take a look around," Alex defends himself.

"Would anyone like a cup of tea or coffee?" Anne asks heading for the kitchen.

"Oh yes that would be lovely, coffee please," Marcus is quick to reply.

"Christ, you haven't lost your touch, have you?" Criss states with a pained expression on her face while rubbing her hand and arm.

"Yeah, sorry about that, I'm a bit jumpy tonight," he apologises.

"You can say that again!" Anne calls out from the kitchen.

Alex sighs deeply, enters the bar and turns the lights on. Re-emerging he says, "Come on, let's go on through and talk."

Anne joins them carrying a large pot of coffee. She pours them a cup each then takes a seat and smiles.

"Well," Marcus begins, "we haven't stopped patrolling the premises since the pub closed and everyone went to bed. We've covered both floors at least a dozen times and so far, nothing, the place is as silent as the grave."

"I suppose that's good really," Anne interjects, "but it doesn't help to solve the mystery."

"Indeed, we were hoping to see or find something by now, anything that would move us closer towards finding these missing people," Criss states.

They hear an alarming crashing on the front door. Glancing up at the clock, Alex sees that it's not yet five in the morning. He gets to his feet and accompanied by Marcus and Criss, heads in the direction of the noise.

Again, there follows a thump, thump, thump!

"Who the bloody hell wants to make all that noise at this time of night?"

Marcus giggles to himself. When they reach the heavy, old door Alex unlocks it, dragging it open.

Initially they are unable to see anything due to the huge flakes of snow ferociously, swirling around, creating an impenetrable wall of white, but as their eyes become accustomed to the light, two figures can be seen standing a few paces back from the step.

"Sorry to be so late old chap," an educated voice states, "but adverse weather conditions have hampered our arrival. Never mind, is there room at the Inn?"

"It's five in the bleeding morning," Alex firmly says, "what the hell do you think you're doing hammering on my door at this time of night?"

"Please ignore my husband. He is having a bad night. Come on in from the weather," Anne diplomatically says from behind the others.

The first man to come forward is a gentleman in his sixties; about five feet ten inches tall, with short grey hair, clean shaven and of standard build. The second is a much younger man, with short dark hair, clean shaven; over six feet tall and much bigger built.

As the older gentleman enters the hall and sees who has invited him in, he says, "Thank you my dear, dammed cold out there, to say nothing of blustery."

"And you are?" Anne expectantly asks.

"My name is Dawson, York Dawson. I'm here to meet a man called Robert. My young colleague here is Tom David."

"Ah yes, Rob said he was expecting you. He lives across there on the other side of the square. Would you like me to go over there and thunder on his door for you, or are you going to do that yourself and wake a few more people up in the middle of the night," Alex grunts.

Criss and Marcus are now unable to control their laughter at the hilarity of the scene unfolding before their eyes.

"To answer your question sir," Dawson explains, "Robert is not answering his door. We went there first."

"Ah what a sensible bloke," Alex quips with a slight nod of his head.

"So with the weather and conditions as they are, we moved on to our alternative plan."

"Got you, well it's just as well we answered the door then, God knows how many people you could have disturbed before you found someone to intrude upon."

"That's quite so, quite so my good man. Now would you kindly show us to our rooms, we have had an emotional day thus far and would like to get some rest?"

Alex turns to Anne, his face, one of total disbelief. She jumps straight in, "Gentlemen, give me one moment, then I'll be back with a key and I'll gladly show you to a room."

She hurries off, but is back in a flash, whereupon she leads their guests up to the third floor where there is a small flat vacant for their use. She ushers them in, apologises for the lack of heat but informing them that the timer on the boiler has been advanced which should quickly take the chill off the rooms.

"This will be adequate," Dawson says, "as I always say, a place to rest ones head in peace, is always a welcome place. Do you not agree Tom?"

"Indeed I do sir."

Anne returns downstairs to find Alex and the officers have returned to the bar. Criss is throwing a fit of the giggles and Marcus is sitting with a wide grin plastered across his face.

"He's a real character, isn't he?" Anne says.

"Well, that's one way of putting it," Alex replies.

Criss erupts, rubbing her eyes with the tears rolling down her cheeks, her laughter coming from deep down inside her stomach. She disappears into the toilets to compose herself.

Alex just stares in her direction, totally dumbfounded he enquires, "What the hell is the matter with her?"

"Oh her," Marcus says, trying to contain his own laughter, "she often does that when she's working, it helps to calm her nerves."

"Bloody odd woman that one," Alex concludes, lifting the coffee pot to pour another drink.

While they are checking over the model of the pub, Clive spots a bulb which seems to fit Duncan's description to the letter. He calls Gary across to inspect it further. The beauty of their find is its location, being on the rear wall of the building and easily accessible.

Meanwhile, Duncan and Julie continue with their search, eventually coming across the others, who they observe have managed to create a hole, and although it has grown to the size of a tennis ball, they are unable to see anything out of it due to the fact that it is dark and facing the rear wall of the building.

Work stops on the hole while they sit around discussing the point they have reached to date. Before they have managed to finish their conversation, Clive and Gary enter the gathering, bubbling with excitement to eagerly enlighten the group of their find.

Michael, having taken some time to consider the various options that now present themselves, decides that the groups should remain constant and continue forward with both of the enterprises they are currently undertaking, the work in the church now taking a back seat and the new endeavours becoming paramount.

Set to go off in their different directions, the three cats come wandering into the room. They immediately spot the hole and cross to investigate it, then after finding nothing of any interest, they walk away, making themselves comfortable on the far side of the room, while retaining the hole within the limits of their vision.

Michael watches their reaction and says to Paul, "Did you see that?"

He nods, "Yeah, what of it?"

"They know, they can feel it, they can smell it."

Paul glances at the cats then back to Michael, "What can they smell?"

"They can smell freedom my friend. The minute that opening is large enough to pass through, you mark my words, they will be through it. That's why they are sat where they are. They are waiting."

"Do we stop them, I mean, do you want me to move them somewhere else?"

"No young man, quite the opposite, let them wait. Someone will have to be first through and why not them. Think about it, we have no idea what will happen if we manage to break free of this place, we could immediately return to our normal size. On the other hand, we may remain as we are now, in which case, we would be in trouble. No, let the cats test the outside world first, with their instincts of self preservation, they will stand a far better chance than us human beings. They are naturally agile, fast, intuitive and vicious if they have the need to be, no, they are actually the perfect choice to send out there."

Paul ponders this for a moment and then says laughing, "So when do you want us to shove them through the hole?"

"Ah, now that's the beauty of it all, we don't. They will know when they can escape, they will make their move when they are ready and it is safe to go. All we need to do is to make sure that someone watches them the whole time. We don't want them going off without us seeing what happens now do we?"

"Gotcha," Paul emphatically states. "I'll watch them myself."

By nine in the morning, Alex has managed to contact Rob by telephone to inform him of his friend's arrival, explaining at what time and how they had eventually arrived at the pub. Rob finds the whole episode rather amusing but as the sternness of Alex's tone registers, so he changes his manner, becoming apologetic and saying, "That is really, rather inconsiderate of them."

Although still snowing outside, releasing wispy light flakes with the sky still laden with the stuff, the storm seems to have passed. Some of the drifts are ten feet high and everything is covered in a picturesque whiteness resembling an Alpine village, with even the church spire enveloped on all its facets.

Alex walks out to the old skittles alley and returns with a shovel, whereupon he meets Marcus and Criss in the hallway.

"I don't think you two will be going anywhere today, so may I suggest you go to your room and get some kip as you've been up all night."

Criss has no objection to this suggestion. She heads for the stairs immediately. Marcus smiles, "Get me a shovel as well and I'll help you dig the snow away."

Alex nods, a wry smile on his face, handing Marcus his shovel. He then disappears for a second time, returning with another one for himself.

As they manage to pull the front door open, they find the drift to be at least five feet high, engulfing the whole front entrance of the building. Both men begin their assault, tunnelling their way through the snowdrift, eventually reaching the lower level on the pavement.

Anne is busy cooking breakfast for the guests, although Dawson and David have not as yet surfaced. She doesn't blame them for still being asleep; in fact she wishes she was too. However, she does note that Isme, Judith, Jill and Grantree all appear extremely tired, worn and haggard. If she was to second guess their appearances, she would have likened it to a late night on the booze, but in their case, she knows differently. She says nothing.

Having managed to dig a path to the road, both Alex and Marcus decide, their hands frozen with the cold, to go back inside for some hot refreshments. Anne having already anticipated this situation has prepared bacon sandwiches and steaming mugs of tea, which she places in the bar as they enter. Marcus sits straight down, digging into the food. Alex smiling thanks Anne, gently kissing her on the head before he ravenously joins him.

Having ploughed through three of the wedges, Marcus looks up and says, "Where did you find a woman like that?"

Alex smiles saying, "You won't find them in the job, not in the police force. Women like Anne are rare to say the least. It took me two marriages to find that one out son. Real women look after their men and the men should look after them in return, work as a partnership you know. What you've got now the majority of the time, is women who only think about themselves and men who do exactly the same, but having said that, it has to work both ways."

"Two marriages, huh I bet that was expensive?"

"Yep but it was worth every penny. I found what I was looking for, so will you, as long as you realise, that a female friend is not just in the sack and they have minds and thoughts as well."

Marcus thinks on this subject for a few minutes, before commenting, "But Alex, you are quite forthright, while Anne, she is so caring."

He roars with laughter. "Of course, she is the other side of me and I'm the other side of her, which is exactly why it works. We argue, but I need her input, that's what takes the edge off me." He briefly pauses and then adds, "You will know if the girl you are with is right, you will just know.

Forget the attraction, forget the sex, forget the things you have in common, forget their social standing. You will know. It will be your heart that tells you." Again there is a pause as Alex finishes with, "This conversation is all because Anne placed a few bacon butties in front of you?"

Marcus smiles, "You're a lucky man, I hope, I pray that one day I will be so lucky."

Alex rises from the table, "Luck has nothing to do with it. Are you up to shifting more snow now?"

Duncan stares at the light bulb, which due to his present dimensions, is comparative to the size of a smart car and says, "It's off at the moment, but we have no idea when it's going to turn back on and I really don't want to be holding on to anything live when it does."

"Hmm," Clive mumbles, "we hadn't thought of that one."

"Thought of what?" Julie asks.

"The time lapse between the lights being turned on and off again. You must bear in mind that we have no control whatsoever over when the power is going to come surging through these cables," Clive explains.

Julie stares at the LED light bulb and intelligently surmises, "If they are LED's, then there is a pretty good chance that there will only be twelve volts of power passing through the wires. That isn't enough to do anyone any real harm, at least I wouldn't have thought so anyway?"

Duncan smiles, "In theory, you're correct. Assuming that everything was in proportion anyway, but as we are really quite small, we have no idea what a twelve volt jolt would do to us."

"When was the last time that they were on?" Gary questions.

"I haven't got a clue," Clive states, "time doesn't seem overly important in here."

"I agree," Julie says nodding, "but throughout the time I've been here, I have noted that when they are turned off, there are two different time periods. Period one, they are only off for a couple of hours, period two, they're off for much longer, perhaps a good eight hours or so."

Duncan agrees with her observations saying, "I've noticed that as well."

"In which case," Gary concludes, "all we need to do is to wait until they come back on next time and observe them until they go out again. This should tell us when the longer period will be."

Duncan nods, "That sounds like a perfect plan. Let's report back to Michael, there might be stuff there which we can help with in the meantime."

They all them make their way back to the others, leaving their gear at the site close to the light bulb. They tell Michael of their plans, who nods his agreement, confirming their idea as sound.

Right up until lunchtime, Alex and Marcus labour away removing the snow from outside the pub. By the time they decide to call it a day, the footpath has a perfectly clear track running from one end of the building to the other, with huge dunes of snow stacked up on either side.

Grantree and his friends are already in the bar. Having questioned Anne over the impending arrival of Dawson, only to discover that he was already there, they are now eagerly waiting to meet him and his younger side kick. Anne has served them coffee on three separate occasions throughout the morning, whilst carrying out her daily chores.

By midday, Alex has cleaned up and is back behind the bar as usual. Marcus has taken himself off to his room, quietly entering so as not to disturb Criss and climbing into one of the single beds, he is very soon soundly asleep.

Fleche arrives as the bells of the local church strike the last chime of twelve o'clock, much to Alex's annoyance. He enters, bounding through the front door with his usual musical, "Morning, morning, morning."

"It's the bloody afternoon you idiot!" Alex yells back.

Fleche tends to routinely ignore this jibe, making his way to his locker, to change his outdoor clothes for his kitchen uniform.

As he walks into the kitchen, he looks straight at Anne, who is shaking her head as she comments with raised eyebrows, "You obviously like to live dangerously."

"Morning ma'am," he replies, adding, "I'm sure I don't know what you mean."

Back in the bar, John is the first customer to come in, requesting his usual, "Morning landlord, a bottle of the wee beastie, if you please?"

Alex places the brew on the bar in the corner which John likes to frequent. He then notices Isme heading for the bar.

"Hi Alex, do you know if Dawson is going to come down any time soon?"

Alex, who by now is a tad jaded due to the early hour in which he was forced to rise, sarcastically replies, "Christ how would I bloody well know? The bloke arrived in the middle of the night. I didn't have time to question him adequately so as to ascertain his movements this morning."

Isme, a little taken aback by this dialogue, turns to his table to join the others, when Anne on hearing the conversation says, "He did come in very late last night, the early hours of the morning to be precise, having travelled for quite a while. I wouldn't expect him to rise until early evening."

Isme smiles, thanking her, not daring to even look at Alex, he returns to his friends.

Just then, Tom comes downstairs and enters the bar. Grantree and his friends are halfway out of their seats when they see him enter, then they slump back down again as they realise that Dawson isn't with him.

"This is one of them," Alex calls over, pointing at Tom.

Tom, immediately feeling rather conspicuous, timidly glances around at everyone present and says, "Good afternoon one and all, but I am merely the apprentice. York will be down later."

His eyes then fall upon the Christmas scene and they narrow. "Now that is an interesting display, especially as it isn't turned on."

Alex glances across to it before going straight to the socket to switch it on. The little lights burst into action as the village scene comes alive.

"Ok it's on!" Canning yells out, as if no-one else could have possibly noticed.

"Great," Duncan replies, "now time it. We need to know if this is the short period or the longer one."

"I hope it's the short one," Julie whispers.

"Me too," Duncan confides, "I want to get back to the job of linking it all up."

Overhearing this conversation, Michael smiles, advising them, "Have patience my young friends. Time is a commodity which we all have. Rushing anything here will only serve to bring our unwanted friend back again and we really do not need that now, do we? Slowly and surely will be the way forward and will provide us with our eventual way out."

Gary walks over to Duncan patting him firmly on the back. "Thus far you have done brilliantly. The old man is right, keep it casual mate."

While they are engrossed in this conversation, Ellie the cat stretches, rising to her feet and sleekly makes her way across to the hole. Once there, she pushes her head in, but as much as she tries, her whiskers tell her that it doesn't quite fit. She withdraws and returns to her warm spot with the two other cats, who have closely watched her every move. No human witnessed her little adventure.

By one o'clock in the afternoon the local farmers have sprung into action, beefing up their tractors with snow ploughs in order to clear a track through the main road of the village.

By now, most of the local people who normally go to work are finished for the year, not that it would have made any difference because leaving the village after the storm of the previous night, would now be impossible. Many have made their pilgrimage to the local hostelry, hell bent on enjoying the seasonal spirit and the picturesque circumstances which they now find themselves in. The pub is heaving with Christmas music playing loudly in the background, the atmosphere electric with anticipation. Grantree and his friends are drawn from their sullen concern over their friend's disappearance to join in with the merriment around them.

Anne has baked a mountain of little roasted potatoes which she places in several bowls on the tables in the bar. Happy people dig in to them at will, some grabbing at the food as if they had never been fed.

Outside the front of the pub, over a period of an hour, a nine foot high snowman appears, built by local people, all of whom have as a group, been rolling a small snowball to create this huge statue. A local artist by the name of Ian takes the time to carefully fashion it, turning the cold exterior of the snowman, into something of a village celebrity. On its completion, most of those present go outside to see the exhibit, quickly photographing it as if it was about to melt before their very eyes. Inevitably, a snowball fight erupts into action with Alex the first to take cover, leaping back into the pub and appearing behind the bar within seconds.

"Just so you know," he says over the microphone, "world war three is occurring just outside the front door. Please feel free to join in."

CHAPTER NINETEEN

By three in the afternoon, those not already exhausted by the snowball fight, have had enough to drink and are making their way home for a late afternoon siesta. The pub finally closes its doors at three thirty, with Anne and Alex still clearing away the debris from earlier. Fleche has gone, his shift finishing at two and being as ever prompt to leave, the chore of clearing up the devastation in the bar has passed to the landlord and landlady.

Grantree and his friends had to be almost ordered to leave the bar to enable it to close, returning to their rooms for a couple of hours. Tom disappeared back upstairs well before this time without anyone seeing him leave. The last person to see him was Anne, and she said that he had been inspecting the Christmas scene with great interest.

Anne is drying glasses and restacking the glass machine for the next wash. Alex is vacuuming the bar, shifting the furniture to one end of the room, cleaning and then shifting it all to the other side before repeating the process. His next task is the front hallway with its polished oak floor which is covered in melted snow. He mops the whole area until it's completely clean and dry.

With all their chores completed, they disappear upstairs with a cup of coffee for a well earned rest, albeit for only an hour or so. Having finished his coffee, Alex glances across to Anne to see she has nodded off. He smiles, gently pushes his recliner back to make himself more comfortable and he too drifts off to sleep.

In his sleep he sees distorted images, faces he knows but can't seem to put a name to. Behind them there is an elusive image, thin and scrawny, which seems to be controlling these people. One of the images stops and his head slowly turns towards him. Alex can feel deep trepidation building up inside of him, but is unable to take his eyes from the illusion. When the spectres head has completely turned and is facing him head on, its eyes are wide open, the pupils large, the whites of the eyes are bloodshot and sunken back inside its skull. The face is drawn with no hair visible and the skin of the neck is almost translucent with the internal organs fully visible. The mouth is down turned, the nose splayed across the face and its ears are pinned tightly back against the sides of the skull.

By now, Alex is experiencing real terror. His complete attention is held by the sight in front of him. He wants more than anything, to get away from it, but he finds himself unable to move. He has lost the ability to turn his head away or to close his eyes from the horrific scene. Suddenly, the figure extends its arms in a pleading gesture. His mouth opens wide, but no words leave, only a high pitched scream which pierces his ears to such an extent that he feels as though the noise will split his head into pieces. Slowly it begins to move towards him, staggering with every step it takes, the muscles in its legs not functioning properly, tottering about as if it could fall at any second.

Then, the figure that Alex had perceived to be controlling the others, lurches forwards, grasping hold of it, snatching it backwards before throwing it to the ground to join the others who immediately shy away, cowering from the tall, thin figure of authority. Alex's gaze falls on him. It seems to be smiling at him with its head tilting from one side to the other.

"Alex, Alex, come on, we're late."

His eyes flicker open to see Anne standing over him. He can feel the beads of sweat on his forehead. In point of fact, he can feel that his whole body is damp with perspiration. He easies himself forward in his chair and holding his head in his hands he immediately notices that they are trembling.

"You ok?" Anne stops in the doorway and asks him with concern on her face.

"Yeah," he replies, rubbing his eyes, "It was just a crazy dream."

He jumps to his feet and heads along the hall towards the bathroom, calling out, "I'm going to get a quick shower and I won't be long."

He hears her sigh, as she heads downstairs.

Anne enters the bar to turn on the lights. They burst forth into action, especially the canopies illuminations which this evening, are actively dancing, varying their brightness. She then heads towards the front door to open the pub for business.

As she opens the door from the bar into the main hallway, she is greeted by Grantree and his friends, all eager to enter. She ushers them through and proceeds to open the main door. Again, she is greeted by people waiting for opening time. She shows them in too and turns the outside lights on, quickly returning to the bar to serve their drinks.

Alex emerges and immediately goes to her aid. As the initial onslaught of people are served and the customers move away to take their seats at the tables, Anne vacates the bar for the kitchen as the food orders start to come in, leaving him in his usual position of hosting the bar.

Firstly John enters and takes his seat, requesting his usual tipple. Then Criss and Marcus enter the room, nodding their hellos and return to Alex before disappearing upstairs to their room. Finally Andy, Graham and Rob stroll in, taking stools around the bar and ordering their drinks with Graham copping the bill.

With the room seemingly settled down and all present supping their drinks, Alex goes into the hall as he hears Criss and Marcus descending the stairs.

"Back again?" he questions them.

"Yes and with your permission we would like to reactivate the bugs which Gary put in place and instead of patrolling, we will listen from our room tonight?" Marcus requests.

"Sure," he says, "if you think it will be more productive, let's go for it."

Both officers smile, nodding and immediately set to work checking the microphones and adding six more in prime locations which they deem relevant for their purpose. For the minute, they don't touch those in the bar, deciding to check on them when the pub closes for the night, not wanting to draw any attention to them.

Alex, once more is behind the bar, serving orders which are coming in thick and fast again.

Twilight engulfs the room and Canning yells out, "Three and a half hours, more or less!"

"I concur," Michael adds, "In which case, that will have been the shorter lunchtime period."

"Which means," Duncan says with a certain amount of glee, "That I have no more than an hour or so to get this thing wired up."

"Can you do it within that time frame?" Gary asks.

"Safely?" Michael adds.

Duncan's lips tighten in thought, "I reckon it'll be tight, but I think so."

"Then it will have to wait until the evening session is over," Michael emphatically states. "We do not need to take any unnecessary risks here. We will wait."

Duncan's frustration and eagerness to proceed is evident, but he bites his lip, aware deep down that Michael is probably right and is after all simply protecting all their interests.

Everybody dejectedly returns to their previous labours. Duncan is the last to move, standing for a few seconds with his head hanging down in dejection. Gary walks past him and pats him on the back saying, "Come on mate, get busy and the time will soon pass."

By eight o'clock in the evening, both the bar and restaurant are pretty full, with the Bell Inn's staff working flat out. A festive buzz fills the air. The Christmas music is cranked up at every opportunity with people singing along to the more familiar songs.

Tom is in the bar. Grantree had asked if he would care to join him and the others and he has accepted, taking his beer with him. Grantree nonchalantly enquires as to if they can expect an appearance from Dawson.

"Possibly, as he has been asleep the entire time since our arrival," Tom replies. "He is exhausted from his last case."

"Which was what?" Isme enquires.

Tom shrugs his shoulders. "That's not for me to tell you. He will tell you himself if he feels the need to do so. You must understand that he is a very private man."

Isme nods as Jill adds with urgent concern, "The thing is Tom, my husband is missing."

"I am aware of that and so is York. Apart from your husband, I understand there are others who are also missing. That is why we are here, hopefully to help you all."

Grantree leans forward and with frustration he pushes, "But when is he going to help, nobody has even seen him yet."

Tom's eyes look out over the top of the glass from which he is drinking and placing it down on the table he replies, "The science of finding people and objects is not one that completely relies on physic ability. I, in fact both of us are aware of your capabilities too. York sensed your powers as he was approaching this building. However, he needs time to adjust to this environment before he can proceed. Time is just a physical notion that cannot be denied, but it is not to be considered as the be all and end all of our lives, it is to be conceived as only part of it."

This statement is followed by silence as Judith glances at Isme and whispers, "Now, that was deep, what did you make of it?"

"I'm buggered if I know," he replies shrugging his shoulders.

Grantree reclines back in his seat, with a wry smile firmly fixed on his face. "So young man, in your opinion, Mr Dawson is simply in preparation then?"

Suddenly the room falls into silence as all eyes turn towards the door. The only sound that can be heard is the music from the CD player and even this seems to have decreased its volume.

York Dawson, dressed in a brown tweed suit with a collar and tie and sporting matching brogue shoes, stands surveying his surroundings and its occupants. His head slowly turns until he ascertains where young Tom is seated and he says, "Your eagerness to meet me is flattering

Grantree, as I in turn have also heard of you, however, your persistence is vaguely annoying. Tom, please if you will join me."

Then he turns his attention towards the bar. Initially, his line of sight catches both Alex and Anne and he gently smiles then his gaze rises to the canopy lights and frowning, his eyebrows drop down towards his eyes which are not flickering one iota. The lights in turn, dim to match his expression before bursting into an impressive array of light, rapidly dancing and changing their colour and intensity.

The audience in the bar is now torn between watching Dawson and the lights. Their heads move from side to side as though at a tennis match.

Dawson lets out a deep breath followed by, "Hmm, so we meet again."

Alex, unable to see the lights from where he is stood, feels a huge responsibility to quell their actions. Under his breath, he concentrates deeply and grunts, "Pack it in will you."

Dawson's gaze shifts from the lights to Alex with a knowing expression written across his face. As his attention returns to the canopy, he commands loudly, "Enough, be still."

The lights instantly return to their usual glow and as he continues to stare intently at them, they finally extinguish. Dawson looks across to Alex and calmly says, "You close at eleven I believe?"

"That's correct," Alex meekly confirms.

"Excellent, in that case, may I partake of some food and drink for both myself and my colleague here and then later, when all these good people have returned to their homes, we will talk."

"No problem," Alex again confirms, handing Tom a menu, "I look forward to it."

Dawson raises one eye to Alex saying, "Is that so, we will see."

He then surveys the bar and spots young Alex, Canning's farm worker, sitting alone at a small round table with his legs extended out to rest on top of another stool. The table is surrounded by three stools in total and he slowly makes his way over to it, quietly asking its occupant, "Would you mind awfully if we joined you?"

Alex stares at him for a second then grumpily replies, "I got mates coming, find somewhere else."

Tom instantly takes a disliking to his tone and begins to move forward but before he can utter a word, Dawson gently pushes him back.

With a smile Dawson says, "Well young man, they are not here yet and every other seat appears to be occupied. If you would be so kind, we would prefer to sit down to eat our evening meal, so we will be joining you."

Alex's eyes widen, his pupils enlarge, anger is apparent in his bodily stance as his stare engages with that of Dawson's.

"In point of fact, you were just leaving, were you not?" Dawson continues, looking deeply into his eyes.

The young lad's eyes open and close, he wobbles slightly before steadying himself by placing both palms firmly down on the table. He stutters a few words then he says, "Leaving... leaving.... yes I was just about to go."

He drags himself to his feet, his eyes never leaving Dawson's until he is across the room on his way off the premises. Dawson and Tom calmly take their seats.

Anne moves next to Alex and whispers, "Now that was impressive. If that had happened to you, Alex would now probably be unconscious," she says as she raises her eyebrows and smiles.

He sighs, "Yeah well, everyone has their strengths, that's what I say."

Silence still reigns throughout the room as Dawson says, "Accommodating young man, don't you know. Now, where were those menus?"

As Anne circles the bar to explain the dining options to their latest guests, the room begins to liven up again with the main topic of conversation this time being the strange newcomer Dawson and his friend.

CHAPTER TWENTY

By closing time most people had already left. Grantree and his friends remained sitting in exactly the same place that they had occupied throughout the evening, having made absolutely no attempt to converse with Dawson at all. Rob is at the corner of the bar with Andy, Graham having previously left saying, "This is all much too emotional for me. I'm going home."

Apart from them, John also remained. By now he was well on his way to alcoholic indifference, but he had no intention of leaving unless ordered to do so by Alex.

Alex surveys the scene just as Criss and Marcus enter the room. He heads for the front door and locks it up. He then closes the bar door, locking this behind him. Finally, he returns to his position behind the bar, picks up his beer and swallows a large gulp of it.

York looks around him at all those still present only hesitating to inspect the locked doors and comments, "By Jove, is this an old fashioned lock in? I've always wanted to be part of one of these."

Tom giggles, glancing over to Alex he asks, "Is that what this is?"

"Oh," York interrupts, "I think Alex would like it referred to as something else really, especially with the two police officers who are currently over there."

Criss is the first person to break the uneasy silence. "What made you come up with that assumption sir, or have your contacts advised you as to our status?"

"Bravo my dear," York jubilantly quips. "Indeed I do have my contacts, most of them are unfortunately now dead, but in this case, your entire demeanour has local constabulary written across it." He hesitates for a second before saying, "Alex, I said we would converse when the premises were closed. This is hardly closed, or do you wish these people to hear what I have to say?"

Alex, who is now sat on the customers side of the bar with Anne and Rob says, "Firstly, let's call it what it is. We are all locked in to this bar and drinks are available to all those who remain here. In the cold light of day it is known as a 'lock in'. Secondly, I have nothing to hide, so you can say whatever you have to say."

"Ah you are a realist. How refreshing that is," York concludes.

Alex slides down from his stool and standing with his hands on the bar, he firmly says, "From what I can gather, you were called here to sort out where these missing people have gone, so is there any chance that you could begin with that deed instead of bending our ear holes?"

York smiles, "That is exactly what I am doing my dear man. You see, I believe that the missing people are your indirect doing."

Now Alex really looks angry and loudly and aggressively he says, "What the hell are you prattling on about? Some of the missing people were my friends!"

Slowly Tom rises to his feet, his whole body charged with adrenaline. Again, York raises his hand and calmly insists, "Please sit down Tom. You are not required to intervene at the present moment."

"Yes Tom, do sit down before you get hurt," Alex grunts under his breath through gritted teeth.

"Please understand Alex," York interrupts, "People surmise that Tom is my protégée, he is not. Tom is ex SAS and he accompanies me solely for my protection." He takes a deep breath before continuing with a smile. "Although, I have to admit, young Tom here is showing definite signs of possessing the necessary abilities for my profession."

Tom smiles, settling back down on his seat.

"Well, I don't wish to do battle with a professional however I do want you to explain yourself."

"Of course you do my dear man, of course you do. We will start at the beginning. To clarify the situation which we have here, we will need to remain both completely factual and logical. I understand that nobody disappeared before you purchased those lights which presently adorn the canopy above the bar. Is that correct?"

After a short silence Rob speaks, "Yes that's about right, isn't it?" he looks across at Alex.

Alex glances over to him and confirms, "That would seem to be about the same time, yes."

"Ok," York continues, "Initially only a couple of people went missing, with almost a complete year passing before there was any further occurrence?"

Anne is the next one to comment with, "Well, more or less, yes."

"No, I beg to differ, not more or less, it was almost exactly a year to the day and nothing else happened throughout the months in between until you once more decorated the canopy of your bar with those lights in time for Christmas. It was after this that the next person went missing?" he adds, tilting his head to one side and raising his eyebrows.

John, who is now shifting uneasily in his seat, adds slurring, "So you're blaming them lights for abducting people? Are you off your rocker?"

York turns his attention towards John, looking him up and down before replying, "In your present state, which is for the better part, inebriated, trying to glean any factual input from you, will be negligible my friend. Obsolete personal attacks are not required either, so will you please be quiet."

John, now definitely looking the worse for wear, stutters, "Waz any... of what he just said.....ingleesh?"

Alex and Anne smile, knowing John to be completely harmless and in his present state of mind also totally out of his depth regarding this conversation.

Then Grantree enters the dialogue. "I believe I have seen what those lights represent."

York smiles gingerly. "No you haven't. What you have witnessed is the master himself."

Marcus raises his eyebrows and glancing across at Alex, he quietly requests, "Can I have a very, very large scotch please?"

Alex feeling he is in for a long night, shrugs his shoulders and returns behind the bar, pouring half a tumbler of whiskey and placing it down in front of him.

Marcus places his hand in his pocket to pay for the drink, but Alex has already moved away saying, "I might be missing something here, but what the hell has this got to do with me?"

York turns his attention back to Alex smiling, "Because whether you like it or not, those lights are firmly tuned in to your emotions."

"What a load of bollocks! What are you trying to say here, that a bunch of Christmas lights follow my bidding? Pray please tell me, exactly why are these people missing?"

York shrugs his shoulders. "They are probably missing because they aggravated or annoyed you in some way."

Alex drains the rest of his beer, gets up and returns behind the bar, placing his empty mug on the bar and grabbing a tumbler, filling it with three shots of a single malt whiskey from the top shelf. "Annoyed me? You are annoying me but you're still here. You haven't disappeared anywhere, so that is all a load of cobblers."

"Of course you are correct in what you say and it is all simply total conjecture. However, I know that I am right because I have met and had dealings with the spirit which is present here now and I know how it operates."

"Spirit!" Rob blurts into his drink. "Explain, what spirit?"

York shakes his head. "This is the problem with group discussions. There are too many things to explain and too many basic questions that require answering before I can continue."

"Well can you please try," Anne asks him. "It's obvious that we all need your advise so can you please clarify everything to us and as simply as you can."

He raises his eyebrows and replies, "As simply as I can. Well, alright then, let me begin. This particular spirit, entity, ghost, whatever you would like to name it, originates from Jamaica. It belonged to a prostitute from the early seventeen hundreds. Her name was Raeni, which means 'queen'. By the time she reached the age of seventeen, she had fallen in love with one of her, now how should I put this, ah yes, clients. The man, who was in his forties at the time, was the owner of a sugar plantation. His name was Louie Trouton and her whole family were employed and kept by him as slaves. The man, Trouton, took her whenever he felt the desire to do so, completely unaware that she had fallen in love with him. As a working girl, she was starting to see increasingly less of her other clients, remaining available just for him."

"So you're saying that this spirit is female?" Anne questions.

"Indeed, my dear lady, in fact it belongs to a woman who was eventually to become infamous in Jamaica as one of the most vicious killers of her time. Anyway I will continue. Trouton, oblivious to her love, tires of her and begins to play the field, taking women at will from all over the plantation."

"Sounds like the plot to a great film," Andy states completely enthralled.

York sighs, glaring at him. "Do you think there is any possibility that I can finish this narrative without any further interruption?"

"Oops, sorry," he apologises.

"Now of course, Raeni knew what was going on but blinded by her emotions, deduced that he was simply testing her devotion to him. However, she also decided that in turn, for each woman that he took, she would seduce the father, enticing them to the remotest corner of the plantation, an old store shed at the northern end of the estate by the stream. Whilst engaging in the sexual act, she picked a suitable moment to plunge her thumbs deep into their eye sockets, instantly killing them."

Anne grimaces and shudders at the thought but Alex giggles, saying, "Jesus, surely they screamed the place down, that must have been absolute agony?"

"I agree," he concurs, "however, no one apparently heard their screams or found their bodies. Having carried out this evil deed, she would drag the corpse into the stream, pushing it out towards the centre where the current was faster flowing, swiftly carrying it down towards the sea. She would then bathe and wash her clothes to remove any signs of her dastardly deed and serenely return to her dwellings."

"How long did this go on for?" Jill asks.

"Eleven months and in that time, twenty two men and two woman were dispatched."

"Why men and women?" someone asks.

"Let me explain," he snaps, a tad agitated, "which is becoming quite a trial with all these interruptions."

Everyone falls silent. "Please carry on Mr Dawson," Jill requests.

He nods his thanks to her and continues. "Initially as the men disappeared, Trouton believed them to be absconding as slaves frequently did, but following the disappearance of the two women, the local militia became involved and they began pursuing their own investigations, therefore suggesting the belief that foul play was possibly involved. Their search uncovered nothing, but after several weeks they found a woman's body in the river. It had remained snagged in the shallows on some rocks. Along with this discovery, came Trouton's realisation that he had previously been associated sexually with both of the missing women. He found himself in a deep dilemma and decided that in the interests of personal safety, he would return to a woman with whom he felt safe, in the knowledge that she had been there before the others had begun disappearing, affording him fewer complication. This may have seemed a trifle naive, as by all accounts he was a man of power and control, but to his detriment he also possessed an insatiable sexual appetite that needed satisfying."

"He wasn't too bright then?" Rob quips.

"Indeed, anyway he pursues this safer option and of course Raeni is only too pleased to accommodate him. During the affair, his mother becomes increasingly perturbed by the fact that her son is installing his whore into the main household and she displays her disapproval. On several occasions, strong words were heard violently exchanged between the two of them regarding this subject. Inevitably, one night a huge argument broke out between them which became so loud that Raeni, who by now was asleep in bed, was woken. She crept downstairs and by the time she entered the main hallway she could clearly see straight into the drawing room where the two of them were standing, heatedly waving their arms around at each other aggressively. Finally as his mother slapped him around the face, he pushed her away with extreme force and sent her crashing into a table, where she landed face down on the floor. Of course, being a fragile, elderly woman, her neck snapped killing her instantly. Louie looked down at her lifeless body and called her name. Realising the worst, he dropped to his knees and began to weep. Raeni quietly made her way into the room, across to console her lover, caressing his head and holding it close to her breast. When he finally regained his composure, the remorse of his deed was replaced by the fear of the outcome. At this point, Raeni chose to tell him about the store shed and how they could dispose of the body, simply informing everyone that she had returned to England. Louie gave this some thought and with a sense of urgency, he agreed to it. They gather up the body, leaving the main house by the servants exit, lugging it to the northern edge of the estate and into the old store shed. By the time they got there, night was beginning to fade away, allowing the daylight to poke its rays through the darkness. They waded into the water with the body, Raeni ensuring that they pulled it towards the stretch with the faster flow, before they released it. As the two of them were making their way back to the bank, it crossed Louie's mind to enquire as to her knowledge of this perfect spot. At first, she implied that she had simply heard of its existence, but as he became more persistent with his questions, not believing her story and realising that there was a lot more to her familiarity than she was willing to say, he lost his temper with her. He dragged her back into the depths of the stream, yelling at her all the time and pinning her tightly towards him so that she couldn't struggle. In a final effort to free herself she brought her knee up with considerable force, connecting with his groin. The pain of which immediately released his grip upon her. Breathless from his hold but free, she tried to reach the bank but as she was about to pull herself up onto it, her hair was wrenched backwards, dragging her down into the depths of the river, his temper now raging with his pain. He grabbed her around the throat and plunged her under the water, holding her there. As her breath ebbed away, she struggled, kicking and thrashing around in a final, wild attempt to free herself. For a brief moment, she managed to raise her head above the water, taking a deep breath she yelled and 'I was only protecting you because of my love for you'! His raging retort was, 'Protect me you bitch, you wouldn't know how to!' He held her head under again until no air bubbles were visible from the surface of the water, when he finally allowed her body to drift away with the current."

"That's one hell of a story," Andy comments tightly gripping his pint mug.

"You can say that again," Rob agrees.

Alex looking perplexed, asks, "So why is she a spirit, I mean how does that work?"

Anne, also thoughtful insists, "Mr Dawson, please continue because I have a feeling that the question you have just been asked will reveal itself at the end of this tale."

"Quite so my dear, you are correct," he continues. "Louie climbs out of the river, staring back at the water to finish watching the body float away. Satisfied that she has gone, he makes his way back to the house. On his return he clears away the evidence in the sitting room before cleaning himself up. He changes the bed linen, searching for anything that may have belonged to Raeni, which he then disposes of.

Later that day, he mounts his horse and gallops it around the plantation, on the pretence of checking on the progress of his crops, but to see if and where the militia were searching. As they had previously investigated the northern section of the estate, he was happy to discover that they were now concentrating their efforts on the eastern side before presumably heading south, so he returned home. Having stabled the horse, he proceeded to the house. On his approach, he observed that the front door was wide open. He cautiously entered the building to see Raeni sat on the stairs clutching a solid, silver candelabra with the candles lit. Her head lifted slowly as she said, 'I can protect anyone whom I please and I will continue to do so. I can also kill anyone I dislike, in this case, that will be you'. With inhuman strength, she launched the candelabra at him, hitting him squarely in the chest. He fell backwards into the colossal front door, which slammed shut under his force. The candles, torn from their holder, scattered in different directions, igniting the heavy brocade curtains and rugs on impact. The blaze didn't take long to gain a hold; the main door from the building quickly became impassable. Louie crawled to the rear of the house in an attempt to exit by the servant's entrance but as he passed the stairs, she leaped from the staircase onto his back, wrapping her hands around his face and pressing her middle fingers deep into his eyes, gauging at his face. As her digits hit their mark, blood poured from the wounds and he screamed in agony, dropping to his knees. She ceased her attack, climbed off him and strode across the room, dragging a carpet which was already firmly alight and tossed it over him like a sheet. It fell on his back. His struggles merely served to entrap him further, his body burning all the while. Raeni burst forth into evil, rapturous laughter. By now, servants and slaves alike were aware that the main house was on fire and had mustered with buckets of water trying to extinguish the flames, but they quickly realised that their efforts were doomed. The door flew outwards from its frame and Raeni, on fire, stood there laughing. She was heard to warn, before falling dead to the floor, 'I will find someone who needs my protection and low and behold anyone who stands against me'. Those watching witnessed a mist emanating from the crown of her head, increasing in volume before finally dispersing along with her life. Dawson raised his eyebrows and sighing dramatically, ended with, "And that was that."

A dark silence followed as the group digested the tale which they had just heard, then Marcus said to Criss, but loud enough for everyone to hear, "Are we sure we want to go to war with this woman, she sounds like some kind of nutcase to me?"

"Well ok, but I still don't understand why she is a spirit and also, how you know all this shit and finally, you said you've met her before. Can I ask where?" Alex asks with confusion.

"A spirit," Isme states, "is a person who has died, normally of unnatural causes and who is not at peace, therefore creating a malevolent energy."

"Yeah, so?" Alex quizzes.

"She died in agony, all the while clearly stating her intentions," Grantree adds. "In essence, she still had strength and purpose, a force to propel her soul onward, wandering until she is able to complete whatever it maybe that she has vowed to do."

"Ok we've got that, but where have you met this spirit before Mr Dawson?"

"I've met her twice before. The first time was in Columbia, South America, in a place called El Carmen. She had chosen the local law enforcement officer to protect. Without going into any details, it finished up with three dead before we reached the other nine people who were missing. The officer himself had no idea that he was the one responsible for causing these people to disappear. The second time was in Boston, Massachusetts in America."

"Gets around, doesn't she?" Anne quips.

For the first time, he laughs openly. "Indeed she does but then she has no immediate boundaries, not physical ones anyway. In America, this spirit chose a taxi driver of Mexican origins, who was a bad tempered person to say the least. He must have invented the phrase 'road rage'. Anyway, over forty people had gone missing throughout a four week period and the police couldn't work out why, so I was called in. At first, I didn't recognise her for who she was, even though the modus operandi was very similar, but when I met the taxi driver, immediately I knew exactly who I was dealing with. You must understand, that Raeni always has a front medium, here it is the canopy lights, in America it was a rosary that dangled on the interior mirror, in Columbia, a battery, operated sixties style model robot which stood on his desk with lights on its head, stomach and limbs."

"I really believe you need to qualify this," Criss says.

"It is quite simple my dear, the lights on this canopy are the physical front to Raeni, they do her bidding, she only shows herself when she absolutely has to, always very cautious never to reveal her true identity."

Suddenly, Anne glances over to Alex, staring at him with realisation. "So what this is leading up to is that Alex is the man who Raeni has focused her attentions upon?"

York smiles a wry, little smile. "I believe so, in point of fact, I'm sure of it."

Silence fills the room for a short time before Alex protests, "Oh come on, this is bullshit, I'm not making these people disappear and besides, where are they going to, go on, answer that one?"

York looks at Tom who is staring at the Christmas village scene, and he slowly replies, pointing his finger, "In there, that's exactly where they are."

Alex doesn't need to turn around as he knows precisely what he is pointing at. However, everyone else in the room except York seems to have the need to look. York simply studies Alex's reaction.

"So, fully grown people are shrunk and installed into a frigging model, by me, not that I am aware of it, and you think that all makes sense?"

His eyes widen and he states, "If we were talking about the organised rationality of the world as we know it, of course not, and that is why you are having trouble comprehending what I have said. However, what you must bring into this equation is that this is a situation where the real world has met the other side, the world of the spirits. This being the case, the 'usual' happenings and goings on change, the whole fabric of the 'norm' alters."

Alex slumps down into a chair and gazes over at the village scene, where the curious people still present in the bar, have now gathered. He places his beer down on the table and holds his head in his hands saying, "This can't be right, surely I would know, surely I would feel something at the very least."

"That is not how it works my friend," York assures him. "This spirit believes that it is protecting you. You become angry, even slightly agitated with someone or something and she will sense it, removing it in order for you to become calm once more. You see, when you are calm, she is calm, she feels that all is safe and serene, a state which she is constantly seeking."

"So how do we get these people back?" Isme asks while methodically examining the Christmas scene.

York gets out of his chair and strolls over to the bar, placing both hands firmly down on it, he lifts his head as he studies the lights. "That is a good question," he sighs, "By now Raeni will know I am here, especially as I have reprimanded her lights. What we need to achieve is for here to embrace a physical form. This will not be easily achieved, as she is fully aware that by doing that, she will finish up directly confronting me, a situation which she has already encountered twice before and lost. Having used the word lost, this is not strictly true as I was not able to lay her to rest, so therefore to date she has only lost the individual battles, not the complete war."

Isme is now looking directly at York and he presses, "So I ask the question again, 'how are you going to get these people back?' I must admit that I am at a total loss as to how they are supposed to escape from their miniature captivity. I've seen them and they are exceptionally well guarded."

York nods a couple of times before he answers. "Those people in the display, when I have dislodged Raeni from her lair, will materialise at exactly the same spot which they were taken from. At least, that is how it has worked on both of the previous occasions."

"Well, then all's well and we have nothing at all to worry about, just as long as it all happens in the same way as it did before," Anne states sarcastically.

Rob giggles and asks, "Is there any danger that you could let me know when this confrontation is about to take place, because I definitely do not want to be here when it does."

"I'm with him," Andy agrees and fidgets nervously.

York, still at the bar, closes his eyes and says, "My dear people, it will not be a matter of time, it will happen when it happens. Attempting to orchestrate an appearance by Raeni will be impossible. By now, she will already be preparing, anticipating my next move."

"And what would that be exactly?" Jill questions.

"To have the medium removed," York simply states.

Everyone's eyes turn towards the canopy lights.

"Yes those, they are her eyes and ears at this moment in time. Remove them and she has no choice but to reveal herself."

CHAPTER TWENTYONE

"They're out!" Canning yells.

"Thank you Mr Canning," Michael acknowledges, having also noted that the aspect has dimmed as the bar lights are doused, "but we will wait for a short while longer, just in case they turn back on for some obscure reason."

Duncan nods excitedly, knowing now that he will be on the job soon enough, extremely eager to see if he can pull it off. Julie smiles at him nodding then resumes her task of heaving the plastic away from the hole. By this point the tiny hole has become akin to the size of a football and Ellie the cat, constantly wanders over to it, only to be pushed away by those who are working. Paul watches with great interest, but says nothing, just maintains his vigil over the animals.

Dan and Clive had returned to the church, where both men took turns at climbing the tower to work on the opening situated there. Like the other team, they have now achieved a hole of similar size with Dan periodically attempting to peer through to see if he can recognise anything on the outside. Unfortunately, he had managed to emerge on the side of the roof closest to the rear wall, therefore he found himself staring at a blank surface. As much as he tried, he couldn't manoeuvre himself enough to free his shoulders as well to gain a better view on the other side. He scrambled back down to the floor of the church, bubbling with excitement to exchange position with Clive who then ascended the tower to continue with the work.

Michael had been travelling between the two groups, not particularly happy that they were split within their endeavours, making sure that everyone was okay and overseeing their progress.

By now, though everyone had gathered back in the room where Duncan had his electrical gear laid out in readiness to power up the laptop, all work on the other projects had ceased and everyone was sitting, intently watching Michael, waiting for his orders to start.

Then it comes, "Ok Duncan, I think we have waited long enough, proceed to show us your expertise please."

Immediately he jumps to his feet, accompanied by Julie and Clive who stride across to the equipment. With penknives, Duncan and Clive begin carving through the wires that feed the bulb. Julies hauls up the cables ready for splicing together as soon as the other two finish their labours.

The rest remain in total silence, watching the others, except for the three cats, who slowly get up, stretching their limbs and then silently, they head for the hole. Ellie is the first one there, sniffing all the way around it. Having inspected the area, she places her head through the hole and glancing left and right, she leaps through, disappearing from view. Within seconds the other two cats have followed her in turn, with Bobs the last to negotiate the obstacle. Paul is oblivious to all of this, completely absorbed watching the electrical work in progress.

Now outside and potentially free, the cats begin to creep along the back of the display, sniffing as they move cautiously along. They make their way slowly forward until they have passed the row of buildings, emerging at the far end where the wires and flexes from the display terminate in an extension lead. Ellie surveys the area in front of her, while the other two contentedly groom themselves, removing the dust and cobwebs from their coats. The room in front of them is pitch, the only light is emanating from the beer engines lined up on the bar, four oval lights in the centre with their respective pull handles standing proud above them. Ellie's ears, like radars, rotate in different directions, listening for anything that may alert her to danger. Bobs and Charlie, still grooming themselves while listening, display somewhat less urgency, allowing the older cat to take the leading role.

Having completed her survey of their surroundings, she leaps down from the extension lead onto the edge of the piano top, gazing down at the drop before her. Bobs and Charlie do not follow her, but they watch as she prowls the extremities of their plateau. Suddenly, she stops, peering hard into the darkness of the room towards the far corner. Her whole body is tense with anticipation. She makes no movement, her ears pricked forward in the direction of which she is looking. The other two sense her concern and immediately they too scan the same area, their eyes wide open and again, not a single hair of their fur is moving.

"Shit, they're gone!" Paul yells out.

All eyes turn to him, including those working on the cables.

"Who's gone?" Duncan replies.

"The bleeding cats, they've gone! And more than likely through that hole," Paul elaborates, getting to his feet and heading straight for it.

Michael's lips tighten, visibly annoyed that Paul had shrugged his responsibilities regarding the animals and says, "I should think that is exactly where they have taken themselves off to. It's too late now, any damage is already done. Not to worry, let's concentrate on the job at hand for the moment."

Duncan switches his gaze from the hole back to the wire, gesturing to Gary to aid him with wiggling the cable back and forth, trying to heat the cut in the wire and hopefully cause it to break. The two men handle the cable, rapidly flexing it up and down, their efforts for a while negligible before finally weakening the arc of the wire. Dan and Canning join in, helping to speed up the task and soon the first wire breaks away from the bulb.

A cry of triumph and sighs of exhaustion can be heard from all four. Immediately they join Julie with her efforts patiently attacking another piece of cable. With all hands now active, in a relatively short time the cable breaks, once more with smiles and exuberant back slapping at their achievement.

Duncan grasps one of the shortened wires, carrying it over to the mains cable, beginning to splice the two together. Gary grabs the other one and watching Duncan work he comprehends how to join the two cables together. He squats down beside him and begins the process of duplicating his actions.

The bar is now completely silent; a pin could be heard to drop. On the far side of the bar, opposite the piano and sitting in an armchair which he had previously positioned before the lights went out, is York Dawson. He is wearing a pair of purpose built glasses with infra red and auto focus capabilities. He sits perfectly still, staring at the piano. He is completely attired in black, with a large skull cap covering his mop of white hair. He can see the tiny creatures darting about on the piano, but every time he attempts to zoom in, they hear it and immediately look across in his direction. He is pretty sure that they cannot see him but he knows they suspect something to be there. He must wait until they have reassured themselves as to their safety before he zooms in again to see exactly what these tiny creatures are.

The canopy lights occasionally flicker, and each time they do, he glares at them and immediately they die back down and go out. Now however, his attention is firmly fixed on the piano and the tiny living things that have emerged from the Christmas scene.

After a while, Ellie snaps herself out of her trance from staring into the pitch blackness at the far side of the room and continues walking around the perimeter on the top of the piano. She passes in front of the display, occasionally stopping and sniffing when something catches her interest. Finally, she reaches the far end of the display, where upon she turns the corner and disappears down the side. Bobs and Charlie see her go, but make no attempt to follow her. They all share the others instincts so there are no surprises for them. They stay exactly where they are, both cats now calmly lying down, purring quietly.

While the others are working, Michael strolls over to the hole and managing to push his head through it he takes a look out in both directions. Firstly he looks left and stares into the darkness, but is unable to see anything. Then he switches to the right. As his head turns in this direction, he feels a soft brushing sensation against the side of his head. This startles him, causing him to withdraw his head quickly from the hole and catch his ears on both sides, making him yell out in pain. Finally freeing himself, he falls backwards landing ungracefully on his rear end. He gazes up at the hole to see Ellie's face peering in, purring at him.

He takes a deep breath and sighs in an effort to compose himself, as he hears Julie laughingly say, "You naughty girl Ellie, scaring that big northern man like that."

He can hear the others giggling behind him as he struggles to regain his composure. He moves back towards the hole to where Ellie is and as he extends his arms to pull her back through, she darts away, back out into the darkness and she is gone.

Ellie, now on familiar ground, and knowing this to be her original route out of the buildings, has soon returned to where she left the other two happily reclining. She leaps up to join them, snuggling down in between for warmth. Her eyes quickly readjust as she stares out into the blackness at the far corner of the room.

York is just able to make out her movement, but remains reluctant to attract her attention. As he watches, he becomes aware that her attention is not focused on him but on something else and whatever it is it's coming from the opposite direction. Caution forgotten, he immediately grabs his glasses to see what this distraction is. Momentarily the mother cat glances his way, but whatever else she has now heard is rapidly taking priority over her attention.

His glasses now primed with their zoomed lenses and autofocus provide him with a perfect image. Suddenly he realises that what he has been watching is in fact not one but three cats. He remains completely still to see what will happen next.

The lights behind the bar turn on as Marcus and Criss enter the room. York nods to them as their gaze falls upon him and he simply says, "It seems all quiet on the western front at present."

Marcus smiles with a shrug, "There's not a lot happening anywhere else in the building either."

York gets to his feet, stretches and removes his glasses. He ambles over to the others at the bar and says, "But it will."

Criss's face shows a certain amount of concern over these words and she eagerly asks, "What exactly are we to expect? What do you believe is going to happen?"

"That's what everyone wants to know my dear, but the answer is far from an exact science. All I know for sure is that within the next two days, this entire thing will reach a head and the final battle will take place. As for how it will happen, well, your guess is as good as mine," he smiles and adds, "Well almost as good."

He then slips his glasses back on, perching them on the end of his nose and walks over to the Christmas scene, examining the spot where he had seen the cats. It was no surprise at all to him that they had gone. He then proceeds to examine the rest of the model. Criss and Marcus watch him, wondering as to what he is actually looking for.

"I thought you said the missing people were prisoners inside the display?" Criss asks.

"That is perfectly correct," he confirms, "but just before you came in, I saw three cats sitting up here."

"Cats!" Marcus exclaims. "Where did they go then, because they didn't pass us on our way in?"

He laughs. "They weren't ordinary cats, they were miniature and they were perched exactly here. That is to say that obviously they were normal once upon a time, but that was before they were sent in there," he adds pointing to the Christmas scene.

Criss and Marcus stare for a moment at the display then Criss asks, "So apart from people, cats can finish up in there as well? How and why?"

He ponders the question for a second before replying, "To be honest, the usual reason that people or things would end up in a place like that, is because the host, in this case Alex, would have become aggravated by a certain issue and Raeni would simply have removed the offensive item from his presence. In this case, it seems that she has removed anyone and anything which disturbed her organisation and control within this building. If I was to hazard a guess, these cats being the pub cats, probably recognised that the display emanated an unusual and strange aura, hence they were potentially causing her a problem and therefore had to be removed."

"But from what you've just said," Marcus quizzes him, "these cats are outside the display and not prisoners inside it at all?"

"Indeed, they have created quite a quandary for me as well."

As the lights are turned back on, the cats dart away, down the side of the model buildings and tuck in behind them for safety. Charlie leads the way, but waits as he realises the other two have stopped. He turns and saunters back to them to see what has caught their attention. Ellie has returned to the corner of the building peering around the corner in order to see what is about to happen. Bobs and Charlie sit tight in their comparative safety, but nonetheless constantly glancing back and forth with their vigil.

Marcus and Criss say their goodnights and start to leave the room as York goes once more to retake his seat in his armchair. Just then, the canopy lights begin dimly flickering. York stops dead in his tracks and the two officers hesitate sensing something untoward in his reaction. He slowly turns, his brows furrowed as he glares at the illuminations, waiting to see what their intentions are. Marcus pulls Criss behind him, his face serious having observed York's strange behaviour.

Suddenly, the lights burst forth with blinding radiance, a constant intense white light. York calmly reaches into his top pocket and produces a pair of sunglasses which he immediately places on his eyes. He puts his left hand into his waist coat pocket and firmly takes hold of something secreted inside.

From deep within the glare of the luminance, he can begin to make out an object pushing forth from the illuminations and as he struggles to see what it is, he catches sight of Marcus returning into the room.

"Go back!" he yells out.

Marcus stops immediately. He glances up at the lights, shielding his eyes and quickly steps backwards.

As York stares at the protrusion, he can distinguish a hand of sorts, with long spindly fingers, protruding veins and elongated talons curving downwards. He backs away until he knocks into the wall behind him, never for a moment removing his eyes from the hand. The hand extends into an arm, within a couple of feet from his face. He can clearly see the fingers wriggling with their attempt to reach him, and the arm muscles flexing, trying to stretch that extra few inches. He remains perfectly still, watching, never releasing his firm grip on the object in his pocket, so tight that it must be casting a lasting impression in his skin.

Suddenly a face frees itself from the light, a distorted, raging face, foaming at the mouth, its eyes bulging, enabling the limb to gain the extra distance required to reach him. York instantly produces the object from his pocket, casting it out in front of his face, he begins to chant.

As though burned, the hand immediately lurches back. The fingers contract to form a fist as the arm withdraws towards the glaring face.

"YOU!" the spectre screams, hissing.

Faster than the eye can see, the fist connects with a table in the centre of the bar, exploding it into a mass of fragmented pieces. York, with his eyes firmly closed, continues to chant, his arms fully extended, holding the object out in front of him.

As fast as the apparition arrived, so it vanishes. The lights die away and the room returns to its previous state. York removes his glasses with one hand, but keeps the other one out in front of him, firmly holding the object.

"What is that?" Marcus nervously asks, as he cautiously reappears in the bar.

York now exhausted, slumps into the armchair and lets out a deep sigh as he relaxes his aching arms. "This is part of a human skull."

"Oh god, that is disgustingly gross," Criss announces from the back hallway.

"Is it alright to come in now?" Marcus asks.

"Yes, she won't be back tonight. She will currently be enacting her plan to kill me."

Marcus enters the room first, closely followed by Criss.

"What was that you uttered young lady? Was it gross? Now why would you consider this object to be gross? It is simply no more than an old bone."

"But it's a bone from someone's head, don't you think that is a little macabre?" She pursues.

"My dear woman, it is neither gross nor macabre," he emphatically states, "it is part of Raeni's skull, an effective amulet because she fears it."

Marcus and Criss glance briefly at each other, raising their eyebrows in disbelief of the current events. Criss poses the next question, "Why?"

York smiles because he was expecting this, chuckling more to himself than anyone else. "Her fear is quite well earned. I discovered where what was left of her body was finally laid to rest and the only recognisable piece that remained was this fragment of her skull. A mass was held over the rest of her remains, to lay her spirit to rest, but I was already aware that her spirit had fled and was now wandering the earth, searching for peace of any kind that she could find. This piece that I possess is the only reminder of her life on earth, a memory that she would rather forget. It also represents the power of the religion that played a part in laying her to rest, something that she totally denies. Therefore when she sees this bone, it causes her immense fear and apprehension."

Suddenly, the door to the back stairs is noisily and hurriedly opened. Alex and Anne enter the room with both speed and urgency. Alex quickly glances around the room, taking in each person present and finally he stares at the remains of the table which lies in pieces in the middle of the room.

His head tilts left, then right, as he examines the devastation. He asks the obvious, "Would anybody like to enlighten me as to why the furniture is now under attack?"

Both Anne and Criss giggle at the way he has posed the question, while Marcus has to turn away in an effort to control his laughter.

"Ah yes, the table," York states, "in my opinion, that was smashed by Raeni's little temper tantrum."

Alex's eyes slowly move from the debris towards York. "You mean Raeni, as in the ghost Raeni?"

"Yes, that is correct."

"She was here, in this room, breaking up my table because she was in a bad mood?"

"That's a trifle over simplified, but in essence you seem to have grasped the situation splendidly," York condescendingly replies.

"Then will you fill in the bloody parts that I'm not seeing, you arrogant idiot," He snaps back.

York sits forward in his chair, not having taken any offence to Alex's pointed remarks he proceeds to provide him with a step by step oration of the events as they took place.

On his completion, a small knocking sound can be heard on the door from the bar into the main hall, with a timid voice asking, "Is everything ok in there, may we come in?"

Anne recognises Jill's voice and proceeds to unlock the door to allow her and the others access to the room. Of course, within seconds, the obvious questions are asked again as to why the furniture is broken. Tom remains quiet, looking at his boss.

York leaps to his feet, stating, "Well I am not prepared to recite the earlier happenings yet again. I must admit that I am quite bored with the story now and I am going to bed for some well deserved rest." He leaves the room without another word, with Tom following closely on his heels.

Marcus is the one who is left to recite the earlier events, his audience mesmerised by the story.

Ellie, who has watched the entire display, now heads back towards the other two cats, strolling straight past them towards their previous means of escape. Bobs and Charlie nonchalantly follow her. They emerge back inside the display just as Duncan announces that his work is completed, everything is finally wired up and ready to be tested.

"Tested!" Michael blurts out. "Please be aware, that we are only going to get one crack at this, so make sure to the best of your abilities that everything is ready and not simply being tested."

He nods, his attention focused back on his work, he starts checking every piece individually.

Clive spots the cats as they re-enter the room and he nudges Paul to alert him to this, who immediately yells out, "They're back, the cats, they're back!"

Everyone turns to look at the objects of his outburst, except for Duncan, who has his eyes closed and with a deep sigh, he inhales. The alert of the cat's reappearance had startled him greatly. Tinkering with electric cables just wasn't good for ones nerves.

"Quieten down Paul," Tara orders, "are you trying to wake the ghoul?"

The cats return to their corner of the room, settling once more to groom themselves.

"Why do you think they came back?" Gary questions.

"Who knows?" Julie replies.

"It was probably something to do with those glaring lights we saw earlier," Canning huffs.

"I am inclined to agree," Michael adds, "something out of the ordinary most definitely happened out there."

Julie walks over to the cats and crouches down beside them, stroking them gently. They begin purring so loudly that it reverberates around the room.

Finally, after having listened to a second account of the nights excitement, Alex glances down at his watch and says, "Come on people, it's nearly four in the morning. Let's hit the sack."

This statement is enough for everyone to head off in their different directions towards to their rooms, an excited chatter buzzing around them as they leave.

When the room is clear, Alex turns out all the lights, locks the necessary doors and then finally heads back upstairs, his bed becoming more important by the second, as his mind is telling him it is time to sleep. As he closes the doorway from the stairs to the hall, through a glass panel he has clear visibility of the rear of the bar. Reflected in the front window of the bar is a single light, one of the lights from the canopy. He sits on the third stair up and watches. At first, nothing happens. It appears to be just the one bulb which has remained alight with a constant illumination. Just as he decides that the whole notion is a complete waste of time, several other bulbs begin to glow, moving along the canopy like a train. He senses a warm sensation, as if a wet flannel had been placed on the back of his neck. He moves his hand to rub the area when he hears a soft voice.

"Don't be hexed by the witch hunter, he cannot harm you. I will take care of him, relax my love."

Alex spins around to see who it is, not recognising the voice. He distantly sees an eerie face as it disappears into the wall. Spooked to say the least, he jumps to his feet and climbs the stairs at amazing speed, entering his flat and locking the door behind him. He peers out of the glass panel here, but sees nothing. He extinguishes the lights to the stair well and moves quietly along the hall to their bedroom. He enters the room which is already in total darkness. Assuming that Anne is already asleep, he gently sits on the side of the bed, removing his clothes, he carefully climbs in under the bed clothes. Immediately he realises that she is not there. He sits bolt upright, turning on the bedside lamp. She's definitely not there; her side of the bed is cold and empty. He gets up, turns on the main light, surveys the room a second time for signs of anything untoward and goes back into the hall. He checks the bathroom, then the spare room and finally the lounge but there is no sign of her.

He wants to call out but is aware that he could disturb their guests. He remains silent, returning to the hall door once more. Here, he looks out again, turning the light to the stairwell back on, trying to see down the staircase. Craning his neck to obtain a better view, he unlocks the door and slowly opens it up. Trepidation fills his heart, his concern for his wife almost consuming him. He allows the door to close behind him, holding it, so that it shuts gently. When the door meets its threshold, he allows it to click shut and he nervously begins to descend the stairs, cautiously taking one step at a time, his eyes darting left, right, up and down, searching for anything and everything that might be lurking around.

"Are you coming to bed?" a voice calls out.

Alex physically leaves the floor at these words, he is so pent up that the voice from the top of the stairs scares him to death.

"Jesus Anne, where the hell have you been? I've searched the flat and not finding you anywhere, I assumed you were still downstairs."

She descends a few steps before replying, "What are you talking about? I was in bed. You came in and then left, god knows why, so I decided to see what you were up to."

Wide eyed, he stares up at her, trying to comprehend what she is saying. At first, he feels the need to protest, fully aware that she was definitely not in the bedroom, but then, knowing there had been some seriously strange stuff happening just recently, he replies, "I'm coming straight up, I'll be two seconds. I'm just checking we're all locked up."

He glances down towards the bar then returns straight back upstairs, securely locking the door behind him. He enters the bedroom to see his wife snuggled up on her side of the bed. He climbs in, sidles up beside her, closes his eyes and drifts off into an uneasy slumber.

CHAPTER TWENTYTWO

The dawn breaks on Christmas Eve. The time is seven thirty in the morning and Anne is already up, in the bathroom showering. Alex slings his legs out of the bed, relieved and happy that daylight has arrived; no more shadows to worry about. He partially dresses, then heads for the bathroom to wash and shave. As he enters, so she leaves, giving him a quick peck on his cheek in passing. He smiles and proceeds to the sink humming, 'T'is is the season to be jolly', and carries out his morning routine of preparing for the day.

When Anne arrives downstairs, Criss, Marcus and Tom are already sitting in the bar. Although a little surprised to find them in there already, she politely asks, "Tea or coffee anyone and would you like it in here or in the restaurant?"

"In here would be wonderful and thank you," Marcus responds.

She heads for the kitchen, putting on the kettle. Then she grabs the keys to open up the restaurant. Having turned on the lights, she returns to the kitchen to prepare for the forthcoming breakfasts.

Alex emerges some ten minutes later, making straight for the kitchen. He can hear voices, both in the bar and in the restaurant, but he still decides to head for the kitchen to see if Anne requires his assistance.

As he enters, he can smell the sausages and bacon cooking, raising his nose to the heavens, attempting to capture more of their delicious aromas. The first thing he spots are the three warm plates all ready for food to be placed upon them and a tray with cups, saucers and jugs laying on the work surface.

Anne smiles saying, "The teas and coffees are to go into the bar and the breakfasts are for the restaurant."

He nods his acknowledgement, lifting the tray of drinks for the bar.

"Morning, morning, morning," Alex cheerily says as he enters the bar, placing it down on the table where they are sitting. He then surveys the room, focusing on the debris from the broken table.

"If you give me an ash pan and a brush, plus the vacuum cleaner, I'll get this lot cleaned up," Criss announces.

He nods and leaves the room. On returning to the kitchen, he sees the three plates of cooked breakfast. He balances the plates in order on one arm and carries them confidently into the restaurant.

When he enters this room, he sees Isme, Jill and Judith all sat at one table. Again he greets them with a cheery 'Good Morning' and places a plate of food in front of each of them. They return his sentiment and without further ado, dig into their breakfast. Alex returns to the kitchen, grabs the ash pan, heads into the hall, pulls out the hoover and returns to the bar to find that they have been busy gathering up the bits and bobs that remain of the table and piling them up in a suitable spot. He smiles, thanking them all for their help.

Gary is sat by the precariously wired up laptop, waiting in anticipation for the power to be switched back on. The others have continued to take turns at the never ending task of widening the hole at the back of the building. Currently, both Julie and Tara maintain that they could now squeeze through the opening but Michael is adamant, that no one is leaving unless they can all do so. Julie points out that if they got through, they could begin working from the other side. Michael, having given this idea some serious thought and taken advice from the others, eventually bows to the idea.

Tara goes first and after some unladylike shoving, she is launched all the way through. A fair amount of laughter and shouting accompanies her escapades but Dan quells the noise as quickly as possible, reiterating the dangers of them being overheard. Re-establishing a more serious approach, they tackle the issue of getting Julie through the orifice. Like Tara, she is able to get her head, arms and shoulders through easily but then gets stuck trying to pull the rest of her body through. Tara tugs from her side and eventually with plenty of pushing and shoving she is launched all the way through, landing in total disarray on the other side.

Clive, who has found the whole episode hysterical, has to remove himself, hiding in the next room, with his hands clasped across his mouth, fervently attempting to control his laughter. Michael smiles to himself, his eyes gently creasing in the corners.

The work on the hole now continues from both sides.

After breakfast, Isme, Judith and Jill take residence back in the bar. This has become a daily occurrence since their arrival, seldom venturing from the building, always retaining their vigil of the Christmas scene.

Today, Tom decides that he will take a stroll around the village to see the beauty of the snow clad wilderness. In its present state it is stunning, placing the village in a beautiful scene akin to a Christmas card. He dons a pair of wellington boots and a thick coat, pulls the collar snugly around his ears and heads out to brave the arctic conditions.

Criss and Marcus, for the second day in a row, walk across to the village square to scrape the snow from their vehicle. They unlock it, only to discover that the battery is dead and the vehicle will not start; a similar condition to an awful lot of cars and vans in the village at present. They return to the pub, slightly dejected, but their moods lighten at the realisation that they won't have to drive the ten miles to the police station, which would have been problematic anyway. They discuss with Alex the possibilities of taking the battery off to recharge it but Marcus eventually decides to call the station to take direction from them and Alex directs him to where their landline is situated.

Returning to the hall, Alex sees York descending the stairs. "Morning landlord!" he booms out.

"Good morning," Alex replies in a much quieter tone, glancing down at his watch to observe that it's past ten thirty. "We can offer you coffee or tea, but breakfast finished over an hour ago."

York passes Alex on his way to the bar, replying with, "Coffee my good man, and a good old fashioned bacon sandwich. I'll take them in the bar."

As York disappears, Alex turns towards the kitchen, muttering under his breath, "Stuck up asshole."

"Make that two rounds of bacon sandwiches and do not mutter under your breath my good man, it's extremely rude don't you know."

Alex shakes his head, this time muttering purposely under his breath, the only would completely audible being 'asshole.'

He meets Marcus and Criss in the hall, who inform him that the phone line is down. There is another snow storm coming in which has already hit Bristol. Alex leaves Anne with the sandwich making, taking the coffee into the bar for York. He turns on the television as he goes, before placing the drink down. Marcus and Criss follow him in. The television flickers on, but initially no channels can be located. Finally one faintly appears, accompanied with static across the screen.

"And the sandwiches," York abruptly asks, "any danger they are on their way?"

Alex, without even turning his head towards him, answers, "I don't know where you've been staying recently, but here we tend to make fresh food, therefore a small wait is inevitable."

Marcus giggles at the agility of his retort. York just simply huffs.

After a few minutes, it becomes evident that the storm is definitely heading their way. It is already wreaking havoc in its wake, tearing down power lines and clouding the satellites out in space, providing a plausible explanation for the lack of television signal.

"Bloody hell, another storm is coming. We'd best start battening down the hatches," Alex states.

"Can my sandwiches arrive before your quest of securing the building begins?"

Alex can feel his patience wavering, something he is trying very hard to control, knowing that it could bring Raeni to the fore and he's really not in the mood for her as well. Nevertheless, he replies, "Your food will arrive when my wife has prepared it. If you have a problem with that, I suggest you sling your hook and piss off into the pending snowstorm."

Marcus and Criss nervously glance across at each other, before looking towards Tom and finally to York. York's eye lids flutter and he smiles, but his stare remains firmly fixed on the canopy lights. "I thought I told you to remove those damn lights," he states.

Alex, who is just about to leave the room, stops dead in his tracks for a second and his head drops, but then as if he hadn't heard the remark, he calmly leaves. Criss audibly exhales, absolutely certain that Alex was going to lose his temper that time.

Marcus glares at York, saying, "What's the matter with you, are you trying to rile him? You know what his tempers like."

Just then Anne enters the room with a plate of sandwiches, which she places down in front of York with a false smile. Marcus, waiting for his answer, sees his hand come up, signally him to wait until she has left the room.

A few seconds later York replies to his earlier question. "Indeed young man, I know exactly what our landlord is like. He has precisely the same make up as the others whose company Raeni liked to frequent, and to answer the other part of your question, that is my intention, to annoy him sufficiently for her to appear."

"Bloody hell Mr Dawson," Marcus exclaims, "you wouldn't like to give us some warning before you instigate this plan of yours, because personally, I really don't wish to be around. All this mystic stuff scares the hell out of me."

Tom smiles, adding, "Please don't worry too much. Raeni will only be interested in Alex and York, Alex, because she will wish to protect him and York because he is her chief threat. The rest of us are superfluous to her interests."

"That's what worries me, the rest of us are simply collateral damage, that's brilliant."

"Protect Alex from what exactly?" Criss questions him.

"That young lady is a question that I cannot easily answer. I am not entirely sure why she chooses to defend the people who she does or how she chooses her subjects, but as I said earlier, the individuals always have a similar temperament."

There are smiles around the room and York tucks into his bacon sandwiches with relish.

The morning moves on, with both Anne and Alex ensuring that everything is battened down in preparation for the pending snowstorm. The radio is full of warnings and the television has so much interference that it is pretty impossible to watch.

Alex has lit the fire and ventured outside to bring in some more logs, which he has stacked up in the huge fire place at the back of the bar. This fireplace is no longer functional but is utilised for stacking wood, enabling it to dry out before being burned. Marcus has been helping him while Criss has accompanied Anne, a friendship building there, as the two of them dig in to the kitchen chores together.

As the time approaches midday, so the snow begins to fall again, just a gentle sprinkling at first but constant in its downfall.

Inside the Christmas scene the occupants can hear the distant voices in the bar, allowing them to conclude that the lights will be turned on soon. The work on expanding the hole has gone well. The smaller built men should now be able to crawl through it easily. Work has currently ceased and the girls are back inside the model. Everyone is gathered around Duncan and Gary who are eagerly awaiting the return of the power to see if their efforts will bear fruit.

The cats, sensing that something is imminent, have taken themselves back out through the hole to the far end of the display, intently watching the goings on in the bar.

Duncan is completing a final check of the wiring to the laptops battery, careful not to touch anything in case the power should begin to surge through the apparatus. Gary is poised to start up the machine the minute that the battery affords him the power to do so, hoping that he can then send emails to anyone who he thinks will actually be broad minded enough to take him seriously and therefore potentially come to their aid. The first one he plans to send is to The Bell Inn itself and the second one, to his station.

Suddenly the lights burst into action. A crackling can be heard from the adaptation in the wiring, causing Duncan to cower away momentarily seeking safety, but on second glance he perceives there to be no visible signs of a problem. Everyone watches as he presses the 'on button' and the laptop begins performing its start up menu. Only half the screen springs into life, but it is enough for them to see that the machine is attempting to work. After a couple of minutes, the main program screen is partially loaded and Gary clicks on his email browser. Having only part of the screen to work with hampers him a little, not being able to see all the necessary icons, but he does eventually manage to negotiate his way around from memory and open the relevant program. Immediately, he types a brief message, explaining where they are and what they consider their dilemma to be.

Meanwhile Michael instructs both Canning and Dan to continue with their work on the hole. Julie and Tara hear his instruction and without being invited, they clamber back through to help the lads from outside. Their efforts are now amplified, working twice as fast as before with a renewed urgency in every movement they make.

Meanwhile, back in the pub and having turned on all the lights except for those above the canopy, Alex heads for the front door to open up the premises. Tom and York are still in the bar and Alex passes Isme, Judith and Jill entering the room, presumably going to join them.

Suddenly the canopy lights, which Alex has not yet plugged back in, burst forth into life. York immediately raises his eyes to the display, while his left hand dives deep into his pocket for the protection of the amulet. Tom remains glued to his seat. He glances over to York, sees what his hand is clasping, before glancing calmly back towards the lights. Isme immediately pushes the two girls back out of the door and into the hall for their own protection.

As Alex re-enters the hall he sees that Judith and Jill are being held back from entering the room. He breaks into a trot and heads straight for the bar. Gazing into the room, he observes York and Tom deep in concentration, not even blinking.

"What's going on?" he urgently asks.

"Your canopy lights seem to have woken up," Tom replies.

"Bollocks, they're not even plugged in," Alex gruntingly explains.

"That's exactly the point that he's making," York concludes. "Now, please be silent if you would, we need to concentrate."

Alex grimaces at the tone of his command, takes a step away and leans against the back of the bar where the optics are displayed, watching the room in front of him subtly change its brightness.

The tiny lights flicker away with a regular pulse then abruptly they flare into an intensely bright red light. Their radiance is blinding. York and Tom calmly remove their sun glasses from their right hand pockets and in unison, place them on.

Gary's head spins around as he hears a distant hissing noise. Duncan seeing his reaction, cups his hand to his ear attempting to raise his audible awareness to ascertain what he is hearing.

The next person to acknowledge the sound is Tara, who forces her head forward, through the hole, her head tilted to one side to push one ear further forward. Julie stops work and remains perfectly still and silent, a fear welling up inside her.

Whoever was next to realise what was happening, is irrelevant, because before long they all become aware of the ground trembling and in turn, they cease whatever they are doing to look down.

Michael glances over to Gary, calmly but urgently enquiring, "How far have you got?"

"Two emails have gone, that's it so far," he replies.

"It will have to be enough for the moment. I think we have company on the way." Michael then turns to everyone else in the room and orders them, "Right, everyone out. We will all meet back at the church!" as he strides off.

Within a split second, each and every one of them drops the tools they were using and they hurriedly disappear out of various exits.

Dan is the last one to leave, after ensuring that all the others have left the room. Turning to go, he finds he is unable to move his legs and he stumbles to the floor. He tries yelling out for help, but of course in his present mute condition, nothing comes out. The hissing sound has increased its volume to become an ear piercing pitch. Locating its origins to be outside the building, he labours in an attempt to drag his body across the floor and towards the nearest exit.

Suddenly, he feels something grab him from around the back of his head, so sharply that he lurches forward, his head connecting with the cold floor. He is thrown bodily across the room, hitting the opposite wall with extreme force. His body slumps to the floor, for a short while not moving, before he musters the strength to lift his head and stare at his attacker.

The being in front of him appears to be enormous, its skeleton clearly visible. There is a skin like substance stretched across its frame, but it appears to be transparent.

The head is bald. The face is without a nose, lips or ears, just sunken areas where these features should be. The eyes are piercing, but with no pupils, just a mass of bloodshot white that bulges from the sockets. The torso is lithe, the muscle tissue pronounced, with the ribs almost bursting through the fabric which is holding everything else in place. The arms and legs are scrawny and the fingers and toes resemble elongated twigs with claws at their extremities.

The spectre begins to move towards him, not walking, but gliding, as if sliding on a rail. Dan still dazed but with an overwhelming need to survive, attempts to drag himself away from it towards an exit, while knowing deep inside that his efforts will be futile. Immediately the apparition is above him, once more clutching him around the neck, but this time lifting him from the ground and staring down into his face.

"Put him down you bastard!" Canning yells from one of the doorways.

The spectre drops him and slowly and menacingly turns its head to face the new intruder.

"Raeni, you may call me by my birth name, not that it will remain in your brain for long as I intend to destroy you for your impudence."

"Yeah?" Canning snears back with bravado, "and what impudence would that be?"

"I have tolerated you for long enough, allowing you to reside within the safety of this domain, constantly trying my patience."

"What the hell are you talking about?" Michael yells from the opposite doorway.

Her head spins around with this latest interruption.

"You presumptuous bitch, you abduct various people and expect a certain loyalty and understanding?"

"SILENCE!" she screams, "you are surplus to my wards requirements. His heart was not to kill you, so I allowed his compassion to influence me. I now clearly see my mistake."

Suddenly, the laptop disintegrates into a thousand pieces, exploding across the room and within the blink of an eye, the wires return to their previous state and the hole is no longer, without even the light which once issued from the original pin prick.

Michael and Canning take cover from the flying debris, shielding their eyes. When the commotion ceases they see that Raeni has gone, or at least is no longer visible. Initially, Canning begins to enter the room, but stops short as Michael gestures him with his hand to remain still. Both men, slowly and methodically survey the entire room, their bodies as still as painted statues, the only moving part being their heads, as their visual sweep takes place.

Canning, having taken the time to scrutinise the room twice, finally steps into the doorway, with his feet past the threshold, but his torso and head remain between rooms. Michael is still examining the area, unaware that he has ventured inside. As he spots him and their eyes meet, the hissing resumes and Michael sees a blur moving rapidly across the room. Before he can yell out a warning, the frame of the doorway is shunted inwards, the plastic cracking and splitting as it is forced into its new position. Canning, on hearing the noise, rapidly tries to reverse his progress into the room but is caught by the imploding structure, his body crushed by the action. His arms reach out, his legs buckle and his face distorts, as the life is squeezed from him, he doesn't utter a word, just a groan, then a final exhalation.

Michael and Clive make their way across, dropping to their knees they stare down at the dead man in front of them.

A menacing chuckle can be heard, followed by a deep, gruff voice stating, "Just a small lesson for you all to LEARN!"

Michael slumps against the wall. "My God, this is not what I wanted to happen."

Clive, eyes welling up with tears says, "Nope, none of us did, but it wasn't anyone's fault, we're playing a dangerous game here and we ain't finished yet."

Michael turns his attention towards Dan. He slowly and dejectedly walks over to him, expecting to find the worst. To all appearances, Dan's body is lying awkwardly on the ground, supposedly lifeless, but then a voice comes forth, "He saved my life, he took what was about to happen to me."

"Dan, is that you?" Michael says softly. "You seem to have regained your voice."

Dan slowly, and by the look on his face, painfully, drags himself up into a sitting position, utilising the wall next to him for support. "Yes, so it appears." His eyes gaze upon the bloodstained and distorted body of Canning and he adds, "You know what, I had him pegged as a complete idiot, instead, he was a very brave man, I couldn't have been more wrong could I? He picked a fight with something he couldn't possibly win, in an effort to draw attention away from me. By God, I was so wrong about him."

Michael nods, his lips squeezed tightly together. "You were not the only one, his actions proved us all wrong." Then he adds, glancing back to where the dead body lays, saying "Can you get up, do you think you can walk? His bravery must not be in vain."

Clive gently closes the gawping eyes of the dead man and assists Dan back to his feet. "Right boss, what's next? We need to get things going again, direction, let's hear some orders from you."

Michael falters for a second, his gaze still fixed upon the dead man. "Orders, hum, I would like to say that would be a burial detail but obviously that is not practical or even possible here. The others should be back at the church by now, so that is where we will head and by the time we get there, I will have had time to think on our next step."

"Is anything going to happen?" Alex questions after ten minutes of nothing occurring.

The canopy lights abruptly extinguish, there total lack of action now very prominent.

"I think it already has," York comments.

Alex glances left and right, then focuses again on York. "Well, I must have missed it. Anyone here see a show of our resident ghoul?"

York leaps from his seat and agitated, he responds with, "Just because the village landlord was not granted a direct visual audience with the turn of events stipulated by the other side, does not mean that it didn't happen."

"What?" Alex exclaims, "What the hell is that supposed to mean?"

Tom calmly rises from his seat, ambles to the bar and explains, "Whatever Raeni was doing, and she was doing something, it was not in here this time. She obviously had business somewhere else."

Isme, who has now entered the bar with the two women, immediately looks across to the Christmas scene. "In there York, do you think it was in there?"

"That's exactly where I think she was. She is not ready for me yet and if there is another domain in which she can flex her muscles safely, it will be in there."

Jill walks over to the display, placing her hands upon it and whispering, "Be safe my love, it won't be long now."

Anne walks through the bar to the window and blankly stares out. "The snow is falling more heavily now, we need to be ready." She simply turns and leaves the room.

CHAPTER TWENTYTHREE

The lunchtime session is steaming, with locals swarming to the pub for a pre- Christmas drink. Alex and Anne are well prepared for this onslaught, having suffered the barrage in previous years, with Fleche, Nancy and Jack, all on duty, ready and waiting.

The weather slowly but surely, severely increases. The winds pick up and the huge, white flakes of snow fall heavier and faster with every hour that passes. At various intervals, people venture out of the front door to check on the conditions, others merely observe its beauty from the comfort of the window.

There is a buzz of excitement in the pub, not only because of the pending holiday, but also because of the bizarre weather. This winter has shown that, the so called 'global warming', is much colder than any expert had predicted it to be, with a December that has so far broken all the records with regards to the volume of snow and its low temperatures.

The residents of The Bell Inn, including Alex and Anne, are feeling apprehensive, aware that everything will reach a head in the next few hours if York Dawson is correct in his assumption, and he seems to be pretty certain of that.

At this moment in time, the man in question is not in the bar. Immediately after the last light show, he took himself upstairs to his room, disappearing without a word. Tom didn't accompany him but joined Isme and crew, who deposited themselves in the far corner of the bar in their usual seats.

Criss and Marcus, despite being tired due to their all night guard duty, are still standing at the far end of the bar, the furthest point from the piano and the Christmas scene.

All of the main players in this somewhat unusual scenario keep casting each other shy sideways glances, attempting not to make full eye contact. Even those on the sidelines, the ones who have witnessed or discussed the goings on, sit or stand pensively feeling that something is afoot. It seems to be Alex who everyone is watching the most, a set of eyes resting on him nearly all the time by someone or other in the room.

Alex can sense this and it makes him feel uneasy. In turn, he glances around to see who has their eyes on him, a deep feeling of paranoia taking place within him.

Being Christmas Eve the bar will not close for its usual afternoon period, the premises will stay open until shortly after midnight to see the Christmas Day in. The staff are all sent home at three in the afternoon aware that they have to return by six that evening. As they leave, the weather outside has turned somewhat wild, with the wind whipping up eddies and the snow forced to drift in its many different directions. They put their winter coats on, pull up their hoods, wrap their scarf's around their necks, don their gloves and brave the elements, all three of them setting off in the same direction, up through the village, away from the square. Anne sees them out making sure the inner door is closed after them, as the weather is battering away at the front of the building and forcing the door to stay slightly ajar.

The kitchens, although not completely closed, are now functioning in a low key mode, just sandwiches and burgers are available until the evening, with most people in the bar having already eaten.

Although now only half full, the locals are mumbling, a little concerned at how bad the weather conditions are getting and whether they should make an early move home, all except for John and Rob that is. John remains forever nonchalant regarding the weather thing and Rob, has no intention of missing the final outcome of the Raeni business come hell or high water.

Slowly but surely, the locals begin to leave, some saying they will return later if the weather calms, others wishing everyone a merry Christmas before taking their leave. Alex sees them all off in turn, finally returning to the bar and the remaining residents, plus the inevitable John and Rob.

"Well ladies and gentlemen. It seems that it is down to us to see the big day in," he announces.

There are a few smiles around the bar, with Isme and table, raising their glasses to toast his sentiment.

"Bunch of sissies," John moans, "No sense of adventure, none of them."

"Oh John, you are a cynic. They have families and children, they should be at home on Christmas Eve," Anne defends.

"I have a family too," John protests.

"Your kids left home years ago and your wife doesn't give a toss where you are, you old fool," Alex informs.

"That's a bit harsh," Rob says.

"It's the bloody truth though," Alex replies.

"Well who can blame her," John concurs. "She wanted Christmas in Yorkshire and I didn't want to go. I can't understand those northern people and its bloody cold up there too."

"It's bloody cold down here, in case you hadn't noticed?" Rob jibes.

"True," he concurs, "But at least here, I can shiver and understand what's being said when people talk to me."

"I've got to agree with John, that's a definite positive there," Alex giggles.

Laughing erupts around the bar, then slowly, as all eyes turn towards the bar door, their tittering abruptly ceases.

"Joviality, what a wonderful concept," York Dawson smilingly states, "One I highly recommend, when business is completed that is."

Alex slowly turns, "Oh, Mr Dawson, how nice of you to join us in our celebrations."

"Celebrations," he retorts, "They are something that will happen later, perhaps tomorrow, if, all goes well."

All eyes are upon him, Alex clearly showing his disdain asks, "Go well? Well if you say so. Bloody hell, so far all you have shown us is a limp wristed fiasco."

York smiles his wry little grin. "Oh landlord, my dear old chap, a man of your intellect could have no concept of the reality of this situation. But never mind, let us listen to you, I am sure you have the insight with which to enlighten all of us."

Alex's eyes narrow, his demeanour altering by the second. He walks out of the main room and re-emerges behind the bar. He places both his hands on the wooden counter and stares hard at York. "You sunshine, even with your damn body guard there, should be careful," he warns, "My tolerance levels only stretch so far."

"Really," York immediately retorts, "Like an old rubber band you mean, one is never sure when it will finally snap."

Alex's eyes begin to glaze, "Something like that mate."

York slumps into one of the chairs, where he continues to taunt. "Well, are you not sure man? A simple yes or no would have sufficed, but no, you just grunt a maybe. How pathetic is that."

Rob and John stare at him wide eyed in disbelief, knowing that Alex is definitely not renowned for his tolerance.

"Come on York, let's not become insulting here," Rob says trying to calm the situation.

York's attention slowly turns towards Rob and he replies, "Oh please be quiet fat boy, there is no defence for a landlord with a personality and basic intellect deficiency."

Anne walks to the centre of the room and with her arms firmly crossed she forcefully states, "Ok that's enough. The bar is now closed, so please all of you leave."

"Oh do shut up woman, you're as bad as the fat boy there, trying to defend that idiot of yours," York continues with his attack.

"Shut your mouth asshole," Alex seethes.

"Oh bugger off you plebiscite," York off handily replies, not even bothering to look at him.

"Plebiscite?" Rob exclaims quietly, "What's he talking about now?"

John, on hearing him, eyebrows raised, replies, "A plebiscite is a word from the Roman era, signifying the masses."

Rob slowly turns to look at him. "I know that, but most people would have simply used the word plebe."

"Oh, I see, yeah you're right, what an ignorant twit," he shrugs, sipping his beer.

Rob's face displays his perplexity regarding this aggressive and limited conversation.

Alex clears the bar in one enormous leap, landing on the carpet with a heavy thud and his fists clenched. Anne instantly steps in front of him, barring his way towards York.

"Oh let him come," York goads him.

Alex, now furious, gently moves his wife aside, ensuring that she is completely clear of the direction in which he intends to go. By now, everyone in the room has their eyes fixed on Tom, aware that he is York's physical protection and will have to intervene before long.

When Alex has placed Anne to one side, he starts to pace menacingly forward, his gaze firmly fixed on York. Suddenly, Tom is out of his seat and moving to intercept Alex. In the blink of an eye, Tom, having received sharp blows to his windpipe, abdomen and back of his neck, slumps to the floor with a low groaning noise. Alex steps across him and continues in the direction of York, who on noting the speed in which Tom dropped to the floor, immediately slips his right hand into his trouser pocket, taking a firm hold of a cosh which he has previously secreted there.

"Oh bravo landlord, your brawn is far superior to your brains I see."

By now Alex is upon him. He grabs him by the lapels of his jacket and with one swift movement yanks him firmly out of his seat. "You are a rude, mouthy little man and I want you and your boy gone from here now!"

As he begins to lift him bodily from the ground, York produces the cosh and crashes it into Alex's head, hitting him just above the temple. Alex releases his grip, letting him go, as he reels backwards, clasping his head in his hands. He drops to one knee and shakes his head, a trickle of blood issuing from a small wound. York also staggers backwards, visually shocked by what he has just done, disgustedly dropping the weapon to the floor.

When Michael, Dan and Clive arrive at the church, everyone, including the cats, are already there awaiting their arrival. Within seconds questions are asked as to Canning's whereabouts. Dan relates the tale and the full horror etches itself on their faces.

Michael waits until the account is concluded before snapping out his orders. "Right, let's get two of you up that tower and recommence the work."

For a brief moment there is only silence, as they digest everything they have just been told then they hear nothing but the orders. Both Julie and Tara immediately walk to the foot of the tower, gaze up at it and like robots they begin their assent. Charlie the cat watches the activity and within seconds is following up behind them, with considerably less effort than theirs. Ellie and Bobs watch as Charlie passes the two girls and then as if he has silently beckoned to them, they follow his tracks up towards the top of the tower. By the time the girls are two thirds of the way up the structure, the three cats are waiting at the hole. Ellie is the first to test the orifice and she passes straight through, immediately the other two follow and vanish from view. Michael smiles knowing that they will be off, exploring their way around, hopefully safely. Finely the girls reach the top and start work immediately, but this time ripping at the hole without restraint.

"Shouldn't we put out some lookouts Michael?" Paul asks with worried urgency in his voice.

"There's no point now. I think we all know that this is going to be our last chance to get out of here, so we might as well all stand together. We will have more chance in numbers now, caution at this point is to the wind," he calmly replies.

Suddenly, a big piece of plastic is torn from the hole in the roof. Unaided it falls to the ground, causing an echo that resonates throughout the whole model village.

Everyone stops, holding their breath, hoping that it hasn't been overheard, a naivety that none of them really believe. Heads slowly move from left to right, all eyes scanning the room which they are in, waiting for what might happen next.

Clive begins to back up. Everyone cranes their heads to adapt their view to match his, attempting to see what he is staring at. The back wall of the church is beginning to bulge inwards, stretching like a polythene bag as it is forced to expand. When reality dawns, they all start to back away. Michael glances up and gestures to the girls to remain perfectly still.

The wall reaches a pitch as two eyes become visible, glaring left and right into the room. Slowly, the head pushes its way through, followed by the shoulders and arms, then the torso, the hips and finally the legs and feet.

Raeni, who is now completely inside the small room, is crouched, her head bowed down, her hands on the floor. She gradually raises her head and stares at the occupants through a furrowed brow. She emits a faint hissing sound as she slowly begins to straighten her body up.

"Everyone remain completely still. Do not do a thing until I say so, then all of you attack together," Michael orders them. He watches for everyone to acknowledge, which they do with nervous hesitation.

Raeni moves very deliberately, only briefly stopping as she inspects the tower, staring up towards the top of it. Her hissing increases in volume. She stares directly into Michaels eyes, a definite sneer stretching across her face. She takes one further pace forward then stops again, as she takes a second look at the tower. Her left arm springs out towards one of the many pieces which form the base structure as she tears it away, flinging it towards Michael. Instantly Gary is across the room to where Michael is standing, intercepting the projectile with amazing accuracy, deflecting it away from him. Again, Raeni hisses, this time her animosity is shared between the two men.

Suddenly, her attention is drawn to the nervous little whimper that emits from the dizzy heights of the church tower which is now violently juddering with its missing spoke. Raeni, now aware that there is someone aloft of the tower, sports a wry grin across her face. She turns and takes a step towards it, placing her huge hands squarely on the structure.

"NOO..NOO..NOO!" echo the screams from the structures apex as Raeni begins to dismantle the lower part of it with apparent glee.

"NOW!" Michael yells out as he strides towards the hideous vision.

Duncan, Gary and Clive instantly react to his command, while Dan and Paul fearfully appear somewhat more hesitant.

Clive is the first one in, using his large frame and big shoulders to deliver powerful blows into the back of Raeni. Each punch and thump that connects makes a squelching sound, with pinkish coloured substance oozing from every point of impact.

Gary and Dan launch themselves upon her. Dan jumps up and grasps her around the neck, yanking her head violently backwards. Gary, like Clive, uses his fists to fight, plus his feet, which are rapidly kicking at the figure.

Finally, Michael enters the affray, with Paul and Dan reluctantly joining in at almost exactly the same time. Raeni's limbs are grabbed, pulled both left and right, all five of them trying to force her away from the now endangered structure.

Suddenly, she turns on her attackers, tossing them off one at a time, like fleas being thrown from a cat. Finally she deals with Clive, who regardless of the demise of his friends remains lashing away at her with all his might. Raeni takes hold of his legs and pulling him off his feet, she holds him up, dangling him in the air while he still attempts to hit out at her. She holds him away at arm's length and violently tosses him into the tower. He hits it with a deafening thud. Picking him up yet again, Raeni holds him up, this time staring at his limp body before finally discarding it, flinging his blood covered remains across the room. It finally comes to rest in the far corner of the room, lifeless.

Gary, completely dazed, clambers back onto his legs, his teeth grinding with the anger building within him. Dan, who landed next to him, nudges him away and begins his way forward for another attack as Gary follows him.

Paul, having regained his senses, goes over to help Michael, who is struggling greatly, having hit the wall halfway up and slumped to the floor in total disarray.

Raeni immediately turns to face this second attack, causing both Gary and Dan to reconsider their approach. They split up, widening the gap between them, forcing her to turn her head in order to see either one of them. She begins a slow, whispering hiss as she apprehends the tactics of her foes, her volume increasing in strength.

Abruptly her noise ceases. Her bodily stance becomes upright and tense, her focus appearing elsewhere, no longer on those present in the room with her, but somewhere else all together. Her head drops forward and slowly swings from left to right. Finally it flips up, her eyes bright red. Dan and Gary back away as quickly as they can, but then, instead of the attack they expected, she turns, dashes towards the opposite wall, crashes through it and within an instant, she is gone.

Totally perplexed, Gary glances around him before moving. Finally, his gaze falls on Clive's limp body on the far side of the church. Again he scans the room for any signs of danger then makes his way over to him. He crouches down and checks for any signs of a pulse. Tight lipped, he turns to the others, who are now all gathered around and he shakes his head, signifying that the man is dead.

"Are you two ok up there?" Paul calls out to the girls.

A tearful, frightened reply comes back, "I think so."

"Can you carry on working, or is there anything up there that should now stop you?" Michael calls up.

"We can keep going," Tara shakily calls down.

"Then get to it girls," Michael orders them emphatically.

"Where did that ghost go to? Did we manage to scare it off?" Dan enquires, anxiously looking around the church.

"Yeah right mate, did you see her eyes? I don't think for one minute we were any threat to her," Gary comments

"I do not know exactly what happened there," Michael replies scratching his chin, "But I did note that she suddenly appeared to have urgent business to attend to somewhere else. The upside is that we now have a new window in which to work, undisturbed. Besides as she is no longer prepared to tolerate us, we have nothing to lose, so let's just go for it and see if we can get out of here."

With eager nods all around, they begin gathering up the debris of the tower to reinforce it.

"You bastard," Alex grunts, his muzzy gaze lifting to a shocked York. "So you want to play do you sunshine? Then that is exactly what we will do."

Anne dashes over to Alex and begins to dab his head wound with a bar towel, nervously chattering to him in an effort to calm him down. Again, he gently moves her aside, clearing his path towards York.

Suddenly, the fire roars into life with the flames leaping not only up the chimney but spilling out from the front of the hearth and into the room, some of them reaching across to the opposite wall. To the mesmerised occupants in the room, the flames appear to creep slowly forward, each lick of fire eerily dancing past their eyes. They strangely avoid Alex who is directly in their path, parting and surrounding him but never touching him. Initially, everyone cowers away from the rampant and seemingly uncontrolled flames, but as the abnormality continues, all eyes remain fixed but without fear.

Then an image begins to form. Firstly a face, followed by the torso, shoulders and arms and finally the legs and feet. Raeni has entered the arena. Her image is aglow, small chards of flame surround her whole being, dancing and caressing her body, as if adoring her very essence. She floats over to Alex and drapes her arms around him, embracing him without his knowledge.

York glances down at Tom, who is still unconscious on the floor, then glares at the spectacle before him. He reaches into his pocket, scrambling for the bone relic, his fingers fumbling to produce the item.

Alex, now securely in the clinch of Raeni, seems to be in a trance, swaying with her movements, his head lolling from one side to another.

Anne cowers away, stumbling and falling to the floor, frightened by both the apparition and the concept of the fire with its licking flames. Criss leaps across the room, grabbing hold of her, ushering her to safety in another room.

Raeni's head turns menacingly from left to right. Her eyes are glowing intensely with various shades of colour, tiny conflagrations issuing from her body, dancing with her every movement.

Finally her gaze rests on York and she emits a gurgled hiss to show her intense displeasure. He tears his fumbling hand from his pocket firmly clutching the relic and thrusts it forward, holding it out directly in front of her. Her hiss ceases as she bursts forth with shrill and piercing laughter, throwing her head backwards in glee. Then it jerks forward, her neck extending until it is only inches away from the object. In the same movement, her left arm swings through the air, smashing into York's arm and knocking the relic from his grip, causing it to ricochet off the wall and land at the foot of the bar. York staggers back from the blow, gasping, clasping his forearm, the collision obviously causing him severe pain.

To everyone's amazement, Rob jumps down from his bar stool and marches over to York, helping him to steady himself. He then turns to Raeni and bellows, "You bitch, pick on someone your own size!" Then he adds a little more nervously, "And you shouldn't come blustering into the room, especially down the chimney, without an invitation."

John starts laughing at the absurdity of it all but rapidly curtails it when he receives a sharp dig in the ribs from Marcus.

"Who and what are you?" Raeni seethes.

Rob, taken aback by this question, utters, "Me, me... I'm just a local who doesn't like bullies."

On his last word, Rob feels an excruciating pain across his face, as she lashes out at him ordering, "Be gone!"

He totters sideways from her power, stumbling into the table which Isme and the ladies are still sat around, flattening the structure until both the table and Rob are strewn on the carpet. Judith, Jill and Isme jump to their feet, stepping back as Rob crashes to the floor. John is off his stool in a flash and both Marcus and Criss move aggressively forwards. Alex, still surrounded by Raeni's caressing arms, seems oblivious to what is happening, gently rolling with her motions. York, sliding along the wall, attempts to sidle out of the bar, his head lowered, hoping that he can't be seen. Anne, now stood at the door to the rear of the bar, watches, terrified at what she is witnessing.

CHAPTER TWENTYFOUR

"One of the girls has managed to get through boss!" Paul yells down to the others below.

Michael looks up to where he is perched, about halfway up the tower and yells back, "Then get up there and take her place!"

Paul immediately begins the precarious climb upwards.

Michael glances around at the others who are still on the ground and stops at Dan. "Up you go lad. Settle where Paul was and wait till the other lass is out, then let us know and take her place with Paul."

He nods, slowly looks at the tower, gulps and makes his way to the base. By now, the damage Raeni had caused has been repaired. He begins his ascent, stopping every few feet, nervously glancing back down.

"Don't look down mate, only up!" Gary calls out, "Believe me, it's safer."

Dan nods and carries on. Although his progress is slow, he eventually reaches Pauls previous position. He lingers only briefly before continuing on up. It's then that he yells down, "That's both the girls out now!"

Michael then looks across to Duncan, gesturing for him to be the next one up.

"Bollocks to that Michael. We need to get you up there, so we'll go up together."

Gary smiles, adding, "You know it make sense. I'll hold the fort down here."

Michael deeply sighs, reluctantly nods and begins his way to the base of the tower. Duncan follows him. Michael starts to make his way up, every step a huge effort, his age and lack of dexterity hampering his movements. Duncan climbs directly behind him, supporting his weight every time he falters.

It takes some time, but eventually, both men reach the staging point, gazing aloft at Paul and Dan who remain grafting away at the hole, with the girls now assisting from the outside.

Marcus launches himself at Raeni, who nonchalantly responds by grabbing him around the throat in mid flight and holding him out at arm's length, not even bothering to acknowledge him. John is the second one in, drawing his chunky fist back, preparing to land the heaviest punch that he can muster. As he throws the potential 'haymaker', Raeni, using the arm that is currently caressing Alex, parries his blow, deflecting its force sideways. John careers across the room, the momentum of his punch carrying him across to the window. He crashes into it, smashing one of the glass panes. Snow billows its way through the aperture, spraying into the room with the force of the wind behind it.

Alex, limply slumps to the floor, appearing unconscious, rolling away from Raeni, only stopping as his limp body connects with the base of the bar. Anne immediately runs to his aid, throwing herself down to protect him, his lifeless body lying face down on the floor. Covering him, she attempts to shield him from further danger.

Isme jumps at Raeni's back, clasping his arms around her neck. Criss dives across the room, leaping low, grabbing her below the waist, forcing her to readjust her stance in order to remain standing. Judith and Jill make their way around the room, rushing past the open fire to take refuge in the other room.

Raeni, throughout this onslaught, focuses her attention on York, who at this point has almost managed to leave the room. She shrugs off her aggressors in one swift, but effective movement and in an instant, firmly places herself between York and his final retreat.

Isme lands halfway in the fire grate, pulling himself out and brushing himself down, his trousers sizzling where the hot embers had already taken hold. John, still reeling from his collision with the window, totters back into the centre of the bar, fists clenched, aimlessly looking for a target to hit. Criss, observing John's behaviour, attempts to avoid him, to gather herself together at the bar. Rob, back on his feet, backs away into the corner and adopts a crouching position, holding his hands across his eyes, not wanting to witness anymore of the violence.

Alex's eyes strain open at his restriction, not realising that Anne is lying directly over him.

"Do you want to get off me?" he grunts.

A smile flickers across her face, "Thank god you're back," she happily whispers, carefully getting up and freeing his body.

When he sees that she was the one holding him down, he smiles and places his hand on the side of her face, saying, "I don't know about you, but I've had enough of all this crap?"

She manages an apprehensive smile and watches as he pulls himself to his feet and adjusts his clothing, tucking his shirt back in to his trousers.

Raeni, in the meantime, takes hold of York, who swings aimless punches at her as she tosses him diagonally across the room. He comes to rest at the base of the piano with a hefty jolt.

"Come on up Gary," Duncan calls down, "I think we're through!"

Gary doesn't need telling twice. He's been feeling pretty vulnerable ever since he was the only one left at ground level. He urgently makes his way to the base of the tower and begins climbing.

Paul clambers through the hole and joins Tara and Julie. Dan makes his way down to help assist Michael on his way up.

The task of getting everyone aloft is a lengthy one, with Michael struggling to keep going, but with Gary, Duncan and Dan urging and helping him the entire way up. Finally, they reach the summit. Dan is first through, followed by

Michael, who is pushed and pulled, then Duncan and ultimately, Gary.

Outside, they find themselves perched awkwardly on the steep pitch of a roof with plastic imitation tiles adorned with blobs of white, intended to represent snow. They can see the cats below, curled up as if waiting for the others to reach them, seemingly bored with the whole business.

On his first attempt at rising, Alex falters and drops down on to one knee, placing his left hand to the floor to gain some stability. He lowers his head and then shakes it, looking through his eyebrows at the scene in front of him. As he tries to pull himself to his feet, his left hand brushes over something on the floor which catches his attention. He stares down at it, soon realising that the object is the relic that York placed so much trust in. He gathers it up and places it in his breast pocket, patting the pocket after releasing the bone, to make sure it has come to rest at the bottom and won't fall out.

With the help of Anne, he regains his feet and rests back against the bar, his gaze never leaving Raeni, who by now has fought off her attackers with ease and is turning her attention back towards Alex, her eyes radiant.

Judith and Jill have entered the bar again but only as far as the piano, to check on York, pulling him into the back area of the bar and out of the fray. He has a sharp gash down his face and the girls immediately tend to the wound, placing serviettes over it and applying pressure.

John, realising that his support has diminished somewhat, assists Rob from the corner where he is crouched and leads him to the bar where Criss, Alex and Anne are now stood.

By now Raeni is squarely facing Alex, her outstretched arms beckoning him to come to her, her whole demeanour displaying undisguised affection towards him. Initially he doesn't move but as he makes direct eye contact with her, he finds himself struggling to ignore her demands. Although his feet remain static, the top half of his body starts to lean in her direction. Anne labours to force him away from her. Criss watching her struggle, attempts to aid her restraint.

With their backs towards Raeni, they hear her begin to hiss as before, aware that this is a warning sign of her growing agitation. Anne swings around to face her, slumping her whole weight back onto Alex and she screams, "Get away from him you bitch!"

John disappears into the back bar to find York, insisting, "What the hell are you doing back here? I thought you were the world renowned ghost killer?"

York, who is still being nursed by Jill replies, "What am I supposed to fight with? I have lost the relic. I have no defence against her now."

"Damn it man, neither have the rest of us, but we are still having a go. Besides, I don't think this bitch is going to simply piss off, we have to do something about her."

York's head snaps around to face him. "Do you not understand? This spirit is dancing between the two worlds, our reality and hers. We are no match for her without tools from her life and the only one we had, is now gone, somewhere in that room."

"Then we need to find it," John emphatically states, turning to re enter the bar.

As he enters, Raeni immediately moves one of her eyes to watch him, the other one stays firmly fixed on Alex. John, aware he is being watched, nonchalantly slumps his bottom down on the piano lid, affording him a pretty good view of most of the room. He slowly and methodically begins to scan the floor, trying to see into the corners.

Observing that everyone is now motionless, Raeni applies her complete attention to Anne. "He is not yours, move away from him and let him come to me," she hisses.

"Over my dead body!" Anne screams back at her.

Raeni lets out a blood curdling laugh and replies, "Very well, if you insist. That will not be a problem."

Suddenly, an outstretched arm and hand wrap their grip securely around Anne's neck, raising her up to Raeni's eye level. Anne, taken completely by surprise, doesn't even begin to struggle until she is firmly entrenched in Raeni's grip, then she lashes out like a woman possessed.

Marcus again attacks, followed by Criss and John. Rob is in the back room, making all the right motions as though about to join the fight, but without actually moving. Alex remains partially mesmerised, labouring with the effort of staying upright. Then Tom, who everybody thought was out for the count as he was still lying motionless on the floor, grabs hold of one of Raeni's legs, pulling it with all his young might. This latest attack seems to cause her a problem. With Marcus, John and Criss launching their bodies at her, while she is trying to hold on to Anne, and with Tom's assault on her legs, she appears to find it difficult to remain stable. The inevitable happens; she loses her balance and begins to totter, releasing Anne as she stumbles.

"She's going!" John yells out.

"Keep at her boys!" Criss shouts with excitement.

Suddenly, the church jolts. The cats are on their feet in a second, scampering off in different directions. The others, who were slowly making their way down the steep roof, now hang on to anything they can see to grasp hold of, hoping that this latest earthquake will cease pretty quickly.

Dan slides down and off the edge, out of view of the others. Gary has a firm hold of Michael, who is on his back, his legs dangling in the air, the only thing stopping him from falling, is the tight grip of the man above him.

The shaking stops as fast as it started. This is accompanied by loud sighs of relief from all around.

"Dan!" Julie calls out, "can you hear me, are you alright?"

There is a moment of silence before he replies, "I'm as good as gold. Luckily I landed on some white, soft cushioning."

Gary stabilises Michael and then makes his way over to where Dan fell from the roof. He cautiously peers over the precipice to see Gary sitting up against the brass hinge of the piano top, which is surrounded by cotton wool to create the effect of snow, with Charlie the cat perched on his lap.

"Are you comfortable down there?" he calls down laughing.

"Yep, I'm just waiting for you lot to catch up with me."

After a short while, everyone is perched on the edge, preparing to take the same plunge as that of Dan. One at a time they jump, until only Michael and Gary remain.

"Off you go," Michael orders, having watched all the others jump and walk away with no visible problems.

"Come on Michael, age before beauty, you go first."

Michael smiles and looks at him. "Gary, I cannot make this jump. You know I'm too old. I'm not sure these old bones would survive it."

"Then we go together and I'll break your fall."

"Young man, if we both jump, it will not be my fall that you will break but more than likely your neck."

"Look Michael," Gary assertively says, "We either go together or we both stay here and find another way out. It's your choice, so you call it. We don't want that lot down there sitting on their thumbs while we tart around up here scratching our arses. They could be in danger, shit, in fact so could we?"

Michael raises his eyebrows and replies, "How eloquently you put that. I don't seem to be able to find fault with your excellent evaluation of our current situation."

He suddenly launches himself from the roof. In the blink of an eye, Gary throws himself down to join him.

The second Michael hits the cotton wool, Dan and Julie leap on him to stop him bouncing around. Once he is steadied and with relief that he is in one piece, he coughs with the immortal words, "That's extremely exhilarating, even at my age, but could you possibly get off me, as I cannot breathe."

Laughter ensues, mainly for his humour, but also through relief that he has survived the fall.

"Yeah, I'm fine," Gary jokes as he bounces off the cotton wool and lands heavily on the wooden piano top. "Crap landing, but all's good."

Even Michael has to smile at this witticism. Abruptly Michael holds both his hands up beside his ears, an action that causes the others to fall silent, as they watch him listening to something. Then the sound becomes apparent to them all. They can hear voices and crashing noises, sounds they haven't witnessed for quite some time.

Instantly, Gary, holding and rubbing his back where he landed awkwardly says, "Come on boys and girls, I don't think we should dither around here much longer."

Michael nods in agreement and points their way down to the left. They have found themselves behind the model village scene and they need to reach one end or the other before they can decide on their next course of action.

Raeni finally crashes to the ground, but not before she and the others battling her, are all dragged through one of the solid wooden tables.

Alex sees Anne drop from her grip. He is quick to collect her up and take her to comparative safety, leaving her to the care of the other two women, he turns and strides back into the bar, back into the affray.

Now focused and without any influence from Raeni, Alex strides over to where the heap of bodies are rolling around fighting, to see Criss tossed out of the pile with force towards the ceiling before crashing into one of the walls. Next out is Tom, as she kicks out with her unhindered foot, catching the lad in the mouth and again causing him to flounder across the room, blood pouring from his facial wound. John, who is winded, crawls to a corner, clasping his chest and panting for breath.

York appears in the arch from the lounge and without delay rushes at Raeni, leaping at her, both feet off the ground, hitting her in the middle and again, forcing her to fall to the ground. While she is falling, she grabs him and pulls him right up to her face, snapping her teeth rapidly up and down. He endeavours, with all his might to keep her away, but after a couple of snaps of her razor sharp teeth, she makes contact and cuts through the side of his nostril. He reels with the pain, staggering away from the fight, only to feel another excruciating pain in his lower back, as she kicks out at him while screeching at the top of her voice.

Suddenly the canopy lights burst into action, their intense light completely filling the room and issuing out into the street with the brilliance. Marcus, who is now in the hall, having been previously thrown there by Raeni, is now on his feet and running back into the bar. He dodges the various bodies in his way, jumps up on to a stool, reaches for the string of bulbs and tears the lights from their securing clips, pulling the whole string down in one yank.

Having traversed the back of the village scene, Michael and his crew following the cats, arrive at the electrical extension leads where the sockets from the models are plugged in. They climb up, and for the first time they are able to see the bar and exactly what is happening within the room.

Raeni, standing directly in front of the fire, slowly turns her head towards the display, aware that they are free.

Isme also senses them but is unable to see what he feels is there. He begins to walk over. Instantly Raeni is stood in front of him, stating coldly, "I will get to them, when I have dealt with you."

Rob, now clasping an ornamental sword which he has removed from the wall, careers into the bar brandishing it around, swinging it to and fro and yelling, "You total bastard, LEAVE MY FRIENDS ALONE!"

Before Raeni can turn, he is upon her, ramming the blade into her chest, driving it in as far as his strength will allow.

"Shit, she knows we're out here," Paul realises.

"That was inevitable," Michael replies, "She was always going to know, it was only a matter of when."

"So what happens now?" Julie questions.

"Now, there's a question which was extremely well put and definitely deserves an answer," comes Michael's usual reply when he is not sure of the situation.

"And?" Gary asks with raised eyebrows.

"I do not have a clue," Michael simply responds, "Not a single clue as to what happens next. That my dear is anyone's guess."

"Oh great and there was me thinking we had a problem," Dan quips.

Gary, who has moved forward from the others, stares down from the top of the piano towards the keyboard cover and asks, "What would happen if I was to jump down there?"

Tara walks over to where he is and replies, "I think you would probably kill yourself. What do you think would happen?"

He turns to look at her, having gauged the drop before him and says, "I don't know, but it occurs to me, that somewhere along this journey, we have to return to the way we were and become normal again."

"It could be a messy way to find out," she states walking back to the others, adding, "Very messy."

Just then, Ellie the cat joins Gary. Like him, she gazes down and lets out a quiet meow before leaping from the top of the piano into the abyss. He tries to grab her before she goes but is too late and is left to watch her as she plunges down the huge drop before them. Just then, the other cats follow suit, leaping over the top of him and following her on her way down. To his astonishment, before his eyes they change, growing, manifesting back into cats of normal proportions.

"They must have known!" he yells back to the others.

"Know what?" Dan calls back.

"The cats, they're back to normal!"

These words echo around them, silence reigning for only a few seconds before Michael says exactly what they have all now surmised and are dreading, "That is the answer then, everyone over the side!" he orders.

"I knew he was going to say that," Tara sighs dejectedly.

Paul smiles, clambers to his feet, clasps her hand and with the others, they head for the edge of the piano top.

Raeni places both her hands on the blade to release it from her chest, as Rob tries desperately to push it in further. Having almost cleared the weapon from her body, she places one of her large hands on his head and begins to squeeze. Initially he doesn't seem to notice, intent on his task of shoving the blade back in, but as the pressure increases, he yelps as the delayed pain kicks in.

The first person to help him is Criss, leaping at Raeni's grasping hand, ripping at her fingers, trying to prize them away. Raeni uses her other hand to snap the sword in the middle, taking the top half of the blade and slamming it into Criss's shoulder. She lurches back with the pain, only stopping when she connects with the bar.

Rob, now buckling with the pain, pushes the remainder of the sword into the arm which is holding him, making her scream as the broken blade travels through her limb. Temporarily she releases her grip to swipe him around the head, sending him spinning across the room, finally slumping at the foot of the old wooden settle which adorns the wall closest to the entrance to the bar.

Suddenly, Raeni's head again spins around to face the Christmas Scene, but this time sporting concern across her facial features, which is recognised by all those consciously present in the room. Next, her eyes flicker to the canopy lights which Marcus is tearing to pieces and trampling on, frantically kicking the broken fragments of bulbs around the room, all life from them slowly ebbing away, as they finally extinguish, the heart torn from them.

Her attention is drawn back to the piano as Ellie materialises, followed closely by the other two cats. Her whole body becomes ridged and her head wrenches back as she screams out in rage, causing the room to shake with the force of her venom. She immediately strides towards the three animals which are now on the carpet, dazedly trying to ascertain their exact whereabouts. For them their animal instinct quickly prevails, not only as to where they are, but also as to their impending danger and within a split second, they are gone, out into the hall and up the stairs to safety.

John, bent forward but on his feet and still labouring with his breathing, staggers towards her. She is now craned over the piano, staring menacingly at the display. He crashes into her, pushing her forward into the models, causing them to dislodge and tumble from their perch on the top of the piano.

Dan, Michael, Gary, Julie, Tara and Paul stand looking down at the huge void before them, not wanting to undertake what they know in their hearts they have to do. Suddenly the decision is made for them, as a massive jolt, followed by the violent movement of the buildings behind them, leaves them with little choice. With the first shock, they clasp hold of each other to gain stability but as the structures begin to move and totter, ready to fall, they all know they have no choice but to jump.

Over the edge they go, holding hands, their eyes closed, inevitability filling their hearts with a paralysing dread.

CHAPTER TWENTYFIVE

Gary senses a gut wrenching pain in his stomach. To him, the fall appears to take place in slow motion and he seems to have time, not only to look down at where he might land, but also to observe the faces of the others. Pain causes him to wince and he releases his grip from the hand he is holding. Looking across at the others, he sees that he is not the only one experiencing this scenario. It seems that they have all released their grip of each other and are individually free falling. He begins to sense that his hands and forearms are undergoing some sort of change and glances down. To his astonishment, they are pulsating and expanding back to their original size and form.

Raeni and John roll along the piano before they finally crash to the floor, half in the bar and half in the lounge.

Alex wrenches the sword blade from Chris's shoulder while Anne presses bar towels firmly over the now open wound as she cries out in pain. Alex doesn't linger. Turning towards Raeni he brandishes the broken blade at her menacingly as he places his hand into his pocket to take hold of the relic, removing it and clasping it tightly. His pace quickens to where she is scrambling to her feet.

John attempts to crawl away, with Judith and Jill frantically tugging at him, while Raeni retains her grip on one of his legs, slowly pulling him back towards her.

Isme, who for the most part has kept out of the way since his initial brush with Raeni and the open fire, rushes into the room and leaps on to her back. The weight and momentum of his movement, combined with the fact that she only has one hand to the floor to steady herself with, flattens her, causing her to slump forwards. This involuntary action leaves her with her head between John's knees. As the reality of her situation dawns she sinks her teeth firmly into his calf and he screams out with the pain, writhing around on the ground.

As Alex follows Isme, he is thrown aside by an invisible force. He collides with the side of the bar and falls back towards the middle of the room. Quick to recover, his head spins around to see what had intercepted his attack. In total amazement he watches as Gary and the others cascade into the room. Michael, the last to land, falls softly on top of Paul, who grunts with a painful groan on his arrival, all simply seeming to materialise out of thin air.

At the corner of the bar, between the two rooms, there is now a mass of bodies, arms and legs, with the new arrivals landing either on top of Raeni or John. It is obvious through the confused looks that none of them have a clue as to what is happening, as they all attempt to quickly scramble away from the mass of bodies.

Jill spots Dan and immediately heads towards him, standing directly on John's chest in order to reach him. Not looking down, she utters a sincere, "Sorry John," as she reaches out to her husband. John groans as his eyes cross from this latest addition of pain.

Raeni places both her hands firmly on the ground and in one single movement she pushes herself up into a crouched position, tossing various bodies away from her as she rises.

She heaves herself to her feet and on her way up she grasps Isme by the throat, holding him out at arm's length with his feet dangling above the ground.

York, whose front is now covered in blood from his nasal wound, rushes to his defence but before he crosses the room, Raeni has turned, glaring at him with a half cocked grin on her face. York, seeing her scowl, stops in his tracks, acutely aware of her power and strength and of the wound which she has already inflicted upon him. With one short, extremely fast movement, Isme is tossed across the room towards York, the room filled with her hissing as she inflicts this assault. York, watching the airborne Isme, tries to avoid the collision, but he is not quick enough as the two men collide heavily, spinning off in different directions and crashing to the ground, with little movement evident from either of them as they land.

Raeni slowly turns her attention back to Alex, her eyes filling with tears, she beckons to him. "Come to me. Be with me," she pleads.

He experiences a deep pull inside but manages to keep his wits about him. The whole room falls into an eerie silence, as the entranced audience attention is drawn to the spectacle unfolding in front of them. Alex slowly begins to step towards her, his hands dropping limply to his sides. Both the sword and the relic plummet from his grip. In his brain, he tries to concentrate and retain control of his world, not wishing to drift into the domain which she placed him in earlier.

Anne feels her hackles rise as she watches the scene, her protective instincts paramount, but as she is about to say something, Criss firmly places her hand on her arm, squeezes it tightly to gain her attention, then shaking her head she gestures for the other woman to stay still and quiet. Having briefly considered her options, Anne sighs and follows the order, and like the others, she simply observes the goings on, still agitated to say the least.

York stirs, looking along the floor with one eye as his head remains on a level with the carpet, his eye suddenly widening as he spots the relic bone lying next to the broken sword in the middle of the room. He looks across to Raeni, who seems to be totally preoccupied with Alex. Now with both eyes fully open, he begins to gradually inch his way forward towards the relic.

Rob, peeping through his fingers like a small child, sees what York has seen and watches with his breath held, his heart thumping so loudly that he can audibly hear it deep within his ears.

John is dragged away by Judith, who having managing to get him clear, slumps down exhausted onto a sofa. Jill and Dan, now out in the hallway behind the bar, are cuddled up with Jill plastering him with kisses all over his head, checking that he is still in one piece. Dan seems totally bemused by the whole thing.

John painstakingly pulls himself up to a sitting position and says, "Bloody hell, I've had it, I could murder a few pints of the wee beastie. Where's mine host when you need him?"

Judith widens her eyes and replies, "In the other room and probably in deep trouble right now."

Paul, Tara and Julie, have managed to remove themselves from the battle, taking refuge in the kitchen, crouched down behind one of the work stations in silence. Michael, with the help of Gary, has secured a small piece of standing room at the back of the lounge, neither man quite sure what to do next.

Alex finds himself almost within the reach of Raeni's full powers and try as he may, he cannot muster the ability to stop the sheer strength of her will. In his head, he attempts to break any eye, thought or emotional contact, hoping this will diminish her grip of his mind, but to no avail.

Inch by inch, York draws nearer the relic bone then suddenly he experiences a sharp and excruciating pain in the middle of his back, instantly stopping his progress. He attempts to turn around to see what is causing it, but can't as he finds himself pinned tightly to the floor. Craning his neck, he recognises the leg and foot that is pushing him down as his eyes move up from this limb to the body and finally to the face of Raeni, who is grinning down at him, her neck extended and head tilted unnaturally to allow her to stare him in the face.

Rob swallows hard, grits his teeth and charges out from his corner, directly at Raeni's back. With her concentration on Alex and her attention on York, she was unable to anticipate this additional attack from him. She totters forward, her weight releasing from York's back, allowing him to lurch forward, his finger tips now only a couple of inches away from his goal, the relic.

Alex immediately drops to one knee, his head flopping weakly down. He shakes his head and as his eyes refocus and his senses return, he slowly surveys the room again to grasp the current situation. The first thing he spots is York. Immediately he can see what the man is labouring to reach. He quickly averts his eyes from him, not wishing to draw Raeni's attention to his line of vision and nonchalantly continues to gaze about the room. As his eyes connect with her, he looks beyond to see Rob over the top of the fire place. He is yelping and frantically trying to get away from the intense heat of the wood burner. Tom quickly hauls him away, both men slumping to the floor in front of the hearth, with Rob still whimpering.

Alex then lunges forward straight into Raeni. He glances down to York, who is now looking up at his advance. Instantly he recognises his attempts to divert her attention away, allowing him to reach the relic unchallenged. Raeni, without hesitation, brings her elbow down firmly into the middle of Alex's back, sending him crashing to the floor, a deep groan issuing from his lips. He rolls away from the scene as Raeni realising who she has attacked, appears to be bordering on displaying remorse. She shifts her complete attention from the others in the room, focusing only on Alex, her arms outstretched, eyes intense and demeanour apologetic. He kicks out wildly at her, too far away to make contact but displaying his anger and disgust.

York has now been afforded the time he needed to gather up the bone relic and is firmly grasping it with all his might.

"You bitch!" Alex yells at the top of his voice, competently making his voice tremor, "I thought I was important to you?"

She freezes without a single movement, only her watery eyes seem to twinkle from a small tear. "No, not you, I would not harm you, I only ever protect you. You are my sole reason to exist."

Tom, having pushed Rob from the room, gathers up the broken sword blade, grasping it firmly in both hands, his intention very evident.

"Well, not anymore, that's frigging obvious, you psychotic cow!" Alex shouts as he leaps to his feet. With a quick glance to York, he grabs the blade from Tom, which rips into his palms, tearing at them as he advances on her, his stare now as cold as ice.

Abruptly, everything pauses as a definite, heavy thump is heard upon the front door. Michael, who is now in the hall, purposely strides to the front door, the only thought in his mind being that long awaited reinforcements seem to have arrived. He opens the glazed inner door, unlocks the front door and swings it wide open.

"Merry Christmas!" heralds a joint shout from outside in the snowstorm.

Two figures, just silhouettes at this point, pace forward and enter the pub, passing Michael with smiles as they enter the bar.

Alex, as angry as he is, pauses, looking at the two people who have just entered. He knows them both. They are local people who he hasn't seen for quite some time, as they have been away visiting some friends in London. They are both artists who live on the other side of the square and at this point they are the last people he expected to see. Ian and Lisa have been partners for years. He is a man in his sixties from Liverpool, in not bad shape for his years and full of life, talkative and slightly deaf. He stands six feet tall, balding on top but wears his hair longer at the back to make up for it. Lisa is twenty years his junior, very slim, long wavy dark hair with a pale complexion and an exuberant personality. The pair of them are frequently the life and soul of the party, having the ability to chat about more or less, any subject that arises.

"Wow," Ian says as his glance takes in the room, "I'm not sure I like what you've done in here. What destroyed it? Has there been trouble here tonight?"

Then his gaze falls upon Raeni and he adds, "Woops, I think I can see the problem. Is the bar still open, we're gasping?" he nervously swallows.

He takes Lisa's hand and strides past Raeni, whereupon he stands up two of the bar stools, which have been strewn on the floor, and they both park themselves at the bar. Alex, totally speechless to say the least, watches them sit themselves down calmly ignoring the mayhem that is all around them.

Marcus appears behind the bar and states, "This is not a good time guys, believe me."

Ian shells his ear towards him, slightly shaking his head as if he hadn't heard and he says, "What was that? Can you say that again."

Lisa repeats Marcus's words, but louder this time, raising her eyes to the heavens, a tad agitated.

"A good time," Ian says loudly with a broad smile. "Yes, that's why we're here, it's Christmas Eve and we want to have a good time, so a gin and tonic for the lady and a brandy alexander for me please."

Everyone is astonished at the new arrivals and their blasé attitude. Even Raeni is staring at them, her momentum temporarily broken.

Then within an instant, Alex's concentration turns from them and back to Raeni, who senses his attention and turns to face him straight on. He can see the sadness in her eyes but remains acutely aware of her danger.

Tom, seeing Alex muscle up to her, suddenly leaps on her back. She falters for a second, one of her knees buckling forward with the unexpected jolt of the attack, her arms splaying sideways to counter her temporary lack of balance. Alex, without any further hesitation, lurches at her and pushes the sword blade as hard as he can into her chest. The blade passes right through and catches Tom in the top of his left leg. He lets out a piercing shriek of pain, immediately releasing his grip on her and falling backwards to the floor, grasping his leg in an effort to stop the blood, shuffling away to a safer corner of the bar, hoping to remove himself from the fray.

With one ear piercing scream she glares down at the blade in her chest. Her right arm whips forward swiping Alex around the side of his head, sending him spinning away, careering across a table and finishing in a heap at the base of the window.

York ploughs in, brandishing the relic, attempting to push it into her face. Initially she cringes, trying to move away from the bone then she lashes out at him. He manages to avoid her blows and backs away.

Raeni glances down at the blade as she begins to giggle, finishing with uncontrollable laughter, with only short breaths breaking the heinous sound for a second.

York stumbles back into Ian and Lisa, clambering around the edge of the bar in order to gain some distance from her.

"For Christ's sake," Ian grumbles loudly, "Someone needs to shut this ugly bugger up."

He leaps from his stool, grabs York's arm and takes the relic from him, advancing on Raeni himself.

At the same time Ellie the cat appears, leaping up from behind the bar with great ease. Her lightening reactions allow her to assess the room and its occupants. Within a second or two she launches herself through the air, landing on Raeni, with all four sets of claws digging deep down into her face in unison.

She frantically shakes her head, her hands trying to grip the cat to pull it away, but Ellie rips into her, biting at her digits and squirming with more speed than Raeni can manage to contain.

Ian dives straight in, grabbing the protruding part of the sword, forcing it downwards, pushing the relic into the wound, then ramming it home using his thumb for pressure. He then retreats as fast as he can, but not before Raeni has managed to kick him, causing him to stumble backwards into the bar.

Ellie releases her claws and pushes herself away from Raeni's head, landing on the floor. She scuttles away, fur flying, back out into the hall. Having done her part, she feels that it's now down to the humans to finish it off.

Raeni remains perfectly still, her head bowed, staring at the wound in her chest. Before the relic was forced in to her body, the only liquid that issued from the injury was a watery yellow and green substance. Now, it is evident to all that blood is trickling out as well. Her head flicks upright, her eyes wide open, her mouth agape, but with no sound issuing. Then she begins to shake. At first it is only her extremities, her fingers and toes, followed by her legs, head and body, until everything is uncontrollably moving faster and faster. Finally, for the onlookers, she appears almost invisible. Her whole body is gyrating so quickly that she doesn't appear to be in any one spot, at any one time.

Gary, who was in the hall with Michael, has now skirted around the bar and is stood in front of the fireplace. He reaches inside the big chimney breast and takes hold of the poker, which he had always previously admired. He clasps it firmly with both hands, wields it above his head and then brings it down with all his might upon Raeni. She has her back to the attack as the steel poker strikes her directly on her shoulder, close to her neck. The blunt instrument is brought down again, time after time, with his frenzied onslaught.

Abruptly, she ceases to shake, her body becoming rigid. He eyes are now closed, her mouth is shut and the chest wound is substantially larger than it was before. Her head slowly turns to where Alex is, her eyes flick open, a tear evident and then with a deafening, whooshing noise, her whole being dismantles and is sucked towards the fire and up the chimney, the sword blade and relic falling to the floor where she had stood.

Ian, having watched her exit, turns to Marcus and says, "Well, that's that then. Thank god all that fuss is done and she's decided to leave, that's excellent. Now can I have a gin and tonic and a brandy alexander?"

Criss starts to giggle with nervous relief, amused by Ian's seemingly, unconcerned and apathetic regard for the occurrences that have just happened. She then glances at Marcus and states, "Well, we've cracked the case and we've found all the missing people."

He raises his eyebrows and looking back at Ian asks, "What the hell is a brandy alexander?"

Briefly, everyone in the wreckage of the room falls silent, looking around at each other in disbelief. Alex slowly rises to his feet as the church bells begin to strike. No one speaks or moves, they simply listen and count. Finally, the bell strikes twelve.

Anne calls out, "Merry Christmas everyone, it's Christmas Day," as she runs across to Alex, caressing his head in her hands she kisses him passionately.

"Merry Christmas," Graham calls out entering the pub. "Saw the door was open so we thought we'd join you."

"Well come on in," Alex welcomes. "Shit, we've just had a cracking Christmas Eve, so why don't you join us."

Grahame and Mandy cautiously walk in, surveying the room which now resembles a bomb site, standing up the chairs as they pass through, they ultimately make it across to the bar.

"May I have a pint of ale and a glass of port please?" Graham requests.

Marcus looks at them blankly and replies, as his fingers dance along the various beer pulls, "I'm a copper, not a barman. I haven't got a clue what a brandy alexander is and I'm not sure as to where, what you are asking for is, either."

"I'll do it," Alex states walking into the hall to make his way back to the bar.

Ann turns to York and nervously asks the inevitable question. "Is she gone for good, is she dead?"

Everyone within ear shot awaits his appraisal of the final drama. He glances at the open hearth and takes a deep breath, his sigh loud enough to be heard by all. "I must admit, my previous meetings with her have not concluded in this way. This was by far the most violent scenario with her that I have had the misfortune of encountering. The use of the relic has always been enough to make her back away and leave in the past but on this occasion, she seemed unaffected by its presence."

Everyone is absorbed, listening intently to his words.

"However," he continues, "At the height of this battle, the relic was lodged into her physical body. Her exit, that we witnessed, was dramatic, but as to whether she was killed or not, I'm sorry I have no idea. The one thing I am sure of is that she will not, if she is still alive, come back here. To date, she has never manifested twice in the same place."

"Good," John calls out from the corner of the bar, breaking the thoughtful silence of the room. He then turns back towards Marcus, who is still behind the bar and says, "A wee beastie my man and be quick to serve it."

Marcus immediately turns to Alex, raises his eyes and says, "Please enlighten me as to what he's talking about?"

Alex bends down, picks up a bottle of the Beast and hands it to Marcus, who tops it and hands it to John. John takes it and placing it to his lips he guzzles down half the bottle without stopping. After he has removed it and taken a breath he quips with a smile, "I normally like a glass, but looking around this place, standards have obviously dropped."

Various people giggle, Alex slowly laughs as the friendly banter of The Bell Inn in Witherford returns to normal.

CHAPTER TWENTYSIX

The pub finally closes at two o'clock in the morning, with everyone who can leave, going home and the guests go off to their respective rooms. Alex and Ann, aware that they will need to open for lunchtime that very day, Christmas morning, clear up the bar as best they can, replacing the furniture from old stuff which had been stored away for future use. By three o'clock in the morning, the bar looks pretty acceptable and they wind their weary way up to bed, their slumber, not the most peaceful, with thoughts of the previous night, echoing and replaying in their dreams.

The snow outside has ceased, the early hours of the morning being extremely cold but with no further snow falling. As the snow hardens, its layers become crisp but it does not turn to ice. It is the first sign that the big freeze may be over.

The hearth and the fire that was ablaze within it, now ebbs with only a few cinders still alive under the charred logs that have managed to survive from the intense heat of earlier. Every now and again, a back draft causes the cinders to glow, almost as if they know they haven't quite finished their job and need to burn the wood that still remains.

Suddenly, a spindly arm and hand flash down from the chimney, out of the fireplace and into the centre of the room. For a few seconds, it seems to grab and grasp wildly at anything that happens to be on the carpet, until finally it finds what it is looking for. As the long, disfigured digits fumble around they come to rest upon the bone relic in the corner of the room, next to the grand settle. The fingers dance around it for a few seconds before grabbing it and clenching it tightly in its fist. Instantly, the arm and hand disappear back up the chimney from whence they came, the chilling laughter echoing around but heard by nobody, as it disperses into the darkness of the freezing night.

———————